OF BLOOD DESCENDED

Steven Veerapen was born in Glasgow to a Scottish mother and a Mauritian father and raised in Paisley. Pursuing an interest in the sixteenth century, he was awarded a first-class Honours degree in English, focussing his dissertation on representations of Henry VIII's six wives. He has received a Master's in Renaissance studies, and a Ph.D. investigating Elizabethan slander. Visit: www.stevenveerapen.com.

OF BLOOD DESCENDED

STEVEN VEERAPEN

Polygon

First published in paperback in Great Britain
in 2022 by Polygon,
an imprint of Birlinn Ltd

Birlinn Ltd
West Newington House
10 Newington Road
Edinburgh
EH9 1QS

www.polygonbooks.co.uk

9 8 7 6 5 4 3 2 1

ISBN 978 1 84697 613 1
eBook ISBN 978 1 78885 350 7

Typeset in Dante by Polygon, Edinburgh
Printed and bound by CPI Group (UK) Ltd, Croydon CR0 4YY

DRAMATIS PERSONAE

THE ROYALS AND THEIR HOUSEHOLD
Henry VIII, king of England
Catherine of Aragon, his wife
Charles V of Spain, Holy Roman Emperor, their nephew
Sir Thomas Boleyn, King Henry's diplomat
Anne Boleyn, daughter to Sir Thomas

CARDINAL WOLSEY'S HOUSEHOLD
Cardinal Thomas Wolsey, Archbishop of York, primate of
England and Lord Chancellor
Richard Audley, his principal secretary
Harry Gainsford, his gentleman
Mr Cornish, his Master of the Revels
Herr Gosson, his Master Painter
Monsieur Visser, his Master Glazier
Monsieur Lutini, his Master of the Strings
Signor Gonzaga, his historian
Anthony Blanke, his guest
Mark Byfield, his trumpeter

IN LONDON
Catherine Blanke, widow and stepmother to Anthony
Signora Gonzaga, wife to Wolsey's historian
Sister Jane, infirmaress at the Abbey of the Minoresses of
St Clare Without Aldgate
Polydore Vergil, former royal historian

PROLOGUE

Pietro Gonzaga's mind was a book thick with margins, daily increased and complicated by the dense, spidery notes one finds in any book worth reading. More writing was added every time he saw something worth recording. Separate chapters recorded everything, each with its own title: of kings; of nations; of the characters of men; of women; of London; of Paris; of Rome; of the Church; of religion; of wars. A historian required knowledge of all. A Mantuan by birth, Gonzaga had been drawn to England, as had many, by the golden world spoken of in Europe. It was a world made new, freshened and sweetened, by the young king, Henry. And, being an Italian and a scholar, Gonzaga had been preferred to courtly service.

As a scholar, too, it was his duty as well as his pleasure to look upon sovereigns. He had looked upon plenty of dead ones – at least, the records of their lives in books and chronicles – but a living one was a rare and glorious wonder.

Two of them was a miracle.

Two of them and a castle and a fleet of huge, hulking, many-sailed warships was Heaven itself.

Gonzaga stood in the crowd of spectators which had

gathered at the Dover quayside. His youngest son, Will, was on his shoulders, the boy's chubby little legs pressing into his neck. His wife stood beside him, clutching the hand of Peter, his elder boy. Bianca was a broad woman and still pretty. She had not, however, come to love England as he had. Its people, she said, were arrogant and haughty and disliked strangers. She had told him this often. Every slight was recorded: the turned back in the market at Smithfield; the kisses offered to every cheek but hers; the voices hurriedly stilled when she entered a shop on Cheapside.

'Are they not fine things?' he asked her. His voice was almost lost to the wind and the excited chatter of the other spectators. That same wind whipped the countless sails of the ships, which rode at anchor out by their jetties.

'No bigger than the one that brought us to this island. And its islanders,' said Signora Gonzaga.

He gave up trying to convince her. Instead, he returned his gaze over the rolling tide of hats and heads to the warships: the *Mary Rose* and *Henry Grace à Dieu* stood proud and tall, their forest of masts dwarfing the littler ships like parents whose chests stood out with pride.

'Well – do you wish to become a sailor, Peter?' he asked. The boy didn't look at him. He rarely looked at anyone directly. Instead, he turned his face into his mother's skirts. Gonzaga had brought his family down from London hoping to spark some interest in the lad. Useless. Peter had developed a love of horses and knew every breed and where they came from, whether Ireland or France or Barbary. He spoke of nothing else – would talk for hours on the subject of horses and no other, and would freeze if his father tried to draw him into some other conversation. 'Of horses,'

Gonzaga thought, was the only chapter in young Peter's mind.

Returning his attention to the ships, Gonzaga began counting the masts. The largest ship, the *Henry Grace à Dieu*, had five. His mind calculated quickly. About 600 mariners and soldiers – their tiny white and dun figures lined the decks. 140 guns, 40 light. Her gleaming brown hull sat too high in the water. One fewer mast might be an improvement. At present, the gargantuan monster of a ship would struggle in anything but the smoothest seas – might be felled by a ripple. He made a note in his mind and filed it alongside the cost of the ship – £14,000 – which his money-minded friend in the Cardinal's service had told him. He was no naval man, no shipwright, but he had accumulated enough knowledge of the history of sailing vessels – from honest history books – to consider himself a good hand.

He knew almost as much about the English ships out there as he did about England's kings.

As if in response to the thought, explosions rent the air. All heads turned from the port.

Dover Castle was a square block of a building with similarly square, turreted towers, all in neat grey stone and glass. It stood proudly on its hill above the port town, ringed by several thick grey walls matching the colour and quality of the castle's keep.

Some of those walls were now sending smudgy fingers up into the hard blue sky. The guns had been set off in announcement of the arrival of the royal party. As a further prelude, trumpets began blasting notes at intervals, growing louder each time.

The rumble of hooves soon made itself felt and heard, as

the standard bearers approached. On the long road down from the castle appeared two riders, one bearing the Tudor Rose on his flagstaff, the other the Imperial Eagle. The insistent trumpets grew more furious.

The two fore-riders passed on, before the crowd, which was separated from the road by wooden railings.

'I see him! Papa! I see him!' Will's thighs tightened, near choking his father. The crowd fell silent.

And then, as one, the cry went up. 'God save the king! God save his Grace!'

Gonzaga didn't join in. He rose up on his tiptoes just as King Henry's head appeared above the heads of the Hydra-like crowd. The king was mounted, of course, and he held up a hand gloved in white. A broad smile split his face and he shouted, 'You know me! I come!' His voice was high and excitable.

His head then turned away, so that Gonzaga could see only the back of a white hat, from which a yellow feather danced.

'Who is he?' asked his son. 'The other one?'

'He . . .' began Gonzaga. He forced himself up a little higher, just as King Henry's hand rose. A white finger jabbed the air ahead. He was eagerly pointing out his ships to the fellow riding beside him.

The Holy Roman Emperor, thought Gonzaga. Charles V. He told his boy this.

'A little man,' said Signora Gonzaga. She said this to the boy whose hand she was holding, but loud enough for her husband to hear.

And she was right.

King Henry rode ahead, turning his head from side to side

again, basking in the adulation of his people. The emperor, moving alone, his attendants keeping their distance behind the sovereigns, gave his uncle-king an odd look. The fellow's eyes narrowed, Gonzaga noticed, and his lips moved, though, if he were speaking aloud, his voice would never be heard by the crowd.

Interesting, Gonzaga thought.

All England was afire with news of the young emperor's coming. All talk was of the new friendship between Spain and its empire and England. But Charles did not look at his uncle with love. Behind his back, in fact, he'd given him a look that Gonzaga would have called unpleasant bemusement.

And then the royals were gone, riding off to board and inspect the great warships, whilst their bodies of gentlemen followed, to no particular acclaim.

It was a foolish thing, thought Gonzaga, for King Henry to show off his navy. If war should ever return between the two kings – and history dictated that it would, at some point – then the emperor would know every detail of England's capabilities.

Yet this King Henry, the ruler of the golden world that had brought the scholar to England, was a man of inordinate pride. The cardinal, too – Gonzaga's master – was a man of pride.

His wife was right, though he'd never admit it to her; the English were a prideful people.

Gonzaga slumped, squatting down just enough to let his boy slide easily to the ground. Excitement still shone on the lad's face. That was good. The emperor was nothing to look at, with his deformed jaw, but the sight of King Henry would last the boy a lifetime. Because, Gonzaga thought, Henry VIII looked like a king.

He had mulled over this during his studies, pondered the question of kingship. He could detail the precise proportions and countenances of every English king, provided that king happened to have been described in a book. Edward IV was handsome and, ultimately, enormously fat; Richard III was plagued by a crooked back; Henry VII was thin and fair but grew wizened and lost his teeth in his dotage.

So what made a sovereign lord a sovereign lord?

A genius of the mind? No. There had been feeble-minded kings, and cruel ones.

A love of justice? The ideal king was a universal king, indifferent in matters of justice to the highest as the lowest. Few met that ideal.

The acceptance of his people? No. There had been unloved tyrants.

The proportions of the body? No. Charles V was misshapen and ugly.

God? Perhaps. Yes. There was certainly some design to it.

Descent from father to son to son to son? Not often in English history.

Descent from ancient blood? Now therein lay the rub, with so few kings descending directly from kingly fathers . . .

In practice, Gonzaga had concluded, it should not matter what a king looked like. What mattered was that his rule was just, his people and his territories protected, and his patronage well disbursed. An ugly, drooling wretch of a man might do all that, his appearance signifying nothing.

But, in truth, King Henry VIII had made it matter.

His Majesty, King Henry VIII, by the grace of God

sovereign lord of England, Wales, Ireland, and France, defender of the faith – he had made a king's face, his mask – call it what you will – matter. His face – his mask – was one of goodly benevolence, of handsome features and generosity.

But Pietro Gonzaga suspected something about what lay behind that mask.

He knew – or soon he would know – the truth of the glorious King Henry's history, from his father's seizure of the throne at Bosworth to the long-dead Lady Margaret the king's mother, through Edmund and Owen Tudor and the ancient high kings. He knew what the genealogists had been commissioned to discover: the descent from the greatest king in English history, Arthur, king of all the Britons. It was a great fantasy of Henry's, proving that descent. Such proof . . . well, all of those who said the king's father was a usurper of no great blood would be silenced. All those men who frowned at the king's lack of a son and looked forward to the next line of kings – even they would not wish to see Arthur's descendant fall from power. It was little wonder the English king had set a small army of scholars to wander storehouses of knowledge in search of some word, some scrap, that would prove Arthur had lived, breathed, and begat a royal line.

Gonzaga had filed away every step through every library which those men had taken. He'd followed their inky paths, had blinked and strained his eyes as they had, and was on the brink of a discovery about King Henry's history which they, even in their zeal to find evidence of the Tudors' descent from Arthur, had missed.

It would take him only a few more weeks.

A few more weeks of following the notes left in faded ink in ever-narrowing margins in unread books in seldom-visited archives and libraries.

But he would do it. He would prove something the scholars had only dared whisper about.

King Henry would have the truth laid before him.

'Let us go, husband.'

Gonzaga turned. His wife had gathered both their sons to her; they were hugging at her skirts. The crowd had thickened rather than thinned, as more people gathered to see the kings come out on the decks of the ships. Signora Gonzaga, scowling, was buffeted and shoved as people fought their way towards the railings by the path. A boy selling nuts bumped into her and spilled some. The little brown balls skittered, bounced, and disappeared among the thicket of hose and shoes. ''Ere, watch it, woman!' he piped.

'Might we go?' she asked, more insistently.

Gonzaga took a deep breath of air thickened and soured with sweat and musk. 'Sì. Back to London.' He had done as he'd wished; he'd borne witness to a little corner of history. The chapter 'Of Kings' had had a little more added. As the *Henry*'s guns fired, sending more smoke into the air, he and his family elbowed their way through the people. Yes, he had just witnessed history.

Soon, he would make it.

Soon.

I

The wherry's oars splashed, dug, and rose, battling the morning current. The Thames had grown quieter out of London, less packed with boats and birds, but the steady, brackish water never gave up its dumb rush towards the city. A scattering of reeds added their own futile resistance, brushing the hull with skeletal fingers.

For a moment we passed into shadow – a brief respite – as the water-gate arched above. And then the sun reclaimed us.

''Ere we are,' said the grunting bull of a waterman. Needlessly, of course. The graceful red towers and gilt cupolas had been visible for a while, the palace haughtily shrugging its shoulder against the bankside trees and the curve of the river. Besides, I knew the road – the waterway, I should say – to Hampton Court, though I hadn't been near it in two years. Nor had I been near any of Cardinal Wolsey's glorious riverside palaces, or city ones, or hunting lodges, or townhouses. I didn't reply but gripped the hard edges of my wooden bench whilst he set to work slowing us down, turning us, or whatever the terms are such men use in their trade. He was good; I scarcely felt the wherry rock and pitch as, for a moment, it caught on the current.

Peacefully now, having declared victory over the tide, the little boat was washed up to the calm of the landing stage. 'A good one that, heh? Fancy a turn in that?' asked the waterman, jerking his head – and nearly losing his flat cap – as we slid past the cardinal's barge.

God save us from wherrymen who insist on making conversation!

I gave him a brief, 'Ay,' and looked politely at the greater craft. It was new: I hadn't seen it before. However, in years past, I had sailed on things like it. It rode low in the water, a great, graceful, gilded swan. At its prow stood a cross, at its stern, a carved wooden cardinal's hat. Near the latter was the enclosed, windowed area – glass, mind you, no horn or oiled paper on a thing like this – where Wolsey might hide from the elements and entertain guests. As we passed the front of the barge, I could see where I might have sat, had I still been one of the great man's musicians: on a red-carpeted dais near the prow, so that my trumpet might blast word ahead that he was coming.

And then the barge was past, and we were approaching the landing steps. These weren't the crumbling, weed-choked steps of London, uneven and carpeted with dog turds; no, they were pure marble, glistening in the hard afternoon sunlight. It was difficult to believe that Hampton Court was even in England; it might have been lifted, from landing stairs to chimney tops, from some Italian romance and deposited on its pleasant bend of the river beyond the smelly city.

It was a city, I thought, to be out of.

With the imperial emperor visiting, the people had gone wild, drinking all day and singing all night, cursing the French openly in the streets and crying, 'God save the Queen! God save the Emperor!' I hadn't taken part in the festivities myself, but I'd heard the cannon being fired from the Tower not far from us in Aldgate, followed by the shattering of glass in the houses near to the citadel of those fool enough – or rich enough – to glaze their windows. And my stepmother had bombarded me with the street news, with all the zeal of a witness, whilst I'd hidden in my bed the previous afternoon, the lockram blanket over my head a barrier against women's jangles.

'And there were big painted shields – you've never seen the like – huge things – and two huge men dressed as Greeks. Great big men, with beards, in furs – furs – dancing and bowing right prettily. And all those arches, right over the street, like canopies, all twined with vines and flowers. And the king – oh, son, the king – he looked beautiful, he did. And the emperor . . . not so very big. Odd sort of face, that one. Sharp chin, too big to be real. Like a mask. Smiling, right enough. But a queer sort of smile, not big and open like our king's. More like he was laughing at all that pomp and prettiness. To himself, like.' Then, hurriedly, 'Oh, but he's good Queen Catherine's nephew and she wouldn't let no man marry her daughter unless he was a right good man, would the good queen. Oh, if only she'd been there, sweet Catherine . . .' And on and on she had droned, sweetening the air of my bedchamber with her grand images and her reveries.

Yes, I was glad to be out of London and its frenzy of holidaying.

''Ampton, residence of 'is Grace the Cardinal Wolsey, Archbishop of York,' announced the waterman, before removing his cap and wiping his sodden brow with it. I raised an eyebrow at him, impressed by his little show of grace. If I'd asked him to take me to Southwark, I'd probably have been seen off with only a sturdy 'fuck off, then' and a leering look.

'And Lord Chancellor of England too,' I said, rising and wobbling down the boat. My legs were stiff, locked at the knee, and my backside dead.

'Ay, ay,' he grinned, holding out a dirty-nailed hand and coughing. I paid him the second quarter of the fare and he regarded me, taking in my age, measuring my worth. I could almost see his mind ticking over what he saw: a wool coat, plain, respectable doublet and hose – the clothing of a young schoolmaster, not a courtier. If I'd told him my name, said, 'Anthony Blanke, of London,' he wouldn't have known it.

Good . . .?

The voice in my head was my father's, full of foreignness, rich in irony, still beaded with love. I blinked.

After slipping the money inside his coat, the waterman grinned again. 'Now get out of it, then,' he said. 'Bugger off.'

Ah, boy – you were so close!

I returned his smile, not troubling to show my teeth, pulled my cap down against the sun and stepped off. 'I'll be waiting, lad,' caught at my back. 'Double the fare, mind, for what I'm losing being outta the town.'

I waved vaguely, waggling my fingers. The steps rose in front of me, gleaming white, polished and fine.

As I mounted, my heart began to race. Strange, I realised, how thoughts can make the heart race – no need to run or jump or ride. Our minds give us exercise enough. I was working myself up into nervous excitement and I knew it. Near two years I'd spent as a trumpeter in Wolsey's household – as long as I'd since been out of it – and I'd left for the same reason every young man leaves service: because I thought the world was waiting outside for me.

It hadn't been, of course.

You might laugh at me for imagining it would. People wish to enter a great man's service, not to leave it. And I'd have agreed with you back when I was just shy of sixteen. Then, I'd had what you might call a godly fit. The idea of early rising, prayer, incense – all of it had become a thing of glory.

Why?

Because a notion had come to me that, as purity was white, as the Eucharist was white, as the Church spoke of the darkness of Hell and God's holy light, then through prayer and a godly life, I might somehow lighten myself. As the Moorish men of Africa had been blighted with blackness as punishment for their heathen ways, so could I undo the traces of it in myself through turning towards the true faith with as much zeal as I could muster. I hadn't told my father this, of course – and had been content to let him use his connections as a former trumpeter to get me in.

Well, we're idiots at fifteen; we have ideas. Before I was twenty, I'd learnt that serving any great man meant resting your head in a den of spies. Even at Wolsey's great court, there was too much danger and too little godliness. It was a world of watchers. It was a place of observing and being observed. I'd finally tired of it during King Henry's sojourn at the Field of Cloth of Gold – that great revel of richness and double-faced waste, when England and France had feigned friendship. Then, it had become apparent to me that our good king was an overgrown child and his people – yes, even Wolsey – his toys. Better, I'd decided, to be my own master.

And, by then, my father had died and thus had no means to counsel me. Nor to say, 'I told you so.'

The old voices of courtly life drowned one another in my head, eclipsing even my father's imagined admonishment.

Did you see the king?

Did you mark that Her Majesty wasn't smiling?

They say the king has a mistress.

Does Her Majesty speak of the king's bastard – did you mark her face at the speaking of him?

His Grace my lord cardinal is sore troubled – he was wearing a frown on leaving the king's presence.

The French dispraise us.

We dispraise the French!

Ugh. Questions and answers, watchers and spies, making currency of every bit of gossip. What would later be smiled at by prate-pies in alehouses and babble-merchant city wives at market was worth money and position at court. And the king himself was the great brewer of rumours. His Majesty didn't give a straw who rose or fell or lived or died; he was doing the lifting and dropping. That was why I'd wished to be out of it. Or, at least, that was the reason of which I'd convinced myself – the chief . . .

Yet here I was, drawn back.

At the top of the shallow stairs, a path wound its way towards the palace. I didn't pause; I kept my head down and set off, crunching over gravel. On either side were planted bushes studded with little red flowers, each opening their petals and sending out a pleasant tang. The greenery was broken at regular intervals by stout, circular columns, painted to look like violet-veined marble. These supported a similarly painted wooden roof, from which were hung banners, alternately showing Wolsey's arms and Tudor roses. This, the water gallery, ran from the Thameside stairs until the end of the pathway. It was a pleasant walk – a walk as fit for a king as a cardinal.

What was that?

I froze, midway along the path.

Something had rustled, something in the bushes. Like a person pushing through them. I thought, too, that I'd seen something – or someone – a figure – hands – parting the greenery, just a little, and letting it spring back. I remained still, tensed.

Fool!

It was my imagination. Or, more likely, some animal at work. I had been in the city too long, had become used to walking about – when I bothered to go out – with one eye over my shoulder against cutpurses. Palaces were something else. Where the city streets were a wild tangle of danger, palaces were neat, enclosed sanctuaries. Order lay within, danger without. Relaxing, I shook my head at my own stupidity and went on. But I moved more quickly than I had done.

As I neared the building, the water gallery ended and the gravel widened into a large open space where some servants loafed – gardeners, I judged, by their dull frieze coats, and red-faced, matronly laundresses trying to regain a little girlhood by flirting and jesting with them.

But it was not the clutch of little figures which drew my eye.

Hampton Court had been transformed from what I'd known – rebirthed, grown up. The place presented a rectangular frontage of red stone and, at its centre, an enormous gatehouse with a grey archway soared up and stood, pristine, against the crystal blue wash of the sky. Banners and pennants drifted listlessly, and carved creatures clung to the gutters, their heads twisted to gaze down at the people three storeys below. Glass windows of all shapes and sizes were set regularly along the front block; dozens of chimneys reached skyward unevenly, and the whole palace was circled entirely by a sparkling blue moat.

The cardinal's country house . . .

I'd never seen anything that fit the name 'house' less. I shook myself free of awe and stepped forward, making for the bridge over the moat. I'd known the place was being rebuilt. For a few months after leaving service, my friends there had written me of the new buildings, of the gossip in the household. But those letters had dried up. On both sides. In fact, I only wrote regularly now to one person, and that in secret. My heart skipped, stupidly, at the thought.

Letters.

For the thousandth time, I felt at my breast. A crinkle met my touch. I exhaled relief, reaching under my coat and drawing out the letter that had brought me here. And then, remembering that strange rustling, I glanced over my shoulder. Free now of the bushes, I had a clear view of the open gardens on either side of the walkway.

And there he was.

A man of about middling height, tending to the bushes, his face turned away from me. Something grey hung at his belt – a brush, most likely. Too far away now to make him out clearly. I squinted, frowning. Then shrugged. A gardener, like the others, just a gardener. I was jumping at shadows.

Shrugging, I turned back to the great house, continued

over the moat's bridge and, instinctively, made my way to the left of the gatehouse arch, scanning for a lower door, a servants' entrance.

It's like you never left.

Indeed. I've found that, even after years away from a job of work, you could step back in and do it again without a second thought. You imagine that you might wave your hand at your old fellows and settle back in, as though time hadn't passed.

Through the little service doorway, I met a rough oak table with a stout, short, swollen-cheeked under-porter writing at it. He didn't rise at my entry, but gave me an expectant look, his quill hovering in the air. I passed my letter to him as little droplets of ink grew too heavy for his nib and fell. Hissing in irritation, he pushed his own document aside, looked over the broken cardinal's seal, and read.

It was the letter that had drawn me. It hadn't come from Wolsey himself, of course, but from some underling called Audley, who must have come after my time. Yet the seal was the cardinal's, and the invitation to be present, today, at Hampton Court as a 'trusty friend' had piqued my interest. Aside from the fact that it would've been unwise to ignore an ecclesiastical summons, I was curious as to why Wolsey should want to see me after all this time, and why all the way out at Hampton Court, when London was rocking with daily news about the Imperial Emperor's visit.

Something changed on the porter's round face, drawing him off his stool and interrupting my thoughts. He licked his lips before speaking. 'Of course. Mr Blanke.' He said my name – my father's name – with remembrance rather than recognition. Once, it might have raised an eyebrow. Old John

Blanke had been a man of some note. His white-toothed face rose in my memory, smiling as he always did, the skin crinkling around his eyes. I shuddered him away. Since his death four years before, I fancied I'd done a fair job of being unremarkable, of blending in. 'By His Grace's orders, you're to go directly to his chambers. What time is it, sir?'

Sir? Very pretty.

'I think . . . around two o'clock.'

'Hm.' He gave a little sour-milk moue, as though I were late, as though I was an inconvenience. 'I'll have someone take you there. Now.'

He slipped out of a door on the far side of the room, leaving me. It was now past dinnertime, I knew. But I knew also that, if Wolsey wasn't with the king, he wouldn't have held a grand dinner, but would keep working through and on into his afternoon meetings.

But what was he working on?

I didn't have long to wait. Almost immediately, the porter returned. At his back was a man I knew. My breath departed me.

'Good morrow, Anthony,' said Harry Gainsford.

It suddenly seemed that the last two years had passed in a blink, though each day of them had ground slowly by. Harry was an old friend – one of Wolsey's gentlemen. I removed my cap and he stepped forward, resplendent in his crimson livery, and offered me his hand. I shuffled my thoughts. We had written, Harry and I, and then, as I'd said, not. Now there hung between us that distance that time causes, that unacknowledged chill. Like a cold breath, almost visible, it seemed to whisper, 'You left. I stayed. We are worse than strangers now.' You had to nurture friendships, I knew – if you let them wither, they became dead things, uglier than if you'd never even met the other person and could happily be polite strangers.

'Good morrow,' I rasped, giving his hand a limp shake.

'It is good to see you, my friend. And you are welcome to His Grace's house with honour.' There was no warmth in his voice, any more than there was malice. He sounded simply . . . dry. Like an old man, despite being only in his twenties. His accent sounded different from what I remembered – it had turned courtlier than ever, high and colourless, as though bleached and beaten clean. I shivered a little, despite the heat, gladder than ever that I'd left service. This is what I'd seen it do to people. It made them hard. It took something away. 'You have been well?'

'Yes.'

'Good. His Grace shall be pleased.' He relaxed, just a little. 'And I am, also, dear fellow.' Sunlight broke over his face, making him much handsomer, much more like the old, soft Harry I remembered from when we were both eighteen and still full of ideas. And then it clouded. 'Come. We perhaps can speak later. You are sought.' He turned on his heel and left the way he'd come. I scurried in his wake.

The door gave out onto a short, undressed passage and thereafter to the New Court. This had been one of Wolsey's additions to the old house: an enormous square courtyard girt on one side by the front of the building, on two sides by new blocks – unfinished these, giving a lopsided look – and on the far side by a block bearing yet another gateway into the second, older, smaller courtyard. It was across the cobbled space and towards this archway that Harry was striding. Being a gentleman, people made way for him – and so many of them. The New Court was a frenzy: grooms leading pack horses; lads sweeping cobblestones; a handful of pedlars crushed by their packs; pages darting about with messages. There were familiar faces too. A ruddy chaplain – Chaplain Chase-Pot, I recalled – was standing by a water butt, his nose redder than I remembered. A lad gave me a cockeyed grin; as I returned it, I recognised him as a former night-soil boy, now shot up in height and dressed in the crimson of some senior position.

Time. Where did it go?

Soft pipe music rose and fell jauntily from somewhere. All was watched over – we were watched over – by the dozens of glass windows which stared down. Mice living in a giant jewel case, I thought – that's what we were.

I've . . . have I missed this?

Passing easily through this Red Sea of servitude, Harry eased his pace as we approached the opposite gatehouse. This was less grand than the new one at the palace entrance – it was far smaller. But it was of the same red brick and, above it, a huge sovereign-shaped lozenge had been set into the brickwork displaying Wolsey's crossed-keys arms, supported by two cherubs and surmounted by a terracotta cardinal's hat. The sun fell on it, making the paint gleam.

Harry drew short. I had intended to ask whoever shepherded me through the palace if he knew what lay in store, but with Harry I found I couldn't. Too many things stood between us: the past; why I had stopped writing; why he had stopped writing. We were strangers and yet weren't – we were something uncomfortable, something in between friends and strangers.

'Through this gate,' he said, 'is the old building. You shall remember it. But His Grace has had his Master of Works refresh it. Hampton Court shall be the finest of His Grace's houses, when it is finished. Finer even than York Place.' Pride raised his chest. 'Very fine. But the last, we fear.'

'Oh?' I said.

'The last of his great works. His Grace wishes not to let the king think he grows vain.'

A bit late for that.

I peered through the archway, into the smaller Old Court. I couldn't see much of the buildings, but did see several knots of men, youthful apprentices by the looks of them, each group keeping well apart. Their heads were bowed in conversation and they were passing around cakes and wineskins; some heads, though, rose at the sight of us, before falling back into their suspicious chatter. Amongst them appeared to be plenty of prentices – a breed of fellow I distrusted on sight, mindful as I was of the Evil May Day garboils, when just such creatures had been the first to indulge their lust for violence, with their cries of 'to clubs' and their delight in savage, mercenary looting. Part of the reason my father had helped me into service when I was younger was that the alternative – becoming apprenticed – meant selling myself into bondage and becoming friends with young brawlers. I shivered. Wolsey was evidently meeting with several men, craftsmen it seemed, and here were their trains of rabid dogs.

Thankfully, I did not see any royal liveries.

'So you're still working for him. His Grace, I mean,' I said.

'Yes. Well, now I serve His Grace's private secretary. Mr Richard Audley.' Harry's chin lifted. I thought of my summons and said nothing, the muscles around my mouth working dumbly. 'You shall meet him. Inside.' He gestured up at the red bricks, dyed rosy by the sunlight.

'Mm. It's very . . . good. All the new works. Good,' I said, cursing my dry mouth and the lame words. Language was a thing you took out and polished at court, sounding it like a trumpet. It London it had rusted.

'I see you have not turned poet in your time away,' said Harry. I thought – thought – a hint of his old, handsome smile appeared, natural and unaffected. And then his mouth fell into its new, imperious lines. The hairs on my arms tickled under their sleeves.

Once, I had thought Harry Gainsford the most fortunate man in the world, well favoured with good looks, charm, and a history to his name. I knew he'd lost his mother, as I had, but his would have been of a quite different complexion. His childhood wouldn't have been one of embarrassment, of looking at the backs of his hands, the little hairs there bristling with difference. Honest discipline would have marked his life from the first swaddling. There would have been solidly built nursemaids to hold his fair hand. Tutors to whip honour into him. His mother, a peaceful woman, conscious of his dress, overseeing his first steps, deciding when skirts were to be discarded for hose. And his late father, of course, always his thin, white father, scourging him with admonitions, demanding perfection in all things – a straight back on the horse at the hunt; a graceful angle to his hat; a mouthful of flattery. I'd envied Harry such a father, such a man of stature and belonging, even if I'd never liked the old fellow.

We are our parents, deny it all we might.

I looked away from him, from that bland expression which made a carving of his handsome face. When my father had died, he'd been a good friend to me. I'd not said a word to him about it when his had gone.

He was two men, now, was Harry: the old, honour-filled fellow, callow and sweet, and this new creature, hard and cold. I had just witnessed the shift from one to another. 'No time for refreshments for you, my friend.' His chest rose. 'The king and the emperor are to honour this house on Tuesday. All must be in readiness. Come.'

I went. Together, we sailed into the Old Court and then pinioned right, turning back on ourselves, and passing through a doorway leading into the back-block of the New Court. Thereafter, I gave up trying to keep my bearings and let Harry lead me through a network of hallways, each one carpeted in red and lined in polished wood and whitewashed plaster. Varicoloured tapestries and glimmering sideboards passed in a blur as we went deeper, farther, closer to Wolsey's inner sanctum. Some gentlemen in liveries identical to Harry's snapped their backs to the walls as we approached, diverted from whatever games they'd been playing. He nodded at them and they back. I kept my head down, as my feet in their plain, city shoes – I'd been sensitive enough not to wear nailed boots! – made barely a whisper as they sank into red fronds.

Again, something like longing rose. This was a life I'd scorned.

But what a life.

Finally, he turned left, into a tiny, box-like square chamber, and halted before a tall, pointed door. The frame was red, the circular handle gilt. 'His Grace's private lodgings.' Again, I removed my cap and swallowed, staring at the door, wishing I'd never come. 'Good luck, my friend,' said Harry. He gave me a tight nod and knocked. The door opened from within and he stepped back.

'Aren't— You not coming with me?' Again, my voice had that appalling, strangulated choke in it. Even an awkward ally was better than none. Harry only gave his head a shake.

I stepped forward, into the gaping, red-lined maw of the room beyond.

2

'And the lady said, "it is not the length of his beard, sir, that troubled me"!' said Wolsey. Laughter erupted from the men who sat around the long, velvet-covered table. The cardinal smiled too, but, I noticed, his eyes remained watchful, shifting around his guests before landing on me.

I had been shown through a pair of richly decorated sitting chambers – with Wolsey's badges engraved on every window, carved into every cornice, and painted on every ceiling – and out into a hammer-beam-roofed gallery so long it ended in a sun-drenched blur. At the nearest end, the usher had bid me, silently, attend on the big table where Wolsey was holding court. I'd already removed my cap and now I bowed my head, but the cardinal had merely paused in whatever jest he was telling to spare me a glance, before continuing as though there had been no interruption. A man in black robes stood behind him, like a stretched shadow, his eyes blank. A little forked beard fanned over his chest. He wasn't smiling.

Now, as the laughter died, the cardinal rose. Sunlight fell upon him from one of the many windows which lined the enormously long, narrow chamber and I regarded him from under lowered lashes.

So many times, in the city, I've heard people whisper about Wolsey. And I've smiled.

'He's a monster.'

'He's come from nothing.'

'He rules the king, and the devil rules him.'

All nonsense. If there was one thing I knew, it was that the king ruled the king. And God alone knew what else His Majesty did. The cardinal, as I'd known him, was a fair man – a man who knew how to make you feel like he was speaking only to you, that you had some private friendship with him.

'Anthony Blanke,' he said, I assumed for the benefit of his guests, each of whom was now deigning to look at me. He sat again and, back in his chair, turned his head to one side and whispered something to the bent head of the man in black. I felt myself shrivel. Wolsey's attention returned to me. 'This young man is known to us from his service some years since. He is son to the king's late black trumpet.' Some murmurs rumbled through the company.

There it was. That, really, was part of the reason I'd never entirely taken to service. As my late father had once been, I'd been the Moor. The stranger. The jewel. Better, I'd always thought, to be a nobody than an oddity amongst the sea of white faces and cropped blond heads of England.

And a littler pool of those faces was looking now, turning to me, white eyes sweeping me.

'You may look upon us, young Anthony. You are welcome to our house,' rumbled Wolsey. My chin lifted. He was gesturing expansively, looking much like a friendly grandfather. The cardinal had that manner about him, the air of a grand old gentleman. He was perhaps a little thicker around the middle than the last time I'd seen him, but it was difficult to tell under his rich violet cassock. He was a well-proportioned man and what must have been his handsome younger ghost still haunted a face weighted and greyed with all the cares of serving a man like King Henry, whose policies whirled. I fancied that he wouldn't have changed much in his manner. During my brief time in his service, he'd been a great man – a great, fair, wildly gesticulating man who held England in one strong palm. From what I'd heard, he'd only grown larger whilst England had grown smaller, the better to be held and caressed and juggled.

At the end of the table closest to me, I noticed, was laid a great banquet of tangy sauces and sweet comfits, of jugs of wine and silver cups. But at the end closest to Wolsey was unrolled, over the velvet, an enormous painted cloth. Rather than the usual scenes from the Bible or Greek mythology, it bore a circular design with a Tudor rose at the centre, green and white sections fanning out to the perimeter. A throned man was painted just above the rose, his crowned head lying flat under Wolsey. The painted figure looked, I thought, a little like King Henry.

'Oh, dear Anthony,' said the cardinal, indulging his guests with a wink. 'You are come upon us in secrecy. A secret conference.' Another wink. Another look towards his man in black. This, I realised, must be the private secretary Harry had mentioned: Richard Audley, he'd said – the man who'd summoned me. 'And privy to secret designs.' Wolsey's good humour departed. 'I know you can keep secrets.' And then he turned again to his guests – there were four other men seated – nodded at one of them and submerged deeper into his high-backed chair. 'I have brought here, today, my master craftsmen. I have already sent them to school, as it were. Each has been in His Majesty's own library at Richmond, reading his fill of ancient history, looking at the great illuminations, that we might better enact our design.' As he said this, I looked at the men, three of whom were studiously inspecting their hands. I wondered if they had studied anything.

The fellow who was still paying attention to me rose in a blaze of colour. 'May I?' he asked, in a silky, high voice.

Though he asked the question of Wolsey, his gaze remained fixed on me. I had not, of course, been invited to sit, and so I remained standing, cap in hand, as the man slid around the table and walked lightly to stand before me. He was wearing the cardinal's livery, but he had outfitted it somewhat, padding it up, stringing blue and yellow ribbons about the sleeves and waist, with jangling charms attached. His eyes narrowed and I frowned, smiled, frowned, looked at the ground.

'He is not so *dark*, Your Grace, as I'd thought,' he announced over his shoulder. His accent was rounded – northern, I thought – as good as foreign to London. And then, suddenly, he reached up and squeezed my cheeks with one hand.

'Hey,' I said. 'What—'

His hand fell away.

'Peace, Mr Cornish,' said Wolsey. 'Anthony, this is my Revels Master. Come, sir, sit.' Cornish stepped away, backwards, cocking his head from side to side like a little pigeon.

'It *might* work,' he said. 'He might do, I mean, sir.' It came out in his northern drawl: 'maaat dooo, Ah mean'. He fumbled back around the table, tutting, muttering, and regaining his seat. Still I could feel his eyes on me.

'I say,' said the man beside him. 'I say, it is me who might have him. This lad was a music man, huh? Son to the king's trumpet, you said, Your Grace, and a trumpet in his own time, huh?' This one I vaguely recognised, both by his long, sallow face and lilting French accent. He was a musician, one of Wolsey's consort. I couldn't recall the name. As though reading my thoughts, Wolsey supplied it.

'You must work together, Monsieur Lutini. Revels and Strings. Dance and music in harmony. Is that not right, Mr Audley?' He didn't turn to his secretary, but the lugubrious fellow gave an unsmiling nod.

'But the man comes under me. By rights, huh?' Lutini protested. 'I have commanded Moors before, in the northern kingdom. Yes, and in masquery also. Four Moors under me, I had, four. I did not come south to share with no . . . no dancing master.'

'This one,' said Cornish, 'is only a *half*-black trumpet. And not in some poor *Scotch* realm, sir. In England! England! He is mine to command. And I am no *dance* master but His Grace's *chief* of entertainments. Is this not *so*, Your Grace? Am I thus to be *slighted* in your own presence?'

'Together,' repeated Wolsey, a trace of irritation now obvious. 'In accord.'

'I still say,' said Cornish, the prodder, 'that he's not dark *enough*. Not for *our* purposes. He must be painted *up*. I must have great painted *masks*. *Fearsome*. No mere cloth or silken things.'

All heads turned to one of the men on the other side of the table – a lean-faced, proudly blond one with hair cropped so close that his scalp shone pinkly through. Apparently unwilling to satisfy them immediately, he drew out a pause. 'The masks,' he said at length. His voice was short, staccato – some kind of jagged foreign, but I didn't know what. Germanic, perhaps. 'Your Grace might commission them.

Good masks. I shall be pleased. To have my men paint them.' He gave me a measured look, before resuming that halting speech which suggested words were expensive. 'At a very good price. A Moor mask.'

At the word 'price', Audley leant to his master and whispered something. Wolsey rolled his eyes.

The bizarre scene into which I'd been invited began to take some sort of shape. The cardinal was evidently holding a meeting of his household's master craftsmen. He had, after all, an entire shadow court at his disposal, and it was said that he paid better wages and thus got more talented men than the king. And together they were plotting some show or other, some pageant.

'I have been unfair,' he said, waving an effusive apology into the air. 'Yes. Unfair. Anthony, we have asked you here to offer you a most special honour. We are hoping to stage a gift to His Majesty. To Their Majesties: King Henry and the Emperor Charles. I have gathered here my Masters of Revels, Painters, Strings, Glaziers, and . . .' He frowned. Yet again, he turned to his secretary and gave a hoarse whisper. Audley gave a minute shrug, and Wolsey addressed the room again. 'Alas, I fear our own dear historian has become lost on his way out of London. Have you had any word of him, Herr Gosson?'

The cropped-haired blond man, the mask-painter, said, 'Nein. No.'

I said nothing.

What the hell has this to do with me?

'Historians,' said the man who hadn't yet spoken – the ruddy-faced Master of Glaziers, it must be. He looked familiar too. 'They think to make their own time, I think? Think we all have hundreds of years to us, yes?' He looked around for agreement, for laughter perhaps, which never came.

'Quite, Monsieur Visser,' said Wolsey. 'The fellow runs to his own clock, it seems.' His voice deepened, growing richer. 'We are minded to bring to life a great spectacle, sometime hence. Entertainments.' He looked upwards. 'The world cries, "Wolsey is a man who can do all." And so, he must be. He must turn from buildings and policy to spectacles. A very merry and pleasant interlude. One which shall entertain our sovereign lord according to his favourite taste. The *Masque of Beaumains*.'

I swallowed. 'A masque?' I asked. 'Here?' Harry had mentioned the king and emperor coming.

'Here? No. No, no. And none here are to speak of it when Their Majesties visit. Secrecy, you see. Yes. Yet we must show our imperial guest the true inheritance of King Henry.' He threw an arm over the table, over the painted cloth. 'You see? Herr Gosson here has begun this design on the Round Table at Winchester. There we will have the masque, when the new-painted table is shown to them. A gift to Their Majesties. A surprise. From our own hand and out of the great love we bear his person.' He let out a long, contented sigh. 'The king has read every word of every book on the subject of King Arthur. Many times over. His Majesty's own physician told me that the king once woke in the night from a dream. A dream in which noble Arthur greeted him as his heir, handed him the glistering sword, and bid him rebuild England. And the king's dreams are portents. My humble gift will be only the beginning. A sign and token that he might revive his own great dreams of proving his noble descent.'

Wolsey sounded, I thought, more amused than awed – as

though Henry was a fond son, to be dandled on his cardinal's lap and entertained in his dreaming. Better that, I supposed, than that the king be taught his own strength and encouraged to use it. He'd have little need for his great minister then.

'What, Your Grace . . . what do you need from me?' I asked.

Wolsey puckered his lips in a mischievous way. And then he shook a finger. 'You know of the old legends, do you not? The tales of King Arthur?'

King Arthur. I'd loved those hoary tales as a child. They'd conjured up a whole world better than the real one – a world you wished you lived in. What English boy didn't dream of being a Knight of the Round Table?

'I . . . yes,' I said. 'I've heard read . . .'

'Then you know of Sir Gareth.'

My mind whirled.

Gareth? Gareth. Gareth!

No good. I couldn't place the knight or the tale, not under six pairs of eyes. Nor did I need to, really. I didn't like the shape the conversation was taking.

Wolsey spared me. 'The Dame Lynette comes to Camelot seeking aid in the rescue of her beauteous sister – though she refuses to tell King Arthur why she needs aid. Oh,' he said, 'but I'm an old man, a poor old priest, not a storyteller.' He looked around the table, again with a show of genial warmth that belied his watchful eyes. They came to rest on Cornish. 'My dear Revels, do go on.'

Cornish licked his lips. And then he stood, speaking with arm gestures to rival Wolsey's. 'The Dame Lynette comes out of the wild lands, seeking help for honour's sake. The Red *Knight*, cries she, must be *battled*. Yet she *will not* tell the king wherefore.' His voice had become a singsong. It was, I thought, as though he were entertaining children. But the men around the table seemed to be enjoying the recitation. Even Wolsey was resting an elbow on the table, his chin on his fist, nodding along with an indulgent smile. Only Audley remained stony-faced: not quite bored, but utterly reserved. 'King Arthur gives her only a kitchen knave, a fair-faced *slave* named Beaumains.

'And so, dame and slave travel together, progressing towards the Red Lands. Through darkness and *danger*, they travail; they battle *Black*, Green, Blue, and *Red* Knights. Beaumains *slays* the Black Knight, brings the others to the love of Arthur, and rescues Lynette's sister Lyonesse, who has been *held* in the Red Lands. And thus, Beaumains unmasks – and *behold*,' he said, almost singing now, 'he is *Gareth*, King Arthur's fair and noble *nephew*.' He bowed over the table, sending one arm jerking out in a flourish.

Oh, Christ . . . 'The Black Knight.' My voice came unbidden and sounded distant.

'Quite,' said Wolsey. 'No man is better fitted. A music man of wit, of skill, of . . . A friend. Tell me, my young friend, what have you been doing these last years out of service?'

'I've been teaching music, Your Grace. In the city.'

'It pleases you; it pays you well?'

Absolutely not. Can you not see my coat?

'Passing well,' I said.

Wolsey frowned. 'Well, what shall please us passing well is your returning to court for this masque. You will be well rewarded. I think . . . perhaps a Master of Music in the city might profit by having young students preferred to him. A bigger place to teach, perhaps? We are good to our friends, especially those who are good enough to remember us after a spell. Yes.'

'I . . . I'm honoured, sir. But . . .'

Come on, think!

'But . . . I'm not worthy of so high an honour. To appear before the king. I am too low for that.' I lowered my head, clutching my hat to my chest.

Wolsey's sudden bark of laughter lifted it. The others joined in. 'Ah,' said the cardinal, wiping an eye with a silk handkerchief – the eye with the lazy lid, I thought, nastily. 'You make us laugh. Yes. You have not forgotten what it is to live amongst courtiers, heh? Unworthy . . . too low. Very good. Very good.' He stopped laughing, and the other titters immediately ceased. His tone shifted to something hard – not threatening, but not to be countered. 'You are as high and as worthy as we say you are.'

'Yes, Your Grace.' I would think of something. This wouldn't happen. There wasn't a chance I'd prance around, black mask on or otherwise, with a lot of dangerously great men and women, gawped at by King Henry and his imperial, pick-axe-jawed nephew. 'Yes,' I said again.

Wolsey clapped his hands, all warmth again. 'Yes. A word I like to hear. Though it always costs me, heh?' A little ripple of laughter greeted him, and he waved it away. 'Well, then, Anthony, I am well pleased we are friends again. You might join our little family at your leisure, as in times past, and all will be very merry. Yes. You shall be under Mr Cornish and Monsieur Lutini. Herr Gosson of the painters shall make you a fine Moorish mask.' He frowned, suddenly, as an air of business descended. 'So we are settled. Monsieur Visser, you will work with the Works' carpenters. And every man to his job and to have each item listed by its expense, yes? My secretaries will keep their eyes on any such expenses. We wouldn't wish any errors, would we?'

No one answered.

'Good,' said Wolsey. 'Then, as it seems the blasted historian will not be joining us, I am afraid we must be finished. We shall find some other scholar to pen the words. We have other matters to attend to, do we not, Mr Audley? That fellow shall not have our commission nor any o—'

'What is this?' barked the glazier, Visser. His rosy face reddened still further under its black cap and escaping sandy thatch. 'I'm sorry, Your Grace – look!'

I turned as Visser and the others rose, and we all looked at the tall window directly behind Lutini and Cornish.

Someone was barrelling towards it, arms swinging.

The table itself, heavy though it was, was jounced, as the master craftsmen scented danger, attack. A musical tinkling of dishes rose. Wolsey, however, gave no appearance of fear – only irritation and curiosity. Finally, though, some animation crept over the private secretary's face: Audley moved from behind Wolsey's chair to shield his master. The figure outside grew larger, taking on the shape of a woman – a large, matronly laundress in a grey smock, the strings of her mob cab flying wild. She reached the window and, with both hands, began beating on it.

'She's dirtying the glass,' barked Visser. 'My glass, my glass!'

She was indeed. Big, smudgy handprints were already forming on the diamond panes between the lead, on the coloured arms which had been installed.

'Open the window,' said Wolsey. 'Open the bloody

window.' His voice was not gentle now, but harsh, freed of its veneer of university polish and returned to something primal.

Its savageness was echoed by the woman outside, whose cries now came through clearly.

'Murder! Help me, help, oh, it's horrible! He's dead! Murder!'

3

There seemed an eternity of confusion, of fumbling, until Visser the glazier managed to unhook latches that allowed the window to open outwards, letting the woman's cries invade the room. She stepped in, her skirts flouncing, her garbled shouts aimed everywhere and nowhere. Someone – it might have been Wolsey himself – slapped her, shutting her up. Audley made a futile, whispered attempt to push her towards the door, away from the company, out of the room.

I remained, transfixed, watching the madness unfold.

The window, like all the others in the long gallery, was made in sections, with panels that could be opened to allow people out into the gardens. To my surprise, Wolsey cried for silence, and then led her to his own great chair at the head of the table. This seemed to have a sobering effect.

'I . . . no, Your Grace, I ain't no . . . I can't be sat down in 'ere. Ain't my place.' She attempted a little bobbing curtsey and then blessed herself. He didn't press the issue, apparently content with having brought her hysterics to an end. His next words threatened to bring them crashing back into the room.

'Mistress, you spoke of death, or murd— *Please!*' He put his arms around her shoulders until she was crushed in velvet. Again, something in him seemed to calm her. Whatever faults he had, Wolsey was good with common people. Whether coercing them or comforting them.

'Peace, dear lady, peace.'

'I ain't no lady,' she sniffed.

'No, you are a fine woman of sense. Now tell me,' he said, 'what is this? What did you see?'

'I . . . Down by the river, Your Grace. Oh, it's horrible. He's dead, dead.'

'Who's dead?' snapped Gosson, the Master Painter, in his strange accent. One of the German states, I decided – some duchy about there. 'Who?' He drew himself out of the knot of craft-masters which had formed near the door back into Wolsey's apartments. Audley hadn't joined them. He remained with his back to the window, his hands clasped behind his back.

'Yes, *who*?' said Cornish, emboldened.

Wolsey threw a dark look at his men and they melted back into silence. The woman, however, looked up at him a little doubtfully. He relaxed his grip on her. 'Perhaps we should begin with your name. What is your name, madam?'

'Mary, Your Grace. After the Blessed Virgin.'

'A beautiful name. Mary. Yes.' His voice was smooth, melodious, the voice of Latin oration. 'What did you see, Mary?'

'Down by the river. I . . . went down to wash. Oh my good night, but I've dropped the linens.' She began to move towards the window. Wolsey reached out and grabbed her elbow.

'Never mind the linens. What did you see there?'

She screwed her eyes shut, either to recall the memory or block it out. But she spoke. 'It's a man, Your Grace. Dead,

amongst the trees. Dead. Slain. There's . . . all about him
there's . . .'

'Go on.'

'Birds!'

I frowned. The master craftsmen began muttering. I
thought I heard 'mad' come from one of them.

Mary continued. 'I didn't see what it was, not at first. Just
a lot of birds all pecking and that. But then I got down and
I saw him and . . . Oh my good night, it were a dead man,
truly.' She opened her eyes and, for the first time, appeared to
take in her surroundings: the great velvet-covered table and
its load of rich foods and cloth. The enormous gallery with its
crimson carpet running the length. The walls, wainscoted to
the height of a man's shoulders. The parade of glass windows,
some looking out onto the blocky green shapes of the inner
knot garden. 'Oh, mercy me, what've I done? What've I done,
comin' in 'ere? I'm sorry, Your Grace, I'm . . . Oh the cardinal,
the cardinal 'isself.' She crossed herself.

'Peace, Mary,' said Wolsey. 'Are you married?'

'Yes, yes. I'm sorry, Your Grace, sorry. My 'usband, 'e'll—'

'I was going to say,' he said, 'that I'm only a man, like your
husband. No more. So becalm yourself. Remain here.' He
looked up towards his gentlemen and then his eyes paused
on me. The lazy one, with its heavy eyelid, twitched.

Assessing. Mind turning. Considering.

'Come, gentlemen. I would see the truth of this myself.'
Without another word, the cardinal turned a violet back and
matching skull cap on us, pushed Audley aside, and stepped,
as though he were a man of twenty and not fifty-odd, over
the low frame and out into the sunlight. As he did, I noticed
that the silk handkerchief was drawn from his sleeve and,

absently, he began wiping the bare hand that had touched the laundress. Audley went after him and the gentlemen craftsmen followed, grumbling.

After a moment, alone with the hapless Mary, who had begun muttering Hail Marys and crossing herself repeatedly, I followed.

* * *

Outside the long gallery was a sea of emerald grass, sloping gently down to the river. To the left, the warm red stone of the building stretched onwards: at its end were the vague outlines of low bushes, punctuated by columns bearing heraldic beasts. Those, I supposed, would be part of the new privy gardens, laid out for those who reached the end of the gallery and wished to take a turn in the sun.

But Wolsey was marching onwards, Audley at his heels, his master craftsmen trailing in their wake. Towards the river, I thought, just as Mary had said. I chanced one last look behind me, debating whether I should stay put or follow. I followed, the grass springing and crunching and sending up freshness underfoot.

Nearer the river, a profusion of trees sprouted, their spreading boughs a canopy of leaves. It would have been a pleasant place to lay out tables and eat, perhaps, on such a day. Pretty thoughts, however, were soon banished.

It was the sound that alerted us all, I think. A shrill, cawing, screeching cacophony.

Birds!

Amongst the trees, with the watery, clean smell of the upper Thames freshening the air, Wolsey paused. His men, too, drew short, their hands covering their mouths, their noses. Even Audley finally looked discomfited. I stepped up behind them, unseen, uncared for, around a pile of wet linen that clung, just as unwanted, to the grass. I had become a thing of no importance, of course, in the glare of what lay amongst the trees.

'Dear God,' said Wolsey. I barely heard him over the shrilling.

The man, the body, the corpse – so many names for flesh – lay on his back. Around him, however, were dozens of birds, so that at first I missed him. Pigeons, corvids, gulls, even – bizarrely – a pair of great peacocks, their feathers trailing the ground behind them.

What might those many eyes have seen if the tails were up?

Some of the birds' heads were darting down at the body, some around it. They threw their *food!* in the air and caught at it. Others were shrieking their disapproval of the competition into the boughs.

'Away!' barked Wolsey. He stomped forward, kicking his cassocked leg out. 'Away, I say, go! Scarce better than beasts!' Some of the creatures threw open their beaks and ca-cawed back protests. But the peacocks strutted off, and most of the littler ones took flight, either skimming away across the neatly trimmed grass or landing on branches to keep watch until the intruders left.

'Dear God,' said Wolsey again. 'It is him. It is Signor Gonzaga. The historian. The scholar.'

As the other men drew back, a chorus of moans emerged. Moving a little closer, I frowned down.

'Dear God,' I echoed. My stomach, empty, since I had brought only a few scraps of bread to eat during the hours on the river, clutched at itself, making my head swim.

The corpse – Gonzaga – was covered in scratches, in bites. Criss-crosses of blood marked his face and his hands. Droppings spattered his doublet and hose, looking like discarded oysters. One shoe was half off his foot. His lower legs, his white hose, were greyed from the knee downwards: wet, I thought, as though he had walked, been led or dragged, through the narrow stream which ran up to feed the moat.

But that was not what sickened me.

It took me a good few seconds to make sense of what I was seeing. Someone – the fellow's murderer – had stuffed something into the dead man's mouth, so that it looked like he was vomiting it up. That thing, I realised, my eyes travelling over it, was a dead bird. Its head and part of its neck had been thrust in, so that the rest of the long, curving body lay on the chest: a great, fluffy mass of light and dark grey. Absurdly, appallingly, two enormously long legs stuck up, ending in four long, clawed toes. There was something obscene about it, about the desecration, about the almost dainty, offended way the bird's feet were poised.

'What is this?' asked Wolsey. He repeated the question, louder, drawing forth more angry chirrups, tweets, and barks.

'A heron?' offered Gosson. No one answered him.

Wolsey turned away from the corpse, his eyes raking his men, sweeping onto me. 'Murder,' he said. 'My scholar has been murdered most foully. In the fair gardens of this, my house.'

Lutini, the Master of the Strings, said, in his broken English accent, 'I knew him, Your Grace.' He looked towards

Gosson. 'As did Herr Gosson, his friend. This man. A Mantuan. He has a wife. Children. He is a loss to us as them.'

Wolsey crossed himself, as did Gosson. 'We shall have them told. Privily.' He licked his lips. And then his eyes narrowed on me. I looked at the ground. We were quite near the body. On the grass, I noticed, was a scattering of crumbs, as though someone had scattered breadcrumbs to feed the birds.

Or to attract them?

Did the murderer wish the man found quickly?

I bent to pick one up and regarded it, frowning, hoping by busyness that the cardinal would forget me. I was to be disappointed. 'A wife?' asked Wolsey. 'Poor lady. And sons? Yes. A great shame to be made fatherless. 'Anthony!'

My heart sank.

'Yes, Your Grace?'

'Your arrival is well timed. In its fashion. I recall that you have good, listening ears and good, watching eyes. I remember them from the time before. Before you left us.' A little rebuke edged his words. I said nothing. Yet it was true enough. When I'd been his trumpeter and it had been my job to lurk in doorways, Wolsey had bid me spy for him, watch for him, listen for him. It was, I'd told myself, what had turned me against service – or at least given me another reason to depart it. 'Some evil person . . . some man evil-disposed . . . has done this. Perhaps . . . perhaps you might be of service again.'

'Surely, Your Grace, the coroner – the king's coroner—' This was Visser, the fat little Master of Glaziers.

'By all means,' said Wolsey. And then he put a finger

gingerly to his lips. 'Hm. Perhaps not the king's coroner. The Surrey coroner. Yes. Mr Dorick. Send for Mr Dorick.' Visser threw me a little look of smugness but remained standing there. 'Well,' barked Wolsey, his mood shifting and arms flailing. 'Send for him! Now!' He paused, as Audley stepped forward, his black robes brushing the grass. With one fist to his mouth, the secretary gave a discreet cough.

'If it please Your Grace, perhaps . . .' His voice descended as he moved to the cardinal, whispering in his ear. It was the first time I'd heard the man speak. His voice was dry, rustling, like a breeze through autumn leaves.

Wolsey's expression changed, high-coloured excitement fading, his features narrowing, turning foxy. 'No. No,' he said, as Audley stepped back, a thin smile on his face. 'Mr Audley here shall write of what happened to the coroner. Yes.' He thrust a look at his secretary.

Audley cleared his throat. 'It is evident,' he said, meeting each craftsman's eye in turn, 'that this has been a most unfortunate drowning. It will be reported as such.' His flat gaze dared challenge. No one met it.

'Quite,' said Wolsey. 'And this . . . ah . . . this drowning. I will review the despatch myself and my good Mr Audley here can take it down for Mr Dorick to sign. That should satisfy the law. And I would not have it noised abroad that anything more . . . unseemly . . . occurred within our house. Yes. His Majesty should scarce bring his imperial nephew to an – an ill-conditioned – a hazardous house.' These words he said as though their taste surprised him.

'As you wish,' said Audley. 'I shall write it and send it by my man Harry Gainsford. Perhaps Mr Visser here will accompany me. To act as witness to what I write.'

'I, Your Grace, I . . .' The little glazier looked at Wolsey in appeal.

'Go!' snapped the cardinal.

Immediately, Audley bowed and began moving serenely back in the direction of the palace. Visser didn't demur further but took off after him, bowing and turning at once.

When we were down to five, Wolsey said, 'And you, Lutini and Cornish – bring up those linens. Cover him.' The two men, either eager to be of service or not to have to look at the corpse, set to work, stepping away and unfurling the wet sheets. They muttered and hissed at one another as they stepped apart and lifted.

'Anthony,' said Wolsey, turning again to me. 'I would have you go to this man's home. Where is it?' he asked, looking at Gosson.

'Birchin Lane, Your Grace,' said the blond man without expression. 'In London. You wish I should go and speak to the Frau Gonzaga?'

'No.' Wolsey remained looking at me. 'Go to the Gonzaga house in Birchin Lane. Tell his wife of this accident. The Fr— the Signora. You understand? Do not alarm the good lady. It is apparent that this is a drowning. Yes. The poor fellow was at the river, was drowned, and washed up here.' He crossed himself again. 'Tell her she will be paid what was due him of his work. That his creditors might be paid. If he had creditors . . . Do you understand me? You are a boy of some wit.'

'Thank you,' I said, flatly.

'That is not a compliment in a servant,' he said, matching me. And then he closed his eyes. 'I cannot . . . In my own house. In *my* house. Who has come here? Who has done this?' He, Gosson, and I all stood back whilst the body was covered over. Instantly, the damp sheet clung to it, making a series of incongruous bumps. Dampness filled the air around us.

Something clawed at my memory. I crumbled the crumb I'd retrieved in my fingers and let it blow away on the breeze. 'Pardon me, Your Grace, but I . . .'

'What?' He opened his eyes and gave me a hard look. Expecting some excuse, I thought, some attempt to get out of this grisly business whilst it still lay bleeding on the grass.

'I . . . I think I saw something.' All heads turned to look at me and I felt my cheeks darken. I kept my head up. 'When I came here. Off the wherry. I thought . . . there was someone. A man, hiding behind the bushes. The water gallery. As though waiting. Watching. Perhaps for Signor Gonzaga to arrive, to . . . to . . .'

'To spirit him off and . . . and do this,' Wolsey finished.

'Did you see the man, boy?' asked Lutini.

'From a great space,' I said. 'It's a long path. I saw . . . he had something grey. A brush, I thought.' My heart skipped a beat. 'That bird. That dead bird, in the mouth.'

A heron.

Wolsey bit at his lip. 'Monsieur Lutini? Mr Cornish? Herr Gosson?' A trio of heads bowed. 'Remain here. I will send some lower persons to remove the poor creature indoors. Into . . . an empty chamber.'

'But the king,' said Gosson, his head snapping up. 'His Majesty. Your Grace, what shall he say of this? This outrage?'

Wolsey pursed his lips, glaring at the man. 'His Majesty shall not be troubled. If he is, I shall know the source. My dear Mr Audley has friends in His Majesty's household who listen for tale-tellers. For men who would breed jealousies and suspicions. With the emperor in England, any talk of violent death . . . it should cause . . .' He didn't finish. He didn't need to. People, if they heard, would say that no Englishman could have done so vile a deed; it must have been some visiting Spaniard. Riots and routs would follow, like night after day. The cardinal's carnival world would be soured to be sure.

Gosson held the cardinal's gaze for a moment before his eyes darted down to the covered body. He sees it too, I thought.

'Good,' said Wolsey. 'See that they do not look under the linen. I wish no word of this to spread. Anthony, walk a little with me. Back to the house.'

Wolsey began moving out of the little patch of trees, heading towards Hampton Court. I kept pace behind him as the magnificent palace rose again into view. So many windows, I thought. Ordinarily, I hated them in any palace, feeling always that I was being watched, commented upon, considered a freak or an outsider. Now, I thought only that it was clever of the person to do their work down under the trees.

Over his shoulder, Wolsey began speaking; his voice came to me on a waft of the heavy perfume which hung around him. 'Naturally, this was no accident. Though His Majesty would be I think . . . happier . . . to hear only that.'

Happier, I wondered – or, as usual, shielded from matters the cardinal preferred to discover for himself?

'I shall pay that wretched laundress well for her silence. You, I would have take a horse and ride for the city. Fast – take a good rouncey from our own stables here. Ay, and a livery from my great wardrobe. Discover if my poor scholar had enemies. Speak to the wife. But tell her nothing. Let us hope that he did, just one – some cruel creditor who followed him here. Or came ahead of him. Speak to her tonight.' The palace now loomed over us, so graceful, so unfit a place for murder. The very idea seemed an affront. Wolsey paused before stepping back into his house. 'I trust you, Anthony Blanke, on the strength of your honesty. I have never heard a word whispered about your time in service, the way some men do when they leave me and seek new masters. And for that I thank you.' He reached out a hand, bristling with grey hairs, and rested it for a beat on my shoulder. Here was favour, of a kind. I was being trusted as a former servant returned to the nest – trusted with service, as I'd once been. That perfume scent fell on me again. 'God bless you. And may He help you bring this business to a conclusion. Approach it, young man, with a certain . . .' His hand twirled vaguely. 'Scrupulosity. And with speed.' He turned away, drawing out that silk handkerchief again, I noticed, to wipe away the touch of me, the inferior taint. And then he was gone, leaving me on the threshold between the teeming life of the palace and the gruesome death beyond.

* * *

I did not take horse immediately for the city. For one thing, I couldn't stand horses – they were useful enough, though not in my new life in the city – they smelled, they were unpredictable, and they didn't listen to me. In my youth, I used to think they thought me some kind of half-breed: a mule. I had been called that once: a mule who lives in the stable and thinks he can out-horse the horses. Perhaps I'd deserved it. My solution to being different had long been to be as much the same as possible – better than the same. I was proud of my high London accent – so different to the Spanish patois my father had warbled without shame, and which still managed to embarrass me in my echoing memories.

I stood before the entrance to Hampton Court, winked at by those many windows staring down on the moat, on the path to the water gallery and river. Still a handful of servants sang as they worked, heedless of the horror which lay beyond the palace. I went from person to person, asking the same question. Gradually, a picture emerged.

A fellow had come up from the river – not me; he had come after me – and had gone off somewhere, not coming up to the palace. With someone? Yes. He met someone. Didn't see who. Don't know who. A man. Down there.

I skirted the water gallery, stepping from gravel to grass, going around the bushes on the other side. When I came to, roughly, where I thought I'd seen the mysterious man lurking, I found a break in the foliage.

He was spying here. Watching. Waiting.

And when Signor Gonzaga had arrived, and the murderer knew he had his man – then, then he had sprung up ahead of him, meeting him at the head of the pathway and spiriting him away. I parted the bushes just a little, putting my face close. The smell of the greenery, strong and fresh, met me. There was the path, the matching bushes and round columns on the other side.

I swallowed.

It might have been me.

Except, I realised, it was never going to be. This was evidently a deliberate attack on the historian. I was nothing; I had been spotted, ignored, allowed to live. Gonzaga, following along behind me, had been taken off. Useless to wonder why without knowing anything of the man. Perhaps the wife could supply a reason.

Or perhaps the other – the man who did it . . .

Returning to the path, I crunched my way down to the water stairs and landing stage. My wherryman was there still, lying down between the boards of his craft, his cap pulled over his blanched nutshell of a face. A good thing, I thought: I didn't relish having to explain that I'd be taking horse for London. But there was another, matching boat, tied up a little farther out along the jetty. Its waterman was busily setting to a meal of bread and cheese, spread out on a cloth on his lap.

'Good morrow,' I said, lifting a hand and forcing brightness into my voice.

'Eh?' He looked up, at the same time folding over his cloth.

I bit at my nail, unsure what to say.

Sweet? Strange.

My hand dropped, sweet-tasting fingers with it. I should have changed into the cardinal's livery before setting off, before asking questions blindly. 'You brought a man,' I said. 'From London. Signor Gonzaga. A scholar.'

The wherryman stood, rocking with the boat. His eyes narrowed on me, taking in my face. I was conscious that I looked like a man not to be trusted. My friend Harry Gainsford – now there was a fine, tall, blond fellow who, with a wink, could have the truth from anyone. 'Mebbe,' he said.

'The cardinal,' I flailed, 'has asked me to discover if the fellow said anything. Was he . . . was he well, in himself? Did he say much?'

The man shrugged. And then he chewed on whatever morsel of food he'd kept in his cheek. 'Nah.'

I frowned. Of course. I had been lumbered with a boatman who would happily talk, as most in London would, and now had come upon one of the rare silent ones. Inspiration struck. I dug at my belt, fishing a coin from my purse, and passed it over.

'Where to?' he asked, taking it.

'What? Nowhere.' I frowned and then saw that he had taken on what passed for a smile. He knew. 'Gonzaga. What did he say?'

He shrugged again. 'Blabber-spout, that one. Clatterfart. Holding a pouch to him. Saying as to how his discovery would change all. Odd accent, he had. French?'

'Italian. A pouch?' I asked, jangling my own with a fist. 'Money?'

'No, sir.' The wherryman lifted a hand and waggled his fingers in an incomprehensible gesture. 'The bigger sort. Leather. For holding papers, like. What a secker-tay would have. But big. Very big.' He mimed the width of his chest. 'Like for one of them books.' He said the word as though seeking to impress.

A book.

A book in a great leather pouch.

I nodded, understanding. Gonzaga had made some discovery, found something. And he hadn't been quiet about it before bringing it to Hampton Court. It might be that which had got him killed: some discovery that would 'change all'. But what would a historian discover that anyone would kill to steal?

'Anything else?' I asked.

He shrugged yet again. 'Nah.'

I nodded once, twice. 'Good. Right.' I considered extracting a few more coins to pass him to give to my wherryman, but then thought better of it. My fellow would never see them. Besides, I had little left. It had already cost me two weeks' earnings to get to the bloody place. 'When your fellow there wakes,' I said, pointing at my old boat, 'tell him the cardinal's men will lodge him the night and pay him the fare home in the morning. And . . . uh . . . Signor Gonzaga won't be returning to London today.'

He bristled. 'What? He told me to wait.'

Interesting.

'Well . . . I . . . you'd better speak to the under-porter up at the palace about that.' I gave a shrug myself, which I hoped said, 'You know what these places are like.' It didn't seem to take.

'You fucking bet I will, lad. Wasting my time. French arse-piece.'

I didn't engage any further but turned my back on him and began hurrying back up the water gallery. The frontage of Hampton Court remained serene, unmoved by all that was going on around and below. This murderer, I thought, might have come by boat or by horse, might be part of the palace's great body of people or from without, from the city. If I hoped to make London by nightfall, I couldn't waste any more time.

The wife, I thought. The wife would know. As Wolsey said, it would be some creditor and the affair quickly ended.

And I was foolish enough then to believe it.

4

Even from the street, I could tell something was wrong. I'd dismounted the horse – a tame enough beast called Abraham – a while back and only just found my footing on the sloping, hard-packed mud, just shy of the central sewer channel. I envied men who could dismount and walk easily. Me, my still legs quivered, and the world spun wildly beneath my feet. My father had insisted I learn to ride young – 'You must if you wish to make your way in da world . . .' – and I was competent, though far from skilful.

It was dull, despite the late summer evening. The city I'd come through was choked with smoke, above and within, making my going slow once I'd reached it. The air was thick with the acrid reek and, here and there, Londoners reeled wraith-like around the dying embers of bonfires. The whole city had gone into a strange kind of extended holiday since the imperial emperor had arrived, encouraged apparently by King Henry. I'd wound my way along streets full of drunken song, ducking under overhanging eaves, between neighbours calling to one another from windows, all the way to Birchin Lane, which ran down from Cornhill to Lombard Street. Here the houses were a little broader, a little less run-down, and fewer revellers were at play. I had no qualms about tying the horse in such a place, and no fear that it would be stolen. Spotting a skeletal frame used to display second-hand clothing for sale in daylight hours, I'd left the panting Abraham there and knocked on doors until I'd been directed to the right house.

And it was this house, the Gonzaga house, that looked wrong.

The darkness.

Though dim under its heavy pall of smoke, London provided a low, hazy, ethereal light. The myriad celebratory fires joined with the spilling glow from taverns and houses. Link boys were escorting wealthier citizens about before the watchmen and the cutpurses began to slither from the shadows. It was not a pleasant light, but a flaring, omnipresent one.

But not here.

Not at this house.

The building itself was set back a little from the street, with a scraggly, fenced square of garden before it. It was narrow but tall, at least three storeys with an attic holding up the sharply pointed roof. A fair town house, I thought – an old place, of wattle-and-daub with timber struts, but proud. Only there were no lights burning in the windows, which were shuttered despite the heat. Not even a tell-tale square of yellow or orange betrayed habitation. A wife and children, Gonzaga supposedly had, but there was no sign of them.

I stood awhile, regarding the place, ignoring the scattered cheers and disembodied roars of laughter that came up from Lombard Street. Perhaps, I thought, the family had gone out, to enjoy the festivities with neighbours. But it was a fool or a madman – or woman – who would leave a house in the city unattended on such a night, even on a good street. Sensible, respectable folk were tucked safely within doors when night fell, keeping the King's peace. Only the roisterers – and idiots like me – were abroad.

I was wasting time, fearful of something, nervous.

Pushing the unease downwards, I left Abraham at the display frame by the stall next door and crossed the garden. At the door, I swallowed and then gave a sharp rap, darting a look behind me as though I might have invited something out of the smoky air.

When I turned back, I saw that the door had opened. But no one stood inside.

'Good evening,' I cried into the void beyond, my voice a ragged whisper. I cleared my throat and repeated it. It came out no braver.

Turn around. Come back tomorrow.

I stepped inside.

A passage lay beyond, like a narrow tunnel burrowing into darkness. I let my eyes adjust to the stuffy gloom. Just about, I could see the passage leading into a room at the back – a pantry, likely – and turning left before its doorway. Keeping a hand on the right wall, I crept in, listening. 'Signora Gonzaga?' I cried. 'Are you at home?'

Thump.

I froze.

Thump-thump.

'Mistress?!' This time I shouted into the darkness. 'Are you hurt?'

The sound came again, heavy and insistent. From somewhere above me. That urge to flee, to run screaming into the street, rose again and submerged. I opened my mouth to speak, closed it, and began creeping down the hall, glad I was still in soft shoes. I chanced a look into the room at the end. It was empty and, in the gloom, the pots and pans hanging on the wall looked deadly. The arrhythmic thudding turned me. Where the hallway turned left, a set of wooden steps rose into shadow. With my neck sunk into my doublet, I put one foot in front of the other, cringing at the ensuing creaks.

The landing at the top of the house turned left, back over the floor downstairs. Hesitantly, I moved into nothingness. My heartbeat had become a frantic thing, rushing and pulsing in my ears. There was no other sound, no further thuds or bangs or—

'Argh!' The cry burst out of me and I was falling forward, my stomach lurching; my hands flew out, hit the ground; I rolled. 'Argh!' I reached out, waving, gasping. I had tripped – something had tripped me. 'Get back! I'm armed!'

The thing was at my feet, a darker black against the shadows, bulky, writhing, living. I kicked at it.

'Mmph! Mmph! Mmph!'

What? What?

I hunched up onto my backside, still sore from the long day's ride. A giant worm, I thought, a great grub.

'Mmph!'

'Oh God,' I said. The wriggling shape was a person, perhaps injured, lying in the hall. I jerked upwards, leaning on the wall, and squinted. And then I hopped over it and felt along the far wall by the stairs. The rough-smooth coolness of plaster met my fingers and I brushed along it.

There!

The smoother, hard line of a window frame. I pulled a hand back and slapped the shutter outwards. It didn't give. I made a fist and punched at it until pain blossomed in my knuckles and it fell open. Diffuse light spread into the hallway, making a dull grey of the floorboards. I turned and saw the figure, unmistakeably human now. 'Mmph!' it insisted. And then it raised two bound feet mermaid-like and thumped them on the boards.

I fell upon it, feeling around the head. A rough length of cloth had been tied around it, forming a gag. Once I'd loosened it and thrown it away, the person – a woman, I could see now, and feel from the hair – gulped in air hungrily and released it in a ragged fury. '*Salva il miei bambini! Salvali!*'

'Mistre – Signora Gonzaga?'

She breathed deeply again. 'My children,' she said, her accent thick. 'Save them!'

Children!

I leapt up and began moving through the house. In the first room I came to, I opened the shutters, letting more of that odd, rusty light in. And there they were.

Both children lay on a stringed box-bed – one about four and still pudgy, the other older and thinner, a boy of about ten with a mop of dark curls. My blood ran cold.

And then I saw the older one move. The littler one followed. Both, like their mother, had been bound up and I freed them. The younger started crying, curling up against his staring brother, trying to burrow under a blanket, away from me. I tried making soothing noises and some inarticulate nonsense poured out. 'Please. You're safe. I mean no harm. Please.' The little boy's crying intensified, whilst the elder squirmed away, not looking at me, his arm curling around a small, straw-and-wood toy horse. Abruptly, he said, 'Do you have a horse from Barbary?'

'Wha— No. No,' I said.

'Oh. I like horses. I know where they come from. Arab horses and Irish horses and Barbary horses. Jennets and chargers and destriers and palfreys,' he said. I narrowed my eyes. Odd child, I thought. His accent was London – as different from his mother's as mine was from my father's. Again abruptly, his subject changed, though not his tone. 'A bad man was here. We were here all night. Bridled like horses.' Still, he was staring down at his toy.

I left them, returning to the hall, and further freeing their mother.

Signora Gonzaga was a handsome woman, plump and pretty, her hair in the low light looking almost as black as mine. Clutching my arm and the wall, she hauled herself up. 'Grazie. Thank you.' She didn't pause for anything more but barrelled past me and into the bedchamber. After retrieving my cap, which lay forgotten where it must have fallen when I did, I followed and found her already gathering the children up in her arms. One clung to her neck, the other around her broad waist, as she sank onto the low bed between them. A muddle of Italian and English words, mixed and indecipherable, swam through the air on a tide of sniffles and tears.

Wildly, I thought: thank God, they're alive. And, on the heels of that: and it must be some creditor, some enemy of this household, that's all.

In the horror, in the excitement, I'd forgotten that I'd come to tell her that her husband was dead.

'Please,' she said, looking up. 'A drink. Ale. Ale. Down the stairs. And lights.'

Only too willing to delay my mission, I did as she bid, returning through the house, opening more shutters. In the pantry I found wooden cups and a jug of sour-smelling ale. On a sideboard were sourer-smelling tallow candles ribbed with solid drips, a tinderbox, fire-steel, and splint. I lit all that might burn until the shadows were banished to corners. And then I returned upstairs, well lit and furnished with ale.

I stood against an undressed wattle-and-daub wall, evidently from an older part of the house, whilst the family – the now-smaller family – slurped their fill. Eventually, Signora Gonzaga burped, a fist held demurely over her mouth. She kissed both heads furiously before standing and bowing her own.

'I thank you, sir. We have lain . . . so . . . since . . . one night. And day. No one come. My husband, he not come.'

Shit.

I took off my cap and held it in front of me, as though I could ward off her pathetic thanks. She would be less pleased to see me soon enough. 'What happened here?' I asked.

To my surprise, her face screwed up in fury and she spat onto a patch of rushes strewn on the floor. 'What you say in this country – fucking thieves! *Bastardo*! I will kill him, what he done to my children, cut his throat myself.' She held up two fists as though to prove it.

'Thieves?' Surely, I thought, no – that was too great a coincidence.

'*Sì*! He come in the night, he say he look for my husband. He know my husband a great man. And he very smiling at the door. And so I let him in. But then he not smiling. He want my husband. He see he no here. And he . . . *Bastardo*!' She spat again. 'I kill him! I find him!'

'Who was he? Did you know him?'

'No! Wicked *bastardo*, brute.' Behind her, the children

began cursing too and she turned her angry face on them. They quietened immediately. When she looked back at me, she said, 'They always the same here. Break in on us from other place. Wish to take what is ours.'

'Did he give a name? Was he English?'

'*Inglese*, yes, he speak English. But no. His sound, I no know. Not Italian. And no name. He was young-faced, not looking a brute. He fool me. Dirty man. Dirty hands, dirty nails. And he smell.' She wrinkled her nose and waved her hand under it. 'And he wearing an apron. Like to do evil work. Dirty work. Dirty man.'

An apron, I thought.

A butcher?

'This man,' I said. 'Did he rob you?'

'He rob my husband. He rob his room. You look.' She studied me a little. 'You from the Cardinal Wolsey, *sì*?'

'Yes. *Sì*. Signora, I . . . Please, come with me. Leave them alone. Please.' She frowned at me, this time peering at my face. I looked at the floor, scuffing at it a little. 'In your husband's room, maybe? Please?'

She left the two boys, who began whimpering. Another hard twist of her head and a stream of Italian silenced them, and then she moved past me, back out into the hall. I followed as she strode down it, turning right at another door near the back of the house. 'Here,' she said.

She remained outside until I stepped into the threshold.

My jaw fell open.

The room might once have been a study. Now it was a wreck. A desk – or rather a board held between two stout boxes – had been smashed in the middle, leaving splintered edges jabbing downwards. Shelves had been torn down and lay amidst the jumble of shredded papers which carpeted the floorboards. A scattering of books – not many – lay with their covers and pages spread obscenely. I thought again of their owner, who had been laid out in an even worse state. I stepped carefully across the room, opening another shutter, and then bent to pick up a book. It was heavy. The title page announced it as *Le Morte D'Arthur*. A few pages on, dense script began, 'In the begynnyng of Arthur, after he was chofen kynge by aduenture and by grace . . .' I put it down. No surprise there; Gonzaga was at the same business as the rest of Wolsey's men.

I turned to his wife.

Signora Gonzaga had her arms folded and she was staring at me, not the room. There was a hardness in that stare, spread across her even features, drawing her thick brows together. I clasped both hands behind my back, squashing my cap, then transferred them in front of me. No better.

I'd had plenty of time to think of how to fashion this news-giving on the ride over. Instead, I'd cursed the horse, watched the road, traced the growing size of the smudgy outline of London's spires and turrets as they grew sharper. Anything, in short, but think of what Wolsey was making me do. Dancing before the royals in a stupid bloody masque, dressed as a fearsome black knight, was starting to look preferable. Almost.

Delay!

'Signora . . . do you know what your husband was about? What his work was about?'

She narrowed her eyes. 'Work?' I nodded encouragement. She only frowned more deeply. 'For the cardinal. For the king. Some time ago, he take us to see the king and little

. . . *imperatore*. But all Pietro talk about . . .' She made expansive gestures. 'Arthur, the king, King Arthur – what he to discover soon. Bah!' She looked on the point of spitting and then something like panic widened her eyes. 'This get him into trouble? He talk of the king putting much . . . uh . . . much monies into his displays of the King Arthur. And the cardinal, his displays and such. All much monies going from your King Henry and his people, to . . .' Her forehead wrinkled. 'The celebrations of Arthur.'

I let silence fall between us. Certainly, I knew that if King Henry had proof of his descent from Arthur, if he had reason to celebrate it, none of us in England would ever hear the end of it. I daresay a new Camelot would be built and painted and gilded inside and out to show the world that Henry VIII was King Arthur's progeny. I could imagine Henry well enough, riding out of the courtyard of a glistering new castle on a high hill – one that would put Hampton Court Palace to shame – astride a white charger, the sunlight picking out the blond hairs in his beard. It would be the crowning achievement of his life, to be known as the heir to our ancient high king.

Get on with it.

I blinked, swallowed, ignored the dull throb of a hunger headache, and said, 'I'm sorry. Signora, I'm sorry. Your husband . . . There was . . . He's . . .'

You're doing great . . .

'He's dead,' I said. 'I'm sorry.'

She drew breath in a sharp gasp and released it in a moan. Her fist flew to her mouth. And then she glanced to her right. She shook her head a little. 'Pietro,' she said. 'Peter, I mean. Poor Peter. Oh. What do I say? To them?'

I bowed my head. And then looked up. 'An accident. The

cardinal, he sends you the Church's blessings and says . . .
all will be well. With you, I mean, for you.' I was flailing; I
wanted out. 'Shall I fetch the watchmen? About this?' My cap
wobbled towards the destruction.

'Watchmen? No. No trouble. Bring no trouble. We fix this
ourselves.'

We?

'But . . . who . . . Your husband, Signor Gonzaga – did
he . . . Was someone . . . Who might have come here and
searched this place? Did the – the "bastard" – did he say what
he sought?'

'He not say.' She gave one hard shake of her head.

I wet my lips. The growing headache had become a flaring
pain at the base of my skull. 'And – did your husband keep
anything here? Of value?'

'His work only. I not understand this. Books and writings
and the history. This man, this creature – he caused this
accident to Pietro, uh? Is this what you say?'

'I . . .' I frowned. 'I don't know. But I'll discover it. His
Grace would discover it and have justice.'

'Justice!' she said, and her eyes widened, grew excited. '*Sì!*
We have justice.'

'You said, signora, that you were attacked – lay here a day
and night. He came last night?'

'Yes.'

'And your husband was from home. Where was he? He
came to Hampton Court today – where did he sleep last
night?'

'At his work. Some – ah – *monastero.*' She thrust her hand
down the front of her brown bodice and drew out a wooden
crucifix on a chain, holding it up. 'Monks. *Monastero.* You

understand? Where he do the studies. The old papers and books. *Biblioteca*.'

'Yes,' I said. 'I understand. Do you know which monastery?'

'All of them!' she barked. 'He go everywhere, searching, searching.' My face must have betrayed me, for she added, 'Uh, last night – I think Southwark, the Priory. He said it must lie there. He try everywhere already and say he find the path. His history, he say, a path to truth, like a sailor who find new world through old maps. Westminster, Charterhouse, Crutch-ed Friars, Westminster. King's library at Rish-mond. Now he say a-ha; the Southwark canons, they have copy. He go there last night.'

A copy, I thought. Of what?

'And he didn't say anything,' I asked, 'Pietro, about what he was studying?'

'Bah,' she said, waving her hands dismissively. 'Ancient tales. Uh, legends. Stories. For your cardinal. *Spazzatura!*' And then, as though suddenly realising that he was dead, her colour rose. 'Oh. *Mio Dio*! I sorry. Sorry. Poor Pietro. I not mean . . . his work, it was . . . it . . .' She began to sob. I lifted a hand, wondering if I should comfort her, trying to recall how Wolsey had handled the laundress. And then I replaced my cap.

'I'm sorry,' I said. 'Uh . . . if you require anything – you can write to the cardinal. He'll be kind, good to you. All of you.' My spine stiffened. 'If this brute who came here, if he . . . We'll discover him. You'll have your justice, signora.'

I had no idea if that was true, but I hoped it would be. It sounded impressive. And I wished it to be true; I wished to do something for this broken family. I gave her a little bow and let her usher me out of the house on a wave of teary Italian gratitude.

Outside, assured by the new widow that if the man dared come back, she'd kill him herself – and I believed her – I retrieved Abraham. I didn't bother trying to mount in the dark. Instead, I began leading him up towards Cornhill. If the watch were out, I doubted they'd trouble to question a man in livery leading a horse. Somewhere – everywhere – bells rang out the late hour.

It had been a long and deeply unpleasant day. I wanted nothing more than some food, something to drink, and some sleep – and not to have to think. And so, naturally, my mind galloped where the horse and I trod slowly.

Strangely, I was not thinking of Gonzaga's murderer, who, I decided, must have attempted to take him at home and, not finding what he sought the previous night – either man or something else – had hastened into the country to await him. To prevent him, presumably, from sharing his discovery with Wolsey and his master craftsmen. Whatever that discovery was, it must have been made in Southwark Priory.

No, I was thinking of another religious house, and the letter-writer with whom I still corresponded.

5

I woke near noon in my own bed, in my late father's house in Shoemaker Row, full of business: a foolish thing for a Sunday. I didn't go to mass with my stepmother – I'd found her still awake when I returned home from the Gonzaga house, quietly led Abraham into our ramshackle stable, and told her I was unwell. I was, a bit, and I wasn't too pleased with God, who seemed to be enjoying setting grisly business in my path.

His history, he say, a path to truth . . .

Besides, in the sudden spirit of rebelliousness, I intended to be quite ungodly on this Sunday. As if in protest, I had refused to think of Pietro Gonzaga. If images of that body and its owner's darkened house and fatherless children swam into my mind, I pushed them away.

I was sitting in our plain little front room, sipping at home-brewed ale and nibbling at a heel of cheat bread, examining the backs of my hands. Stupid of me, not to wear a pair of gloves, even light ones. I swore I could see my hands taking on that dull walnut look. All that sitting in the glare of the sun had done me no good. I'd have to take care of that, and I had heard—

The door banged open, and I stood up as my stepmother huffed into the room, her face red. 'Anthony,' she said, kicking it shut behind her, making the cheap painted cloths on the walls flutter. My father had chosen them from the stalls by St Paul's. It was here, in this room, that he would hold his evenings of 'da hospitality' – which too often devolved into his unashamed foreign dances and chants – and from which I'd scurry upstairs to hide away under good English woollens.

I pasted on a smile. 'Good morrow, mother.'

A good woman, my stepmother, a good honest woman. She was broad and hen-like, and never seemed to care what anyone thought of her. I admired that. It must have been that lack of care that led her into marriage with one of the only black men in London, and certainly the only one in Aldgate; and a man with a child, too, though I'd been over ten when they were wed. Sometimes, I imagined she must have been what my own mother would have become, though she'd died in getting me. Though my father had been dead and gone for two years now, my stepmother wasn't shy about him. She was, naturally, never ashamed of him, never embarrassed. I'd asked her once, affecting to be offhand, whether people had talked when she'd married. 'Yes,' had been her answer. 'They said I'd been a cunning wench catching a man who knew the king's own court and its folks.' It wasn't the answer I'd expected, but she wasn't giving anything else.

'I see you found the bread,' she said, wiping sweat from her brow. Strands of blonde had darkened and clung on obstinately. 'Another hot one. You're feeling better, then?'

'Yes, mother,' I said. It was what my father had bid me call her and I liked it, having a mother who fit in. 'Much.'

'Good. Good. Though you shouldn't miss mass like that.' I belched, shrugging. 'Honestly! What's got into you, boy?' She sounded more amused than annoyed, as she moved over to me and gave my head a peck, before starting to clear away the remains of my meal.

'I'm not finish—'

'You're finished. No time for the priest, no time to stuff your face. You'll have noticed I cleaned up the muck you tracked in last night, when you were still a-bed this morning.' This came with a mischievous smile. 'I swear, I don't know what gets into you. It's going to court again.'

'It wasn't court. It was the cardinal's—'

'Just like the last time you came back from court. With a rebel's spirit about you. You watch that.'

I rolled my eyes. It was a common enough complaint of hers – that I'd left service with a wilfulness about me. My stepmother took in lodgers, when she could, and she had firm ideas about how wilfulness should be treated under her roof. 'Yes, mother,' I said, in a singsong tone. With her free hand, she swiped at me and I ducked, laughing in spite of myself. I stayed sitting as she disappeared, but her voice drifted in from the pantry.

'You know what I heard?'

I got up and went to stand in the low doorway, one hand on the frame. 'What?'

'That the king and the emperor are hearing mass at St Paul's today. And then a great feast at Bridewell. So, it's another holiday, so everyone's saying. It's as though a midsummer moon's seized everybody. Ruling their brains. Folk are so merry at the in-coming of this Spanish emperor that they've neither eyes to see nor good legs to stand on! Might go and revel myself, God-spare-me.' Clatters punctuated her words as she busied herself finding a water jug amongst the collection of hanging pots and pans over the hearth. I sometimes wondered how God had time to smite and save and judge, so much time must He spend sparing my stepmother. 'But no word on the queen. Give us the queen, that's what I say.'

I bit at my lip. The second Mrs Blanke had, I knew, an inordinate love of Queen Catherine, whom she'd never spoken to or been near. It might have been because they shared given names, I sometimes reasoned, or perhaps because my late father had come to England in the queen's train. I, though, was loath to hear her bring up the queen: not because I disliked that good lady – quite the opposite; she is a fine woman – but because I couldn't be bothered telling my stepmother, for the thousandth time, what colour the queen's hair was, how short she was, how graceful, how kind. I sometimes felt that Catherine Blanke was as heartbroken when I left service as she was when my father died; I had cut off her link to news of her idol. 'Well, then,' was all I said.

'Give us women the queen,' she persisted. 'God gave us the queen and you lads the king, that's what I say. Here, go out and fetch me in some water, will you?'

'I'm going out,' I said. Then I licked my lips. 'Here, do you know anything about King Arthur?'

'What?'

I repeated my question, not sure what to expect.

'Know? Of course. Your father used to sing ballads about him. Let me see . . .' She looked over her shoulder with an appearance of being about to sing.

'Never mind the words. Did you ever hear of King Henry's . . . his descent? From Arthur?'

Looking back to her pots, she said, 'Oh, yes. Heard the king once said that he was the right king of all the Britons. English,

Welsh. Even the Scots up north. Because he was Arthur's son. Well, not son, but you know what he meant. That he'd make England all anew, all as it was then, whenever then was. All Camelot and ladies and knights. Bring the old days back. Old ways.' She snorted. 'Still waiting to see the rolling hills and handsome young gallants on steeds. Still look outside and see horse turds tramped into broken paving stones. And not all horses', neither. England all anew.' Another snort.

I took this in. None of it was surprising. I'd heard as much myself about the king's frenzy for the ancient king. It was no wonder, really, that Wolsey planned to delight him by celebrating it.

Much monies into his displays of the King Arthur.

'Water?' she said, interrupting my musing and punctuating the word with a nail tapped on a pan.

'I'm going out,' I said, sliding my hand down the lintel. This drew something under her breath which sounded – fairly – like 'lazy'. 'Um,' I said. 'There were no letters, were there?'

'What? Out . . .' she rose, setting the pantry things jangling again, 'where?'

'Just out. I . . . I have business.' That was flat. The truth was, I'd had no music students in . . . I couldn't say how long. My trumpet hadn't held a note in months. I was too long out of the court to retain any of its glitter amongst the citizens and burghers wealthy enough to provide musical tuition for their brats.

'Well, you can take care of business, whatever it is, after you fetch us in water. I have enough to do, God-spare-me. You know what I didn't expect when you came back to live in this house? A great big strapping three-year-old babe. Your father knew how to pull his weight.' I had the grace to look abashed – and to feel it – as she rhymed off a list of chores, each aimed at smartening up the house or myself. I followed them and, when I'd finished and returned to find her sitting on a stool with a cup of ale herself, she said, 'And I hope you don't do business in your shirtsleeves?'

I looked down at myself. I'd splashed water on the shirt. 'Of course not. I'm going to change.' As she began muttering, I went out into the front room and up the rickety steps, not returning until I was back in the cardinal's red livery. The rush of redness, blocking my vision, was becoming familiar again. I'd been so proud when I'd first donned it, years ago now. I'd been so ready to pray, so stupidly hopeful of the purity of the Eucharist and innocent lambs' wool and angels and manna.

I drew short as I clattered back down and found her standing there, one hand on a hip, an amused look on her face.

'Business on a Sunday,' was all she said.

'I'm going to see a friend.'

'You look very well turned. Clean. A friend, is it?' A bolt of fear jolted through me. Had she discovered my cache of letters, thumbed the pages? There was nothing in them, of course – a bland litany (the right word, believe me) of devotional works read, new posts appointed, old ones lost, the plight of the local poor – but they were mine alone to read. Their author was my friend – the only friend from my days in service with whom I'd kept up a friendship, if friendship can be maintained in black and white. Yes, they were mine to read.

To cherish.

I ignored her question and moved towards the front door. My hand was on the ring when she caught me again. 'A friend who writes letters out of the Minories, is it?' I froze but didn't turn to her. 'Be sure you take her something. If they'll let you in there. Something useful, mind.' Her voice was growing closer and I did turn, to find concern on her face. 'Be careful, son. Have a care of yourself, I mean.'

'It's just a convent.'

'I mean this friend there. She's a nun, isn't she?' I shrugged, unable to meet her gaze. 'Just . . . remember that. Don't go chasing after the moon. It'll never get any closer to us.' I looked up, to find her staring at me, her expression blank. Still I said nothing. To my surprise, her face broke into a smile – a determined, mischievous one. My back bumped the door as she reached up and grasped my elbows.

'Wha?'

'Shh, and listen to your old step-dame. People will talk, out there, if they know what you're about. If they think they can read your heart and make sport of what they find there.' She paused, as though considering what to say next, her fingers still burrowing into my sleeves. Eventually, she fetched a sigh. 'Always do, gossip-aunts. But don't you listen. You just be . . . friends . . . with them as make you smile. You never know. God-spare-you.'

★   ★   ★

The House of the Minoresses of St Clare Without Aldgate was, not surprisingly, just outside our ward of Aldgate, across the street from the tall, spired hulk of St Botolph Without. A tall grey wall surrounded the complex, hiding it from the world, cloistering its company of nuns within. I had been inside once, just before I'd left Wolsey's service, but since then had only exchanged letters with one of its sisters. I can't say what made me wish to see her again in person. The pull of the past, perhaps, as I'd pulled against the tide of the Thames the morning before and gone backwards.

At the gatehouse, I knocked and waited.

Prior to coming, I'd visited the barber and then the apothecary, in search of something to bring, some offering, some gift. I'd gone first to a street vendor in Old Jewry, who sold what he claimed were true gold items lost by some rich merchant's wife after the old fellow had fallen on hard times. From him I'd bought a little gold filigree ball. And then I'd gone into the headily scented apothecary's and bought a thin net bag of lavender, sage, and peppermint. The bag fit snugly into the gold ball and made a pleasant-smelling pomander. With a chain, it could be secured at the waist.

But that was not all I'd bought.

'What do you mean?' the wizened apothecary had asked. 'As an unguent, you mean?'

Heat creeping into my cheeks, I'd coughed. There were other people in the shop, waiting. 'I've heard of it . . . for lightening. You know. Like people . . . might use. At court.'

'Ah,' he said, 'I know what you speak of, young Blanke. Most sovereign, it is, against the sun. Against the brownness the ladies do hate.' He sniffed. 'Nettle seed, cinnabar, decoction of ivy leaves, ground saffron. You couldn't get better from any court man. I'll mix it up.' And he did, whistling and humming. The other customers – a heavyset woman with a mewling infant on her hip; an old man; a servant on some errand – all stood watching as the apothecary handed me a little stoppered wooden jar.

As I handed over my coins, to pay for the spice bag and the lotion, I said, 'It's for my wife. The unguent. For my wife.'

He looked at me as if I were a fool and then, I think, realisation dawned. 'Right you are, lad,' he smirked. 'It will do your wife's fair skin wonders. Odd you kept news you'd taken a wife quiet . . .'

Now, waiting outside the convent, I could feel both packages bulging in the purse at my belt.

Just hand over the correct one, by God.

'Good morrow.'

I jumped. To my surprise, a man stood at the gatehouse door, which was divided into sections. He'd opened the uppermost one and leant out. He was middle-aged, I saw, and in clerical dress. Strange: I had never thought about it, but men must be present in a convent every day. It was hardly as if the nuns could say mass themselves. 'Good morrow, Father. I . . . I have come to speak to one of the order here. One of the sisters. Her name is Jane.' My heart fluttered as I said it. I had noticed that my old friend Jeanne had begun signing her letters 'Jane'. 'She's French,' I offered. And she was – formerly a lady of the French royal court. I'd met her briefly in Wolsey's service, when she'd sought and been given a place in an English convent. I'd since thought of her as a kindred spirit. We'd both left service; we both had a little strangeness about us. Not perfect symmetry, perhaps, but close enough to kindle a spark of likeness. Close enough to make me think about her often, to write her back, to keep her scribbled writings close to me, always.

The priest appeared to have been looking at me more than

listening to me. And his eyes had fallen on the crossed-keys badge on my livery. 'But of course. You're a cardinal's man?'

'I am,' I said, without a spur of shame.

Rather than answering, he opened the door. I stepped into a small chamber. This was as far as I'd gotten on my previous visit, all that time ago. I'd had no thought of going farther then. The idea was vaguely wicked, lurid, like wishing to peek beneath a woman's skirts. The priest was opening a door across the cell-like, grey-walled room. Over his shoulder, he said, 'They don't forget here that the cardinal pressed the Court of Common Council to help restore the buildings after the fire a few years back. A cardinal's man is always welcome amongst the sisterhood.'

Good old Wolsey.

I followed the priest's swishing cassock out into a vast open space: a square of green surrounded by slate-roofed buildings. The smoky smell of the city had receded in the gatehouse and now disappeared entirely. Instead, a good, fresh smell filled the air: herbs, grass, and just a whiff of incense. I might have been in the country, so well did the thick walls curtain off London.

Rather than strike out across the grass, he turned right and led me to a door farther along a gravel path on the same side as that we'd left. 'Sister Jane,' he said, 'is our infirmaress.' I knew that she'd been nominated for that position and smiled, as though it were my own victory too. 'She might see you, I think, and will be free until Sext. She will treat your wounds, if she can.'

My wounds?

Of course he thought that was why I'd come – for free medical treatment. Rather than explain – it was none of his damned business, anyway – I simply let him knock on the door before pushing it open. He stood back, smiling, and I stepped inside.

At first I thought he'd made a mistake, or that I had. Jeanne – Jane – was a tiny figure, far smaller than the pleasantly plump girl I'd known so briefly a couple of years before. She was wearing a dun-coloured, shapeless habit and a dark grey veil edged in white, which hung down on either side of her face. That face, too, was scarcely recognisable. Had she not eaten in the last two years, I wondered? Her once square and stubborn jaw was now drawn, so that her heavy cheekbones seemed to slide inwards and right down to her chin. The cheeks beneath those cheekbones seemed simply to have been wiped away or worn down. Her eyes, always prominent, were now enormous. If remaining in service had made my old friend Harry Gainsford hard, leaving it had made Jane something less than she'd been.

'Anthony,' she said, more confused than pleased. 'You . . . have come here? Has something happened?'

I stepped into the room. It was an infirmary, to be sure, with two wooden-boarded cot beds, neither one with even a straw mattress. A shelf was nailed to the wall, and on it were lined up, sentry-like, jars with neatly inked script on each: GYNGER, CYNAMON, RUE, SAUNDERS, and SYROP. She stepped back, alarmed. I saw her gaze slide past me. The priest remained in the doorway, and I turned to see him smiling genially. Naturally, I realised, I wasn't to be left alone with one of the sisters, cardinal's man or otherwise. I don't know why I'd expected anything else. This was a place of discipline, of order – of watching and being watched, for the good of all, moral, physical, and spiritual.

'Are you ill?' she asked.

'No, I . . .' I turned to the priest. 'Sister Jane is an old friend. I came to tell her that . . . I might be going away a while.' Such was the best excuse I could find, anyway, for getting in to see her. 'In His Grace's service,' I added, with a heavy dose of meaning. To my irritation, the priest only deepened his smile, bowing his head.

I cursed to myself. Nothing inhibits free talk between two people like a third person, and I wanted very much to be alone with her, just for a moment: that would keep me going for another year or two.

For a moment I wished to push the fellow backwards. Instead, I settled for staring him in the eye for a beat. And then another, and another. If sight had power, if what the poets wrote about the beams of the eyes were true, he'd have been thrown with some force. Instead, he blinked gently, until he looked, to me, like an idiot. And, mirror-like, I felt like one.

'The cardinal's service?' asked Jane, turning me from my fruitless staring contest. 'I thought you had gone from it. Your letters . . .'

I smiled at the word. Her English had improved, so that there was only a pleasant whiff of French airs. I had seen that in her own letters, the improved spelling, the confidence. Ridiculously, annoyingly, my heart swelled. 'I did. His Grace called me back. Only for a little while.'

'I understand. You will see your friends again. Harry the gentleman. Mark the trumpet.'

She remembered, I thought, with a thrill. She remembered that, when we met, I'd had friends and a life at Wolsey's court – a position.

'I saw Harry,' I said. And then, with another look over my shoulder, I dug at my waist until I could feel pitted roundness. Carefully, so as not to draw out and drop the other thing, I produced her gift. 'I brought you this. For friendship's sake.' I held out the gold ball.

She took it, frowning down. And then she smiled. It looked painful, that smile, on such a thin, wasted face. 'This is kind, Anthony. There was no need. A kindness.' And then she unclasped the ball and extracted the bag. 'This is good. Our garden here has no such mint. This will be very good for digestion, when we have the complaint here.' She held the emptied ball back for me.

'But I . . .' My throat turned dusty and I dry-swallowed, taking the thing.

'So kind,' she said.

'I . . . I've liked reading your letters.' I licked my lips, feeling a stubborn jagged hair the barber had missed. The gold was warming in my hand. 'It is good to see you.'

'And you.' Her smile was becoming perfunctory.

I'd rehearsed all manner of pretty speeches, but they fled me. I looked around at the shelves and shutters. 'It's a shame,' I said, 'that you don't see much of London.'

She gave me a half-amused look. 'London. London. London is like Paris.' She shrugged. Full amusement crossed her face. 'If Paris were built by blind men with empty purses.'

I tried to smile too. 'You're . . . I hope you're happy here.'

'Happy?' Confusion wiped away her amusement and she looked at the priest. Half-turning, I saw him smile. 'I gave my life to God. We have a library here. We read good works. What else is there? What is this happy?'

'I think,' said the priest, butting in, 'that what our Sister Jane means, Mr – Anthony? May I call you Anthony? I think what she means is that she is happy. This is a good place. A safe place. A place of devotion. There is order here, as close to perfect as we can have in this sinful world.'

Suddenly, and ludicrously, I felt unsafe. Worse, I felt soiled, caught between holy and holier. 'A library,' I said, grasping at the word. 'Jeanne – Sister Jane – I . . . the cardinal's business . . . I . . . I've told you before about why I left the last time? That rich men's courts were places of intrigue . . . of . . . of creeping dangers?' I couldn't remember what I'd told her, if anything.

Her hand rose to her throat, her sack-like gown bunching. 'I remember. I recall the dangers of great courts.'

'There is . . . trouble . . . touching a family connected to the cardinal's court.' The opportunity to present myself as a hero arose and I'm ashamed to say I took it. Better a hero than a rambling fool, come with no news. 'I saved a woman and her children. They had been attacked by a wicked man. A man I think has done murder.' Both spines stiffened, two pairs of hands making the sign of the cross, so that again I was caught in the midst of holiness. 'He has murdered a historian, a scholar, who sought books amongst the library at Southwark.'

'Library?' This was the priest. It was like the word had taken on the power of a charm.

I turned, irritation drawing my lips down. 'Yes.'

'Pardon me, son. I . . . was this poor murdered man seeking books in other libraries?'

'I . . .'

'Yes. Yes, he was.' I realised that my tale was misshapen,
its beginning and end on backwards. But I was loath to lay it
all out. I waited a few beats. And then I sighed.

If you cannot trust a priest and a nun.

Briefly, I poured out the whole story, from my arriving
at Hampton Court until leaving the Gonzaga House. 'And
so,' I finished, 'it seems the historian was seeking his truth
everywhere, following a path, his wife said. Until he went to
Southwark, found whatever he found, and was killed for it.'

'Was this poor murdered scholar at the Crutched Friars
yesterday evening?' asked the priest. 'Late?'

I turned to the man properly. 'What? I . . . no. Not unless
he was a ghost.' I regretted the words, as they brought on
more signs of the cross. 'I mean, the historian was murdered
yesterday. It was *yesterday* I was at the palace. At about two
o'clock.'

'Ah, forgive me,' said the priest, running a hand through
his grey hair and then making a vague gesture. 'I see. It is
only that . . . I was at the Crutched Friars yesterday. It is but
a stone's throw from here. I spent the night. I am chaplain to
the brothers there and the sisters here.' I felt my blood run
icy. 'And in the evening a man craved entry to the monastery.
He said he was a scholar, hoping to see the library. Insistent,
he was. And rude in his demands when we refused him. It
was late. We did not know him. Did not let him in.'

'Who was he? What did he look like?'

'A young fellow,' said the priest, holding up his hands.
'Pretty enough in the face, as youths will be. But rude and
hard in refusal.'

Wicked bastardo, *brute!*

'Was he dirty?' I asked. 'Untidy, dirty?'

'I couldn't say, sir. I paid him no mind. Beardless, you know, lady-faced, young, looking. About . . . I should say about eighteen or so. Built well enough. He looked . . . yes, I should say he looked like he'd had a long ride. Spattered from the road, you know.'

A long ride, ay, as I'd had. From Hampton Court.

My mind was whirling. The creature had turned Gonzaga's study upside down in search of something. He had killed Gonzaga for it. And now he was following in the dead man's footsteps. Had the historian not had it, whatever was sought? It didn't make sense. Why kill him, then? A chill ran through me. As I was riding through the city, seeking that house, or perhaps as I was leading the horse home, the lurking murderer had been out there too. He must have ridden hard for the city after the killing.

'What is this?' asked Jane.

I turned to her. An urge came upon me to reach out and touch her, to gather her up, in fact, and carry her out of the place, carry her home.

And feed her.

'I have to go,' I said. 'This man, the man at the Crutched Friars last night – he might be the one I seek. Going where Signor Gonzaga went before. I'll have to go there now.'

The priest coughed behind me and I spun. 'What . . .? Father?'

'I think, son, that you will not get in there this day. The friars are bound over to prayer on Sundays. You say the dead man went to . . . where was it? Southwark?'

'Yes,' I said. Already, in my mind, I was running down the

street in the direction of the Crutched Friars, battering on the door, demanding entry.

'And the murderer is now doing as the dead man did?' I screwed up my face, shaking my head, nodding, making inarticulateness a study in expression. 'Then perhaps he went to Southwark first. And perhaps he got in there. He did not get into the Crutched Friars.' He cleared his throat and held up a gnarled finger. 'Does a bird swoop down to a trap on the ground when no bait is there?'

'Does a trap spring up from the ground if it has not caught anything?' asked Jane, stepping towards me.

I looked between them. 'I don't know what that means.'

'It means,' said the priest, 'that if this murderer you speak of, this man I saw – if he is following in the dead man's steps, then so must you.' He gave a sage little nod but didn't meet my eyes. 'But not today. Today is the day of rest.'

In support of him, bells began ringing out, from the convent's spire, from St Botolph's Without, beyond its walls – from every corner of London, turning the air wild with cacophonous music. 'We must go,' said Jane. 'Anthony. Have a care in this business.' She reached out and took one of my hands in her frail little white ones. She squeezed once before letting go. A memory stirred. Once, we had danced together in a temporary palace in the Pale of Calais, where we'd met during the Field of Cloth of Gold.

I've told you before about why I left the last time?

In truth, I knew that I'd left service, at least in part, because, after that great event, Jane had come with us to England and taken up in her convent in my stepmother's ward. Even if I knew I couldn't see her, I'd wished to be close, to breathe the same airs. We do nothing, I suppose, for just one reason, but for a whole raft of them, each more foolish than the last.

My heart surged again as I looked at her.

Could this be the same girl?

We all three of us left the infirmary and I watched as she hurried off to her devotions. Her life was one of strict order now, of an hour for rising, hours for prayer, a minute, presumably, for eating, and hours of sleeping. It was the kind of order I'd known in the cardinal's household but stripped down to its elements.

I left Jane and the safety of the convent, sure now that the dirty man, the shadowy, faceless, nameless murderer, was abroad in the city streets.

And I'd been set to hunt him.

6

'This way,' said Brother Humphrey, shuffling ahead of me, reluctance weighting every step.

I followed.

After a fitful night full of crawling, writhing, slithering dreams, I'd elected to come down to Southwark and work my way home via the Crutched Friars. I had no need of Abraham – a horse was a rich man's or a fool's property in London – and had walked down to the Customs House water stairs to hail a wherry across the river. Ordinarily I avoided Southwark. Lying outside the city, it was where strangers lived, and I was no stranger. But, in my head, the Priory would have answers of some kind: answers as to what Gonzaga had discovered, and to whether this murderer had been in pursuit of the same thing.

The plan, as nebulous as the rest of my life was beginning to feel, seemed especially fruitless when looking at Brother Humphrey, who fumbled with keys ahead of me. The priory itself was not unlike Jane's convent: closed off, curtained from the muddy, smoky, smelly sprawl of Southwark. Neat, grey stone walls enclosed neat, grey stone buildings. The place, however, was small, clinging to the side of the huge, slate-roofed church of St Mary Overy, the central tower of which looked like a middle finger raised to London Bridge and the city across the water.

'In here,' Brother Humphrey said, opening the tall, thick oak door and stepping in ahead of me. The room into which he showed me was large, vault-like, with a painted ceiling showing a dull, reddish brown between its beams. Every wall was lined with books, stacked on their sides, the edges of their pages turned outwards. Low cabinets divided the room, each packed with more books stored the same way. There must have been hundreds, I thought, a thousand, more. The smell of them was heavy – a slightly damp musk, like fallen leaves drying out in the bright sunshine that sometimes follows rain. The monk went off – a black canon, I'd learnt from my wherryman, an Augustinian – in a swirl of crisp white linen to a lectern with an open book spread on it.

'Give me a moment, please,' he said.

As I waited, my gaze wandered the room. It fell on another lectern, this one standing between a pair of cabinets. A slanting column of sunlight landed on it, falling from a large, diamond-shaped window. I moved over to it and ran my finger along the edge of the polished wood, shrinking a little at the heat from the sun.

'Here, sir,' said Brother Humphrey. I looked up and began stepping towards him. The keeper of the library, I'd found, was neither pleasant nor unpleasant. He was a man of indeterminate age, somewhere between thirty and fifty, with a V of hair over his high forehead. It made his tonsure seem all the more useless. Absurdly, a memory of something my father had once said about monks rose into my mind. The tonsures, he claimed, were a result of monks being torn between God and earth. God had them by the head and our world by the feet. The earth always won, leaving God holding a little patch of hair between His mighty fingers.

I tried not to laugh at the foolish image. As though he could read my mind, Brother Humphrey frowned. 'Signor Gonzaga,' he said, 'took from the place one book.'

'You let men take books?' I asked.

He frowned and I realised I'd made a mistake. 'He was a scholar and an historian.' His narrowed eyes landed on my livery. 'Employed, sir, by your master. He was trusted.' He shrugged. 'And the man made his mark here. And the book.'

My heart leapt.

'Oh! What book? What did he take, Brother?'

The monk looked torn between the chance to be helpful or obstructive. He appeared to opt for the former, however grudgingly, and he bent low over the open ledger. After licking his upper lip, he said, 'It's here. P. Gonz.'

'Peter Gonzaga,' I said. 'And the book?' Not waiting for his answer, I hopped over and stood in front of the lectern, so that our heads were both bent over it in opposite directions. The page was filled with neat, inked columns and lines, like a book of accounts. At the top – the bottom – was the inverted signature in one column. Next to it, also upside down, was 'G. Cass.' Brother Humphrey's thick finger, its nail clean, was helpfully poised next to it.

'Who is G. Cass?' I asked.

'That is a book,' said the monk. 'The book he took.'

My heart was racing now. 'Which book, though? What is it?'

Brother Humphrey, apparently sick of me now, stepped back from the lectern, into shadow. 'I cannot say.'

I was as sick of him. I hadn't come all this way to be disappointed. 'What do you mean, Brother? You're the keeper of the books here. You . . . you must know.'

He breathed out slowly and a little colour rose in his cheeks. 'I keep the books, sir. Keep them. I don't sit reading every page that passes into these walls. I read devotional works. Here,' he said, waving a billowing white arm, 'we have a storehouse of knowledge drawn from everywhere. From every time. A place for scholars to read.'

I could have shaken him.

Stubbornly, I refused to accept this. 'But . . . you have to know. G. Cass. What is it?'

'I've told you, young sir,' he said, evenly, 'I do not know. I know where the prayer books are kept. And the old accounts of the Priory. Signor Gonzaga visited and asked to know where our history books lay. I showed him.'

'Where? Where are they?'

Tutting, the monk led me to a cabinet. The volumes within it were heavy. My burst of boldness fled. I had no business with great historical tomes. My preference was for old myths and romances, and, in truth, I hadn't read a book since I'd first left the cardinal's services. Even if I could have afforded one, I couldn't have justified the expense to my stepmother or myself. I decided to try another approach. I swallowed, before smiling. 'I'm sorry, Brother. I've been rude.' He inclined his head. 'Signor Gonzaga has . . . he's had an accident.'

The monk's head shot up. 'And the book?'

'It's been stolen. His Grace my lord cardinal would like to know why.'

I thought I saw a little fear clutch at the monk. Whether it was due to my summoning up Wolsey or the loss of a valuable book, I didn't know. 'The cardinal,' he confirmed, in a low voice.

'And so we'd like to know what Signor Gonzaga was about. An accident, you understand?' I was laying it on a little thickly, I knew.

Brother Humphrey shook his head. 'From the first, from the moment he arrived . . . two days since? I think two days. He came in the afternoon and worked all evening. These books,' he said, lightly stroking the cabinet, 'he had them all out. Left the place in a fearful mess. I had much to do, putting it all in order.' He cleared his throat. 'From the first, Signor Gonzaga said that his interest was in the lineage of the king.'

'The king?' The masque, the Round Table painted on the cloth before Wolsey, the book I'd seen in Gonzaga's study: all bombarded me. 'King Arthur?'

'No. Yes. I mean – the man was set on discovering the true lineage of King Henry. Our king, by the grace of God. Our good sovereign lord. Of proving his lineal descent from King Arthur and the Welsh Britons. These books – and I suppose the one he took – they're ancient texts. They chart the lost histories, ancient kings, high kings, from the times of the old Romans, I should imagine.'

'G. Cass,' I muttered.

'Perhaps the book's title and author. G . . . I cannot say. Cass? That sounds like the start of a Roman name, does it not?'

I had no idea. I wasn't a scholar. I had a vague memory of a Greek myth of a Cassandra, but no more. I looked up at the monk. 'The book was worth a lot? Rare?'

'Indeed, sir. They all are. It's why we keep them safe here. Only for well trusted gentlemen and scholars.' A little regret coloured his words. 'Such a loss. In the hands of thieves, I suppose, who'll know nothing of its worth.'

'Has anyone else been here? Asking to see the place?' I had intended to lead in to this question carefully. But no matter.

'Other than Signor Gonzaga?' he asked. I nodded, too eagerly. 'No, sir. Not until yourself. Only he these past . . . I cannot say. A good while. Visitors seeking the library are rare. The other Italian used to come. But not in a long time.'

The other Italian?

'Who is that?'

'The king's historian. Signor Vergil.'

I had no idea who that was, but I stored the name away. And then I began sorting the rest of my thoughts, trying to stack them like books. Wolsey had intended for his pet scholar to play a role in devising and writing a masque on King Arthur. The scholar had set himself on proving a link between that king and ours. He had dived into libraries and archives across London, and ended up here, in Southwark Priory, where he had been led to a book – G. Cass. – about ancient history. Roman maybe. And then he had taken it, gone to Hampton Court, been murdered in a bizarre way, and had the book stolen. The murderer had taken the book and was now tracing the means by which the scholar had found it. That meant . . .

I didn't know what that meant.

But others might. An abbreviated book name might mean something to someone with the brains, the education, to root it out.

I exhaled. There was no need to spend any longer in the Priory. The murderer hadn't come here. There was no need; he'd had the fruits of the place from Gonzaga's own hands. I forced a smile, feeling in the twitch of my cheek how ghastly it must look. 'I thank you, Brother Humphrey. And apologise again that I was rude.'

He smiled too, a little more naturally. And then it faded. 'Peace, lad. I'm only sorry for the loss of a book.'

I bowed my head, acknowledging that loss, and then let him show me out of the library, through the rest of the building and grounds, and back out into the street. There were no hearty professions of mutual thanks or desires that I visit again on either side. I was too intent on setting aside what I knew, for now, and tracing a path to the next place I had to visit.

More monks.

I stepped out of the shadow of the priory wall and onto the broad, rutted street that led the short way northwards to London Bridge. I considered walking, but already the crowds approaching the bridge from the south were heavy: men were driving sheep and goats; here and there some friars' bald heads were bobbing; saucily dressed women were touting for business with merry songs and exposed upper bosoms.

I decided to shoulder the expense of another short boat trip and began picking my way through the hot stink of animals, the nip of sweat, and the dry reek of the street. Here, a wall had chalked on it, 'Alleyn ys a whoremaster.' There, more proclaimed, 'Mystress Gyles sells bad ale.' For the illiterate, there was a crude drawing of a moustached man's face with pointed horns curving upwards from either side of his wavy-lined head. Southwark, I thought, smiling in spite of myself.

A huge, chattering mass of people thronged the water stairs, too, and I had the vague impression that something was going on. But I was too busy thinking, working myself into confusion, to pay much attention. It was only when it came my turn to step into the wherry that I was jolted back into the living world.

The boatman, I saw, as I opened my mouth to give him directions, had begun rowing me upriver, not to the north bank. 'Begging pardon, man,' I said, 'I wish to go north. Custom House Stairs.'

'What's that?' he grunted. He didn't stop plying his oar. In the wrong direction. I half-rose, making the boat wobble. 'Sit down, for Christ's sake!' I did. We were too near the bridge, too deep into the more turbulent waters there, for argument. If he had to take me further upriver to the north shore, I'd bear the extra walking. And pay him less for a longer journey I didn't ask for.

When the prow of the wherry sank, gratefully, into calmer waters, we joined a whole flock of similar craft riding the waves, resting. ''Ere we are,' he said.

We haven't gone anywhere, I thought. We had simply ducked under the bridge and come to rest, still at Southwark. Before I could speak, a great cheering broke around me, above me, coming from the other boats, from the houses and shops on London Bridge.

What the . . .?

And then I saw it.

King Henry's royal barge, almost as grand as Wolsey's, was crossing the river ahead of us, sailing downstream towards Southwark. Dozens of oars plied the water on either side, rising and falling, propelling the vessel through the glassy, sun-dappled water. The reddish faces above green and white liveries remained bowed.

The king.

Henry himself had come out from under the canopied

seating area in the rear and was standing. As I watched, he held up a hand to the crowd. Behind him, I could almost make out the stick figure of the emperor, still seated, apparently content to loll in the shadows. The cheering intensified, so that I felt that the bridge behind me might crack under the weight of it. I pressed my hands over my ears.

And then the red-and-gold barge was turning, its Tudor rose pennants stubbornly tugging rightwards. King Henry turned too, not rocking or quivering with the movement, so that he remained steady, facing the great crowd. An enormously tall, handsome man, he was quite visible in his suit of cream and gold. In a moment I was transported back in time, as though borne on the wings of majesty into the past. Images came riding through my mind.

King Henry VIII on horseback, riding through the hot, the horribly hot, afternoon sunlight on a windy day in Guisnes, his ruddy, baby-like face looking up at the palace. This I'd seen as I stood between him and it, invisible – a bauble, like the plaster animals and the glazed windows.

That same king, younger still, the first time I'd seen him, his stockinged legs spread apart, his chin upraised. How we'd all fallen to our knees as he stood by a charger in the courtyard at Hampton Court. What a god he'd seemed – what a man beyond men. This I had seen, and I'd thought: I'll serve him one day. I'll be his toy, his tune-peddler.

Henry, seeming less a king, walking with his arm around the neck of the Duke of Suffolk, his great friend, as though they were brothers, in the yard at York Place. It was sunny then too – it's always sunny in memories, always summer. Still, I'd thought to serve him, to have him look upon me with a friendly eye. My father had served a king; why not?

And Henry – still Henry – his name now sounding hard and rounded in my head, like a cannonball, barking orders at my lord cardinal, making the old fellow bow and buckle and turn inwards on himself. Cardinal Wolsey had been an old man when I'd joined his household, old to me – an old man, but a proud and great one. By the time I'd left, I'd seen him age – not greatly, not horribly, but bit by bit. It was as though the king's service had joined forces with time in a plot against him, agreeing to fill his life with cares. Gradually, I had learnt something of Henry VIII, through seeing Wolsey bend and warp to his tune, through seeing the cardinal's bombastic ways straitened, his forehead turned rippled, his eyes reddened from toil and worry. Somewhere, somehow, the king had ceased to be a man who liked things just so. He'd become one for whom if something wasn't perfect, it wouldn't do. And the cardinal's response had been to become an ever more protective, ever more worried, ever more secretive father to his sovereign lord.

This, too, I had seen and, seeing it, seeing what the king did to his servants, how he made them something less than they had been, I'd learnt to fear him – more than an honest subject should fear his dread sovereign.

A cry flew across the water, seeming to ripple it, to churn the white caps. My memories, my images of the king as I'd seen him in the past, cracked and broke apart and blew back into the past.

King Henry was shouting back at us, matching the crowd's excitement, but his words were lost in the din. I could see his smile, though, almost aggressive in its happiness, splitting his white face in two, his red-gold beard divided from his small, joyless eyes.

Like a child, showing off. Like a boy playing at King Arthur and his knights.

For all that he looked a magnificent prince, for all that he was cheered, and for all that the day was already hot, I shivered.

I didn't trust King Henry, whom I'd once cherished a dream of serving.

There was something under the beautiful, graceful exterior, something cold and cunning, like a serpent hiding in a bowl of ripe fruit. I had indeed had ideas – great, gilded, glistering ideas – of being a king's man, before I'd left Wolsey's service. Yet, during that brief year or two with the cardinal, my fantasies of royal court life had been shattered by the games I'd seen his courtiers play, the gossiping, even the spying on the queen and her ladies he appeared to encourage.

His court was a place of scheming, of whispering. My dreams had died on seeing the king's court in all its dark corners and hidden doorways and windows and stairs leading up, leading down. You see too much caught between stairs and lurking in doorways.

I might have wished to be something other than I was; I didn't want to be made less, to become a listening schemer in a court of vipers.

Nothing fills the gap of lost dreams quite like resentment and distrust. To me, King Henry's smiling face had become a mask, and he a player, a mummer, who feigned friendliness and gentleness but, in secret, when that mask was off . . . what little feeling might lie behind it. Only a man without feeling could make Wolsey less than he was. Only a man without feeling could rule a court full of secrets and spies and busy, watching listeners.

As the barge began to leave us, washing into the calm of a private landing stage, my boatman turned. As the cheers around us died, he said, 'Well, sir. Whattaya fink?' He gave me a strange look, half-curious, half-proud. 'You come all the way to England for to see our good King Harry, I'm guessing. Whattaya fink?'

'I was born in London,' I said.

'What's that?'

'Customs House Stairs,' I barked.

Disappointed – good! – he began plying the waters again, and finally taking me where I had wished to go all along. Had I known what I'd meet there, I should have scolded his tarrying with a vengeance.

* * *

After debarking, I began making my way back through the city, through the crowds of hawkers and vendors. Not having eaten since breakfast, I bought a meat pie and crunched it, unsurprised that it was more crust and juice than meat. The remains went to a scrawny dog, picking its way down the gutter that ran riverward, its head occasionally darting into the sludge.

I could tell there was something wrong before I reached the Crutched Friars.

It was the quality of the crowd, the air of frenzy and panic and awe, all intermingled. And then I saw, rising above the walls of the friary, above the steeple and gabled roofs within, a thin, black column of smoke, fading to grey as it battled the cloudless sky.

Pushing my way through the huddle of panicked men, women, and children outside St Olave's Church, I made my way towards the tall surrounding wall. Snatches of conversation met me, coming sharply through the general gasping and moaning:

'Is it burning?'

'Water!'

'It's aflame!'

'Peace, fool – it's a little fire – see the smoke!'

'Fire!'

And then I was in the thick of the people, some of whom were standing gawping, others pushing away, pushing against me.

Goddamn it!

I gave up my weak attempts at resistance and forced my way on towards the friary. Fewer people were near the wall – nothing of the smoke could be seen from directly beside it. I pressed my hands to the warm stone and began edging my way towards the gatehouse. There, my new friend, the priest from the Minories, was holding people back. Our eyes met at the same time.

'What's happened?' I asked, shouting over the coiffed and hatted heads of a group of news-sniffers.

He didn't answer at once, hesitating, and then he jerked his head for me to step forwards. I did, and, once I was by his side, I asked again. 'What happened?'

The priest opened his mouth to speak. No sound came out. His eyes widened. And then, 'There! There he is!' He raised a black-clad arm up, pointing over the heads of the crowd. I spun, looking out over the waving sea of heads, rising up on my tiptoes.

And then I saw him.

Perhaps it was premonition, a touch of prophecy, a turning of a key in my mind: call it what you will. But, standing far back from the edge of crowd, against the low wall of St Olave's, was a man of middling height, his thumbs hooked into his belt, wearing a fustian coat with its collar turned up despite the heat. His hat was pulled down over the top of his face, so that I could see nothing. And then his head, bent low, turned in my direction, like an animal scenting danger.

Or prey.

Icy fingers tickled their way up my back.

I threw myself into the crowd, shouting, trying to part them, not hearing what I yelled. Before I could take three steps, I was being shoved backwards, buffeted, turned hither and yon. When I twisted back around, rose up again, he was gone.

Yet, I felt, it had been the one I sought. He had been standing watching whatever was going on in the place he'd been rebuffed from two nights before.

And he had seen me.

I tried to push back against the crowd, to break free of it, to give chase. But it was useless. Not only was I at the mercy of the growing throng of fire watchers, but I hadn't seen the direction he'd gone in, whether south to Tower Street and the river, up towards Lombard Street, or deeper into Aldgate. Defeated, I bowed to the inevitable, letting the muttering, shouting crowd wash me back towards the priest, towards the friary.

I didn't bother trying to speak any further with him.

Instead, I nodded at the gloomy interior of the gatehouse. He understood, and together we slipped inside and succeeded in pulling closed the door. He dropped a bar across it. Instantly, the chorus of voices beyond dimmed.

'That man – he came back here, didn't he? The murderer, he was here.'

The priest mopped his brow with a fold of his cassock. 'I . . . I think so. I just came myself, when the alarm went up in the streets. Such a concourse of people.'

'What's happened?' I asked again.

He stood regarding me for a few too many beats. I had time to look around the gatehouse, so different from that at the Minories. A few staffs stood against the wall by the door, with crucifixes topping them: the kind of things carried when the friars ventured abroad. But they were the only nod to austerity. Here was no self-flagellating barrenness, but a well-furnished space with settles, boards, and even red-and-green wall hangings. The latter, I noticed, covered only one wall; the other walls had square, clean-looking patches. It was as though someone had made a desultory attempt to undress the place. The priest must have caught my wandering gaze; he looked abashed, staring at the polished wooden floor. When he spoke, his voice was out of tune. 'I . . . I lied.' He crossed himself.

'Father?'

'This house . . . When I said you should not come yesterday but today . . . that the brothers here take their Sundays with great solemnity . . . I lied.' He looked up at me and I saw tears glistening in his watery eyes. It was my turn to look away. 'In truth . . . this house is not as it should be. There is sometimes some . . . some slackness. In the running. Less poverty and want than is . . . fitting. I thought . . . if I warned the brothers to clear things, to make a good showing when a cardinal's man paid a visitation . . .'

My head jerked up. 'This is no visitation, nothing like that. What I told you was true. I'm seeking a murderer. A bad man.'

The priest nodded absently. 'And for my lie, my attempts to mislead . . . I . . . this other fellow came back, and I was not here to refuse him. The brothers must have allowed him entry. And he . . . he—'

I began to push past the priest, ignoring his clutching hand as it reached my elbow. Out of the gatehouse and into the courtyard, I found several red-faced monks rushing to and fro, the pails of water in their hands slopping over, their faces red. They were heading in the direction of a grey tower building which stood out as taller than the other jumble of tenements that made up the friary.

The priest's voice caught at my elbow. 'The library,' he said. It was unnecessary. I could see that the black smoke was pouring from a window high in that square, grey tower.

Together, we crunched our way over the grass, ignoring the anguished squeaks of the brotherhood. They were, I noticed, sleek and well fed, like pampered pet dogs. I passed through the open, arched door of the tower and, finding the narrow, winding stone staircase in a corner – this was bare and uncarpeted, at least – I stood back to let a monk waddle down, his bucket empty, and leave the way we'd come in. His voice drifted in at our backs.

'Soft, lads. She's quenched. Lay down, lay down!'

Some cheering followed.

Ignoring it, I began turning my way up the dizzying stairs, the priest a shadow at my back.

Emerging at the head of the staircase, I found a library much like that in the priory at Southwark, albeit more cramped. And this one did not smell of books and mustiness, but of burning.

And something else . . .

The source of the great panic lay on a blackened lectern, which had somehow survived to remain standing, a proud, charred skeleton. I stepped over to it. Mercifully, the open window seemed to be sucking out the worst of the smoke, so that only a thick pall of fug hung shroud-like over our heads.

On the ruined lectern lay what was left of an open book, its innards completely burnt away. Thin smoke still drifted from it. I reached down.

'Stop!'

The priest's voice made me jump.

'It might be hot yet. You don't want to get burnt.'

I eyed him with suspicion. He seemed to be in earnest. And then, after a cough racked my throat, I stood back and let him use his cassock to gingerly lift the edges of the book cover. The whole thing collapsed back to the burnt wood in a sludgy fold of wet ash.

Goddamn it.

'What was this?' I asked, more to the thick, smoky air than the priest.

'I cannot say,' he said. 'But we shall discover it. I will fetch up one of the order.' He fled the room. Once alone, I stepped beyond the lectern, towards the window, wishing for nothing more than good, clean air.

What's that?

I felt it at the same time it caught the tail of my eye.

Yellow?

On the floorboards, squashed down, were several small piles of . . . I leant, my eyes narrowing. Mud, of some kind – dried mud. And footprints were crushed into it. Odd, odd, odd. A man fleeing, a thief in the night, might leave the marks of his passage: footprints in the mud, or the like. God knows, I had been scolded often enough for tracking dirty boot prints through the parlour of the house in Shoemaker Row.

But these prints went nowhere; they led towards the window, towards the wall.

And I had seen no such marks on the curving staircase.

My head swam, confusion and the sour tang of smoke making a powerful admixture.

It seemed – it must be – that the man had come into this place carrying his own

. . . *yellow dirt?*

. . . muck, with the intention of pressing his footprints into it and then setting a fire. It made no sense, it was ludicrous, like a madcap game. I might even had've dismissed it as such had he not killed a man and terrorised his wife and children. I thought again of the birds, which had been deliberately attracted to flock around the unfortunate Gonzaga's corpse. It seemed that this man was leaving messages, carefully arranged messages, for the man set to discover him.

Unfortunately for my murderer, the man set to discover him was a fool without the book-wits to decipher such messages.

I stooped again, retrieving a handful of the packed yellow

filth. After sniffing it – no scent . . . a little earthy, perhaps, like mud, not strong – I tipped it into my purse, where it could keep company with my diminishing store of coins.

I then turned back to the burnt lectern. This was far from odourless. It stank, not just of smoke, but of something thin, needling and sour. It seemed my man had also brought something to help him set the fire.

Footsteps and voices drew me up, making me feel, unaccountably, guilty. I folded my hands behind my back as the old priest drew a frowning monk into the room, his head bent.

'Good morrow,' I said. Neither man responded. 'The man who did this,' I said, 'who let him in?'

The monk looked up. He was young, I noticed, perhaps younger than me. That was good. I suddenly felt a weight of authority gather in my throat. 'I did,' he said.

'Do you know what this book was?'

'Can't say. Same as the other man was reading. The Italian.'

'And what was that?' I asked.

The monk shrugged, and the priest barked, 'Answer him, Brother!'

'I can't say,' the monk persisted. 'Something in Latin.' He looked up. Light came into his eyes, hope. '*Getica*! That was it. Pleasant name. That's what the Italian asked for, back when he was coming here.'

'What is *Getica*?' I asked, looking from one man to the other. 'Is it by someone Cass? Cass something?'

'Can't say,' said the monk again. The urge to slap him rose and fell. I was fairly certain that striking a holy man, even one of a degraded order, warranted divine retribution, and God was already having sport enough of me.

I let the matter drop. The scholastic bent of this madness was all beyond me; it could keep, could be shifted from my shoulders to those of a man fit for scholarly thinking. 'Tell me what happened here.'

With much prompting from the priest, the monk unfurled his tale: of a man coming to the friary just an hour or so before – when I was watching the king, perhaps – and begging entry. Claiming himself a scholar. Nothing odd in that. He didn't mention having made an attempt on Saturday night. He was allowed in, shown up here, and appeared to know what he was looking for. The monk had shown him to the pile of books – the unchained ones, the non-religious ones – which the Italian had consulted. The Italian, Signor Gonzaga, was, the man claimed, his friend and master. Nothing odd in that. And then the young library keeper had left him alone, to retreat downstairs to pray and fast and attend his devotions.

And drink wine and do God only knew what else.

Then, madness.

The man had flown downstairs, out into the courtyard, and forced his way from the building. This had been just as the priest arrived. And the smoke had been smelt, sighted, and the panic descended, the people outside seeing it first, beating on the doors, the monks all a-flurry fetching water up and down the stairs.

I digested all of this, and was still doing so when the monk, hope again crossing his face, caught me. 'Sir? Sir?'

'What?'

'I forgot his name.'

My mouth fell open. 'He gave you a name?'

'Ay. Mr . . . let me see, get it right . . . strange name.' That urge to strike came upon me again, stronger. 'Mr Caledon.'

I repeated the name twice, looking first at the monk, then at the priest. 'Does the name mean any— do you recognise it?'

Twin shakes of the head.

'Shall we write some report for the cardinal? To show the king?' asked the monk.

'No,' I said. Any report would never reach the king. Wolsey couldn't tell His Majesty of any new matter – not without revealing he'd hidden the strange death at Hampton Court ahead of the royal party's arrival. 'I'll carry the news.'

Both monk and priest looked relieved.

I didn't have much to carry, in truth, but it would have to do. I took a last look around the room before making to leave, on a wave of protests that no more strangers would be allowed into the friary; that they were truly a good order in need of the gentlest rebukes and reforms; would I please speak kindly of the place to His Grace; and remember God's law that it's always better to say nothing than to speak wickedly.

Once finally free of the place, I took a look around the thin crowd. Now that the excitement of a fire had burnt itself out, only stragglers remained in the street. Some women stood in knots before St Olave's, their chins wagging, their glances occasionally directed over my head. Farther up the street, where it turned down into Seething Lane, the upper shutters of houses were open, men and women hanging out, pointing.

I tried to look everywhere at once.

What if this Caledon hadn't fled?

What if he'd watched me approach the friary, go in? He was leaving messages for someone, to be sure. It would make sense that he'd been remaining outside the building to see who appeared: to see, in fact, who had been set loose upon him. It stood to reason, I thought, that he was still nearby now, watching for me to come out.

And I had advertised my presence well enough. I was also, to my chagrin, a man who would be easy enough to find, easily noticed.

Oh, the dark man? His house is hard by the city wall.

What is he, some kind of Spaniard? Lives on Shoemaker Row.

Worst all all: *Oh, it's the* Moor *you're after? Everyone in Aldgate knows where the Moorling lays down his knotty head.*

I hurried away from the Crutched Friars.

* * *

'It won't work all at once, young Blanke. Er . . . tell your . . . wife. It won't work all at once. Takes time.'

Again, I was standing in the humid spice scent of the apothecary's shop in Aldgate High Street. Thankfully, however, there was no one else in the place but me, the proprietor, and a stuffed lizard hanging from a ceiling beam. I stood away from it, nearer the counter, and frowned. 'I didn't come about the unguent,' I said. In truth, I'd slathered the stuff onto my face and forearms before sleeping the previous night, washing what hadn't rubbed onto my lockram blanket off in the morning. 'She'll wait,' I said.

This seemed to relieve the apothecary. His lined, bearded face relaxed. A smile appeared, and his nostrils flared at the prospect of selling me something else. He was to be disappointed. I pulled up my purse and unstrung it, before sending the powder flaking over my open palm. The coins I held through the leather. 'This stuff,' I said. 'Can you tell me what it is?'

He frowned. 'What?' Leaning over the counter, he grasped my wrist in a knotty vice.

Startled, I yanked my hand away. I hated being touched, still less suddenly. Clumps of yellow skittered over the counter. 'Hey!'

'Yellow?' he asked of the air.

'You've spilt it!' I cried.

He ignored me and began sweeping the stuff across the counter towards him with a cupped hand. When he'd got it to the edge, he leant down and rose up with a small, glazed earthen dish. Into this, he brushed the surviving powder. Lifting the dish to his moustaches, he sniffed. 'No smell.'

I could have told you that.

'What does that mean? Is it mud, some spice?'

He stared down at the dish, his jaw working under its straw-coloured thatch. 'Not saffron. Sulphur, perhaps. Might be sulphur.'

'What's that?'

'A base element. We use it in many things, in this trade.' He cocked an eye at me. 'In some whitening unguents, even. Must be kept well away from fire. Else it makes a bad stink. Very bad. Poisonous.'

I swallowed, staring down at the stuff. If a stray spark had lit it, then . . .

'We shall see,' he said, and then he turned away again,

ducking through a low doorway and re-emerging with a flaming taper.

I hopped backwards, hitting the lizard, sending it into a creaking sway. 'What? What are you doing? You said—'

'Soft, lad. It's only a little, very little. You might cover your face, though.' I began to mumble protests, but I did as he said. Standing well back, he did the same with one hand. With the other, he stretched out, holding the taper like an artist's brush, until the flame prodded gently at the powder in its dish and . . .

I shut my eyes, bracing for the bang, the flash, the pop . . .

Nothing happened.

After a few beats, I looked. I moved back towards the scarred counter, staring down. The yellow powder had blackened, but it hadn't flashed or burst into anything. The apothecary shook out the flame and then frowned down. 'Curious,' he said. 'Strange. Not sulphur. But perhaps made to counterfeit it.'

The door opened behind me and I spun. It was just a man in a good doublet, a merchant by the cut of him. He gave me a sidelong glance, his nose in the air, stepped to the counter, and began drumming ringed fingers. 'I would speak with you alone, good sir, on a matter of privity.'

'Yes, sir,' said the apothecary. And then, to me, 'Sorry, son. I can't help you. You bring me some yellow dust – what can I say? It is yellow muck of no worth that I know. But not true sulphur. It has merely the appearance of it. If someone sold you this as the true stuff, they cozened you. Good day, Goodman Blanke. Tell your step-dame I wish her well.'

'But I—'

'Good day.'

Dismissed, I stepped back out into the sunshine, pulling my cap down to block it. It might, I'd thought throughout the day, undo the good work of the unguent.

As I wound my way home, I considered the oddity. Perhaps this Caledon had wished to give the appearance of having left trodden sulphur without any danger to himself as he lit a fire near it. But it was bootless to try and make sense of a murderer's doings.

I had a name.

Doubtless, it was a false name. But between that and the knowledge I'd secured of what Gonzaga had been up to, trying to establish proof of King Henry's descent from King Arthur by digging through ancient pagan texts, I felt I had something to carry back to Wolsey.

And that, I thought, as I turned into Shoemaker Row, was exactly what I planned on doing the next day. Already I had had enough of monks and libraries and stumbling around London after a learned – for I realised he must be learned – madman. If Mr Caledon the sulphurous – or non-sulphurous – knew what I was about, I'd trail him no further. If he was going to have at me, he would have to follow me well away from my stepmother's house.

All the way to Hampton Court, in fact.

7

The palace had been busy a few days previously. Now it was a buzzing, whirling confusion of colour and noise. I'd come by horse – for speed, yes, but, I realised, I shouldn't have been able to take a wherry even if I'd wanted to. Every boat in London must have sailed upriver, bearing clerks, servants, Spaniards, grooms, pages, physicians, all.

The king and the emperor are to honour this house on Tuesday.

I'd deposited Abraham at the stables, which lay down near the river, on the main road from London, and then come up into the New Court. And there I was lost. Through the service gatehouse – the porter didn't meddle with me this time – the courtyard seemed to have shrunk, surrounded on all sides by its finished and half-finished buildings. But it was the people who caused the illusion: the great concourse of people.

I wandered a little, looking, almost certainly, like a fool. But that didn't matter. No one, you see, was looking at me. In the midst of the chaos of the arriving royal parties, no one cared. Conversation hummed around me, much in English, some in Spanish; some from male servants, some from female. Hampton Court had been invaded, occupied – a gentle manner of invasion.

I smiled as I moved about. I'd missed the feeling of being lost and unremarked upon amidst a great company.

Throughout the previous two years, I had, in honesty, gone out very little. I had no friends to go out into the fields with, running or singing and picking flowers. I'd remained at home, in my stepmother's house – my house, really, coming upon my father's death, though we weren't lawyerly people – writing and reading my few letters, teaching music when my stepmother managed to drum up business. There had been no reason to leave London. Until Wolsey's summons, I hadn't even gone much beyond Aldgate.

I had missed it, I realised, being part of a colourful, rich, moving world: a world of life, even if it came with death alongside. I was weary of being small, of not mattering. Here was life, in all its noisy, sweating, shameless pride.

'Anthony?'

I smiled around. *Someone with my name.*

'Anthony Blanke!'

I turned, pulling off my cap.

'Anthony Blanke, well, if it ain't!'

'Mark? Mark!' I cried, a grin pulling at my cheeks. Before I could say anything more, he had hurled himself at me, wrapping his arms around me. He was, like me, in the cardinal's livery, so that we made a little red ball. I let him have his hug awhile before wriggling out of it.

'I heard you'd been back here, and I didn't see you.' His low London accent climbed above the general chatter. 'Good to see an old face instead of all these dirty blooded foreign scraps and foreign-talking prentices and arty-tarty bastards. You don't half look thin, man. Ain't there no food out there in the big world?'

I laughed. Mark Byfield was one of my best friends.

Was.

When I'd been a trumpeter for the cardinal, he'd been my twin, as little as we looked alike. Together, we'd flank doorways and blow Wolsey into dinner, or out of conferences. It was just such a position that, Wolsey had once told me, would make me an excellent watcher and listener. Men who lurked in doorways weren't seen. He might have taken up Mark as his creature since, but I suspected not. My friend wasn't a creature of ambition, and most certainly not a fellow to keep his mouth shut and his ears open. He was, in truth, pleasantly plain-speaking.

Plain-writing, too.

Ah. As I've said, when I first left service, I'd written to my friends. With Harry Gainsford, stiff formality passed between us, until mutual recognition seemed to pass on either side that we now had little in common. With Mark, though . . . Letters had come in the first months and, judging by their childish, laboured scrawl, they had cost him much to write. Sometimes they were even written in other people's hands – which must have cost his purse – with only his name messily added at the end. I'd stopped writing replies. Letters had still come, ignoring my lack of responses. I'd intended, every day, to write back, and found reasons not to: there'd be no one travelling to York Place or Hampton Court to carry a letter; I might have better news tomorrow – I'll write then; I'm tired. With luck, I thought, he might be discreet enough not to mention my rudeness.

'It's good to see you, Mark.'

'And you, man. Could've written letters, you great piss-wit. Cost me loads to pay folk to carry mine.'

Again, I laughed. He didn't sound angry, nor even annoyed. 'Sorry, man,' I offered. 'Busy teaching music.'

'Don't matter. Music master, were you?' He let out a whistle and then rubbed his thumb and forefinger together. 'Much money in that?'

Not so's I've noticed.

I made a little noncommittal sound.

'Reckoned not. What else you been doing with yourself?'

At this, I laughed – loudly, long, and genuinely.

What *had* I been doing with myself? In truth, my days had become a pleasant enough blur of rising, praying, eating, teaching – sometimes – and sleeping. It was fine. Once you got used to a life, the days just seemed to trip over themselves in their race ahead. Orderly disorder, I considered it. Even the things you used to enjoy – a drink at a different tavern, market days and fairs – started to become a chore, interfering as they did with the comfort of . . .

. . . *being a merrily shiftless bastard.*

'One of my students taught me to juggle apples,' I said, still smiling and raising my palms. 'I got to three of them. That kept me going a good three weeks.'

Mark gave his own grin. 'Bloody hell. That's wild. You'll be making use of that now you're back. Cardinal loves a juggler.'

'A few more months and I'd have been walking tightropes for him. Anything to occupy me.'

Mark's smile faded. 'Here, are you back, then? In the service?' He retreated a little to take in my livery. As he stepped backwards, he bumped into a man in Spanish-cut doublet and hose.

'*Tener cuidado!*'

'Key your own dado,' he snapped, giving the Spaniard's back a fillip. Tutting, he turned to me. 'Think they own the place, them and the king's men. And the cardinal's bloody foreign crafters and their strange muck. Forget it's our house and country, don't they?' He gave a dark look after the departed Spaniard. 'Our lads'll show 'em whose house it is. Got some fine lessons on who owns England in store for 'em, I heard.'

I didn't pursue that. I could imagine how much the foreign servants would be tortured for being strangers, the mockery and scorn and pranks. I didn't need or want details. Mark brightened. 'Come on,' he said, 'let's go somewhere quieter and talk.'

I hesitated. 'I – I need to speak to the cardinal.'

'Some bloody chance. His Grace's closeted with,' his nose rose in the air and his voice heightened, 'His Majesty King Henry and his Imperial Majesty Emperor Charles.' He dropped it again. 'I'll send word. It important?'

I cursed inwardly. I didn't want to lie to Mark. But I couldn't see any way of avoiding it. And then inspiration struck. 'He's making me be in a masque. A secret masque. For the king and emperor, at . . . Winchester, I think he said.'

'Oh, that. Everyone knows about that.'

'What?'

Mark laughed. 'You think even the cardinal could keep something like that secret? I know – everyone knows. The king's lads know, and the queen's ladies. Them Spaniards, they'll know. The cardinal wouldn't plan any surprise for the king without His Majesty knowing about it – in case he didn't like it, like.'

'I . . .'

Mark tapped his nose. 'King Henry, he's a good one for showing surprise where there ain't no surprise, you know?

His Majesty'll jump and cry out and say, "What is this?"'
Mark mimed putting his hand to his heart. 'But he'll know all
about it and not want to spoil that it's meant to be a surprise
for no one. Good man, the king. Good player.'

A good player indeed, I thought.

'And he knows how to play delighted,' added Mark, with
a wink.

I cast a glance down at my hands and thought of the king
playing, mumming, feigning delight.

'What you standing looking like a damn fool for?' Mark
asked. 'Come on. They're making that masque stuff over
there.' He gestured towards the completed new northern
range, a vast expanse of red brick and glass climbing up to a
slate roof. 'I'll take you to them lot. It'll be quieter than here.'

I followed him through the courtyard, through the
bustle of laughing, chattering underservants. As we
slipped through a doorway and into a long, narrow hall,
I found that he was right. His voice, when he spoke, took
on the quality of a proud fellow showing off his new home.
'Up yonder are the new kitchens. Can serve us lot down
here and them lot up in the old court. King's rooms are
up there. Oh, well, well.' We stood back against a wall
as a serving woman – a girl of about eighteen – came
hurrying along the hall. She went carefully. In her hands
was a wooden bowl full of cherries. She went in the
direction Mark had indicated, towards the kitchens. She gave
him a sideways look and then, over her shoulder,
another little glance. When her back was to us, he sucked
in his cheeks. 'Bet you don't got none women like that in
London,' he smirked. 'All trulls and tails up there, eh?'

I smiled, thinking of the convent and the woman

who couldn't have tasted a cherry in years . . .

'Must be nearly time for dinner,' said Mark. 'Them lot'll want their little dainties first. Won't be a cherry tree not naked by the time they go off to Windsor.'

The serving woman disappeared through a doorway at the end of the long hall. 'Heh,' I said. 'I wonder what the king will do when he reaches the bottom of the bowl.'

Mark laughed. 'The king . . .? When you're the king, there ain't no bottom of the bowl.' He took a breath. 'Come on. This way.' He led me to a flight of stairs and up to the second floor of the building, where another long hallway was stacked on top of the first, and then into a large chamber at the end.

Here, the vinegary smell of paint and the dull tick-tack of hammering filled the air. At the far end stood what appeared to be sections of stone wall, grey and made of neat bricks.

Yet something was wrong with them.

My mouth fell open. The great slabs of wall were each as thin as a hand. The rectangular bricks, slotted neatly one atop the other, were illusions painted on canvas. The Master Painter, Gosson, was standing back from them, watching intently as a cropped-headed young craftsman poured dirty-looking, powdered grey paint into water buckets whilst another leant in, ready with a brush. One section, only half-done, showed remarkably real-looking bricks fading into the blank whiteness of canvas. Gosson's mouth was working. 'Ja,' he said. 'Ja . . . ja.' He would be a rich man, I thought, when news of his work spread. All involved in making the masque would. He saw me looking and turned from his men, blocking my sight of their work, a hand on each hip. 'This pleases you, trumpet?' I shrugged, moving away from his hard, blue gaze.

Elsewhere, men were kneeling on spattered drop cloths, nailing boards together, for what purpose I couldn't say. And closer to us, away from the sour tang of the painting, stood the other master craftsmen. Dumpy little Visser, the glazier, was at a window, opening and closing it. And Lutini, the musician, was arguing with Cornish, the Revels Master, who was waving a sheaf of pages in his face. The first two were dressed in their plain crimson liveries and white hose, but Cornish had outdone himself in a ridiculous mustard doublet and matching hat, a white feather bobbing from it. Scatterings of each man's suite of servants stood about, those who weren't engaged in work looking bored. Cornish's fool capered, failing to induce either laughter or enthusiasm.

'This your lot, then?' asked Mark.

'Yes, I'm afraid,' I said.

'Heh. There's the fool. Love me a bit of the fool. Once saw him steal off the cardinal's plate and run away and hide under the table. Sat there munching. His Grace – he just laughed and laughed.'

'A marvel,' I said. 'Soul of wit.'

'Heh. Well, then . . . I'll see if the cardinal can see you. Send word. It important?' he asked again.

'Yes.'

'Right.' He turned back into the hall, leaving me in the doorway, before shooting a look over his shoulder. It came with an enormous, natural grin. 'Good to see you again, man.' And then he was gone, leaving me to the madness of the masque-planners.

'*Here* he is,' shouted Cornish, breaking off his argument. 'Lurking in *doorways*. You, boy. Come. Here. *Now*.' He jabbed a dainty little finger at the rush-strewn floor and I stepped towards him. 'Settle a dispute, would you? You come from the town. Would you not say that these false walls should be whitewashed in *pink*, as the better sort do? Not this cruel, hard *grey*. Would that not give a *taste*, would you say, of Camelot?'

'I think the grey looks well enough,' I said. Behind him, I saw Gosson and his young painter turn and raise their hands in salute.

'Pfft,' snuffled Cornish through his nostrils. 'Well, you *are*, I am sure, not from the *better* part of the town. You can *read*, I suppose?'

I removed my cap. 'Yes. Uh . . . sir.'

He thrust the pages at me and raised his chin. Replacing my cap, I took them and scanned the page. In a loopy, flourishing hand, with plenty of blotting, was an incomprehensible series of directions, descriptions, entrances and exits, something about a tower. 'Well?' he asked. 'Young man, I know you are no *scholar*, but I'm sure you can see that this is a work of great thinking and craft. Yes?'

I nodded blankly, handing the pages back. He swiped them from me and waved them before Lutini's face. 'You see?' he cried. 'Even a *trumpet* knows the worth of my skill.'

Lutini put his hands to his temples. 'Is trash, I say. Trash, trash, trash.' Cornish began spluttering, one hand over his heart, and the music man turned to me. 'You were a trumpet, boy. You see there – he has no music. The man forget to place the music. What is a masque without it has music?'

'I,' announced Cornish, stepping away from us and brandishing his paper in the air, 'am an *artist*. Not a . . . a *tune*-peddler. You wish *music*? You *add* music, you . . . musician.' He thrust the pages at Lutini's chest and let them fall to the floor. And then he stormed off to the window where Visser was now tapping and then listening to the glass. Lutini bit his thumb towards him.

If these were master craftsmen, artisans, makers, then I was sorry to be part of them.

Lutini, grumbling in Italian, bent to retrieve the papers. 'Trash,' he said, rising. And then he squinted at me from under his thick eyebrows. Trying to work me out, I thought. Though I was beneath him, I was not yet fully a member of the household but a guest of sorts. Low and menial, yes, employed, to be sure, but something of a guest who demanded a measure of respect. Yet I was seemingly neither one thing nor another. A nor-this-nor-that. An in-between. A shade.

A mule.

I turned my hat in my hands, staring down at it. 'You and me, we play. We show him where music stands.'

I swallowed. Cornish was sailing towards us again. He ignored Lutini and grabbed my elbow, yanking me away. 'I would have my player,' he said, 'my evil Black Knight.' I had no choice but to give way, though I chanced a dumb look at the music man. I had no loyalty to any of the craft-masters, but neither did I wish to make enemies of either.

Frankly, I had hoped that the affair of the murderer, of this Caledon creature, would have put paid to my involvement in Wolsey's stupid not-a-secret secret masque. Releasing me near the tall window, Cornish clapped his hands together and shouted into the room, 'Come, my dear fellows. We might have no more *players* to hand, but I should like to run through my work.'

Gosson bent to his painter, exchanged a word, and jabbed

a finger at a canvas before wiping his hands on a rag and marching up the hall towards us. 'The great tower will take time,' he said, gesturing towards the chunks of painted cloth and board.

'And a *bower*,' said Cornish. 'We *must* have a bower. And can any of your men paint a dragon?'

'There's no dragon in the tale,' said Gosson, in his heavy Germanic accent.

'There *will* be,' smiled Cornish.

The painter whistled. 'We can make anything living and real. A dragon.' He counted on his fingers. 'That will be a cost. As high as the Round Table, ay. A dragon.'

'I'm seeing,' said Cornish, staring at nothing, one finger to his temple, 'flames from its nostrils. Great fangs. Cruel eyes.' He refocused on Gosson. 'I – *I* cannot be troubled by such vulgar things as expense. His Grace shall bear the expense of it. A *monster*, Herr Gosson, I would have a monster in nature!'

'A dragon,' said Gosson, a smile crossing his face, 'he shall have.' His dark eyes pooled, like drops of fish-oil spreading. He turned away and returned to his squatting painters, bending his head to them. Some laughter shot up, either at the prospect of plundering Wolsey's purse or at Gosson's liberal sharing of it.

Cornish shouted after him, 'And we must have a night sky!' He spread his hands in the air. 'A night sky, *twinkling* with the *owl-light* of stars! I will not have his Imperial Majesty think us *niggardly*.' He turned to one of his servants – a bearded man in black – and held out the paper. 'Add a dragon to my Red Lands. *Fearsome*. Fetch up more supplies from the city if we require them.' The fellow took the pages in ink-stained fingers and moved off to a sideboard tenanted with ink and quills. 'Now,' said Cornish. 'Let us see if Camelot stands where it did. To work!'

I'll spare you the tedium of the next few hours, and myself the horror of reliving them. It is enough to say that our chaotic rehearsal was a tireless round of argument between the master craftsmen: of Visser arguing with Gosson over who had the right to paint glass and make designs on it; of Lutini and the extravagant Cornish of where music should go. I was forced to pose in various states of anger and threat; to be fitted for masks which would hide my whole face, given I was, apparently, a poor sport for not making *fearsome* sausages of my lips; to move about non-existent settings with Cornish's servants, who were pressed into service in the roles the great lords, ladies, and gentlemen would play in the masque proper.

It was hideous.

Naturally, I was relieved when a pair of household servants brought us in trays of crumbly cakes and jugs of good wine. My mouth was only just full when Mark arrived to find me standing alone, apart from the masque-makers. 'Cardinal'll see you, man,' he said.

'Now?' I asked, in a shower of deliciously sweet crumbs.

'Now.' He cast a look around the room and whistled. 'Jesus. Be some sight when this is laid on.'

I swallowed, looked at the sideboard, and palmed one last cake for the walk. And then I bent my head to his. 'Ay, if these men can ever agree on any of it. Like fishwives arguing over how you take the bones from a turbot.'

He clapped my back, sending more flakes of pastry from my lips, and led me towards the door.

'Where do you think you're *going*, boy?' shouted Cornish,

moving away from his own small crew of attendants, dropping an empty cup for one of them to retrieve. 'We are not done here. Far from it.'

Before I could answer, Visser, the glazier, moved away from a window embrasure, leaving a handprint on the dyed glass. 'If he go, I go! Foolery. I have enough, enough, of you men bet . . .' he grasped for the word, 'betwitting each the other. Enough!' His features twisted into a scowl. 'They say the cardinal to make no more great houses when this one finished. Bah! Me and my men as soon to be turned out for want of work. And now, I think, good!' His little burst of anger fled, deflating him, and he sighed, turning back towards the wall. 'Tsk. The windows in this place, they not close tight. Poor work. I see from without. Come!' Ignoring Cornish's offended spluttering, he snapped his fingers. Instantly, the workmen who had been hammering nails into wooden panels – building windowed false walls, I guessed, ready for painting – rose as one, brushed woodchips from their aprons, and followed their master from the room.

The Revels Master turned on me and Mark instead. 'Traitors!' he barked. 'The cardinal will hear of this . . . this . . . treachery is what it is.'

Mark moved to stand before me. 'My friend here is summoned by His Grace. On great business. *Sir.*' He gave a sarcastic bow.

God bless Mark.

We fled out into the narrow hallway together, on a wave of fresh argument, blown on hot air out of the disagreeable Cornish. As I walked, I munched on the purloined cake. It began to sour in my gut: not because it was bad, but because, suddenly, the weight of the Caledon affair and the prospect of laying it out before Wolsey sat ill on such light stuff. Worry crept over me: I would forget something, some crucial detail, of the last wild few days in London. Memory battled memory: yellow dust; G. Cass; fire; Caledon; Gonzaga's wife and children; the late King Arthur; books. They concocted, like a mixture of foods in the belly, eaten in the wrong order, causing pain.

Mark kept up a stream of conversation, diverting me, as we made our way through the palace. I lost track of the chambers, the stairways, the twists and turns; I knew only that we didn't go back outside, nor did we go to the cardinal's privy chambers or gallery, which I assumed were now in the hands of one of the royals.

'Here,' he said, drawing up. His voice was changed, turned low. 'Inside.' He knocked on a narrow wooden door and stepped back. As I slipped inside, he pulled it closed behind me, leaving me alone with the cardinal.

8

Wolsey was reclining on a settle. He was in his red robes, looking like a great pool of blood. One arm was held up over his forehead, as though protecting it from the light which didn't reach him from the windows on the other side of the chamber. It was a large room, well-appointed with its tapestries, carved wooden ceiling, and sideboards of polished plate, its windows facing down onto the New Court and its great fumble-jumble of lower servants. I jumped as I realised that Richard Audley, Wolsey's secretary, was in the room, too, half-hidden in shadows along the side of the wall with the door I'd just come through.

'Ah, Anthony,' he said, without looking, somehow knowing it was me. 'It is a weary business to entertain a king. To entertain a king and his queen and an emperor. Pah!' He threw down his hand, opened his eyes, and heaved himself up. 'From London, yes? You have missed nothing beyond honest labour here. Our poor Signor Gonzaga was, it appears, foully deprived of life. Strangled, like a wicked woman, by some stronger creature.' I saw, in my mind, those clinging little children and their fierce mother, swearing revenge. 'What news?' asked Wolsey.

He did not remain seated as I unravelled the whole story as best as I could, from entering the Gonzaga house on Saturday night until leaving for Hampton Court as the sky turned pale that morning. 'And Your Grace's horse, Abraham, is back at home,' I finished. I felt lighter, suddenly. Wolsey had not, to his credit, interrupted me once, nor asked for any points to be gone over again. But he had risen and begun pacing the chamber in his marvellous stately gait, rubbing at the cornices around the windows, tapping his side, waving me on silently when I hesitated, always in motion, like a great red sun rotating on its sphere.

'There's no more, Your Grace. I don't think.'

'Good. Good. Yes.

'Mr Audley?' He turned to address the fellow, who hadn't moved an inch from his position against the wall, not even when Wolsey had passed him. 'Go and take up your pen. Omit nothing.' Audley inclined his head, looked at me without expression, and then bowed his way from the room, closing the door softly behind him. 'I might wish to revisit the tale later,' Wolsey explained, drawing my attention away from the door. 'I think far better in the deepest part of the night, when there are fewer other matters.' He took a deep breath, raising both hands to the side of his head and then dropping them. 'Madness,' he said. 'To kill a scholar and burn books. Do you know what burning books signifies, lad?'

I felt an itch creep up my neck. 'Uh . . . it makes people wish to read them?'

A long pause drew out between us. I had stumbled, I thought, made an error. And then Wolsey barked laughter, hearty and genuine. 'You might be right. That it might do.' He shook his head, wiping his lazy eye with a finger. 'Ah, but no. It simply serves to stop them being read. To destroy what they contained. And that burnt book in – where – the Crutched Friars? Perhaps something in it, whatever it was, pointed to Southwark. And so this Caledon would have none of it.' He resumed his stately pacing. A knock came at the door. 'Be gone! Leave us!' He barked. Whoever was there went away in a whisper of footsteps.

'Does the name . . . I guessed it was false. Do you know it, Your Grace?'

'Hm? What? Caledon? No. No. And yet . . .' He chewed on his jaw awhile, his eyes narrowing. 'Not a name. Not a man. A place. Yes. Caledon. Caledonius. Latin for the Scotch race. A Scotsman?' He wasn't speaking to me. His face was bent to the carpet, his hands knotted together, the thumbs circling one another furiously. Inspiration appeared to strike him and he looked up – not at me, but at a tapestry on the wall. I followed his gaze, followed the stitched, furiously coloured threads which wove together to show Jesus and his disciples enjoying their last supper. 'The Scots . . . the French. The French. By God, as close as lovers, ever.'

I scuffed at the carpet. Whatever he was saying, whatever he was thinking, was beyond my compass. 'Anthony,' he said. Excitement coloured his words. 'Tell me, my young friend, do you know how a king comes to be?'

'What? I . . .'

'Answer me truthfully, boy. How does a king come to be a king?'

I scented a trap, felt danger. My eyes widened and my heart began to skid and skip. 'God,' I said. He rolled his eyes to the carved ceiling; they flitted about the painted roundels up there. And then he made that rolling motion with his hands – the one he'd made whenever I'd faltered in my tale-telling. *On man*, it said – *on*. 'I . . .' The schoolroom yawned in my mind: hornbooks and ink and the piping yawn of a dozen voices repeating the monk's words. Now, as then, I said, 'King Henry, eighth of that name, was born of King Henry, seventh of that name.' And, as then, I looked for approval and found none. I cleared my throat. 'Kings come of kings. Father and son.'

Wolsey had docked beside a large fireplace, the red sails at rest. 'Yet our king has no Henry of his own. Not yet,' he added quickly, his eyes flitting to the door. They came again to me. 'Only a fair maid, fit to marry the emperor one day.' This he said too loudly. 'And so, where does this leave your little reading of kings?'

I folded my arms across my chest, crushing my cap. 'Well . . . fathers and sons . . . and daughters. Children. Heirs. Royal heirs.'

'Blood royal!' cried Wolsey, pushing himself away from the fireplace. I remained rooted to the spot whilst he went to a sideboard, picked up a candlestick, put it down. 'The right of descent.' He turned to me and appeared disappointed in my stupidity, in my lack of revelation. 'I set Gonzaga to work on King Arthur, that he might learn of the man, find some fitting matter to please the king. His Majesty is hotter than any king of England has ever been on proving the truth of descent from that ancient king. Such proof – it would still any seditious tongues that speak against his family. It would prove the rightness – the godliness – the rightness of everything.' His voice had been rising. It calmed. 'It was Gonzaga who first wrote us of the tale fit for the masque – the king and his honourable nephew.

'And yet now you tell me he went beyond his commission. That he intended to find some – some evidence – some written proofs – which would prove that our sovereign lord was of right noble descent from that king of the old days, that king of all the Britons. Ha! A task even that proud, clucking old fool Vergil disdained as a fool's errand. The student sought to outdo the master, it seems.' His voice took on a faraway sound, and he said something I'd suspected myself. 'Yet . . . yet . . . if it could be done . . . His Majesty once said that he would build a new Camelot if such signs and tokens came to him.'

'Yes, Your Grace,' I said. Again, I was looking down at the squashed, scarlet-coloured cloth in my hands. Vergil, I thought. Signor Vergil. The monk at Southwark, Brother Humphrey, had mentioned that name.

Wolsey sighed, evidently admitting defeat, deciding that I would have to be led, kicking and screaming, into understanding his vast mind. When he spoke, his voice was low. 'There are men, Anthony – ay, and wicked princes – who would speak ill of our king, our good King Henry. Who would speak ill of his high blood and right.'

I looked up, worried suddenly that I was being tested. 'I know of no such talk,' I said. It was true. Whilst I didn't trust the king very much – whilst I thought he was a good deal more serpentine than others – I'd never been fool enough to say so to anyone. And nor did anyone else seem to see it, or even sense it. All thought that the king was a paragon, as I once did: a great, golden god of a man.

The cardinal clucked his tongue, flexing and unflexing his grey-haired hands. 'I would it were not so. Yet . . . yet . . . You recall the French king?' I did. When I'd been with the court in France, we'd been promised universal and everlasting peace between England and France, with the Spanish and their emperor left out in the cold. Nonsense, of course – as I'd learnt, kings, of any race, were double-faced. My stepmother kept up with the courtly gossip, inasmuch as it touched on her idol, Queen Catherine, and so I knew that the great wheel of politics had turned right about several times since then. At present, as the emperor's presence in England showed, Charles was in and King Francis was out. It meant nothing to me. It would be the opposite story in a month, a year. My father had once told me that all kings were children, and so it seemed. Like children, they played with toys; but their toys were not little wooden poppets but real men. Like children, they huffed and sulked and turned their back on men who were their friends yesterday; but those friends were nations. Like children, they spoke behind one another's backs, spitting insults and running away; but now those insults sparked wars. They were children, to be sure, but of the spoiled, petted kind, with whole courts and kingdoms to indulge and entertain them.

'I remember King Francis,' was all I said. And I did, for more than yesterday's politics – a tall, ugly man with a nose like a generous doorstop. At the Field of Cloth of Gold, he had looked at me as though I were a strange jewel and bid me dance for him. The only good that had come from that particular humiliation was that my partner had been Jane, then plump and pretty . . .

'Mm. Yes. Now I say nothing against that Christian sovereign, of course.' Wolsey waved away the idea. 'Yet I own he might have wicked men about him, wicked counsellors, who would . . . misjudge . . . their king's wishes. And, to trouble this loving accord between our king and the emperor, they – not he, they – might send one of their tamed Scots into England to make mischief. Yes. Yes. Sowing seditious seeds and double-hearted fruits. Yes.' He moved on again, back to the window this time, rubbing at an invisible piece of dirt on one of his sleeves, which were carved and dyed into a diamond pane.

I inclined my head. Wolsey. It was like Wolsey to leap to some great continental conspiracy, to imagine foreign agents lurking, looking to upturn whatever his policies were. And yet I could see his point, and he certainly had a far sharper mind and a deeper well of knowledge than I.

Yes, I thought, warming to the idea. If proof existed that King Henry came of ancient kings, of true descent from King Arthur of the Britons, the French king would seek it. So might his friends the Scots, who had, I knew, their own king. Either nation – both nations – would profit by seeing King Henry reduced, or at least kept in the state he was. Either – both – would seek to see such proof lost, buried . . . burned.

'It would make Her Highness the Princess Mary much fitter the prize than she is, even now,' said Wolsey, still looking out the window, 'were it demonstrated that she comes of such stock.

'Ah, the French. The French, the French.' He turned from the window and crooked a finger. 'Come here, lad.'

No, thank you. Fine where I am.

I dragged myself across the carpet, around the settle, and into the circle of his perfume. It was mingled now with sweat. 'Your Grace?' The scent invaded my mouth, drying it. I fought the urge to choke.

'You see out there, across the way?'

I stood on tiptoes, trying to get a good view out over a slanting lead bar. And then I gave up, looking through the pane below instead. The windows of the room he'd chosen looked down on the courtyard, so, I guessed, that he might spy on arrivals. The New Court spread below us, three floors down. Hundreds of circles marked out drifting hats. In the corner, a mob cap rose and fell as some serving women drew water from an old well. To the left, the tiny figures of the two royal guards flanked either side of the gateway through to the Old Court, where the cardinal's lodgings – the royal lodgings – lay.

'Directly across,' said Wolsey, tapping the window. I looked, whilst he produced his silken handkerchief and wiped his finger. 'The southern range.' I nodded, taking in the unfinished wing of the new building. Only two storeys were present, the flat roof sealed with tar. At least another level would have to be added, I supposed, to complete the place, and a slate roof set above to match that on our side. 'Over there, in the finished chamber, is a fellow – a friend – of mine. A good man at the joust; likely you have seen him in the past. He is a firm friend of France. He knows all that passes in the French court. His daughters were there. You might speak with him.'

I looked down at my livery: scarlet, not fine crimson. I could feel disbelief making a mask of my face.

Wolsey laughed. 'I have the means to win you his credit, young Anthony. It lies in his daughters. Both have played in masques before. Both are well favoured enough. Hmph. The elder, too well favoured . . . Go to him and beg that he allow his fair girls to play before the king in our little masque. And then – with craft, you know – see if there is anything in his chambers that reeks of France. Or, if you will, speak to him of that realm. With a care, of course. Yes.'

Still, I must have looked doubtful. 'I . . . but . . .'

Wolsey's face hardened – not angrily, not aggressively, but firmly. 'Anthony Blanke,' he said, 'I have done you no small honour in giving you my trust, because I know that no man can hear of matters like a low man.' This he said without any trace of insult. 'You have jetted about London in pursuit of a murderer in my name. And you have discovered what the creature has done – and likely why. Do not stand there protesting in silence that you are a mindless dolt. I do not believe it. Close that gaping mouth and do as I say. Now.'

I swallowed. He was right. I wasn't a fool – I wasn't going to lumber into those chambers on a false pretext and, in passing, say, 'And, my good fellow, would you mind telling a low trumpet from the city if you know whether the French king has sent a Scot into England to kill people and steal a great discovery?'

I would think of something.

'Good man,' said Wolsey. 'Now go.' I started for the door out of the chamber and his voice caught at my back. 'Halt, lad. It is I who is the fool, truly. The fellow's name – your new friend across the way. It is Boleyn. Sir Thomas Boleyn.'

* * *

The name had rung a bell. It must have been, I supposed, that I had indeed heard it read at jousts during my previous time at court. Yet I remembered nothing of the man, could recall no stories of his nature. He was not like the Duke of Suffolk (whom everyone said was ambitious and grasping, behind a broad smile and feigned simpleness); or Sir Thomas More (kindly, you know, if a little prone to preaching); or Sir

William Compton (a dirty pander, so the stories had run in Wolsey's household).

If Sir Thomas Boleyn was a courtier, he had given the scandal-mongers little to stock up and sell on.

I had mulled this on my way downstairs, across the New Court, and into the stunted southern range. It seemed odd, too, that Sir Thomas had found himself lodging in a building under construction – it would mean sleeping with the great weight of the not-yet-done hanging overhead, dangling.

I brushed down my front, straightened my cap, and knocked on the door. I glanced down the hall as I waited. Like the lower section of wing opposite, this one had a long hallway with doors set at intervals, leading, apparently to courtly lodgings. My attention was drawn from the distant end of the hall, nearest the western range and gatehouse, to the polished oak as it slid inwards on well-oiled hinges.

My hand flew to my cap, pulling it away. 'For Sir Thomas Boleyn, from my lord cardinal.' For added obsequy, I dipped a knee.

A gaunt usher stood in the doorway, his rose-coloured doublet brushed to a sheen. 'Halt,' he said, disappearing back inside. I was conscious of the windows at my back. On this floor, they gave out onto the courtyard below. I wondered dimly if Wolsey was spying from his own window, looking out across the courtyard to see if I was dancing to his tune. Likely not. For one, he'd have no doubt of it – for another, someone had already been knocking on his door craving his time even when I'd been closeted with him.

'Come.' The usher had reappeared, and he threw the door wide. I stepped inside and looked around the room. It was an outer chamber, like any other – save that much of the household stuff appeared to be packed. Only one carpet had been unrolled, and it lay with a corner messily tucked up. A couple of braziers were merrily smoking with herbs, the better to ward away the smell of fresh whitewash which still soured those parts of the wall not hidden by linenfold panelling. Wooden crates still stood around – these, too, made me shiver – and on the other side of the room, servants were polishing windows. Others stood open, letting the watery, summery, greenery-filled air into the room. Those windows, I thought, looked onto the gardens and the river, not far from where Gonzaga was found. I shivered.

'Sir Thomas,' he said, looking at my livery rather than my face, 'will see you in his bedchamber.'

'An honour indeed,' I said. It was, though the honour, I supposed, was intended for Wolsey. I followed him to a door on the left of the room, skirting the carpet as he opened the small door without a knock. I had to duck through it, as he did.

'His Grace Cardinal Wolsey, Lord Chancellor, his servant,' the usher announced. And then he bowed, left, and closed the door.

The little bedchamber was, at least, fully furnished. A big, soft-looking featherbed stood in a corner, on a canvas mattress resting on woven rushes. Tapestries depicted scenes of animals – hares seemed to leap about prominently in most of them, though they bore strangely human faces.

I went down on one knee, sinking into the thick weave of a blue carpet. But my eyes rolled upwards, regarding this Sir Thomas Boleyn, friend of the French, father of two lusty daughters.

He was a dull-looking fellow of about fifty, with a broad,

long face, lengthened still further by a rusty beard which fanned out over a black doublet. As if to equal his big face, his sleeves were well padded, and slashed to reveal some silken white folds. He was seated on a small chair, a book in his lap with a finger to mark his place.

And there was suspicion in his eyes.

He saw me looking and it faded. Placidity washed all expression from his features so that he seemed to be staring at nothing.

Say something, goddamn you.

He hadn't invited me to rise, and so I didn't. Instead, I spoke. 'My lord cardinal sends you his good wishes and the good wishes of all his house. And welcomes you to his home.' Still, the man was a statue. 'And His Grace wishes me to ask . . . to request . . . to ask . . . if you might spare your daughters to play in a masque. Before His Majesty. And his Imperial Majesty. A masque.' I looked up, frustrated now, floundering, furious at this silent man.

Silence spread between us, uncomfortable and growing worse.

'My daughters?' he said. Relief washed through me.

So you can speak, you old goat.

'Yes, Sir Thomas.'

'Yes.'

He seemed to consider this, his face twisting into a thoughtful frown. I supposed this was a piece of theatre. 'Yet only one is here at court.'

Then send for the other; do you need me to write out the request for you?

'His Grace bids that the other be brought.' Two things were

becoming rapidly clear to me: Sir Thomas Boleyn was too clever to be led into saying or suggesting anything himself; and he wouldn't take a broad hint if it were administered by enema.

He smiled. 'I will do as His Grace requests, naturally, and thank him for the honour he does my house. Most warmly do I thank His Grace. He has been a good friend to us all. To my young Nan. And I trust will continue thus as she marries into Ireland.'

'Yes, Sir Thomas,' I said again. I assumed that this Nan was the other daughter. What she had to do with Ireland I didn't know – presumably the reference was for me to carry back to Wolsey: a little spice to go with the unbearably heavy sweetness of his gratitude. 'The masque,' I said, 'is to be of King Arthur's nephew, Gareth, in his guise as Beaumains the urchin.' This availed me of nothing but his blank stare. And then, finally, something flared, making his eyebrow twitch.

'The expense. Of bringing my Nan to court. Naturally, we thank His Grace for shouldering such an expense.'

Niggardly bastard.

'Yes,' I said. I cleared my throat, preparing a lie. 'Much of the masque will be in French. His Grace understands that both your daughters speak French.'

He narrowed his eyes. 'Naturally,' he said again, in that smooth voice. It was odd, Thomas Boleyn's way of speaking. There was a lulling charm to it, a friendliness, but so brittle one could almost shatter it with a finger, like pressing the ice on a puddle. My plan, insomuch as it had existed, had turned on him being a proud and boastful man, like most courtiers. I had thought that, at the mention of France and his daughters speaking French, he might have set out their talents, their connections and friends, touting for them, holding up his French credentials like an old bawd showing off the new gowns and bonnets of his whores.

Nothing.

I was stuck. Butterflies danced within me, feasting on the decaying morsels of cake and fluttering drunkenly. Soon the perspiration would glimmer on my brow.

'I think His Grace should like to kn—'

A dull crash shot through the room, distant but distinct.

Boleyn sprang from his seat, looking past me. I fell into a huddle, scrabbling at the carpet, righting myself. 'What the devil? Wotton! Wotton!'

There was only a second's delay before the door to the bedchamber was thrown open and the usher fell in. 'Sir Thomas!' he cried, his eyes darting from Boleyn to me and back again.

'What devilry was that? What black deed?' Before the usher could answer, Boleyn had pushed past him, leaving the little room. I followed, the wide-eyed usher in my wake. The outer room had emptied, rags and buckets of water lying where they'd been dropped. Nothing else was broken, nothing amiss. The crash had come from without, from farther away.

And there was another sound now, filtering in from the door to Boleyn's lodgings, coming from out in the New Court.

Screaming.

9

The servants fled farther down the hallway as Boleyn emerged from his rooms. Other doors had opened too, disgorging their brightly dressed tenants, who immediately went to press their faces against the windows looking down onto the New Court.

'Sweet Jesus,' said Boleyn.

He was standing immediately before me, his face chalky in the pooling light. He began fumbling at a catch on the window, cursing and muttering until he released it and threw the thing wide. 'What news?' he called down. 'What has happened?' His voice was lost. With the opening of the window had come an increase in the cries from below. The screaming had faded to a collective anguished moan.

Forgetting myself, I leapt beside the bulk of Boleyn and looked out.

One floor below us, on the ground, the great mass of people had moved away, moved over towards the northern range where Wolsey's room was, and where I'd spent the day being posed and measured and asked to look black and fearsome.

What devilry was that?

Across the way, directly beneath that wing, the crowd

had formed in a semicircle – a great forest of people with a clearing just beyond it.

And at the centre of that clearing was a body.

I could not see from the window who it was. It appeared to be a man, lying like a puppet with its strings cut. Looking up, I could see more open windows, more faces and torsos leaning out. The chorus of cries and shouts was formless, like a consort of musicians playing blind.

'Someone has fallen,' Boleyn said blandly. I looked away from the spectacle and up at him. His expression was anything but bland. He was unblinking, and his lips were twisted under his beard. His eyes were darting almost imperceptibly from side to side, up and down, missing nothing. Out of the side of his mouth he hissed, 'Go, Wotton. Discover the truth of this.'

Before the usher, who was at our heels, could react, I began walking quickly away. I didn't look back, didn't stop, until I had reached the ground floor, left the southern wing, and reached the New Court. Only one woman, detached from the crowd, seemed still to be screaming, and a pair of her fellows were trying to slap her out of it. She was, I realised, Mary, named for the Blessed Virgin, who had found Gonzaga.

It's really not her week.

Crossing the emptied area, from which the two royal guards had not moved – only their heads turning – despite the chaos, I thrust myself into the crowd. 'Make way,' I said. 'Shift, make way!' It was no use.

'Who is he?'

'Turn him!'

'Leave him!'

'How did it happen?'

There was nothing else for it; I dug into the mass of people – I pushed forward with both hands and parted them, pushing them back, pushing myself forward, swimming through the swamp of men and women until I reached the clearing.

There, some of Wolsey's men had formed a circle around the body. Among them were Harry Gainsford and Mark. Harry saw me first. Something crossed his face.

'Anthony,' he said. 'Take my place, would you? I will alert His Grace . . . about the nature of . . . Take my place.' He fled, leaving a gap, and I filled it. I turned around and looked down.

You!

Lying on his front on the cobbles, his hat down at his feet, was Visser, Wolsey's Master Glazier. His voice to me, returned in all its Flemish-sounding hauteur.

If he go, I go! Foolery. I have enough, enough, of you men betwitting each the other. The windows in this place, they not close tight. Poor work. I see from without.

What, then, was he doing inside the building? How did he come to be thrust out of it?

He had evidently fallen from an upper floor. His neck was twisted so that, though his body was on its front, his tousled grey head was bent too far to one side. The side that – mercifully – I couldn't see, must have been a mangled pulp. Small pieces of shattered glass lay about him, some coloured, others clear. Worse, a pool of blood had formed beneath the fellow, spreading out from his head, from his middle. I traced the wandering paths it had made between cobblestones, running in every direction, looking like the inside of a man's wrist writ large, writ in red.

I looked up. Still, heads were poking out of windows all along the palace wall, looking down. But one, directly above on the uppermost floor, was shattered. The sunlight, which danced about the other windows in a dazzling reflection, met only blankness there, only darkness.

In my mind, I heard that sudden crash again. I imagined that second between standing on sure ground and dropping, the lurching of the gut, the sudden loss of surety, of safety, hurtling downwards, knowing that it couldn't be stopped, that death was coming at a bone-shattering gallop.

Ghastly.

If he had fallen.

If he hadn't been pushed.

I chanced a look at the crowd. It had not thinned, but neither was anyone in it trying to press on us. Bending down, I gently lifted Visser at the middle. He was stout, but not tall. I managed to get him a little off the ground without rolling him over, just a little, just so that I might see—

My hand jerked backwards without my willing it to.

Visser's corpse slumped wetly back into its pool of crimson.

I couldn't do this. I was no stranger to corpses; a week didn't go by in London without some unfortunate being carried through the street in a cart. I had seen my father freshly laid out, embalmed, his skin turning from a rich chestnut to waxy grey beside the linen fold of the shroud. But this – a corpse mangled and broken and bloody – no.

Harry's voice cut through the crowd, his courtly accent arcing and slicing through the babble. He was coming back, and at his heels were two men with a plain oak table-board and a dirty drop cloth – one of the ones that had been used in our rehearsal room earlier, I guessed, when the painters and Visser's own carpenters and glaziers were at work. Those of us standing around the body moved out, letting the two fellows set to work in retrieving the corpse. Every head in the crowd seemed to crane in towards us. Some men were on tiptoes. Others had hoisted some of the kitchen lads, the runners and gong-scourers and spit-turners, onto their shoulders.

'His Grace does not like this,' said Harry in my ear. 'It is rather bad. Looks rather bad. With Their Majesties here. He said . . . would see you. He's called the others.' Others? I wondered. There was no emotion in his voice; he sounded a little like Sir Thomas Boleyn – a good, careful creature of the court. My former friend also knew, of course, that Wolsey had set me watching and listening to who came and went through doorways before.

He led me into the northern block. When we were indoors, he said, over his shoulder, 'His Grace will be along soon. He is with His Majesty. Mr Audley has gone with him to inform him of this accident.'

Accident, I thought. Sir Thomas Boleyn's colourless 'naturally' formed in my mind.

Harry left me in one of the long hallways on an upper floor: the same one Mark had brought me to after the rehearsal. Now it was filled with whispering men. They fell silent on seeing me and I glanced around them. They were the master craftsmen's men, keeping in huddles to themselves: glaziers with glaziers, painters with painters, poets with clerks, lutenists with rebec players, the red-eyed fool alone. I kept my eyes on the floor, tracing the rushes. As I reached the door, I heard voices rising and falling within. Hesitating, unsure, I paused before pushing it open and stepping inside.

Cornish, the Revels Master, was collapsed on Wolsey's settle, weeping and making guttural, anguished sobs. Gosson, the painter, stood aloof, his arms folded and distaste on his flinty face whilst Lutini spoke with his arms. All gave me a brief look as I entered, Cornish's sobs ceasing as he half-rose. On seeing it was only me, he resumed, as did Lutini.

I went over to the window across the room, passing the grand fireplace, and looked out. Already Visser's body had been covered. A servant stood by, just outside the ring of Wolsey's men, with a bucket of water. Lifting my gaze, I looked across and tried to find the hallway of windows in the southern range. Sure enough, a figure who was almost certainly Sir Thomas Boleyn stood there, looking out, though the distance was too great for me to read his expression. I remained there awhile, watching, thinking, until the body was carried off on its makeshift stretcher and the servant began watering the blood. I could see it, below me, turning from rich wine to cheap stuff, losing its power to horrify, to discomfit. It ran farther between the cobblestones, spreading wider, as through trying to run from the huge creature with the bucket who would destroy it.

'His Grace, the Lord Chancellor,' barked a voice at my back. I recognised it as Harry's.

I wheeled, in time to see Cornish leaping up, and Lutini and Gosson backing towards the tapestries, their caps in their hands. I backed towards the window, thought better of it, and made for a patch of wall wainscoted up to my waist.

Wolsey walked heavily into the room, his face hard and

set. He proceeded to his settle. Looking down at it, his frown deepened. His handkerchief appeared in a flourish and he dusted the cushions down before sitting.

And then he whipped us all with silence – a long, unhappy, admonishing silence. The cardinal, I thought, might have given lessons in the art to Sir Thomas Boleyn. One cassocked leg immediately began jiggling up and down, rapidly, a hand patting it, a slippered foot drumming the floor. It was as though one side of him resented being held still, forced down. Yet the movements were silent.

I could see that it was wearing on Cornish. Eventually, he could take it no more. '*Poor* Monsieur Visser,' he said. 'Oh that poor, poor fellow. He was my *friend*, Your Grace, my *best* friend. What shall I *do*? How am I to go on with *anything*?'

'Your best friend?' Lutini laughed, without humour. 'Pah! You not exchange five words with the man. You cry for pity, you dancing—'

Wolsey rose and the two rivals stopped brabbling. But the foolish argument had broken the floodgates.

'We to be all in danger!' hissed Lutini. 'He shall come for us next!'

'Someone wishes this masque stopped. They have killed my friend Pietro and now this glazier to silence us. You must not stop it, Your Grace – we are still to be paid,' chanced Gosson, pushing himself away from the wall, making the Last Supper table ripple.

'Silence!' Wolsey shouted. 'You, Anthony,' he said. There was no warmth or familiarity in his voice. 'Open that door. Call my secretary.' I did as he asked. As soon as the door slid open, a jumble of heads thrust forward. Audley's was chief amongst them. His tall, trim figure swept in after me and went to a leather-covered table laden with papers, inkpot and quill.

'To Mr Dorick, Coroner of Surrey, etc. We greet you well,' began Wolsey. He was, I realised, beginning to frame a letter. 'Hm. Yes. Regret, etc.' He lowered his hands, which had been dancing in the air, and turned sharply to the secretary. 'Audley, a word?' The fellow carefully put down the quill and went to him, inclining his head. A whispered conference took place before Audley returned to lean over the desk. Wolsey cleared his throat. 'Hm. Yes.' His hands began to ply the empty space in front of him again. 'Another accident of mischance, etc. etc. Mr Jehanne Visser, sometimes called John Visser, by birth a Fleming, etc. etc. When . . . what was it?'

Audley turned his head. 'Inspecting the windows, perhaps, Your Grace?' His voice was low, dry. 'A tragical thing indeed. Most sad.'

'Hmph,' said Wolsey. 'Ay. Inspecting the windows at this our house at Hampton Court, the said John Visser did fall, a most tragical accident, through the said window to his death. With these our blessings, on Tuesday, the 10th day of June.' Throughout, Audley scribbled, his quill making a jerky, scratching sound. 'Make a fair copy. Send it to the coroner to sign and seal. Go. Now.'

Audley sanded the page, turned, bowed, and left without a word.

And then Wolsey stood. 'An accident,' he said. 'So the case rests. Yet the king mislikes of it. Too many eyes saw this one – too many to be bought or dismissed before he could be troubled. He mislikes any whisper of death or accident. He will not tarry here. He would move on to Windsor in a day or two and go from there to Winchester. Cruel and purposeless death. He mislikes of it.' We all stood silent. 'Yet, like the other . . . we see some devilment here.' He raised a finger and began jabbing at the air. 'Does it stand, I ask you, that a Master Glazier should be fool enough to topple from his own construction?'

No one spoke. And then I remembered – something, I thought, that didn't fit.

'Pardon me, Your Grace,' I said. Wolsey spun in a whirl of red.

'Speak, boy – and do not waste my time.'

I swallowed. 'Mr – Monsieur Visser – he – he said that he was going to check the windows. From without. Said they weren't closing properly, or something. So . . . so he should have been outside the palace, looking in. Not inside, falling out.'

As I said it, an idea formed.

Outside . . . looking in.

Did Visser see something going on in one of the rooms? Did he hear something through an open window as he inspected the glass from without? If so, what did he do next? I tried to trace his path: huffing his way outside, going around the building, climbing a ladder, perhaps, still huffing. And then freezing. Squinting. Cocking an ear to the glass. And hearing something he shouldn't, seeing something amiss.

And then?

Why, then he should have run to the cardinal with it.

My eyes widened. I heard again that knock at the cardinal's chamber door, after I'd told him the long, rambling tale of my adventuring about London.

Be gone! Leave us!

I couldn't say how much of it was true or how far fantasy fashioned my thoughts. I was spared having to do either. Wolsey himself went to the door, opened it, and began muttering to someone outside. A chorus of voices rose and stilled. And then, closing the door, he began pacing. 'Monsieur Visser's workmen,' he said, 'say you speak true. Yes. The fellow was inspecting windows without. Those opening into the north of this house.'

'Which room? Which chamber?' I asked, too sharply. Wolsey gave me a stern look. 'Your Grace,' I added, with a head-bow.

This appeared to satisfy him. 'A closet. A private room for meditation. Empty, untenanted. And, of a sudden, he descended his ladder and cried urgent business with me. They heard no more of him until the great cry rose.' He was, again, winding his way about the room, his robes billowing, his arms making little pinwheels. He paused, putting a hand to his forehead. 'This man was murdered,' he said at last. 'I am beginning to think . . . Yes . . . I am beginning to think that someone does not wish this masque to go forward. Does not wish any celebration of our king's friendship with the emperor of Spain. Nor any cheering of his descent from King Arthur.'

'But it must!' spluttered Gosson, stepping forward. 'It must! The tales of Arthur are true. Our king his right heir. The tales are true! We shall not be silenced.'

'This creature – he murder again to stop it – he come for the rest of us next!' cried Lutini.

Cornish issued a long, drawn-out 'Ooh', before affecting a swoon. No one paid him any attention.

'Enough!' barked Wolsey. 'You will do as I say. You will be guided by me in all things.' He folded his arms over his big chest. 'Mr Cornish – get you gone. Some wine, perhaps, will steady your fragile humours.' This he delivered with contempt, but Cornish didn't seem to mind. He bowed, before fleeing the room.

'Herr Gosson and Monsieur Lutini? Take your men and question them. Discover if they saw anything amiss. Go. Now.' They did.

I dreaded being left alone with Wolsey. His mood was frangible, apt to blossom into cold fury. 'Anthony,' he said, 'you will escort me next door. Yes. I think next door.' I preceded him out of the chamber on the upper floor. The only remaining men in the hallway were his – clerks, secretaries, chaplains, and a smattering of household officers. He gave them a withering look and they melted back. Together, we went a little way down the hall. Wolsey paused before a door, nodding at me to open it for him. I did.

Inside was an unfurnished chamber, its tiles bare and the plaster of its upper walls blank, some streaked with grey smudges from an unlit fireplace. The room was noisy, though, filled with the diffuse chatter of the servants in the New Court below. Across the room, I could see that the window hung open. Its lead frame was intact, but pieces of glass were missing.

We crossed to it. Wolsey, his hand wrapped in his handkerchief, reached out and pulled the big frame in and out. It moved smoothly, quietly. It was well oiled. 'From here,' he said. 'He was pushed – thrown – from here.'

I could see it. The fellow had come to speak to Wolsey, been rebuffed, and waited in this room. Until . . . until . . .

'I think he saw something, Your Grace,' I said. 'Or heard something. It might have been him who knocked on the door when I was with you. And he came here. Waited.' I looked at him for permission to go on and he nodded, stepping back as I reached out for the broken window. 'The window – see,' I said, pushing it hard, 'swings out. Fast. Hits the bricks and breaks. Maybe Mr Visser going through it made it do that.'

'Perhaps. Yes. It might be. But who, boy? Who wishes this great celebration disrupted? Who wishes this masque stopped?' His eyes widened. 'You . . . you spoke to Boleyn? You learned something of the French, I trust?'

I swallowed. 'No, Your Grace.' I looked out the broken window. 'I was on the point of it. And then this happened. I only had time to ask about his daughters. For the masque, as you said.'

Wolsey drew in his cheeks, moving away from the window, back into the chamber, his back turning on me. 'Then forget that course. For the moment. We have thought better of it. The masque,' he said, giving a humourless little cough of laughter. 'The masque. Boleyn. He might bring the younger daughter. The elder . . . we have thought better of it. The elder might insult the honour of the emperor and the queen. We shall think on that. We shall send Mr Audley to speak with Sir Thomas. He will be a fitter messenger for . . . delicate . . . Yes.' He turned to me. 'You, boy, you might go. You have practised your part. We have no more need of you.'

Thank God!

'And,' said Wolsey, fixing me with a look, 'it has not escaped our notice . . . certain things.' He lifted his chin. 'You come here – and he kills, this creature. Chance, perhaps. You go to London – and he works such mischief there. Hm. You come again – and again he kills. I put little faith in chance, young sirrah, little enough at the best of times.'

He thinks I'm a curse.

'Now I do not say that you are a curse, lad,' he said, startling me. 'Merely that this creature appears to know that we have allowed you a measure of interest in this affair. And with the royal family so near to us, across the way,' he gestured vaguely at the window, 'perhaps you might do us meet service in . . . leading the creature elsewhere. In the city, perhaps. Yes. The authorities in the city might help you catch him. Already I have sent word to the great houses of religion to apprehend any stranger attempting entry under any false cloak or colour.'

'You wish me back in London?' I asked numbly. It was a perverse thing, but I had turned from wishing to be away from Hampton Court, when it was my choice, to wishing to remain when it was thrust upon me. One way meant escape. The other tasted of disgrace.

And, I realised, Wolsey was right. This creature, this Caledon, had followed me, or I him. If I returned, I should be putting my own head on the block. I might get two leagues towards London and find myself meeting with another one of the cardinal's 'tragical' accidents.

But I had no say in the matter. If Wolsey wanted me gone, I must go.

'It is our wish that for the better protection of this house and yours, you return to your lodgings,' he said, inclining his head. 'You need only attend on us if . . . if you and the London authorities chance to catch this creature. And, of course, for the masque.'

My *better protection*?

Yet, I thought, an idea rising in my mind, I need not make things easy for the mysterious Mr Caledon.

'I'll be pleased to go, at Your Grace's command,' I said, 'if I might beg one favour. For protection on the road . . .'

* * *

Abraham was a remarkable horse. It wasn't his speed or his grace that marked him out, but the fact that, despite being a uniform brown, across his rump was spread a large, heart-shaped patch of white. Abraham was my horse, or he had been. The grooms knew it down at the stables by the Thames, and so anyone else who cared to discover it might know it. If, that was, such a questing, clever creature as Mr Caledon didn't already know it.

My plan was simple but, I flattered myself, rather cunning.

I had no great desire to be murdered on the road, left bleeding and forgotten in some nameless hamlet or woodland on the way between Hampton Court and London. Nor did I wish to be involved in an unfortunate wherry accident and subsequently nibbled at by eels.

Yet, I suspected, Wolsey was right. The murderer of two men was at Hampton Court and had been in London, as I had been. He knew what I was about as well as I knew his ugly business, and the steps he'd taken. It might be that he'd followed me on the main road down from the city – or perhaps he'd seen me ride up, having got to the palace ahead of me. It really didn't matter. What mattered was that, if he should try and follow me, he should be misled.

There were two principal ways, I knew, of reaching the city by road. The main way, the way I had taken on my last trips to and from London, ran along the Portsmouth road, crossing the old wooden bridge at Kingston and thereafter passing through Putney, Wandsworth, Clapham, and so on into Southwark, from where the city proper was only boat or bridge away. It was a fair journey, the road well peopled and every high street encompassed.

And then there was the other way. This I did not know as well. Running through mostly countryside, the road passing the odd rural village, it formed part of the great western highway. It would lead north from Hampton Court, up through Twickenham and Syon, broadly following the meandering curves of the north shore rather than crossing the Thames. Its great waypoint, I knew, was near Hammersmith and the bishop of London's estate of Fulham. There lay a coaching inn, commonly called the gateway to the west, on the Goldhawk's Road. This name had always stuck with me; it sounded beautiful, though I knew the road itself to be as dusty and barren as any other.

This was to be my way.

But I would set a diversion, if Caledon the killer should have it in mind to follow me.

The Hampton Court stables were not lavish, but they were large. They appeared to have been built in a good-sized old cottage, the insides of which had been ripped out to allow room for stalls and paddocks. If ever the place had smelled of cooking, of hearth and home, that pleasant odour had long been replaced by the reek of manure and the earthy stench of hay. The place was noisy, too: not with a master and servants, but with whinnying, with men coming and going, taking and leaving horses, returning from the city with messages, leaving on errands. No great notice should be taken of the details of my departure, the direction I went in. I stood, looking at Abraham, his dull, black eyes staring dumbly through me.

'I'm here, man,' said a voice at my back. I turned away from the low wooden door.

And my mouth fell open.

Mark stood before me. I had told him everything that had passed, from the murder of Gonzaga to the death of Visser; I trusted him implicitly. My plan was thus: I had made no secret of my going, sharing the news about the New Court with faces I knew and some I didn't. But Mark would wear my cap, ride my horse, and take off for London by the primary road through to Southwark.

I, meanwhile, would take the more troublesome and – I thought, wary of thieves as well as murderers – more dangerous route to enter the city from the west. If our murderous Caledon set off in pursuit, he would be stymied. Likely he would follow Mark, who would be riding my horse. I had even stuck an extravagant heron feather I'd found floating about the gardens in my cap and worn it as I'd prattled about my taking off for the city. This I would exchange with him also. There was nothing I could do about the more conspicuous difference between us.

But apparently Mark had found some means.

Jesus Christ, Mark.

He stood in front of me, his white teeth gleaming in a face spread thick with soot. His hands had been coated in the stuff too, so that he resembled a gong-scourer after a hard day wriggling through a sewer drain.

'Here,' he said, passing me a dun-coloured bundle, 'just as you said, man.' I barely looked at it: the canvas doublet

I'd asked him to secure – workman's weeds. I just had time to register that it was covered in smudgy black fingerprints, before I looked again at his face.

'It's good, ain't it?'

I swallowed. It was far from good, to my mind. I had seen Mark dressed up similarly before, at the behest of the French king, supposedly so that he might better play my twin. What King Francis – and apparently Mark – failed to notice was that I was not the black of coal dust. Nor had even my father been so dark. 'I . . .'

'I mean, from a distance, it'll look right, won't it? If this bastard gives chase.' He stopped smiling; the flash of white disappeared. I had told Mark enough of what was afoot, and he had leapt at it. Wolsey had given him permission to go, though not a command. My friend seemed to read my distaste. I couldn't hide it.

He meant well.

'I thought it might help,' he said. 'Had the craftsmen up in the palace do me up like a . . .' He looked at the sanded, hay-flecked floor. '"A Moor," I said. Do me up like a Moor, like. Wouldn't spare me no proper paint powders, so I thought, bit of soot . . .' He smiled up, waggling his fingers next to his black face. 'Then had a bit of a lark with it – scaring the hell out of people. Went to see if I could have a bite of that lass's cherries, if there was any left. And she screamed and she said, "Demon!"' He seemed to realise I wasn't enjoying his tale. 'Scared. On account of the glazier. On account of . . .' He gestured at his face. 'See, cos he dirtied me up, like.' He looked down again. 'I mean, well, dirtied, ay, with dirt, soot, like, but I don't mean that Moors are – not that you're really even all—'

'It's fine,' I said, a little throatily. I gave myself a little shake. 'Fine. But if you say that you're my proper twin again, I'll have to cut out your tongue.' He laughed, but I didn't join him. 'Remember, this fellow is dangerous.'

'Pfft. Let him try it.' He struck a pose, fists up. 'I'll kick him in the cods. Then rip 'em off and feed them to him.'

I shook my head more firmly. 'No. Just ride on. Don't stop.' It was Mark's job to be a false hare, not a hound. My hope was that, if Caledon did try and follow, he would realise he had been duped and return, perhaps even try the other road, or the river – either way, we would be ahead of him. Doubt filled me, suddenly. The craftsmen's servants had been in and out of the stable; I should have told Mark to forget the whole scheme and ridden with one of them. But it was too late. Still, I might wait on someone riding with a message for London and go with him. But no. I had concocted the scheme, begun it, and now must ride with it.

'Well,' he said, interrupting my regrets, my doubts, 'I'll get going. Love a bit of London, me. Might find meself a girl there. Don't come troubling us if I do. This my horse, is it? Well, yours. You know what I mean.' He didn't wait for an answer; he unlatched the gate and went to Abraham, stroking downwards, between his eyes, whispering. Mark knew horses better than I did. He had the wit to do all the things I'd been told to do but felt foolish doing: talking to them as though they understood English; never releasing the reins; keeping the spine straight.

I helped him get Abraham saddled and dressed. Occasionally I looked over my shoulder, now that we were setting the thing in motion. But no one was interested. No one was lurking in a shadow or an empty stall, no one was paying undue attention. A groom was shouting at a lad who was forking hay. Another lad was grunting as he hauled a trough of water through the resisting sand on the floor, even as the horse's head swung down eagerly. A trio of men in royal liveries was standing around laughing, as one of them told some tale or other, punctuated with obscene-looking hand gestures.

We were not being watched.

'Right,' Mark called down. His round, blackened face beamed down, making him look childish. I removed my hat and held it up, its new feather tossing around. He took it and passed down his own. Straightening it on his head, he said, 'Right, then. See you in London.' He grinned, throwing me a salute, and then began edging Abraham out of the stable. His crimson back, I saw, smiling, gave way to Abraham's broad, white-flecked rump.

When he had gone, I set to work quickly, taking off my crimson livery doublet and tying it into a makeshift pack, before putting on the canvas one and taking another horse. Wolsey had indicated where I might find a fast one, a jennet, accustomed to carrying messengers. And then, hurriedly, trying not to catch the eyes or attention of any of the men in the stable, I hopped up on a mounting block, bent low over the beast's neck – *keep your spine straight and stiff* – and nudged the brute forward. It went as bid and, as we emerged into the sparkling, early-evening sun, I set off on the opposite road from the one Mark would have taken.

No one was coming down towards the stable, not that I could see.

But if Mr Caledon was up there, in the palace, watching from one of those innumerable windows, he would already have seen Anthony Blanke, his feathered hat on his head, his horse's white spot bleached further by the sun, off on his way to Kingston. I could wait to see if he appeared, to see if I might recognise him from that brief glimpse of a turned collar and a hat pulled low, but I thought better of it. If I lingered, I risked giving the game away – and besides, any man who came down could cry ignorance, and I had no proof of anything against anyone.

Taking the great western highway, I quickly realised my mistake. As soon as the horse's hooves touched good riding road, the brute shot off, bolting, cantering.

Fucking horse! Fast messenger's horse?! Fucking Wolsey!

I braced myself for a wild ride.

I should have seen the selection of such an animal, I suppose, as a kind of portent.

10

Finally, I thought. It was growing dull, as the squat coaching inn appeared, a little grey box on the horizon, hazy in the fading day. The Goldhawk's Road shrank towards it. I continued on, just about accustomed to the rhythmic ache that had settle into my bones. To the right, a tree-lined avenue branched off, presumably on its way to the bishop's palace that oversaw the area. I ignored it, rocking onwards.

I was tousled, sweating, thirsty, hungry, frightened, bored, and thoroughly, utterly irritated. The horse – its name was Gideon, I'd remembered, though shouting that hadn't calmed it in the first hour of the journey – had slowed. That was in no way due to my mastery; the brute had tired itself out and now dragged its legs grudgingly through the rising clouds of dust.

It's a further irritant, on tiring journeys, to have the goal in sight. The coaching inn never seemed to grow larger, and so I gave up staring between Gideon's ears. Instead, I sat back, ignoring the sawing feeling that sliced into each cheek of my backside.

Stupid horse. Stupid Wolsey.

Stupid me.

I had time, now, to think. In the preceding hours, my thoughts had been occupied by worry that I was going the right way; fear that my plan had failed, either because Mark was in danger or because I was still being followed; and a rising panic, too, about what might fall out in the future. Two men were now dead in Hampton Court, and the murderer seemed to be a ghost, moving invisibly between palace and city, unnoticed, unremarked upon.

Murder ran screaming into my mind.

Accidents, Wolsey had called them. And he'd get away with it, because he was Cardinal Wolsey, and he had spies in every household and great chamber in the realm, each ready to report on anyone who said otherwise. I'd heard that the king had spies in Wolsey's house too, of course, but the jest ran that they were paid twice – once by the king and double that by the cardinal, who bid them tell Henry's people only what His Grace permitted.

No, people wouldn't ask questions. Even the king, I supposed, would have little interest in the deaths of a pair of master craftsmen. At best, he might lament that he'd never be able to poach them for his own service.

But death was death, I thought, trying not to look at the dark woodlands that had sprung up on either side of the road. In there, deer would be hunted by the bishop and his guests; their hooves would skip over branches and bracken, their liquid eyes wide in terror as they sought safety and life.

Death was everywhere, hiding, lurking. It watched over cradles, it hovered over battlefields, it gambolled about woodlands, and it was godfather to accidents and murders. It might surprise you to know just how much death there is in a great palace. Maids died in childbirths they'd tried to hide, along with their babes; there were fights – one time, at York Place, a groom had fought with another, striking him, and killing the poor lad stone dead with one punch. It had been an accident, he'd claimed; he didn't know how a little strike had done so much. Death had come for him too, though; he'd met it at the end of a rope. And, as Wolsey knew, there were true accidents. I'd heard tales of a spit-boy who fell into the flames at Sheen, though I didn't credit it. Most definitely, though, a workman had been killed years back, during the first round of building works at Hampton Court, when a loose stone from the old house had fallen on his head. And an old woman called Joan – she wasn't on Wolsey's staff, but she lingered; I'd seen her; we'd nod at each other – went down to the river to wash or pick flowers and fell in. She was found, face down amongst the reeds. Poor old Joan.

Yes, in a small household of five people, years might pass without death visiting. In a great palace, hundreds of people, swollen to over a thousand during royal visits . . . things happen. Death follows a crowd. Like merchants and pedlars, he rubs his bony hands in glee at the thought of a great band of people, some stupid, some without luck, some evil-minded and preying on others, and he swings his blade high.

But these latest deaths, of Gonzaga and Visser, were no accidents, however imaginative Wolsey's embroidering of false reports to be signed by the coroner.

A murderer was abroad. Someone of the court, someone who could pass in and out as freely as I could. I was an in-between, of sorts, neither a master nor a lowly domestic. This murderer might be likewise. Yet, I thought, he must also be educated, skilled in learning, which would indicate the better sort, the courtly: a man who was two things at once.

As birds rose squawking into the sky – disturbed by God knew what in the trees – I tried to rein in my thoughts, to make sense of them. The coaching inn, I saw, had grown a little larger, the night a little dimmer. Gideon seemed to sense it – perhaps, I thought, horses could smell things we couldn't, and already he'd picked up the scent of oats or other horses. He picked up his pace and I straightened.

What really troubled me was the nature of the murders. A flock of birds brought by crumbs, staged like a scene in a masque; a fall from a great height; and still there was the strange issue of the false sulphur. It all meant something, but I didn't know what.

Useless to speculate, I thought. Until the fellow could be drawn out into the open and caught, his antics would be shapeless and mad. And either I would draw him to London and call up the watchmen to take him there, or Wolsey would have other men watching. Probably he had paid informants in the king's own household guard. Let them worry about Hampton Court and Windsor and Winchester.

And then, all at once, the coaching inn ceased to be a little grey box. It was, in fact, a wattle-and-daub building on two storeys, with a neat, grey-slated roof. The road I was on branched around it – on my left it ran between a jumble of tumbledown hovels, and on my right it ran riverward, through rolling fields spotted with trees. I could just about make out some parish church spires, the occasional grey- or red-tiled roof, and dots of thatch here and there. That was my way: on to London.

'Come on, you,' I said. Gideon, apparently desirous of a rest and cheated into thinking he'd found one, refused to move. He came to rest with his nose pointing to the side of the inn, where a timber archway led into, I assumed, the stables beyond. And that, if he had the magnificent horse-sense I'd ascribed to him, would be where his water, oats and brushes – and possibly a mare with low standards – would be.

Tough.

If I had no romantic life, neither would a damned horse. I shook the reins. 'Come on,' I hissed. We were too close to London and it was getting late. I didn't want any trouble at the city gates. Besides, I couldn't leave Mark up there on his own. I'd said nothing about lingering – and he would be as worried about me as I was about him. Grudgingly, Gideon began to move on.

'Wait! Halt!'

I jerked in the saddle, twisting. The voice – a woman's voice – had trumpeted into the air behind me.

'Yes? What news?' I called down.

She was a broad woman, matronly, her face pleasant. Frizzy red hair framed it, escaping her coif. Her eyes were narrowed, running me up and down, and she bit at her lip. 'Is it you?'

'What?' I had drawn Gideon to a halt easily. His head had again swung around to the left, the big nostrils flaring. He whinnied. 'Is what me?'

'Sir . . . are you . . . what's your name?'

Why should I tell you?

It was a risk, revealing your name, revealing anything, to strangers. But this was no trickster, no cozener. I judged her to be something of the inn: the tapster's wife, perhaps. 'Blanke,' I said. For no reason, I kept my voice low, as though hiding it from the empty road.

'Ah, it is you,' she said. 'Begging your pardon, sir. I have news for you.'

'News?' I asked.

She disappeared back into the inn before re-emerging a moment later, brandishing a piece of paper. 'This come for you.'

Mark, I thought. And then: oh God, what's happened to him?

'What is it?' I asked, my mouth dry. 'What does it say?'

'Can't say, sir,' she said, holding it away from her and frowning at it. 'Couldn't read no letters of men what come here even if I wanted to. Which I don't. Not none o' my business, sir.' She shrugged, holding it up to me. Leaning down – carefully, warily – I plucked it from her. The paper was good quality, veined like the inside of a pale wrist, very white against my fingers. I cursed myself for not having found gloves.

'Who brought it? Is he here? Young man – my age? Brown hair? Round face?'

She shrugged. 'Feller brought it up out of London. Not long since. Didn't see him. Passed it to the ostler.'

I glanced round to the stables. 'Is he here? Might I speak to him?'

'The ostler?'

'Either,' I said, annoyed now.

My irritation sparked something in her. 'Ostler's away for the night. No one staying except a merchant's wife and daughters for the west. Are you lodging or not, sir?'

I ignored her, cast one last frown towards the stable, and then unfolded the letter.

Anthony ye trompet. Mete me at ye syne of ye Boars Head. East Cheap. Your verie gude freynd, Mark.

The writing was not his, I saw immediately. The spelling was poor, but not his manner of poor, and the script itself was rather better than his. It was neat, the letters joined up. This all, of course, meant little. Even when we'd written one another, Mark had often had someone else write the letters; he was no great lover of reading or writing. But even then, usually he had appended his own scrawled name. The 'Mark' here was in the same elegant hand as the rest.

'Are you lodging, then?'

I looked away from the note, back down to the woman. She was standing with one hand on her hip. 'No,' I said. 'No, I'm for London.'

Her arm fell as her chin rose. 'Very good, sir.' And then a smile spread across her face. 'London, is it?' I nodded. 'Wait here, sir.' Again, she darted into the inn before hopping back out, her skirts and apron bouncing. No letter this time – a large, heavy stick was in her hands. I recoiled a little at the sight of it. 'Going up to London, you say, love?' Her voice was pure honey now. 'You don't want to be going abroad in the streets, love, not at this time. You ain't got no sword. You take this, sir. Only a groat.'

A groat!

I sighed. She was not going to let me go without giving her something. Besides, she had done me a service and it occurred to me that I must owe her. Wolsey had, thankfully, paid me off after I'd told him of my plan; his treasurer had furnished me with a good bag of coins, enough to let me live well a while, in fact, and still return to court for his masque. I folded the letter under my doublet, passed her down the money, and forced myself to take the staff. It was a striking staff, meant to beat away footpads, horse thieves, or any other saucy jack who fancied making mischief. It could be lethal, if wielded against a head, painful applied anywhere else. I tucked it into my belt, behind my back. It would force me not to slouch on Gideon, anyway.

I nodded my thanks, but she had lost interest in me now that she'd had what she wanted. She disappeared into the coaching inn and this time she stayed there.

'Come on, you,' I said to Gideon. Doubly uncomfortable now, I managed to get him moving, and we began our final clop into the city, the dust we cast up now lying heavy on the descending, windless night. The sky above was a darkening canvas streaked with growing fingers of smoke.

I would, as it turned out, be glad of the stick up my back soon enough.

11

I descended into London down the long sloping road. Dismounting once I reached the bridge spanning the stinking Fleet River at Farringdon Street, I moved on towards Ludgate itself. It was a fool's game, to remain in the saddle in London; if you weren't careful, you'd split your head on one of the jutting upper galleries of a house or civic building. Still, I could see the appeal of the river. I'd far rather be arsenumbingly bored than bone-rattled and sore.

A pair of men in city livery were standing hard by Ludgate. As I approached, one bent down just underneath the crumbling stone archway and began fumbling at something. The other man turned, his heavy face crinkling. A hand rose to paw at his beard. 'Hold!' he shouted. I paused, apprehensive, and then realised that he wasn't speaking to me. The iron grille of the portcullis had descended about a yard. 'Well, come, man, if you're coming! Quickly!' He began waving me on, tutting, as though he had better things to do.

I quickened my pace, leading Gideon down towards the closing maw of the gate. It remained suspended, its sharp points hanging downwards. The other porter must have managed to halt its progress.

'Who goes there, sirrah, your name?'

I told him and then added where I'd been and who I worked for. He shrugged this away, holding out his gloved open palm for the toll. I paid, and he waved me on. 'Hurry,' he said. 'It's gone eight already. We're not slack here, you can tell His Grace, should he ask. Not slack at the Ludgate.'

I nodded and went on, passing into the shadows of the old gatehouse and emerging back into the light. Once I was through, I turned, and listened to the men bark at one another, my porter slipping inside just as the portcullis began falling to the ground in a fit of sudden, uneven drops.

I thought of the Master Glazier as the metal points sank into their old, well-worn holes in the muck.

I was safely inside – just. Sealed into the safety of the city itself: a place where, if something should happen, there would always be someone around to hear me scream.

Dimly, I wondered if Visser had considered himself safe at Hampton Court, if Gonzaga had. It was feeling safe, going about your business without thought or care, that made you easy prey for the wicked. On that cheerful thought, I turned away from Ludgate. As I did so, I felt the letter crinkle against my breast. I had read and reread it whenever Gideon paused, until the elegant, careful script – the slanting A, the looping thorn, the curly-footed M – was printed in my mind. Something troubled me about it, but I couldn't say what. It was like seeing a piece of music written out but set at the wrong note. I banished the thought.

You fool, Anthony Blanke! You bloody great piss-wit!

The thought came in Mark's own voice. It struck me, all of a sudden, why he might have sent a letter up to the main coaching inn on the road he knew I was taking. Our plan, from the start, had been half-cocked.

See you in London.

We had agreed to meet in London, but we had neither of

us actually said where. By his faster route, and with his better horsemanship, he would have reached the city before me and found himself a lodging house. Then, all he'd have to do was send word up to the inn by anyone travelling that way. It was a busy enough route, at least during the day. And it couldn't be missed – it was the only road in from the west. I relaxed, as my shoes squelched onto the dirty, un-cobbled slope, into the darkness of London, where the only sky was a narrow sliver carved out between high rooftops.

But Mark knew where I lived, I thought. He had written me.

Two years ago. Until he stopped because I didn't reply.

I was arguing with myself, intent now on finding danger. My father had once said of me that I was only happy when I was finding reasons not to be happy. Loath as I was to admit it, I supposed it was true. It needn't even be happiness I soured; if a matter was going to plan, I must find some crack, some disorder or danger or flaw.

It was no surprise that the old man forced himself into my mind. As I turned right into the narrow Creed Lane, I could see over the crooked line of rooftops the enormous spire of St Paul's, stabbing into the twilit night like a beckoning finger. I knew these streets. When I was little, my father used to take me on walks around the area, around the churchyard, along Carter Lane, which I was making for. They never seemed to change.

The memories of him came hard. I imagined he might step out from any of the narrow lanes between the houses. The whole place had a dreamlike quality, as will any place that loomed so large in childhood. It perhaps seemed a little smaller, the old houses now vaguely threatening, looking apt to tumble down, rather than simply enormous and never-ending. I might almost have heard his voice, its Spanish accent heavy: 'Up there we have da greatest of the churches. Da finest. You keep out of the church, though, when you grow. No life in poverty. Come. We look at the colours. Tonight, maybe you earn a tale of the Greeks. If you good.' There was always a story, whether I was good or bad, usually sung. But before that, we'd wander the churchyard, marvelling at the gaily painted cloths, laid out for display like ships' sails stained by a rainbow. 'You see – all dyed in all colours by magic.'

Yes, I could almost hear him.

A tear pricked in the corner of my eye. I hadn't been ashamed of him then. Not as a child. I hadn't carried him on my back as I later had, weighting me down in service . . .

A wave of raucous laughter, bursting from above, broke the spell.

'Get you home to bed, horse-boy!' someone shouted. It was a woman, leaning from an upper window. A fat man was at her side, an arm around her waist.

He hiccoughed, raising a wooden tankard. 'To t'king. And t'emp – emp – Spain. And fuck the French!' The woman wriggled against him and a narrow column of ale hit the muck of the streets, splashing, forming a sucking puddle. The pair began shouting at one another as they disappeared into the pool of light of their shutter.

I hurried on, intent now on reaching Mark, of getting home. I passed the turnings for Paul's Chain and Sermon Lane – gloomy tunnels, they were now, and noisy too – until I reached the Old Change. Here, the houses faced the eastern rump of the cathedral. Accordingly, they showed finer faces to its grace: thatched roofs were fewer and tile or slate more common; the whitewash was fresher; most of the shutters were sensibly shut or open with a friendly candle set in a dish against the evening. Any coloured cloths they might have sold during the day were now securely locked indoors.

I might reach Eastcheap by any number of routes. The streets of the city were numerous, but if you knew your way, there was rarely a dead end. It was an old saying that you could easily get lost in London, but if you kept walking long enough, you'd find whatever you sought.

If the thieves or the watch didn't get you first, was the end of the jest.

Because there's no difference between the two, would be added, invariably, by that one tiresome fool who never met a jest he wouldn't explain.

My mind was wandering. Exhaustion seemed to wash over me with the promise of a bed, with the lure of being so close. I had, I realised suddenly, made the winding journey twice in one day again, like a begrimed messenger. I'd risen before the dawn and would, with luck, be home before the summer day finally released its waning grip. The thought spurred me on.

The Boar's Head.

The thought was a tonic. I opted to turn south, riverward, and led Gideon down Lambeth Hill. It sloped down to the vast length of Thames Street, where the going was, I fancied, safer. Here one was never far from the riverside palaces of clergy and nobility, nor from those houses of fine burgesses and aldermen which thought to pick up a little glister by proximity.

I quickly realised my error. Though the street was broad and fine, it was lit along its length by numerous bonfires. As on my last entry into the city, people were dancing around them. They were gypsy-types, I realised, or affecting to be, out to try and earn a few pennies putting on entertainments for the revelling populace. And the wealthier the residents they paraded themselves near, the richer the pickings.

I kept my head down, ignoring the sudden eruption of cries, the blast of dreadful and tuneless song from dozens of unrelated men and instruments, the cackling mirth. When I did look up, I saw a crowd in strange animal masks: men were done up with greyhound snouts and lions' manes; women were gyrating wildly, eagle beaks thrusting grotesquely from their faces. Some little children were wearing greenery – woven leaves – with dark masks from which hung forked tongues; these were sitting on the ground or lying sleeping, looking for all the world like the bigger creatures had slain them. The whole makeshift pageant was frightening, lit more by the licking flames of a bonfire than the evening sky. There was no need to guess at its significance. It was a dumb show in the flavour of the court but with none of its gilding or fair words: the great beasts of England and Imperial Spain dancing in victory over the beaten, hideous Francis I: the salamander of Europe. We were many miles away from the court now, I thought, but only a hop from its mind. From the houses on either side, people were leaning out, standing on rickety galleries, throwing coins and cheers to the parties of masked dancers.

I considered finding a means of getting back up on Gideon, but before too long I came upon the turn for Dowgate Street and turned, gratefully, away from the unpleasant bustle and feverish revelry.

Not far now.

Thank God.

I turned right up St Mary Botolph Lane – a shortcut – hurrah – and began moving up towards Candlewick Street. The houses here were quiet again, shuttered. I passed by a couple; I could see the street which would bleed into Eastcheap.

''Alt. 'Oo goes there?'

The voice froze me. I released Gideon's reins. They flapped downwards. I began to turn. Something pressed into my lower back. 'Don't you move,' the voice said. 'Put yer 'ands up.' Strangely, I wasn't afraid. Instead, a cold kind of fury flared. I was close, so close, to finding Mark. The canvas of my doublet pinched further, just to the left of the staff.

The staff.

'Where's yer money? Yer coins, stranger, where's yer coins?'

I swallowed. 'In my purse.'

'Ay? And where's yer purse?'

'I don't know,' I said, my eyes intent now on the street ahead. It would take a very strong blade to cut through canvas and linen, I thought. 'All around my coins, I suppose.'

My attacker fell silent, apparently confused. 'The fuck you mean?'

I wheeled, pushing forward at the same time, hitting him in the chest.

A rascal prentice, just a lad, no older than me!

He recovered, hissing curses, and braced his legs, well apart. I fumbled at my back, stupidly, grasping for the staff.

My right hand closed around its end and I jerked. It lifted. Caught. It was stuck, the striking end caught in my belt, trapped. He pitched forward, jabbing at the air, and I hopped back, nearly falling. His blade, his dagger – I saw it wasn't a dagger.

A stick!

It was no more than a crudely sharpened stick. Unless he could get at my eyes, it was worthless, more to cause fear and alarm. Small wonder he didn't want me turning round. I forgot the staff. Instead, I lurched forward. He paused, wary, his spotty face darting left and right. And I brought up my knee, hard, between his legs.

Kick him in da cods! Men always weak there.

The lad yelped, grasping under his patched, untucked shirt, cupping his cheap hose. Slowly, I began twisting the staff out from where it was caught up. It came smoothly.

Holding it before him, I said, 'Go away! You . . . you shit. Go!'

His eyes wide, he began hopping away. When he had got part-way down St Mary Botolph, he paused, hunching over, putting his hand against the crumbling plaster of a house. 'You . . .' he breathed, 'dirty . . . filthy . . . black . . . ape . . .' Another gasping breath. 'Kill . . . you!'

I moved forward, holding the stick high, and he fled, disappearing down an alleyway between two houses. 'And stay gone!' I yelled at the empty air. My heart, I realised, was racing, beat skipping ahead of beat. Some windows began opening above.

'What news?'

'The watch! Call up the watch!'

I ignored them, willing my heart to slow. I might,

indeed, call up the watch. If they could catch the hapless, foul-mouthed rascal – a generous if – then he might hang.

No, I thought. I might see a man hang for murder, and gladly, but not for a failed attempt at thievery. Had he wounded me, had it been my home he'd broken in on, perhaps. But not this, no matter what he'd said.

I began leading Gideon onwards, resuming our journey. 'Much help you were,' I said, just for something to say. My voice was cracked, not far from tears, and I regretted speaking. I carried the weight of those hateful words up to Candlewick Street and so on to Eastcheap.

★ ★ ★

I knew the Boar's Head. It made sense that Mark would go there; it wasn't far from where he'd have entered the city via the bridge, and, as he'd said, he loved a bit of London. I was only glad he hadn't tarried in Southwark, inviting me to meet him in one of the less orderly hostelries – one of those which prided itself on its ability to provide a warm bed and warmer flesh to fill it. I'd no wish to find him locked in the bare arms of a Flemish frow.

I didn't have to enter under the archway to the side of the building; a groom was in front of the place, watching a group of men tumbling, coloured streamers dancing about their heads as they did so. Invasion, I thought. London had been invaded, was being occupied, by revelry. When people spoke of the king bringing a golden world, this was what they meant.

'Stable my horse, will you?'

The youth threw me a sullen look. 'Inn's closed up. Old Rawle won't let no one in past eight.'

Rawle, I thought. I remembered the man – a stringy, pinch-faced fellow. I'd drunk in his place once, back when my stepmother had sent me out to see what the competition for board was like.

I tutted. 'Him. I'm a guest. Already. A guest of a gue—' This was stupid. 'Stable the damn horse, will you?' I reached down and lifted my purse, digging in it for a coin. This worked its charm, and he took Gideon. I followed him into the innyard at the rear and watched as he led the beast off to be stabled. Poor old brute, I thought. I hadn't been kind to him. No ostler appeared to fetch my bags – or bag, rather: my entire luggage consisted of my livery rolled up into an unseemly ball. Carrying it myself, tucked under one armpit, I pounded on the door to the street-facing hall.

There was no answer. I tried again. Then, after a beat, I leant to it. From inside came a jangling chorus of laughter and song. It seemed that those Londoners who weren't still revelling outside had moved their good cheer indoors. I leapt back as the door opened.

'Who goes there?' asked a ragged, haggard face. 'None admitted past eight.' Sunken eyes roved over me. Suspicion glinted. I didn't blame him. Already, I could smell the city smoke clinging to me, mingling with my own sweat and the reek of the road.

'Mr Rawle?' I asked, using the gentle voice I used whenever I was near the court or its people.

It had an effect, much as the coin had worked on his groom. He stepped back, letting the door swing inward.

Orange light bloomed around him, dancing, casting his face in shadow. For a moment he looked demonic.

His name came back to me as his face resolved. I stood back a step and something like recognition tilted back his head. 'Good morrow. I am a guest,' I said. 'Of one Mark. Trumpet to His Grace Cardinal Wolsey, the Lord Chancellor of England and Archbishop of York.' There was more, but this seemed to suffice. Prissily, with a thin finger, he brushed a string of dark hair behind an ear.

'But of course, sir. You're – ah – let me see – you're the trumpet. Anthony. I recall your face, to be sure. Been my guest before, yes?' I gave an unsmiling incline of my head. 'Climbed up in the world, I think. Your chamber's been appointed for you, sir, special.' He managed a little bow and I swept into the light, feeling quite as grand as his obsequiousness suggested. No matter my filthy canvas doublet and spattered hose. I was a cardinal's man again. That meant something.

'Very good,' I said. 'Lead on, then, Mr Rawle.'

Rawle fussed at the door behind me, making a show of locking it – you are safe here, his slow movements said; there is security – and I had time to look around.

The hall of the inn was spacious – bigger than I remembered it. A central hearth burned merrily, leaking its smoke up to a hole in the ceiling. A trestle table stood a short distance from it, and in the firelight around it I could see a whole group of people, most clutching tankards. Women's heads lolled against men's shoulders, which were rocking with laughter. A new song was being got up – some ballad or other – and there was an argument brewing over the right words. Good natured, I thought. This wasn't the kind of inn for riff-raff rascals. The table itself was heaving under the weight of elbows, of cooked meats and glinting tin dishes of dried herbs.

'This way, sir,' said Rawle. The door locked tight against the night, he led me to the other side of the chamber, away from the company, speaking over his shoulder. The tip of his nose angled sharply downwards. I remembered suddenly why my stepmother had had me drink in his taproom.

I'll bet you tuppence his ale is watered. Heard complaints of his house at the market. Anything to save money.

Her words brought an unbidden smile to my face, and I fought it. Rawle seemed not to notice. 'You shan't be troubled by the noise, sir,' he said. 'Not where you are. Very good rooms we have, sir, nice as any in London or without. Sheets not touched since the laundress, sir, linen, all sweetened. And your friend waiting, a fine bed for you both.' He began climbing a wooden staircase, hissing a little as his knee creaked. 'Weather's going to break, I reckon, sir. Always feel it there.'

'There's no need to go up with me, Mr Rawle,' I said. 'I saw the stairs up when I was last here. I can find my way.' He gave me a grateful look, tempered by a little hesitance. His eyes lingered on my face before passing to my doublet.

'Well, I . . .' He trailed off, looking down and over the crowd of guests, judging whether they were safer unattended than I was. I stepped around him, blocking his view a moment as I gained a higher step. The staircase creaked. His decision made for him, he said, 'Very good, sir. Very kind. As you wish, sir.' I waved away his thanks, impatient now; he broke them off and gave me directions to the chamber instead. And then he filed back downstairs, throwing an occasional glance back up at me, a simpering, suspicious smile curving his thin face. A little demon descending to hell, I thought. I shook the image away. The man had done nothing to offend me.

The staircase led into a doorway that opened out onto a gallery, which ran the length of the building. A wooden railing afforded a view out over the innyard I'd come up from. It was deep in shadow, now; looking up, the greyish blue was being washed away, in uneven strokes, by dull lead.

The chamber Mark had appointed – had Rawle mentioned Mark? I didn't notice; I was tired – was at the far end of the upper gallery. The room must face out over the street itself, I thought. I shuffled along to it, my legs heavy now. Already I could feel that bed. I would stay here tonight, I decided, with Mark. Home could wait.

I knocked on the thin wooden door.

No answer.

I tried again. It had worked on Rawle, after all. When Mark didn't reply, I looked down the gallery, wondering if I'd misheard – if I was so tired now that I'd got the wrong room. I didn't relish having to go back down and check. How foolish I would look then! No, I decided, it was the right room. I banged again, louder, and called, 'Mark, you lazy swine. I'm here. Open up.'

Still there was no response.

Cursing, not yet worried – for surely he was in there sleeping – I reached down for the iron ring. The door would likely be locked against incursion but . . .

It slid open, slid inwards, smoothly.

'Mark?' I asked, stepping into darkness.

Light suddenly flared. My mouth fell open. I would have screamed, had I been able to believe what I was seeing.

12

It came at me with a torch. Fast. 'What . . .?' I asked, stupidly. The creature – the man – the thing that wasn't Mark lowered its head. Light played over its features. I saw a snout, tusks, the jagged line of fangs. From just below the eyes, the thing ceased to be a man and became an animal. The body, however, was man enough. Of middling height, dressed darkly, a – *blood!?* – stained apron tied around his waist – and coming at me.

Shock and exhaustion rooted me to the floorboards.

This is not real.

My mouth was agape. In one hand the man was wielding a flaming torch. From the other fist a blade glinted, like a long, crooked finger. It was the sight of it that shook me into action. 'No!' I cried.

This is *real. Must've got Mark!*

He raised the blade – a dagger, I saw, an old quillon dagger, sharpened, lethal. Reflected flames danced along its length. Foolishly, I reached up and over my shoulder, my fingers searching for the reliable hardness of my staff. The gap between us was cleared. The dagger fell, slashing at my forearm, slicing through the soft linen of my shirtsleeve. Pain burnt brightly in a thin line. I yelped, kicking out. The man hopped back, his flame flaring. I could feel wetness begin to soak my sleeve.

In or out?

In or out?!

I was still in the doorway, my arm raised. I cried out again.

You shan't be troubled by the noise, sir. Not where you are.

I shouted across the gap between us. It was narrowing again. 'Stop! Where's Mark? What've you done with him?'

The brute ignored me. He might have been smiling behind his tusked mask. It was a boar, I thought wildly; he had purchased a boar mask. Fitting, for the place. A jest.

Say something, goddamn you – speak!

I stepped backwards. I was trembling, bleeding. Fear, which I hadn't felt when the foolish thief had assailed me, washed over me now. Coldness joined it, making the shaking worse. Hardness buffeted my back. The staff dug in. I had hit the railing of the gallery which hung out over the innyard. My eyes widened. My attacker stood in the doorway now. He swivelled his head from left to right, his snout stabbing at the air. His dagger, though, had disappeared. Careful of the torch, he reached out with a grimy hand.

Dirty man. Dirty hands, dirty nails. And the smell.

That smell washed over me now: a sour tang mixed with road muck. He was going to drag me into the room, I realised – drag me in there and kill me. I didn't think. With my good arm, I grabbed onto the wooden railing and swung over the side. I hung on for a beat or two, heat searing through my arm. I couldn't remain there, even if I'd wished to. My body was pulling me down. My palm began to burn too. I let go, rough wood scratching, tearing at it, and dropped.

The fall was short but hard. Strangely, no pain hit me, not at first. But still I was shivering, wildly now, uncontrollably.

On my back, I stared up. Light bloomed, and in its glow the hideous boar mask appeared. He stood up there, staring down at me, unmoving. I rolled onto my side. Then the pain made itself felt, tearing through every joint. I tried to cry out again, failed, and rolled farther.

If you can get down, he can get down.

I looked up again. The light was gone.

He's gone.

But no. He had extinguished his torch, but a bulky dark shape writhed and twisted in the dimness of the night. He was climbing over slowly, lithely. I forced myself to my knees, twisting my head around. The stable, I thought – the little groom. But the doorway was closed. Probably locked from the inside. The lad would be asleep in there. Even if I beat on the door, he would take fright, would ignore me. No hope of the inn's door either. It had taken me long enough to make myself heard the first time.

I looked up again. He was hanging by the arms from the railing, moving hand over hand towards a pile of hay lying neatly against the inn's inner wall. Pain seared up my arm again. I felt blood drip onto my hand. It looked dark, brown against the soft paleness of my palm. No good. No means of fighting him. No ability to, either.

I lurched away, surprised that my legs worked under my quaking body. The city, I thought, the watchmen, someone. He wouldn't dare strike at me out in the open. Staggering still, my good arm in service again to bear me up against the stone of the archway, I passed out into Eastcheap.

It was deserted. The lodgings above the locked shops were mostly shuttered, with just a few candle flames blinking here and there. I might shout up for help, and be met with, at worst, the soft closing of windows or, at best, witnesses to my murder. No good. No use.

Lose him.

I held my arm tight across my belly, pressing the burning wound to the canvas doublet. It wouldn't absorb anything, but it might help stop the bleeding, stop the tell-tale drips. Looking round, I saw nothing. The archway was gloomy, an empty barrow against one side of it. I began moving, going right, and swung myself around the first corner, into St Clement's Lane. Still, no one. But it was only a short, shambling jog on to Lombard Street. Surely, I thought, there would be people there. I went, ignoring the racking shakes which only intensified the pain.

Past the quiet houses of St Clement's, Lombard Street stretched left and right.

There!

Up on the left stood a couple of men, just at the entrance to Birchin Lane, where the Gonzaga house lay. I considered going there, wildly thinking of its mistress's promise to kill the man who had robbed her of a husband. No. This creature, this demon – he seemed to know my movements. Doubtless he might expect me to return to one of his old haunts. Sticking close to the buildings on the left, grey-looking now and silent, I made for the pair who stood just beyond the lane.

'Help!' I cried. 'Help me!' Laughter subsided and the two heads turned in my direction. I held up a shaking hand as I approached them. 'I'm attacked!' I gasped. Even my voice was ragged now. My throat hurt, as though something had scratched it. 'Help.'

One of the fellows rocked on his boots. His head tilted

backwards, and he tried to focus on me through bleary eyes. ''S this then?'

''S a Moorish – Moor – t-tumbler. Clown,' said the other, reaching out to steady himself against the wall of the building whose rump end stood on the corner of the two streets. His friend slid backwards, whistling and clapping his hands. 'A jig for us, lad, a,' he hiccoughed, 'jig!'

Jesus Christ.

Both men were drunk. Not acceptably drunk but roaring with it. Useless. I might bleed to death, even without the boar-man finding me, before they sobered. ''Ere,' said the first drunk, 'comes another. Mask.'

Panic bloomed. I turned.

Sure enough, my attacker had given chase. I considered throwing myself behind the drunks, childlike, seeking protection. Their crazed laughter prevented me. 'Caledon!' I shouted. He had stopped just after St Clement's Lane and stood watching, as though deciding whether a blood-feast of three was worth the risk in the open street. I didn't fool myself that use of his false name would give him pause. Yet, madly, I wished him to know – to know that I knew something of him, that he wasn't the only one who could give chase.

And then I began moving, more quickly. A fierce desire to live had overcome the pain and the fear. These were my streets. This my city. I knew it. He might, too, but I didn't care. I would put my streets between us. Amazingly, unfathomably, I found that I could run. My legs, despite the drop, remained loyal. And run I did. Up Lombard Street and around the squat, ancient St Mary Woolchurch to the Poultry. Amidst the jumble of houses and streets there, onto Cheapside, my shoes skidding on the muck, which seemed to resent my passage, to always want me to slide downwards to the sewer channel. The buildings around me melted together, leering over the tunnel of the street: two great, lengthening walls of sagging grey plaster; an endless hatch-work of black cross-beams; an unbroken sea of suspended thatch and slate.

Lightness came upon me, a kind of mad ecstasy, as I reached Cheapside. Surely, surely, on busy Cheapside, people, help . . .

I halted, stumbling, and this time I did fall. The sloping ground took me into the filthy gutter. I sat there – I don't know how long – as the thin trickle of filth hit me, soaking my hose, desperately trying to find its course and continue on its long journey to the Thames. I stayed because I'd realised my error.

Just ahead, Cheapside, the busiest shopping district in the city, the richest, beloved of wealthy mercers and wealthier patrons, had not a soul in sight. Nor should it. Mobbed by day, the whole street was packed with shops. Very few houses stood on it. Even the merchants who still lived on the street kept their fine houses behind the shops, not above them. Tears pricked in my eyes and I blinked them away. It might have been pleasant under other circumstances, to see it so peaceful. I began hobbling, my sense of excitement, my burst of wild fury, deserting me, and began moving in the direction of the Great Conduit. The moon was out overhead, a milky, disinterested sphere, pitted and cruel. My feet began to drag. I don't know why I kept going. The watchmen, perhaps; if they were anywhere in the city, if they weren't dozing in the Guildhall, they'd be patrolling the spice houses and goldsmiths of Cheapside.

Passing under the forlorn triumphal archways which must

have been erected for the emperor's visit – plain wood now, the gilding chipped away and stolen, the vines and flowers stripped – I saw the Great Conduit, the marker of one end of Cheapside. Its turreted head peeked out just above a row of locked wooden market stalls. It seemed a good place to – *die* – cry out for help, for the watch.

Before beginning to stagger towards it, I turned around. The streets behind me were silent. That terrible shivering seized me again, as though a great beast, a dog – *a boar* – had taken me in its jaws and was jerking me from side to side. My gait was lopsided now, my head light. Still I went. My legs, so loyal, had begun to rebel. I dragged them onwards, not turning again.

Where is he?

I expected the creature's sudden descent. I expected the street to split open, spitting him up. And then I tried to force away the fear. He was a man, like any other, just a man. Perhaps, I thought dimly, he had given up. He had meant to take me in that chamber, and I'd frustrated his plans. Perhaps he'd given up.

And then, ahead of me, I saw something. I froze.

Light.

I thought of the boar-man's torch and my head swam. And then, gradually, the light began to resolve itself into several smaller ones. Two, three, four . . .

My heart leapt. I put my hand out to the stone lip of the Great Conduit. I could hear the soft tinkling splashes of its pipes, the low, steady rush of water. The watch, I thought – the city watch. The lights had stopped somewhere up ahead, perhaps as far as Bow Lane. I shuffled away from the fountain. No, they were farther away still – they were moving away –

they were at Bread Street. 'Help!' I called. My voice came out small, shrill, was lost among the silent, disapproving shops.

I forced myself to focus on the lights. They blurred again, joining, separating. I willed them closer, bending my feet to that will.

I opened my mouth to try a louder cry. 'Hel—'

I was flying.

Falling.

Sideways.

'No,' I gasped.

I blinked up, trying feebly to turn, to twist myself, to raise my arms against my face.

And there he was. Leering over me, that snout. The ground slammed into my back. I winced at the hard, punching weight of the staff as it pummelled my spine. Light bloomed, bringing to life the narrow Ironmonger's Lane. How? I wondered. How had he got ahead of me, around me?

He is a devil, a demon, an unnatural thing!

And then I cursed my dazed fall into the sewage gutter – I nearly laughed up at him. Stupid pig, I thought; I'm the stupid pig. And now I must pay for it.

You lured him from Wolsey's house indeed. The cardinal will be happy.

That odd lightness came upon me again, even as I saw the torch in his hand, making him more devilish still. He wasn't really going to kill me, I thought – I wasn't really going to die. I rejected the idea, refused it outright. I'd been tired – I *was* tired – I was just going to sleep, to be knocked out for the night. I'd wake up again in the morning and go on. Perhaps this was a dream, a hideously lifelike dream. I wasn't going to die.

I was still thinking it, still kicking weakly up, still feeling fresh courses of blood stream down my arm, as voices filled the air not far away, shouting, calling out.

I'm here, I thought, but didn't say.

The voices were growing closer, certainly closer, I thought triumphantly. And I was still thinking that as he lowered the torch and set me alight.

13

There was pain. Everywhere, there was pain – in sudden, fiery bursts and in low, dull aches. I didn't know a body could experience so many forms, from the narrow, slicing jabs of it to the sudden, racking seizures, to the all-encompassing furious scourging. It can come in waves so intense that you think you must die; you wish you would die. Pain is death's black trumpet. It announces the coming of the end.

Strangely, the pain wasn't within me; I was within it. It was as though I was wrapped in a blanket pierced all over with hot needles. Death, I supposed, must be the seamstress, working furiously with a thousand bony fingers.

And sometimes there were voices, making themselves heard over the agonies.

My stepmother.

Was I at home?

Mark.

Was I at the cardinal's court?

And a French accented one. Jane.

Was I in Heaven?

The voices came in snatches, sometimes raised high, more often low. I couldn't see. I thought I might be opening my eyes, or trying to, but nothing appeared. And when I tried to move, to wriggle, I found that I was locked up tight, as though bound, as though in a winding sheet. Sometimes, through the pain, I accepted that I was dead. And it occurred to me that I must have been bad, very wicked, to have deserved this fate. This, I guessed, was purgatory. It was a place of constant pain, jabbing everywhere, and a lack of movement, the body unrigged from the mind. Yet the mind worked. I could hear those voices; I was aware of myself.

My name is Anthony Blanke and I was born in the reign of King Henry VII of England, son to John and Eleanor Blanke, deceased.

But I had been a miserable son: an insufferable little imp. I'd pretended to be a Spaniard, an Italian, anything to explain my appearance. The Bible says we should honour our fathers and our mothers, and I hadn't honoured my father. This, this unfathomable, painful, immovable state of being – this was my punishment. A condign punishment. I deserved this. I wasn't scared. If this were to be it until Judgement Day, until enough prayers and masses had been said for me, I would bear it.

I deserved this.

And then I was being moved. I could feel my lips being parted. I had a mouth, still, though I couldn't see it, couldn't touch it. Something invaded it, poured down my throat, going down the wrong way, and I began choking.

The voices rose again.

'Have a care!'

'Sorry, man.'

Before I could try and speak, the warmth began to flow again, more gently now, and I swallowed, and swallowed, and swallowed. And then I breathed. I wished to speak, to bring the voices back.

'He sleeps. It is better.'

No. No, I don't want to sleep.

Useless to resist. I faded away, letting the pain dull, just for a little while, just for a beat.

* * *

I didn't know how long this waking and drinking and blindly hearing voices continued. But somewhere, in the course of it, my mind began to return more clearly, the fog lifting, the fantasies of death fading. Even the pain, too, began to recede. It never went altogether, but it became something it was possible to imagine being borne by a living body rather than a repenting soul.

I was alive.

Suffering, damaged in some painful, indefinable way, but alive.

With that knowledge, I was able to endure. The voices were still indistinct – my ears seemed to have been swaddled, like my eyes, but they were there, and they were familiar. And thus I could think, even if speaking through a throat that was parched and sore and occasionally filled with foul-tasting liquids was too difficult.

I've heard it said that after a cruel assault, you forget what happened. I hadn't. The journey from Hampton Court into London, certainly, had become lost in a fog. If I'd spoken to people – hadn't some rogue prentice come at me? – the memories were indistinct. But from the moment of opening the door in that inn – yes, the Boar's Head, that was it – I could remember every stuttering step, every shuttered house, every turn from Eastcheap up to Cheapside.

I could remember the tusked mask.

I could remember the dagger's thrust and the torch's flame.

The murderer had fooled me, lured me to the inn, and then chased me through the streets. And there he had wounded me. Yet now, somehow, I was elsewhere, wrapped and protected and girt about by the soft voices of my family, my friends. And so the endless dark cycle of sleeping, drinking, hearing, not seeing, spun on. Until, just as I felt the strength to speak – the desire returning – blinding light seared my vision.

'Have a care,' hissed a voice. The darkness fell again. 'Let me.' I felt a weak smile creep over my lips. It hurt but just a little. It was Jane speaking, Sister Jane. I had grown to hope for her voice during the darkness; the other voices, welcome as they were, were just preludes to her voice, gentle and caressing, like a silk sheet rippling in a soft breeze. 'Close the shutters.'

Softer fingers were prodding at my head.

The light assaulted me again, too bright, too much. I screwed my eyes shut; dancing shapes twirled, colourful and bright against the darkness. I blinked a few times, willing them away. And then I could see.

A thin face was peering down at me, dim light making a halo around it.

Jane!

'He wakes,' she said. Her teeth, looking huge against the narrowness of her lips, were drawn in a smile. Her eyes twinkled.

'Yes!' This from another voice, Mark's, somewhere else in the room. 'Shall I fetch his stepmother?'

Jane didn't answer him. Instead, she said, 'Can you hear me, Anthony?'

I made a little sound in my throat. 'Here, let me give him a drink,' said Mark. And then more liquid was being forced down my throat. Some of it splashed, running down my chin. Yet, when it reached my neck, I couldn't feel it. It must have become lost in the wrappings. I choked the stuff back.

'Mmph,' I said. And then, as a whispered conference began somewhere above me, I coughed. 'I'm here,' I said. 'I'm up. Awake.'

'Anthony! Welcome, man, welcome back!' said Mark. Jane disappeared from above me and his round face hove into view. He was grinning. Too falsely, I thought, too brightly. 'You're looking good, my friend.'

'What – what happened?' I asked. My voice sounded rusty in my ears. I meant: why am I not dead? 'Where am I?'

'You're in my convent,' said Jane. 'Mr Byfield here and your stepmother brought you.' A little shyness crept into her voice. 'I've been tending you. I've bled you. And applied the poultices. Rose honey, vinegar, egg . . .'

'She was going to coat you in dung,' said Mark. 'I said no.' Jane began to protest, but Mark spoke over her. 'But you're alive. Thanks to her.'

'What hap—'

'And me and the watchmen. Lazy bastards. I got them up.'

'You can speak with him later,' said Jane.

'No,' I said. I tried to sit up and slumped back down. Lying there, with their faces floating above me – it made me weak, a victim. But dizziness, itchiness, and a thousand fiery fingers pushed and kept me down.

I could see now where I was: in the little infirmary room into which I'd been shown on my last visit to the convent. The plain plaster walls were scrupulously clean, but they looked grey in the half-light. I'd been put on one of the little beds. Looking down, I could see that I was, indeed, swaddled. My whole body was encased, cocoon-like, in linen; even my arms and hands had their own wrappings, all neat and pinned. 'Tell me. Now. Please.'

Jane, her smile fading, inclined her head and stepped back. She almost seemed to retreat into her habit. And then she shrugged, turning away, going to a shelf, and beginning to jab at things with quick, careful movements. A tinkling of bottles and jars drifted over.

'You didn't come home,' said Mark. 'I got to your house – thought I'd better go there, like – and spoke to your step-dame. She wasn't happy. Said you'd be getting yourself into some trouble or other in His Grace's service. But she fed me. Good woman, her. And we waited. It got dark. Got late. Got so as we thought they'd be locking up the city pretty soon. And you didn't come.' His voice was hearty, excited. 'And so she said to me, you go and look, go and find him. Bring him home. Well, I didn't need telling twice. Said I'd rouse the watch, say there was trouble. Woulda ridden the upper road all the way back to Hampton Court, if I'd had to.' Solemness overtook the cheer. He moved away from me and returned a moment later, his head sinking. I realised that he must have moved a stool. 'Them watchmen – lazy bastards – they were in the Guildhall. I had to use the cardinal's name to get them up and out. But it worked. So we set to work. Planned to go out and down the streets. Down Aldermanbury, Milk Street. Were gonna go eastward up Cheapside.' His voice had definitely flattened. I thought of the little band of torches ahead of me.

'Then,' Mark went on, 'one of the lads heard something. Or saw something. Right down Cheapside. We ran for it. And then we found you.' Alarmingly, a sudden burst of cheer rose in him. That too-bright smile reappeared. 'And there you were. Lying at the arse end of Ironmonger's Lane. And so we . . . took you over to the Great Conduit. Got the fire out. Good thing you were wearing that canvas, man. It . . . it could've been worse.'

I remembered the torch. The fire. And again I looked down at the linen.

Mark hurried on, as though eager to bypass the most interesting parts of the tale. 'And then I carried you home. You were . . . I carried you home, with the watchmen. And your stepmother said you'd a friend here. Sister Jane. And, like she said, she's been your nurse. Your old stepdame and I, we've been coming too.' His brightness became intolerable. 'Cardinal Wolsey – I wrote him, sent a message up. He'll be right happy to hear you're back with us, so he will.'

I breathed out, my eyes still on my bandaged arm. As if in response, my arm twinged along the cut. 'He'll be happy,' I said, 'that that Mr Audley doesn't have to write the coroner . . . informing him that I "tragically, accidentally" burnt myself to death trying to fry an egg.'

Mark exploded in laughter. 'Here,' he said, 'you can still jest. I've missed the old dark-humoured Anthony.' Then his grin faded. 'It's good to see you up, man.'

What aren't you telling me?

It could've been worse.

'That creature tried to kill me,' I said. And then, in full,

I relayed what had happened, from the false letter inviting me to the Boar's Head, the murderer in his boar mask, to my trying to make for Cheapside on my search for the watchmen.

When I'd finished, Mark let out a low whistle. 'Jesus. So we didn't fool him. Or did we? Maybe he is some demon.' Jane, across the room, wheeled, crossing herself and making little gasping noises. 'A boar mask?'

'I saw people in masks,' I said. 'Revellers, down on Thames Street. He might have bought one. Altered it, maybe. But . . . how does he know all he knows?'

'Demon,' said Mark, with a firm nod of his head. 'We didn't see no one but you when we reached you. He'd disappeared. There are folk who . . . who can know things they shouldn't know. By charms and sortileges. Wicked folk.'

I considered this. When I'd been lying in my shroud, for however long it had been, I'd thought a great deal about this. 'Perhaps,' I said. 'Or . . . I thought . . . at first . . . I thought maybe it was a man with two sides to him. Living at Hampton Court, working there. That was how he could kill the scholar and the glazier. But now . . .' My thoughts were too many. I shuffled them. 'Visser,' I said, picturing the fat little man obsessed with his windows. 'I think he saw something. Something he shouldn't have, when he was inspecting the windows from without.'

'Like what? The demon dancing with a devil? Summoning it up, like?'

'No, no.' I tried to shake my head. It brought a wave of pain. 'Maybe . . . maybe it's not one man. Two men. Maybe more, even. Maybe Visser saw them talking. Heard them. And he went to tell Wolsey whatever he heard or saw. But he got sent away. So he went into the other room to wait.

But one of these men found him. And pushed him out the window.'

'Two men?' asked Mark.

'Or more,' I said. I was growing convinced of it. Visser could hardly have seen much if there was only one fellow involved – he couldn't have been doing anything suspicious by himself, wouldn't have been talking to himself. But if he was discussing what he was up to with someone else . . . If Visser had heard what that was . . .

'A conspiracy,' said Mark. Awe came into his voice. Fear mingled with it.

'That was what the cardinal thought.'

'The damn Frenchies,' Mark snapped. His fist thudded on the bed. 'They're up to something.' Beyond him, I saw Jane stiffen. Her already colourless face paled further, and she turned her back on us.

'Mark,' I hissed.

But he was off. 'Well, the cardinal's right, then. Fucking French. Wouldn't put it past them. Here, there was a masque put on at Windsor on Sunday. Whole city's heard about it – all fired up for war now, folk are. Idiots.'

Sunday!?

'That's where the court's gone.' My heart skipped a beat at the word. 'A masque with a real live horse. A wild one. To be tamed by King Henry and the emperor. The horse is that big-nosed, hatchet-faced French king.'

This time, the tinkling sound across the room became a clanging, a thud of glass on wood. 'Mark,' I said. 'Remember Sister Jeanne.' The use of her old name, before she had come to England, made his eyes widen.

He twisted his head round and rose from his seat, pulling off his cap at the same time. 'Oh. Shit. Sorry.' She ignored him, continuing to make noise at her shelf of bottles and herbs. He looked at me in appeal and then back at her. 'But . . . I mean . . . I mean, you ain't even French no more, Sister.'

Jane wheeled around. 'In the service of God, there is only this one Christendom. Not French. Not English. No, nor Scots, nor Spanish. Only one. You would divide us against ourselves. This is . . .' She shook her head. The anger faded. Sadness replaced it. 'It is a shame,' she said. And then, her hard little chin rising. 'I am French. And there is nothing wrong in that.'

'Christ,' said Mark, turning back to me. He had the sense to look abashed. 'I've a big damn mouth, is all. Talk, talk, talk, and don't do no thinking, sometimes. And then bury it with more talk, talk, talk.' He grinned suddenly. 'Like I'm doing now.'

The tension in the room faded. I took a breath. 'How long have I been here?'

'Days,' said Mark. 'Near a week.'

I considered this. Too long, I thought. Time to be up. 'Well,' I said, 'the cardinal thinks something's going on. The French and the Scots, trying to – to ruin King Henry. To stop Wolsey's own masque. To deny the king's coming from King Arthur.'

'Scotch,' said Mark. 'As bad as the French. Frenchlings, them lot are.' He laughed. 'Here, you should ask Lutini. The Strings Master.'

'What?' I sat up, ignoring the pain this time. 'What?'

'Lutini – the musician. King of the Strings.'

'I know who he is! What about him?'

'Ay, right. No need to be like that. Well . . . he's French, ain't he?' I shrugged. 'And he come down from Scotland. I heard that years ago. Worked for the old Scotch king, until King Henry and Queen Catherine done him in. We woulda been brats at the time, but you must've heard Lutini prattle about his time serving a king. It's all he ever talks about. Gives himself airs, like. Prick.'

Something registered, dimly. When I'd first returned to Hampton Court, when I'd first heard about the masque, Lutini had said something about having commanded Moors. He hadn't mentioned Scotland, I didn't think – but perhaps something about another kingdom. A northern kingdom – that sounded familiar. 'Lutini,' I said. As Master of the Strings – harps, lutes, and rebecs were the most prized, the most expensive instruments – he was master of all secular music in the cardinal's household. Even Mark, a trumpet, had nominally to defer to him. He would have command of a whole host of servants: men who could go anywhere, passing in and out of the court, returning to London for repairs, perhaps.

'Lutini done something?' Mark asked. 'You don't suspect—'

'No,' I said. 'Nothing.' I filed away the suspicion. That's all it was, I realised. If I wanted proof, I'd have to find it.

And that is what I was going to do.

I sat up properly. 'These swaddlings,' I said, sucking air through my teeth. 'Can they come off? I can walk, can't I?' A little blossom of fear bloomed. I saw that Mark's face had grown falsely cheerful again.

'Course you can walk, man. She says you're not . . . ah,

seriously . . . hurt. Not deeply.' He turned to Jane. 'Can . . .
can they come off?'

She turned from her shelf and glided towards me. There
was no false brightness there. She looked quite serene. 'But
of course. I can do this now. And you will further recover at
home. At home, the walls heal.'

'Uh – I – I'll go outside. I'll go over to your house, man,
wait for you there. Uh – I'll open the window first, give
you some light.' He hopped off the stool, punched open the
shutters, and beat a retreat towards the door, nearly tripping
over his feet. 'See you there, man. Don't get lost on the way.'
And then he was gone.

What's your hurry?

'What is it?' I asked Jane. 'What aren't you telling me?'

She licked her lips and met my gaze. 'Anthony, I . . . I'll
remove the linens. Tell me if you feel pain. And I'll stop.'

She set to work before I could think of anything to say. It
was a tedious process; she unwrapped me slowly,
methodically, placing each pin in a tin dish she brought
over from the shelf. My worries faded as I watched her.
She was so tender in her movements, so careful. Her bony
fingers moved gracefully. Memories of the old Jeanne stirred.
Though I'd only known her briefly, she had then been a
creature of the French court, trained to dance, to sing, to
play, as all courtly women were. Even in her new austerity,
she retained that grace – it clung to her like a second skin; it
sang in the incline of her head, the straightness of her back,
buried under its shapeless habit. I wished that a strand of
hair would escape the veiled hood, brushing her forehead.

'Your arm,' she said, breaking the spell, 'was cut. Yet
the fire sealed it. I've washed it, many times. There's no

corruption. You've had very good fortune.' As she spoke, she lifted my stick of an arm and began to unwind the bandages. Round and round they went, in an unfurling stream of grey. Gradually, the grey began to grow streaked with yellow, and then a weak, watery red where the unguent and lotions had soaked through. An unpleasantly sour-sweet tang rose into the air, killing off the more distant scent of rosemary-scattered rushes, catching in my throat.

'There,' she said. 'And now your breast.'

'But you've not finished,' I said. My eyes were playing tricks. There was still something on my arm.

And then I saw. I saw what Mark had been trying to avoid discussing, to bury under his cheerfulness. I let out one long, anguished howl.

14

I might almost have laughed. How long had I rebelled against the dark, honey shade of my skin? How long had I silently cursed God for branding me, for painting me with strangeness? How long – even until his death – had I resented my father for being the agent of it? I thought of the little jar of ointment I'd bought from the apothecary – the stuff ladies use to whiten and lighten their already fair skin. Laughter threatened again.

'Do not be a baby,' said Jane. Her voice was curt, even, the voice of an infirmaress used to dealing with complaining, whining patients.

A baby?

An urge to retrieve the linens came upon me, to wrap myself head-to-toe in them and never be seen again. Above all, I didn't want her seeing me like this – and yet there she was, continuing to reveal my breast, working her way up to my face.

My face!

'Oh, God,' I moaned. 'Oh, Christ.'

'Enough of this, please,' she said. 'The arm can still be used, as ever. You are fortunate. No corruption. Don't move, please.' The tip of her tongue darted out between her lips, looking very pink, very determined. Solemnity had brought it out: care for her work. For me. I looked away from her. Unable to resist, my gaze found my right arm again.

My skin had lightened, to be sure. Through patches of sticky, stinking poultice, I could see that. Only a line of blackness remained – a crusty, dark brown line which ran from the outside of my wrist, curving to the inside of my elbow. Around it, the rest of the arm was lost in a blotchy, irregular patchwork of pink and white swirls and whorls. I thought of pigskin, for some reason, stretched out and cured. It didn't look burnt; it looked broiled, drained, washed out.

I had seen, occasionally, those who had received burns wandering the streets of London. Most kept well covered, going to live off the charity of monks. Occasionally they left the monasteries, clinging to the walls, as people made wide circles around them. There was an old blacksmith, too, in Aldgate, who had been burnt at some point. His face was a mottled mess of patchy pinks and reds, similar to my arm, and his left eye was milky and sightless. No hair escaped from under his hat. My arm, now, looked hairless too. I compared it to the left, unburnt one, which was still covered in dark fluff.

I could see my torso now, my breast, as Jane continued. She put her arms around me briefly every few seconds, unrolling, unleashing the horror beneath.

Oh, God!

Parts of my chest were fine, looking as they always did. But as my gaze travelled upwards, I saw more of that dread discoloration. It began just above my right nipple, and seemed to carry on upwards, as far as I could see below my chin. Upwards, I thought, to . . .

'Your face is untouched,' said Jane. She had stepped back.

Her scent – clean, like fresh linen – went with her, leaving me in my own sourness. 'Mostly.'

'My face,' I echoed. I raised my left hand towards it. A terrific itch had come upon me with the removal of the linens. It was everywhere: my right arm, my chest, my neck. The back of my new, bad hand was wild with it, as though insects were buzzing there, biting me. I could see that burnt skin stretched from thumb to pinkie, only stopping at the knuckles, where my faded, tawny fingers sprung out, quite unruffled by the sudden ruination of their base.

'The marks – they go up your neck from your breast. On the right side, they go until your chin – just below. Not deep. The left is unharmed. Untouched,' she said.

I swallowed. 'Will it fade? Will it go away? With time?' I was pleading. 'Have you seen it fade, in people, burns? You must have seen it.'

'No,' she said. There was no pity in her voice. I moved my good hand over my itching chest, trying to protect myself, to hide the hideous flesh from her.

'Will I be like this for the rest of my life?' There was challenge now. Anger. A desire not to believe.

Jane didn't answer at first. She cocked her head to one side, studying me. 'You might thank God,' she said, 'every day. You might thank God that there *is* a rest of your life. These wounds are – they are on the surface only. They are not even the deep burns of . . .' She frowned, as though looking for the words. 'Soldiers, cannon, and such. You will have only some . . .' Her cheeks drew in and a slight crease appeared in her brow, as though she were searching for the word. 'Some miscolouring of the outer flesh. Better that than flesh be lost. Burned away. Men at their metalwork suffer worse, sometimes. I'm afraid we have no mirrors here. I cannot show you your face.' A smile broke across her face – that ghost of her old self stirring. 'But I assure you. Your sweet face is unmarked.'

Mirrors!

We had a mirror at home – a little old thing of polished steel. That, I decided, would be getting smashed in pieces soon enough, if I'd the strength.

I had the grace to turn my frown away from her. But still I kept my arm up. 'My clothes. Clothes. I have to go.' I was determined. As stupid – as pointless – as it was, I didn't want her seeing me like this any more than she already had.

'Your friend – Mr Byfield – he brought a shirt and doublet. Hose too. From your home.' She turned and went to a shadowy corner of the room, returning with the bundle. 'I will leave you. Now you are restored, it is not meet I should be alone with a man, with you. Abbess Alice gave me dispensation to tend the sick, not the lusty.' Again, that flash of a smile. 'And certainly not a handsome and sweet-faced old friend.' To my surprise, she winked, and then left with a soft click of the door.

That wink might once have delighted me. Now it shamed me.

Miscolouring of the outer flesh, indeed.

On the surface only.

I was a monster.

I was now the kind of man that others would cross the street to avoid.

And the worst of it was that it all seemed so deserved. My mind returned to that stupid, bootless cursing of my darkness, that whining desire to look like everyone else, to be as white and pink as they were. Now I'd had my answer to that.

As I dressed, the pains emerged. My right arm was the worst, where the slash wound its way through the scarring. My legs ached at the knees too, either from my fall, my running, or my week of inactivity. I was rough in dressing, deliberately rough, welcoming the pain, demanding it. It was as though, in my fury, I was compelled to lash out. Deprived of any better target, my own body would do.

Once I had the doublet laced up over my shirt and the hose tied up at their points, I set about covering up those bits Jane had said were marked. The collar of my shirt was turned up, as I'd seen the man who'd done this to me turn up his. My right sleeve was not folded back and pinned; I allowed it to dangle down over my hand. If she spoke truly, if my face was unmarked, then I might not be quite the monster I imagined. I might be hidden.

This, I decided, was how I would dress from now on – every day.

Before leaving the infirmary, I walked in circles, working feeling properly back into my legs. It would be easy, now, to retire from life. I wouldn't live well – I wouldn't teach, or be sought as a teacher, probably – but I could hide away again, doing nothing.

But there was something I wished to do still.

Something I wished very much to do. My right hand curled into a gnarled fist, the freshening skin tight and sore over the back of it.

* * *

'How could you take me there?' I asked Mark.

He was sitting on a stool in the front room of my house. I was standing. My stepmother had gone out, after smothering my cheeks in kisses and assuring me I looked fine, to fetch in what she cheerfully called 'a feast'. I'd had to dissuade her from inviting the neighbours round to share in it. My good hand fastened on my left hip. Twin tear tracks had stiffened on my cheeks; I hadn't even felt them run down. 'How could you?'

'What?' He was lounging, his legs spread wide. A dish of bread and bowl of honey sat on the table before him. Some of the stuff still stuck around his mouth, in a little stream down to his chin, as though he were a child.

'To Jea— to Sister Jane.'

'Your stepmother said – you were hurt – it's a convent. She's an infirmaress, ain't she? Did good work?'

'But – her – I wouldn't have had her see me like this.'

'Like what?' Mark rose, stepping towards me and putting a hand out. He dropped it. 'She's seen you worse off, man. I mean, she'll have had to change your sheets, won't she? Catch your piss.'

Jesus!

'I . . . I . . .' I was clenching and unclenching my left hand now.

'Easy, man. You're only just up. Sit down.'

'I don't wish to—'

'Sit the fuck down!' Mark snapped. Taken aback, I did so. As a final show of anger, I pushed the wooden dish away, sending it skittering across the table. It bounced off the bowl of honey with a muted thud. 'Good. You're going to upset yourself. For nothing. Them marks ain't nowhere near as bad as your custard mind seems to think they are.' Mark put his back to one of the cheap painted cloths and folded his arms over his chest. He looked at me awhile and I matched his stare. And then he dropped his attention to the floor and began scuffling idly at rushes. 'You and this nun,' he said. 'You got something going on?'

'What?'

'You heard me,' he said. 'You hear about nuns . . . monks . . . all them lot. You hear stories.'

'Sister Jane is a friend,' I said. 'A friend. Like she always was, even before she went into the convent.'

He seemed to digest this for a moment, frowning, and then looked up. Scratching at his chin, squeezing it between thumb and forefinger, he said, 'I saw how you looked at her when you come to. When them bandages come off.'

It was my turn to frown and look away. 'I don't know what you mean.'

'Yes, you do.' He coughed, drawing my attention. 'Know what I think?'

'I think,' I said, 'that you're going to tell me.'

Mark smiled. 'Ay. I think, Anthony Blanke, that you ain't ever happy. Not unless you've got something to trouble you. You make things to trouble you, I mean.' He took a breath, watching to see if I reacted. I said nothing. The words had weight; they were familiar enough. Apparently judging that he had license, he ploughed on. 'You've got yourself a liking fixed, an affection. For that French nun.' I began to protest and he held up a hand. 'No, no. Hear me. You chase that nun so you can be all woe-is-me. It's your meat and drink, that.' Here he swallowed and looked into a corner of the room. He rolled his tongue around inside his cheek for a few seconds.

'And because . . . it's like . . . because if she don't love you back, well, it's because she's a nun, not because . . .' He didn't finish the thought. He had no need to.

Seeking what I could never have seemed to be my way. Master of my own misery, I was – an idiot.

That itching began prickling over me again.

'Nonsense,' I said.

Mark sighed. 'If you say so. I'm just trying to help. Help you see things you won't.'

I looked at him. Poor Mark, always smiling, uncaring of the world. I stood up, jogging the table with my knees. 'Thank you,' I said. 'You saved my life. Thank you.'

'Oh, bugger off,' he said. He took off his cap and began scratching the back of his head. 'I mean, it weren't me alone – it was that nun of yours. And the watchmen. Proper fools they are, but they come out when I made 'em. Only sorry we didn't find the bastard having at you. That demon.' He held up his fists. 'Wouldn't have tried nothing on me. Wouldn't have taken the both of us. Even if he is Master High-and-Mighty-Worked-for-a-King Lutini. Or one of his minions.'

I smiled, despite myself. 'We don't know that,' I said. Then I sighed. 'We don't know anything.'

'Hmph.' Mark, relaxed now, stepped towards me and lifted a hunk of bread, dipping it into the honey. As he lifted it, thick streamers of the stuff stretched into the air. Some dripped onto the table as it went into his mouth. 'Reckon,' he said, through mouthfuls, 'I better get my arse up to . . . Windsor. See . . . 'f anything's happ'ning.'

I nodded, vaguely. And then I remembered something. 'The horse. Gideon. I left it at that inn.' It would still be there, I supposed. The law said that if a horse was abandoned, the man who found it must care for it for a given time – I didn't know how long, but it was a good while – before he might sell it.

'Boar's Head, you said?' he asked.

I nodded. 'Mm. It was where the bastard took a room. Where he lured me. The man who owns the place might know something. Rawle. His name's Rawle. A lean-cheeked crow.'

'Don't know him,' said Mark. And then something dawned in his eyes. He gulped down the bread, already well chewed, and said, 'Here, you ain't giving up, are you? You're going after him still. I'm sure the cardinal'd let you off with it. After what happened. Sure he can have some other jack put out on the hunt.'

'I'm going after him,' I said. I looked down at my dangling cuff. I was going to find him. I was going to – *kill him* – see him hang.

I wasn't going to be chased again. And I wasn't going to hide from the world, at least not just yet. This time, I was going to hunt.

'Well,' said Mark. 'Let's go. Before your stepdame brings a whole shop back here. Ay, and the neighbours too.'

Together, we left my house in Shoemaker Row bound for Eastcheap.

* * *

Eastcheap by day was a mire of laughter and merriment. The tumblers, jugglers, and roisterers had made their way up from Thames Street, it seemed, to try their luck with the crowd of city wives and maids who spent their days touring the inner city. We were still around the corner from the Boar's Head, walking along Gracechurch Street, when a creature on all fours bounded out between two houses.

'Woof!'

It was no dog. I recoiled at the sight of the mask, my heart racing erratically. Mark burst out in laughter as the tumbler shook a cloth tail. 'Look!' he said. 'Bloody clown!' The man-dog got to his knees, yelping, holding out two brown-stained hands, just like a begging dog. Mark dropped a coin down. The fellow barked his thanks and then began scampering off, back into the darkened alleyway.

'Hey!' I shouted, the snouted dog mask still in my mind. 'You! Wait!'

I stepped towards the mouth of the alley and Mark put a restraining hand on my arm. 'Don't bother,' he said. 'You won't get no sense from a clown. He'll talk nonsense just to trip you.' He was right. But I cursed it; I cursed the whole air of strange, unpleasant unreality which had descended over London these past days and weeks. It was becoming a fool's paradise – and a dangerous one at that. 'I love a clown, me. Knew exactly when to wag his tail and when to bark, just then. You can't learn that.'

I rolled my eyes and said nothing.

Rounding the corner, we passed on to Eastcheap and through the archway that led to the stables. I swallowed down the fear that ran through me. It was just as gloomy in the daylight as that night. The abandoned barrow stood just as it had before. Crossing the innyard, we went to the stables. Sure enough, there was Gideon. The young groom was asleep on a patch of hay, a raggedy blanket over him despite the day's rising heat.

'You,' I said, nudging him with a foot. It felt good, kicking out. My legs hadn't suffered too badly from being laid up. 'Up. Now.'

'Easy on him,' whispered Mark, as the lad began murmuring. 'Don't frighten him or you won't get nuffink.'

I kicked harder. 'Get up!'

He did, springing up quickly, wiping his eyes with a grimy sleeve. He wore no doublet – just an old, coarse woollen shirt. 'Masters?' he said, looking between us. If he recognised me, he gave no sign of it.

'This is my horse,' I said. 'I was here. In the night.' I tried to think. 'Last week. I came late.'

The boy moved to stand in front of the low door to Gideon's stall. 'Sir? This is Mr Rawle's horse.'

'Not yet it isn't,' I said. 'Nor ever. It is Cardinal Wolsey's own beast.'

The boy's eyes widened as he mouthed the cardinal's name silently. He began opening and closing it, making inarticulate sounds. 'Ugh, leave him,' said Mark, tugging at my sleeve. 'Let's see this Rawle.'

He led me out of the stable – though I cast a dark look back at the frightened lad. As he crossed the yard, Mark said, 'You need to damp yourself down, man. If you don't want a knife in the ribs.'

I didn't answer him. Instead, I stepped ahead and into the inn's main door, which lay open and welcoming. Rawle was inside, laying a carpet across the table. I saw it soak up spillages as the scarred wood disappeared under its sea of brown wool. 'Mr Rawle,' I said.

The fellow looked at me. He recognised me, I could tell, immediately – though he likely saw only a lost horse. He let the carpet fall and began pressing down on it with a fist. His other hand rose to push a string of hair behind his ears. 'Sir?' he asked, no commitment to anything in his voice.

'You remember me?' I asked. Nothing but a guarded look. 'I'm the one who climbed up in the world. A cardinal's man. As is my friend.' I stepped aside to let him see Mark, who had put on his livery. At the sight of it, Rawle crumpled.

'Pleased I am to see you, sir,' he said, sounding anything but. 'Your pack – your own livery – I have it still. Have had it laundered too. And your horse has been tended to. The price will be—'

'Cardinal Wolsey thanks you for your expenditure,' I said. A battle seemed to go on inside the man's mind: to fight for the money he'd spent or to leave it. He opted for the latter, his shoulders sagging. As a rule, I wasn't one to play up my court connection, not like some. I was happy to do it now.

'It's my pleasure,' he said. 'Anything for my lord cardinal.'

'Good,' I said. 'His Grace requires some knowledge. Of the man who took the room on the night I came.'

Mark stepped forward. 'Take us up to the room, will you?'

It was unlikely there would be anything there still, but I shrugged. 'Yes. Now. Please.'

Rawle did as he was asked, leading us up the creaking wooden staircase and along the gallery. I kept my gaze fixed ahead, not daring to look over the short drop. When he reached the room, he opened the door and went in ahead of us. 'We've had no gentlemen in here since,' he said. 'Everyone's flying west, down to the court.'

Good, I thought.

The room was quite big, stretching all the way over the wall below, with shutters that would look down on Eastcheap.

There was a wooden board set on crossed planks against one wall, a pressed tin dish and a full tallow candle sitting on it. A good wooden stool stood beside the makeshift desk. A casement had been knocked into the plaster before the window, with a short length of brown carpet folded neatly on it. The bed itself was a feathered affair, fit for at least two, squashed cosily onto a stringed wooden frame.

'As you can see, sir, a fine room. Though neither you nor Mr Mark slept here.' His eyes narrowed.

'What?' Mark asked. His chest rose. 'Bastard knows my name.' He turned to me. 'He knows my name.'

I put my good hand on his shoulder. 'We know that,' I said quietly. 'He knows everything. It's how he could write a letter feigning it came from you. He knows.'

'Demon,' said Mark, shaking his head. 'I'd . . . it's just . . . hearing it . . .'

I dropped my hand and addressed myself to Rawle, who was looking at us now with real interest. 'This fellow, who gave you that name – what was he like? His nature, I mean.'

'What?' asked Rawle. 'He was your friend, wasn't he? Said to send up the Moor to his room. Said you were friends.'

'He was a trickster. Hoping to cozen me,' I said. 'I escaped. You've had a trickster, a cozener, under your roof, sir. A great enemy of my lord cardinal.'

Rawle frowned, scratching behind his ear. 'I . . . I . . .'

'What was he like?'

'Oh . . . a rotten one, sir. I could tell that immediately.'

'Not too rotten for a room,' said Mark.

Rawle glared at him. 'You can be sure I had him pay in advance. Been fooled by young prentice knaves before – or they've tried. Didn't like the look of him. Young. Beardless,

- 212 -

like yourselves. But younger-looking, like a lass. And the mess he made.'

'Mess?' I asked.

Rawle gestured about the room. And then he went to stand by the casement window. 'Here,' he said, putting a finger to the plaster. 'Right here. He'd written some nonsense. In dirt. Must have scraped it from his boot.' I looked. The wall had been cleaned recently. There was a different sheen to parts of it, marking out the paths the cloth had taken.

'What did it say?' I asked.

Rawle moved his tongue in his cheek. A dimple appeared. 'Conana . . . Conanus . . . something like that. Looked like church language. I washed it away. Dirty brute. And there were drawings. In the same wet muck. A boar. Tusks, you know.' He bent a finger on each hand and held them up beside his cheeks. I shivered, right down to my boots, and itched mightily. 'Quite well done. You won't find a trace of them, sir. This is a clean house.'

'A boar,' said Mark. 'Conana.'

'A jest,' said Rawle. 'I fancied, anyway. The Boar's Head . . . a boar. Perhaps he was wearied in waiting for you to come. For this . . . this cozenage.' My eyes widened. I looked to the side of the washed wall, to the window. One of the two shutters was open, letting the street chatter in.

Had he sat there, on that folded carpet, in the dark – or perhaps with a candle lit – watching for me? Had he seen me entering the yard and known to light his torch and ready his blade?

'Is there anything else?' Mark asked. 'We're trying to find the lad. On Cardinal Wolsey's instructions.'

'No, I . . . I mean, of course, if it's for my lord cardinal, if there was anything else, but I . . . no. He was a dirty young man. I did not know his accent – he spoke English, though, fairly.'

'With an accent?' I asked.

The fellow chewed on his jaw for a second. 'The lad spoke fair English. Odd accent – foreign, maybe? A trace.'

Maybe.

'Dirty?'

'Ay. His hands, his clothes. But that's common enough a thing. With travellers.'

I nodded slowly. He was right. Caledon – Mark – whatever he called himself – had been dirty at the Gonzaga house too, even before he'd killed the historian. He must have ridden all the way from Hampton Court then as well: he was a comer and goer. But was this young man working on someone else's orders?

The glazier, Visser, might have seen thrower and stone in conference.

Or mind and hand, or mind and weapon.

'Did the young man seem educated?' I asked. 'Learned – that sort?'

Rawle shrugged. 'Polished enough.'

I accepted this, putting my bad hand with its trailing sleeve behind my back and giving him a little bow. 'Thank you, Mr Rawle.'

'His Grace thanks you too,' said Mark. 'Good man.'

We returned downstairs; I received my livery; and we were able, with Rawle's grudging help, to convince the groom to release Gideon to me. As we walked home, Mark began to muse about the conspiracy, about Monsieur Lutini being a French-Scot, about witches and wizards. I was glad when a troupe of masked fools silenced him, forcing us to wind our way through, waving open hands and bells on sticks in our faces.

Before we turned for home, I sent him on with Gideon and bid him take his own horse back to the cardinal; he was right – he'd been away long enough. He might, I suggested, tell His Grace that I was recovered and still set on his business. He hesitated, he demurred, he tried to stay with me – but off he went to Aldgate.

I, however, went wandering through the city, in search of the man-dog. It might be, I thought, that my attacker had purchased his mask from this clown or one of his company. I could at least get a good look at the thing, to judge its quality. In my mind, the boar mask had been fairly well made – better than the cloth-and-leaf efforts I'd seen on Thames Street. It was the sort of mask you'd find in a good city house, purchased especially by a wealthy merchant bent on keeping revels in high state; the kind of thing you'd see in Guild pageants; perhaps even good enough for court. He could have stolen it or bought it anywhere, if he had the money. Unable to find him, I eventually bought a hobby horse, its head mounted on a timber shaft.

I'd decided to go to the Gonzaga house. I had no reason to – I didn't think the wife could help me. Yet, in my dark mood, I felt drawn to darkness, to sadness. I got as far as the door. The sound of children's laughter from inside prevented me from knocking and I left my gift, stepped away, and began heading home myself, keeping my head down, feeling certain people could see through my clothes.

To take my mind away from that course, I thought about the mystery I was set on by the cardinal.

This, really, was why I'd wanted to part with Mark: for time alone to arrange my thoughts, to sort through what I knew.

The key, I decided, was to understand what this creature had been doing. It didn't matter if he was doing it alone or on orders. There was a pattern to it, a shape. There was reason. As I'd known all along, I was just too stupid to know what it signified.

The birds around Gonzaga; they were a message.

The book Gonzaga had found, 'G. Cass'; that was why he'd been killed.

The false sulphurous fire; it was a message.

Visser had seen something; that was why he'd been killed.

The Boar's Head inn and the boar mask – the name, 'Conan-something'; they were all a message.

But for whom?

I was following him, seeking him. That's why I must be killed.

Amidst the jumble of names, another occurred to me. A man named by both one of the monks I'd met and Wolsey himself. An Italian name. That fellow certainly wouldn't be stupid. He would have exactly what I lacked: knowledge.

And I felt very sure now that knowledge was the key that would unlock all.

15

A drooping-eyed young servant was clearing the cobbles before the cathedral's eastern rump with quick, resentful darts of a broom. 'Signor Vergil? Polydore Vergil?' I asked. His chin jabbed to his left, up the Old Change.

He let the top of the broom handle rest against his chin. 'Left. Tall house.'

I nodded my thanks.

St Paul's Churchyard spread in a lazy semicircle, all around the southern walls of the great, spired cathedral, up and around its eastern end. In the morning light, the greenery and cobblestones were bathed in freshness, the heat rising, bringing the smell of new grass and hard stone up to me. It was tempered only with my own slightly sour smell: my stepmother had bought me lotions and poultices to ease my itching, and they lacked Jane's fair rosy scent. The shops facing the cathedral were already a blaze of reds and blues and yellows. The voices of the shopkeepers rose and fell. 'Who will buy?' competed with, 'Step forward and look.'

I began moving up the street, hugging the low wall of the churchyard, as the steeple's heavy-tongued bells lolled.

I had worn my livery. Rawle had been as good as his word: the doublet was laundered, smelling fresh and clean. It didn't cause too great an itch when it bore down on the shirt beneath; it was soft and supple. My legs, too, hadn't suffered too badly – a little stiffness from lying down, some aches – but I took a perverse pleasure in those. Mark had gone, having stayed at my house in Shoemaker Row and left for Windsor with the dawn. I hadn't told him of my plan.

The king's historian. Signor Vergil.

That proud, clucking old fool Vergil . . . The student sought to outdo the master.

I'd learnt a little something of the much-storied Vergil from, of all places, my stepmother. In the morning, after we'd waved off Mark, who saluted us from his horse and clattered out into the street, we returned inside for breakfast.

'Have you ever heard,' I asked, more for something to say than in any expectation of a good answer, 'of an Italian, a Signor Vergil?'

'Vergil?' she asked. I nodded. 'Oh, yes.' I looked up. She was busying herself with a wooden jug, tutting at the scum which had somehow managed to settle across our ale despite her constant skimming in the little still-room out by the kitchen. 'Oh, yes. I remember him.'

I stood. 'How?' I asked. My stepdame, as much as I loved her, was hardly a scholar.

'He's a name enough,' she said. 'Would *you* forget the name Polydore Vergil? It's not Tom Smith, is it?'

'Polydore . . . Who is he? What've you heard?'

She set the jug down and turned to me, frowning, tightening her apron strings. 'Vergil,' she said. 'Vergil. Your father and I . . . we talked about him.' Light dawned. 'Ay, I remember.' She picked up a spoon and lifted the jug again, as though movement helped her think. 'When he was news, this Vergil, I asked your father if he knew him. From his old days. And he'd seen him, too.' The stirring slowed.

'Your father . . . he'd seen everyone who was anyone, he had.'

'What was the news?'

'Hm?' I repeated the question. 'Oh. That. Ay, Vergil. This is going back a bit, mind you. You would've been a boy. Before you went into the cardinal's service.' I began drumming on the table with my left hand, willing her to hurry up. 'This Vergil was an Italian, like you said. He was some kind of scholar for the old king and the new. Wrote books for them.' She said the word 'books' as though it were vaguely distasteful, a little louche and suspect. 'And then, a few years back, his name was in everyone's mouth.' She shrugged.

'Why?'

She frowned, and her stirring intensified. 'I can't . . . He was locked up in the Tower,' she said at length. My heart skipped a beat. The Tower wasn't all that far from us. It was a crumbling, ancient place, in need of being built up again or torn down. My father used to tell me that Julius Caesar, the king of the Romans or whatever they had for kings, had built it. 'He'd . . . Oh yes.' She had turned a queer look on me. 'He'd said something. Maybe written something. Against your master. Against dear old Wolsey.'

'What?' I asked.

'Can't say. No,' she said, putting down the jug and spoon finally. 'I really can't. Can't remember. It would've been the usual, no doubt.' She took a breath. I could imagine. Plenty of slanders were whispered, shouted – maybe even written – against Wolsey. I supposed some might even be true.

'But he was let go?'

She shrugged. 'I suppose. Still lives in London. I've heard the name spoken sometimes. He's a name, like I said.' One of her cheeks inflated and she blew out air. 'Why?'

'Cardinal's business,' I said.

Some argument had followed. I wasn't well enough yet for any business. I should rest awhile. I needed to eat to build up my strength. She'd fetched some ointments and lotions for me from that sweet Sister Jane – shouldn't I stay in bed with those on, under a plaster? I'd waved all of this off and she'd admitted defeat.

Thereafter, I'd wandered down to the river and enquired of wherrymen about this Italian, this historian, this name. And so, I'd found that he lodged somewhere in the churchyard of St Paul's.

The house the servant had directed me to was large – it looked a little like a countryside house had been lifted by a giant hand and dumped in the city. In transit, it had perhaps become a little squashed inwards and stretched upwards, until it took on the look of a skinny, somewhat crooked old man, leaning, grumbling down over the neat garden before it. I cast a look down at myself before I took the path up to the stout front door. The crossed-keys of my livery were bright in the sun. I didn't intend to frighten the fellow but supposed that if he'd once been locked up by Wolsey, he would fear him now. He must be old, weak, if he had served the old king. Probably he thought he lived now in easy comfort, writing his books or thinking his thoughts or whatever aged scholars did. I could scare him if I had to.

Once, the prospect of doing so would have been appalling.

Reaching the front door, I rapped. I had only a short time to wait. A grizzled head appeared as it was opened.

Old servants for an old man, I thought. Good.

'Signor Vergil?' I asked. The steward stood back, tilting his head. His eyes narrowed, focusing on my face before travelling downwards. And then they widened, fixing on the livery. 'I come with a request from my lord cardinal,' I said, without expression.

The man's voice, when he spoke, was light, jittery. I felt cheap. My right hand curled, stinging, beneath its hanging sleeve cuff. 'Yes, sir. Please, sir, come in.' He bowed, pulling the door wider, stepping away.

A narrow reception hall opened up. Good tapestries covered the plaster walls. Men on horseback rode nowhere across flower-filled fields. Soldiers with round shields marched without moving. Here and there women in flowing white danced and lounged, their poses fixed. A little table stood in the centre of the hall, fresh flowers overspilling it. Their scent filled the room.

'I'll tell – inform – the signor of your coming, sir,' said the usher, barely above a whisper. He bowed himself away, before turning to a door set in the wall between the Roman soldiers and some dancing ladies. He didn't, I notice, ask my name or my business. I supposed, with my coming from Wolsey, it didn't matter. Possibly he felt it could be nothing good.

I crossed to the flowers and lifted some, crushing red and white petals in my right hand. The scent of roses grew harder, more livid. I let them fall. Roses had been part of my treatment, or rose oil, or rosewater.

My treatment. Still, I thought, there would be some remedy that would restore me fully. Jane could . . .

If she don't love you back, well, it's because she's a nun, not because . . .

Perhaps I had been afflicted for the sin of lusting after a sister of Christ.

No. I lifted my hand and sniffed. I'd been attacked by a man, not struck by God. And I was going to find that man. And this fellow, this Vergil – he was going to help me.

As though in agreement, the door opened, and the steward reappeared. He was biting at his mottled lower lip. Nastily, something pleased me in that. I'd heard it said that those who are monstrous on the outside become monstrous inwardly – and I crushed away the thought as I'd crushed the petals. 'This way, sir, please, sir.'

I followed him into a long, narrow room with a long, narrow table: a dining room, I supposed, for when the scholar entertained. Along the right wall, he led me to an open, doorless archway, and so deeper into the house. Through there, we went upstairs, along a gallery, passing servants who pressed their backs to the walls, and up again, until I could feel the house beginning to shrink, to cower down over my head. I felt suddenly as the petals might have: that I was being carefully enclosed. The smell up here was of dry plaster, like a clean stable.

Eventually, when I judged that we must be somewhere under the roof, he paused at a thin, low door, knocked on it, and said, 'Inside here, sir.'

I thanked him and went in.

To my surprise, the space opened up ahead of me and to either side. We were, indeed, just below the roof; I could see beams criss-crossing overhead, the underside of the matting and netting and plaster which held up the roof slates. The space, which might have been divided into small rooms, for servants perhaps, had been turned into a vast library. Books were everywhere. Many were in cabinets, their burnished gold edging making the cases shimmer in the light spilling in from open horn cut low in the walls, but others were stacked on their sides in tottering piles. There were three wooden lecterns keeping company amidst the piles. Hope fluttered. I could envision now a thin, majestic, swan-like old man, his beard trailing, unfolding a book with delicate white fingers, placing it on a lectern, pointing. But the book of my imagination was empty, unmarked. I couldn't imagine what it might tell me.

I jumped as the door closed behind me. At the same time, one of the lecterns moved. It was, I realised, a man: it was Vergil, bent over a little, his back to me. The figure rose up, turning to me.

How different from the image I had conjured was Signor Polydore Vergil. The old man was short, dressed in dark robes. At he turned, I had a glimpse of a nose which dropped to a sharp point, dominating a seamed, beardless face. He seemed sprightly enough; old age seemed to have leapt upon him unawares, clawing lines into his face – though he was not quite the eighty years of my imagination; he might have been in his middle fifties. He was hatless, as well he might be in his own home, and his grey-white hair hung in a fringed curtain down past his ears. Instinct bobbed strong in me: all thoughts of intimidating him fled. My cap was in my hand and I was bowing without thinking; the old man might have been the cardinal himself.

Stepping around a pile of books which reached to his waist, his movements lithe, Vergil approached me. 'Good morrow, friend,' he said. His accent was Italianate, sounding a little like Signora Gonzaga's, but it was nowhere near as strong. There was firmness in his voice, belied only by the slightly wary, deepening of lines on his brow.

'Good morrow,' I returned.

'You come from His Grace, my lord cardinal?'

'I do, sir.'

'I see. And what brings you hither, friend?' He sounded business-like, as though I were intruding on his valuable time. I was, of course, but he might have hidden it. This, perhaps, was his concession to the fact that I came from an old enemy.

I had considered how to answer this question – or one similar – on the wherry journey upriver. Then, I had still been toying with the idea of frightening him. I felt now that this wouldn't work. Yet, my plan then had been to tell him of the murders, of the brutalities and the strange signs. Talk of murder should scare anyone. I would still ask for his thoughts on Gonzaga and Visser, but I'd lead up to them.

'I understand,' I said, 'that you were friends with the late Signor Gonzaga, a historian in the employ of my master.' My words sounded hollow, like a child pretending to authority.

Vergil crossed himself. 'Yes. Poor Signor Gonzaga. He was my student, once. I've written his wife.'

I bowed my head. 'Do you know, sir, what he was doing? His work – his scholarly work?'

Looking up, I saw Vergil frown. 'Scholarly,' he spat, rolling his eyes.

'Sir?'

'He trod his own path, that poor fellow.'

I swallowed. 'It might be,' I said, 'that my lord cardinal set him to work. To write some history of King Arthur. For a masque.' Something passed Vergil's face. His eyes narrowed in – what? Contempt, perhaps. Scorn. He was looking at me as though I were a fool, beneath him. 'And he found, we think, some proof. Of our King Henry's descent from King Arthur.'

'Bah!' Vergil struck out, bringing his gnarled fist down on top of a tower of books. 'What is this, boy? You come to me with fairy stories and fond fancies. What is this game?'

'I . . .' felt trapped. 'I . . . it's true. He found them. And he was murdered for it.' I licked my lips. 'Most brutally, fearfully.' I tried, and failed, to lace the words with menace.

'Murdered?' snapped Vergil. And then realisation dawned. That look of contempt deepened. It was directed towards my livery. 'I see. Accident. Murder. May God have mercy on him.'

Who – Gonzaga or Wolsey?

'Murdered,' I repeated. 'Horribly murdered.'

Vergil looked back up towards my face. His slate eyes had hardened. His lower lip and chin jutted. After a rapid flaring of his nostrils, he said, 'Do not attempt to frighten me, Mr – what is your name?'

I didn't want to give it. I felt smaller than ever. 'Blanke,' I said.

'Blanke,' he repeated. 'Blanke. Blanco. White. You're the late black trumpet's boy?'

'Yes.'

'Hmph. Hmph. Do not presume to frighten me, son, for I won't be frightened. Not by some mad tales. I've read enough of them. You say Gonzaga was murdered. I will believe you. I will believe that your master has . . . That the truth has . . . been suppressed. For the sake of . . . I'm sure my lord cardinal had his reasons.' Again, that sneering dislike, just tamed, like a snarling dog yanked back on its leash. 'Tell me what happened.'

Keeping my head low, I told him: about Gonzaga's death and the birds; about Visser's fall; about my own assault by the boar-man; about the sulphurous – or falsely sulphurous – footprints – and about the mysterious book: 'G. Cass'. He interrupted me often, criticising my confused style, my weak descriptions. But interest began to replace contempt. When I'd finished, he said, 'And whom does your master suspect is behind this?'

I hesitated before answering.

'Spit it out, boy!'

'The French. Maybe. French-Scotch.'

Vergil cackled. 'The French! Yes. I see how his mind works. Some men think all strangers have been created only for the discomfort of the English.' I didn't answer this. His head rocked back, his eyes on the roof. 'G. Cass. Hm. And you say that the book burnt in the Crutched Friars by this Caledon was unknown?'

'Yes,' I said. 'It was burnt, gone.'

'Hm. Imprimis,' he said, a thin finger jabbing into the air, 'a murderer is at work. Item: he has killed a man and left a message. That man sought some knowledge of the legendary King Arthur.' He laid emphasis on the word 'legendary'. 'Item: he has visited sundry libraries and burnt a book. Item: he has taken a book which was borrowed by his victim. Item: he has killed again. Item: he has left sundry messages. These he wishes well understood.'

I nodded, impatiently. 'But those messages,' I said, 'what do they mean?'

Vergil stroked at his chin. 'Let us examine them. Come.' He turned away from me, apparently knowing that I'd follow, and moved left and right as he wandered through his forest of book piles. I decided to try another approach. Forcing levity into my voice, I said, 'Do the books not dampen, sir? Up here. In the rain, I mean . . .' I trailed off as he looked over his shoulder at me, his nose a sharp beak.

'They survived the Tower. They shall survive this realm's endless rain.' Then, turning away again, 'My servants are sent up with tar and buckets at the first spot. And they labour under my watch. If anything is spoiled, they are dismissed.'

I closed my mouth.

Soon enough, he reached the far wall, where a single stool sat, like a giant clawed insect. He sank onto it. 'I think better in comfort,' he said. There was no seat for me. I folded my hands over my stomach. 'Firstly, lad, I say that your master is wrong.'

I looked down at him. 'His Grace,' I said, 'won't like to hear that.'

He matched my glare. 'I'm not afraid of threats, young Blanke. Weak men make threats. Don't try to threaten me with your master's name.'

I blinked first, looking away.

So much for your career as a hard-faced man of interrogatory.

'Nor will I be lured into any Catonic speeches.' His head tilted backwards.

'I . . . don't know what that means,' I said.

'No. Of course you do not. I say the cardinal is wrong,' continued Vergil. 'As Gonzaga was wrong. And so we start with him.' He took a breath. 'He was my student. A fellow of some moderate learning. He hadn't the makings of a great scholar.' He spoke quite honestly, without emotion. 'He lived by the old creed. Of books. Finding all histories from books.' He thrust his chin into the room behind me. 'Books. Fine,

fine. But books tell us only what men of the past wished us to hear. The truth? The truth is something else. It is in the privy letters, etched on walls and glass, the things never put in any books. Books of history – they are like hearing the tale of an execution only from the judge, who never went to it. Never saw the dulled axe, or the drunk headsman, never counted the strikes missed. Books are good only for what scholars write in the margins. The hidden histories, secret, you see? The notes and questions.

'Consider Gonzaga. The cardinal says he died in some tragic accident. Ipso facto, he died in an accident. Even the king, I imagine, has been told this, and those around him watched lest they should say otherwise? Hm. Yes – His Majesty might find he has no need of . . . great men . . . if such men do not shield him from dark matters and enfold him in entertainments instead. Should some writer of history wish to tell the tale, then it is the truth: Pietro, or Peter, Gonzaga died by fortune's hand. Yet you, Mr Blanke, tell me another tale. You say he was murdered. Which is true?' He raised a leg under his robes and brought his foot down on the floor, banging it, and looked at me with challenge glittering in his grey eyes. 'Which is true? Answer me, boy!'

'He was murdered, sir. As I said.'

'Ha! There – you see? The history books telling Wolsey's – my lord cardinal's – tale would tell it falsely. Unless some later man – some scholar – writes in the truth by the tale. You understand?'

I did, but I didn't see the point, unless the old man meant to show off, to make a fool of me. 'Yes, sir.'

'Don't frown. Stand up straight.' I relaxed my face and straightened without thinking.

'This I could not get Gonzaga to see. Books, books, books. These were all he thought necessary to discover any history. And they misled him. As they have misled your cardinal. Perhaps misled the king, and the late king.'

I opened my mouth to object, but he silenced me with a glare and said, 'I have made clear, young man, that I will not be frightened. By you or anyone. I will not.' I closed my mouth. 'Good. You say Gonzaga set out to prove our king's descent from King Arthur?'

'Yes, sir. And he found it. In this "G. Cass", perhaps. The murderer wishes the proof suppressed. To deny King Henry's claims.'

'Be silent, boy.' He tutted. 'G. Cass.' He rose, stiffly, from his stool, and put his hand against the wall. 'Bah!' He wheeled. 'Nonsense. Nonsense, nonsense, nonsense. Gonzaga can have found no such proofs because . . . because there was no King Arthur.'

My arms fell to my sides. Mad, I thought. The old fellow was cracked – he'd lost his mind amongst all these rich old books of lies and margins. 'I don't—'

'King Arthur,' he said, one hand, formed in a fist, sailing through the air. 'Merlin, Camelot, the Round Table, Guinevere . . . it is, all of it, a fantasy. A fond fantasy. Fables made for children. Nonsense. No new Camelot shall ever be made. No such king of the Britons ever was, nor any such place.'

'But that's not true,' I persisted.

You're lying, you mad old knave.

'Ugh,' he said, half-turning to me. Contempt had returned, and it had sovereignty of him now. '*Boys*! You ill-witted, sheep-shearing English boys!'

'But King Arthur was real, as real as – as the king's own father. And Gonzaga found the proof, in Southwark Priory. A book,' I added lamely, already forgetting his contempt for books.

Grudgingly, Vergil breathed out slowly. It came in a phlegmy whistle. 'The book you seek,' he said, 'you foolish young pup, is Cassiodorus's history of the barbarians commonly called the Gothi. G: Gothi, their history. Cass: Cassiodorus, the Roman scholar.'

My heart leapt. 'That, then – what is it? Does it prove that—'

'Peace,' said Vergil, holding up a restraining finger. 'I have not read the book. I thought it lost.' He shrugged. 'Yet I doubt it proves anything of any Arthur, because, I tell you, that king is a fable. A fantasy.'

'But—'

'Will you let me speak? Good. I have not read the book. There was a summary of it, I believe, in the Crutched Friars.' Before I could say anything, he said, 'Which is undoubtedly what Signor Gonzaga's murderer destroyed. Commonly called *Getica*. Perhaps some old notes in its margins directed him to Southwark. But whatever he thought he had discovered, it would be worthless to any true master of history. As I said, matter prepared by ancient men who wished whatever falsehoods they fancied preserved.'

'Are there any more copies of the book, this Cassiodorus book about the . . . the . . .'

'The ancient race of the Gothi. Not that I know of. There might be some copies of the *Getica*, its summary, in the realm.' He shrugged. 'Common enough. Of no interest to me. None. Trash. Trash which leads men into error. Makes them fancy great discoveries in pages of lies and falsehoods.'

I fought the urge to put my head in my hands. I had the name now, of the book Gonzaga had found, and which had likely got him killed, only to be told that it was worthless trash.

Or so this man thinks.

I wasn't so sure. How many people, I wondered, believed – rightly – in King Arthur, and how many stood instead behind a crackpot old Italian living in an attic room and expounding strange theories? Gonzaga must have believed in what he found or he wouldn't have taken it. His murderer believed in it too and had killed him for it. Whether or not Polydore Vergil accepted the truth of King Arthur, everyone with a mind not soured by overmuch ink certainly did. I kept this thought to myself.

'The man who murdered Signor Gonzaga means to spoil the cardinal's masque. To deny our sovereign lord's descent from King Arthur. Which,' I added quickly, 'the cardinal says His Majesty believes in.'

'Kings!' spat Vergil. He licked his lips. 'They say that princes' minds are not as other men's. Bah! What they mean is that they *should not* be. Follow me.'

Sighing, I did. This time he took another path through the books. He ended at another wall. Against this one was resting something I had seen only very rarely – even the cardinal didn't bother with them in any of his palaces: it was a rectangular portrait in an orangey-coloured metal frame. It showed a gaunt man with a thin face and hooked nose. Dark clouds of paint marked out the hair on either side, tumbling from under a plain, black hat. His white fingers, folded before him, held a rose. It was lifelike, but small: far more lifelike, I thought, than any tapestry I'd ever seen, or any image painted on a church wall.

'You are looking, my boy, at the old king. Our present king's father. Henry, seventh of that name. Do you not tremble?' asked Vergil.

I frowned down at the painting, unsure what I was supposed to say, and then looked back at the old man.

'It is a copy,' he shrugged. 'Not very well done. The finest artists, the true masters, are in my old country. The creatures here . . .' He made a face. 'Left to me. I prefer not to hang it. Not to look always at un-good, indifferent things.' He nudged at it with his slippered foot. 'That king, now in his tomb . . . he was a man fulfilled. I have made a study of his life. From various sources – not books alone, not written or printed matter. From speaking to those who saw. To those who were there.

'When that king came to this realm, in 1485, he came from Brittany with Frenchmen at his back. Through Wales, he went, under the banner of the red dragon. This, he claimed, was the standard of the supposed King Arthur.' Vergil's voice, I noticed, had taken on the stentorian quality of a man speaking to many, despite my being his only audience. He began gesturing as he spoke, marking out pauses with a palm cutting through the air. 'And so, it was proclaimed, Henry Tudor was of the rightful lineage of Cadwaladr, the last of the ancient high kings of this island. And Cadwaladr was, of course, descended of Arthur.' He cleared his throat and said, more powerfully still, 'Cadwaladr's blood lineally descending,

'Long has been told of such a prince coming,
'Wherefore, friends, if that I shall not lie,
'This same is the fulfiller of the prophecy.'

He laughed, without humour – just a sharp, old-man yip.
'Weak, is it not?' he asked. 'Weak of verse and poor of
sentiment. Those lines were declared on the old king's in-
coming to England. And the cry went up amongst the
stupid rabble, the sheep: this our king is a king by prophecy,
descended of King Arthur. Bah! Prophecies. A force given
colour of truth by our dear late king.'

I measured his words for a whiff of treason, of
scandal, but found nothing but an old man's haughty
arrogance. 'Prophecy,' I said. I knew the word. I echoed the
lines of verse. 'Fulfiller of the prophecy. But he was, the old
king. He became king. Rightful king of all England. In my
father's time.'

A little stab of inferiority jabbed at me. My father had
come to England with Queen Catherine, when she was to
marry Henry VII's son, another – new – Arthur, who would
have been king had God not taken him. 'Your father,' said
Vergil, looking at me a little more intently.

I looked away. My father, I thought: captured out of Africa.
Carried out of Spain. I was a creature of a history murkier
than the golden tales of prophecy and lineage. I twisted my
head to a pile of books. None of them would include the likes
of me. Not even in their margins.

But this man knew, this historian who looked beyond
history books. I could see it in his rheumy, grey, interested
eyes.

And my attacker had known it. Probably he thought less of killing me than of killing an Italian and a Fleming.

'Could your father write?' asked Vergil, raising a gnarled, heavy fist to his chin. 'Did he leave any observations of England?'

'No,' I said, ignoring the rising heat which crept up my neck, burning through the right side.

'A shame,' he said. He gave me a long, sharp look, his eyes like polished daggers. 'A great shame. You ought to dig yourself, into this past. You should be proud of having such a father, coming from strange lands with a headful of strange knowledge.' His tongue, looking frosted, looking scaled, darted over his lips. 'Yes. Proud.'

I couldn't help it; I lifted my hand and loosened my shirt collar, scratching at the flaking skin. Pain protested only for a moment; relief followed.

'Hm,' Vergil said, still watching me over his hawk-like nose. 'Oh. Of course.' Phlegm rattled in his throat and he coughed it away, his hand still before his face. 'We were speaking of prophecy, yes. For a reason, boy, for purpose.

'You say that the late king made the prophecy true, as the verse does. By becoming king, he proved it.'

'Yes,' I said.

'And therein lies my point. Do you see?' I said nothing and he shook his head a little, frustrated . . . 'His late Highness, King Henry, was a man, like any other. I saw him often enough. I watched as his hair grew less. As his teeth dropped. As the bones began to show in his face. A man, like any other.' He waved away my sputtering protests. 'Oh, yes, it was God's will that he should reign, yes, I've no doubt of it. But he was a human being, a man. Do you see? A man made the prophecy come true. And men trumpeted it. Men like your father. And now – now prophecies grow like weeds, waiting for men to fulfil them. Now any fool can take up a pen and scribble a prophecy. And any other fool can hear it and pick up his sword or anything else and seek to make it true. A prophecy, I say, should be torn up at the roots wherever it is found.' He mimed doing just that, leaning over and tearing at the air, throwing a handful of emptiness over his shoulder. 'This hunger to gaze into the future . . . it infects many. All kings suffer it. And . . . perhaps . . . this murderer of yours . . . seeks to take advantage of that hunger. To feed it, I might say.'

This murderer of yours?

'What do you mean? What prophecy? What is he doing?'

Vergil took a deep breath and began moving back through the room to his stool, leaving the long-dead Henry VII to his dusty spot against the wall, his dusty gaze falling again on dusty books.

The old man creaked down onto his seat. 'You spoke to me of signs. Birds, boars . . . sulphur . . . Caledon – the name, yes?'

'Yes,' I said. 'Please, sir, do you know what they mean?'

He inhaled again. I got the sudden impression that he was enjoying himself mightily. Perhaps he saw few people, had few subjects to torment with his vast knowledge. 'Perhaps,' he said, on a wave of breath.

Frustrated now, annoyed, I said, 'You'd better tell me, then. Now.'

From under his thick brows, his eyes twinkled up. 'Recall what I said, boy, about threats. I am no friend to them. But for that young fool Gonzaga's sake, I shall help your master, if I can.' He tilted his head back. 'Now, bear in mind that I speak from memory.' Another deep breath, more laboured this time, as though I'd tired him. 'Come here.'

Reluctantly, I stepped towards him. His black-robed arm reached out, reached for my own arm, and I pulled it away. 'For the love of God,' he said, 'I have read medicinal writings; let me see.'

Fuck off!

'No.' I wasn't going to bend, not for him or anyone.

'Boys!' he said. 'You say a man in the guise of a boar did this? This Caledon? And the neck, I think, too?'

'Yes,' I said, through gritted teeth.

'Hmph. And the name on the wall. Conanus.' I nodded, but stepped no closer to him. Thwarted, he said, 'Now, allow me a little license. My memory is large but it is not perfect.' He stared out into the room, working his tongue in his cheek. 'Yes. From Conan shall proceed a boar . . . a war-like boar . . . that shall use sharp tusks.' My heart began to thud heavily in my ruined breast. He looked at me again, his eyes narrow. 'The Arabians and Africans shall dread him; for he shall pursue his furious course to the farther part of Spain.'

'What?' I asked. 'What are you talking about?' My hand rose up over my breast.

The Arabians and Africans.

I cursed inwardly, my mind searching for a rebuff.

You ill-witted, sheep-shearing English boys!

Yes! I would take even that, and in an embrace.

Vergil didn't answer directly. Instead, he again looked into the middle distance, his eyes crossing slightly. He looked, I thought, like a mad old seer – the kind of fool who peddles nonsense about lovers and marriages to girls on holidays. 'One of the three great trees shall spread, killing the other two by the multitude of their leaves: and then shall it obtain the place of those two, and shall give sustenance to birds of foreign nations.'

Birds!

Peacocks, herons, ducks, doves – all the birds drawn to Gonzaga's corpse spread their wings in my mind. 'There was a heron,' I said. 'In his mouth. Its feet out.'

Vergil licked his dry lips. 'Feet? Birds have claws, talons, and toes. A heron . . . yes . . . shall come forth. She shall cry together all the winged kind and assemble her all manner of fowls.'

'Yes! That's it!'

Vergil gave me a dark look. 'Death shall follow. Nor is that all – far from it. A maid,' he said, 'shall emerge from the wood of Caledon. Wherever she shall go, she shall make sulphurous steps, which will smoke with a double flame.'

Sulphur!

'What is this?' I broke his spell, moving directly in front of him. Without realising it, I'd reached down and grasped the front of his dark robes, was gripping them, shaking. 'What are you saying? What is this – how do you know it?'

Contempt came riding back over Vergil's face. 'Do not handle me, boy,' he said. 'I will not be handled.'

I maintained my grip for a moment before letting the heavy wool fall. I stepped back. Swallowed. And then I repeated my question: 'What is this?'

'Nonsense,' he said. 'Drawn from the old *Historia Regum Britanniae*. A book in twelve volumes. Of history, or so it guises itself, of the kings of this island. Author: Geoffrey of Monmouth. Filled with such tripe.'

Another book.

'But – what you said – all of that – that's what he's doing. Even the names, he's getting the names from the book.'

'Indeed.' Vergil rocked forward on his knees, hanging off the stool. 'As I said, young man. A man making prophecies come true. Just a man, like any other. Or men.'

'But why?'

He rocked back, waving the question away. 'Why? How should I know why? I am no grubbing murderer, no madman. Find him and ask him. Before he . . . let me see . . . before he makes the corn wither. Before he has the flocks of Cambria and Albania drink dry the wide Thames. Ha! These foolish prophecies, boy, come from the *Historia* – they are, together, called the *Prophetia Merlini*.'

Merlin, I thought. An image of an old man – not unlike Vergil, but with beard and moustaches where the historian was clean-shaven – reared up in my mind.

'Given such foolish provenance by one John of Cornwall and included by the said Geoffrey of Monmouth, who should have known better, in his book of fancies. History. Bah! Fables meant for mimps and mops.'

'Where?' I asked. 'Where is this book? Do you have it?' I turned to the room, looking out over the little city of books he'd assembled.

'Peace, boy. No, I do not have it. Years ago, I read it, and read it, and read it. Such time wasted. When the old king bid me help him prove the old tales of Arthur. I told him as I've told you: there was no King Arthur. No, nor any Merlin. It is all trash, meant to entertain and blind the unthinking. I haven't thought of the prophecies in years. I daresay few have. Only foolish believers would be quick to think of them. These days, unless it is in print, unless it is bound in covers and made by press and sold – *sold* – then no one thinks of it.'

'But Gonzaga – the birds – the boar.'

He rose, slowly, grunting, to his feet. 'I shall grant you,' he said, 'this man you seek – it is clear he has read or heard the prophecies. And, as the old king did, he is making them true, in his fashion. For what reason,' he added quickly, 'I cannot say.'

'Where can I find the book?' I asked. It, I realised, was what the creature was working from. It was his plat – his design – for the murders and sacrileges he'd been displaying.

'I do not care,' snapped Vergil. Then, more kindly, his eyes on my livery, he said, 'Perhaps in one of the cardinal's libraries. Or the king's. It has been much copied, written by hand.'

The cardinal's libraries.

The cardinal's household, I thought, where the mind behind these murders lurked.

'In English?' I asked, adding a belated, 'Sir?'

He gave that nasty old smile again, showing his good, sharp teeth. 'You read no Latin?'

'No, sir.'

'No. No, of course you do not. A monks' school, was it? Learning letters from a man with small understanding himself, no doubt. English whelps. Yes,' he said, 'I should think you'll find the trash in English. In the king's court, most certainly.'

'Then I'll go there,' I said. 'I'll find it.' I had my answers, I realised – answers as to why these grisly affairs were shaped as they were. Yet still the whole thing lacked sense, lacked reason. If Vergil was wrong – I was sure he was wrong – and Gonzaga had found proof of the king's descent from King

Arthur that had to be buried, suppressed – whether by the French or the Scots or any other enemy of King Henry – then why draw attention to the histories, to the prophecies? All of his messages . . . the murderer had wished them to be understood, and it had only been that no one did, no one bothered to discover the meaning. But why?

Find him and ask him.

I remembered to thank Vergil, tightly, and bowed my way from his presence. He seemed a little disappointed, as he raised a hand and gave a cross between a dismissal and a wave. And why not? He was losing his inferior plaything. Doubtless I had enlivened an afternoon spent reading books he felt were beneath him.

By the time I'd escaped the house and stood in the garden, the sun was high overhead. It would, I thought, be shining in now, letting the old Henry VII enjoy a little warmth.

If I could find that book, I thought – *it has been much copied* – then I would have a window into this creature's madness. I might even trace what he planned to do next. And then – then – I would have him. And I would do more than simply ask him why.

16

I've heard it said, and it's true enough, that London isn't truly a city. Rather, it's a collection of parishes and towns that, over time, have burst their boundaries and blurred together, like the boughs of trees forming one great canopy, one great metropolis.

Windsor Castle, however, is very much a city, enclosed from the shabby little town by its heavy stone walls. The gatehouse – King Henry's own construction – was a massive archway cut between two mammoth octagonal stone towers. It was, like everything the king did, a display of strength, of power, of the God-given rightness of his reign.

And of his descent, I supposed, from King Arthur and his world of prophecies.

Only foolish believers would be quick to think of them.

I'd judged it too far to ride to Windsor. I was still raw, still flaking and itching. And there was no need. For a small fee I had found in London that numerous barges were daily plying their way upriver, and at speed, transporting spices and goods to the court. For a larger fee, I bought passage for myself and Gideon. And then, after the tedium of unloading, I joined a crew of swearing, sweating workmen as they hauled and pushed barrows heaving with coffers up the mutilated path, through neat meadows and parklands, to the castle itself.

Through the great gate – I wasn't stopped; all was a

whirling confusion of transit – I led Gideon into the Lower Ward. The size of the place stopped me, as it always had. Unlike Hampton Court, Windsor wasn't diminished in stature by a sudden in-pouring of people, by an army. It roared to life with the influx. It rose up everywhere, imperious, greater than ever.

My fellows from the barge deserted me, huffing off to wherever their orders took them. Ahead lay a vast green, with carved columns bearing gilt rampant lions and begging hounds. From their paws, pennants dangled, dejected. Cloisters lined the inner wall to my left, stretching off. Despite its distance across the green, St George's Chapel lost none of its grandeur; the long, enormously tall building, with its columns painted in King's Gold, its leaded glass windows and its carved saints staring placidly from their niches, dominated the Lower Ward.

My business, however, wasn't in that particular palace. It was to the right, up the sloping hill. My chest and arm eased with ointments and my legs feeling strong with purpose, I joined the throng of singing servants in moving upwards, in the direction of the ancient keep, the Round Tower, which squatted in the Middle Ward of the complex like a fat, half-burnt candle. The crowds grew thicker and the shadows heavier as we all rounded the tower's circular moat. I was unremarked upon throughout; it was pleasant, to be one of the crowd. It was a different feeling to being part of a mob on a London street; here, amidst the singing and the oaths and the occasional orders barked from senior household servants, there was a sense of being in something together, of being part of the machinery of the court.

The royal apartments, where Wolsey would be, had their

own stables in the paved and scrubbed Upper Ward. After passing Gideon off to a groom – my livery told him who the beast belonged to – I gazed up at the mellow, gold-hued stone of the lodgings, their countless windows glimmering in the early evening light. My experience of Windsor was limited – I remembered standing by doorways rather than where they led to – and so I had to ask around. The news, which was shared willingly, was that His Grace was arranging a conference set to convene the next day with a whole host of great men: the king, the emperor, the imperial chancellor, English bishops, English earls. And Sir Thomas Boleyn. Everyone remembered good Sir Thomas, champion of the joust. Everyone was at Windsor, apparently. Windsor was, a breathless page boy told me, the centre and heart of the whole world.

I was eventually allowed inside, through a gateway hung on either side with the arms of our king and the Emperor Charles. Through there, I passed into an antechamber hung with tapestries and into a long gallery on the right. There, I could see immediately, I was expected to wait. A trailing queue met me – petitioners, I supposed. Men in red velvets and feathered hats kept company with tradesmen in brown and dun doublets. Some ladies stood, the backs of their boxy headdresses dangling gauzy veils. An usher was passing up and down, almost bent double in submission when required, taking names and business.

When he reached me, he looked only at my doublet. 'Cardinal's business,' I said.

'Mm,' he nodded, vaguely touching a cap which he kept firmly on his head. He moved away, up the crowd. Eventually, he disappeared into a doorway at the far end of the gallery.

Time began to spin on. Mutters, yawns, and under-the-breath curses punctuated it. Through the windows on the left, I could see the shadows thicken, stretching out from the trees and fountain of a courtyard. When the usher returned, he made straight for me, and made to pluck at my sleeve. I yanked it away. 'Come,' he said.

Thank God.

Ignoring the bemused, disgruntled look of my waiting fellows – male and female – I was led down the gallery, bemused myself that my appearance must have told the usher who and what I was. A broad stairway lay in the next chamber, panelled entirely in wood, with a purple carpet covering the middle portion. By some magician's hand, Tudor roses were woven into it – huge, almost as wide as the carpet, and repeating, perfectly, all the way up.

Up those stairs were the king's chambers. The king.

I kept my head down.

'Is His Grace lodging within?' I asked. For effect, I removed my cap and held it in my left hand. 'Will he see me now?'

'See you?' The usher, a round little man in the king's own livery, stopped just as he was passing the foot of the staircase. 'Certainly not. His Grace is at work. His secretary, Mr Audley, has been told of your coming.'

Ugh.

I could see the thin, black-clad ghost whispering in Wolsey's ear. 'Will he see me, then?'

'Certainly not. Mr Secretary Audley is at work.'

Oh, for fu—

'Then where are you taking me?' I snapped, jamming my cap back on. He didn't answer and resumed his sedate march onwards. I followed, muttering to myself now, as he turned right into a doorway.

I gasped.

Great halls were nothing new to me. Hampton Court had one. York Place had one. Even, I remembered with a chill, the temporary palace erected at Guisnes, when the king had met with King Francis, had had four. Still, it had been some time since I'd set foot in such a place.

The ceiling soared overhead, carved in a honeycomb of wooden beams, with brightly painted medallions and designs painted in each recess. The space was wide, vast, and echoing with the chatter of dozens, maybe hundreds, of voices. The usher did not break his pace. He walked me right down to the lower middle of the hall, away from the end which boasted the raised wooden king's dais with its highly polished thrones of estate under their cloth-of-gold canopies.

'Here,' he said.

'What?' I asked. I was still tasting the splendour, already feeling it, like the first sip of heavily sweetened wine.

He kicked at a straw-bed on the floor. 'Your lodgings. You're well favoured, I see.' He gave me a look up and down. 'Mr Audley will see you in the morning. Be sure you're washed. That collar turned down. And that sleeve tidy. You look like you've ridden here in a day.'

Close, I thought. I'd left London on the barge at first light.

Still, the fellow was looking at me with distaste. He turned away and busied himself somewhere in the room, returning with two black strips of leather. 'Wear these,' he said. 'You're not on the road now.'

He handed me the soft leather and hurried off, back down the hall in the direction of the gallery. I sighed. The air was heavy, full of drink and laughter. I looked about for Mark, or even Harry, for they would be sleeping somewhere in this place too.

Just like the old days.

But I couldn't see them. And a strange kind of shyness had crept upon me. Despite the feeling of homecoming, of returning, I was out of place. I belonged here and yet I didn't. The faces had changed, so many of them, even if this part of the hall was the cardinal's men's lodgings. Wolsey's service had moved on in my absence. The fellows would be laughing and gossiping about things, people, about which I knew nothing.

I kicked off the shoes I'd put on in the morning without even thinking about them. Good, solid shoes, not a far cry from boots. I really was back in courtly life now, I thought, looking at them, in all their muddy, flaky shabbiness. Normal things, good for London and good enough even for the cardinal's house. They were like stiff little cages for my feet, meant to keep the world out. But the things I'd been handed – they were like the slippers of the nobility: gentle gloves meant to embrace the foot and keep the softness in. And the king – he would have softer things yet – kidskin. Every step he took must feel like his feet were being kissed.

I bedded down, keeping on just my shirt, amidst the farts and snores and belches of a hundred men. Just as I used to do.

★ ★ ★

Washed at the communal ewer – well, the bits that showed – and back in my livery, which I deigned to brush down, I found myself standing before Mr Audley the next morning, in a wainscoted chamber in the block of apartments across from the great royal lodgings. Though there was a seat, the man stood, looking prim and gaunt, his hands clasped behind his back.

'Anthony Blanke,' he said, in his low, dusty voice. 'You have returned, as I was told.'

'Yes, sir. I slept well,' I lied. His dark eyebrow arched; he hadn't asked and didn't care.

'His Grace was pleased to hear that you are unharmed. Mark the trumpet told him of your accident.'

Accident, I thought.

Started already, have we?

'Yes,' I said. And then, because I didn't like him, I said, 'I drew the bastard away from the court, though. Good service, I think.'

To my surprise – my horror – Audley smiled. It was unpleasant, as though he'd seen others do it but had never quite mastered the act himself. 'Did you, though, Anthony Blanke? Did you?'

'What?' I asked.

Audley's chin rose, his forked beard twitching. 'Perhaps, briefly, you did. Yet there have been troubles. Worrying troubles. Regarding His Grace's coming masque.'

My blood froze. That infernal itching began, across my chest this time. 'Not another murder,' I said.

'No,' he said tightly, his eyes boring into me. 'Not another accident of that nature. Yet others. Touching the said masque. And it has riled the craftsmen's wild prentices, ungovernable mercenaries – they brawl amongst each other more than ever. His Grace has had a time preventing the ugly nature of these outrages reaching His Majesty.

They would interest the king much. Trouble him in his mind.'

Then cancel it! Stop it! Put an end to it!

Even as I thought it, my mind rebelled. I didn't want to be in the stupid masque – it could be discarded, for all I cared. But this Caledon creature apparently wished it to be; his goal, I thought, was to bury all talk of King Henry having come – *blood lineally descending* – from the ancient kings. And to hell with what the bastard who had attacked me desired.

'What's happened?'

Audley shrugged. 'Some sacrileges. Wicked pranks and japes.'

'What like?' I asked. And then, 'I have to speak to the cardinal. I discovered – Mr Audley, I found what our murderer has been doing. The birds, the boar mask – did Mark tell him about that? The powder that looked like sulphur. He's working from a book of prophecies. He's making them come true. I don't know why. I need to speak to the cardinal. I need to get to a library – is there a library here? I need that book.'

Audley stepped backwards, as though I'd run mad. 'Peace. You speak wildly.' I had succeeded, I thought, in confusing him – though I hadn't meant to. 'A book? Library?' I watched as he regained control, his brow unknitting, his jaw regaining its usual, in-drawn, taut lines. 'I shall speak with His Grace. I will see if we might have some more fitting man to consider . . . books.'

Anger flared. Once, I might have squashed it. 'You don't approve of me, do you?' I asked. 'In His Grace's service. You don't like it.'

Blandness met me.

'It is not for me to question His Grace's desires. I approve or disapprove of nothing. You will now come with me.'

He glided smoothly past me, his robes coming close to my new shoes but not touching them. Opening the door himself, he sailed on. I followed.

Through the lodgings we went, with Audley only stopping when he came to an open door from which angered voices carried. 'Here,' he said. And then he began moving back in the direction from which he'd come.

I stepped into the chamber: a tall, well-windowed room with rush matting on the floor. Three men were arguing in conference at the far end, whilst closer to me gaggles of younger men – apprentice craftsmen, inferior music-men cradling lutes, the sly-eyed fool, clerks, and tumblers – were following their masters' leads, their fists upraised.

I kept my head low and my cuff down as I slid towards Lutini, Cornish, and Gosson. Their argument was taking place against a strange backdrop, I noticed: no tapestry or wall hanging, nor even one of Gosson's painted scenes, but a tawny cloth.

'The Black *Knight!*' said Cornish. He had been in the middle of saying something else as his gaze fell on me. I said nothing. Across the room, his slack-jawed fool, Patch, began repeating the words, with the same inflection. Cornish ignored him. 'Isn't it just wicked, wicked, *wicked*? I do believe there is some *curse* raining down on us. Some *dread* affliction!'

I didn't answer him, but my interest must have shown on my face. Gosson looked at me as though I were a devil, as though I'd been causing whatever mischief had happened in my absence. Rather than speaking, he pulled away the tawny sheet from whatever it was covering.

A great red dragon reared up in a cloud of vinegary stink.

Part of a painted scene, the beast was rampant, yellow, orange, and red flames licking outwards from between white fangs. It growled and roared silently against the background of the huge canvas: a swirl of rolling green fields dotted with trees, looking far out of kilter in comparison to the size of the monster attacking them. Something about its eyes drew me. They were bright yellow, with black slits; they seemed to be staring right back at me. They seemed, for a moment, to be telling me something.

Dragons . . .

I was still looking when Cornish began whining, 'My dragon! My *beautiful* dragon! Ruined!'

I could see what he meant.

In the middle of the beast's belly were several gaping, ragged tears, the canvas strips flapping down like windless pennants.

'It was this way this morning,' growled Gosson. 'The beast strikes again. My red dragon torn in pieces.'

Lutini spoke. I looked at him, at the soft brown eyes and gentle brown curls. I resisted the urge to turn and look at his lute players. 'There has been much, huh? Such . . . what is your word? Desecrations.'

'My fair copy *stolen* on the way from Hampton Court,' cut in Cornish. 'It was found *drowned* in the moat there, *ruined* by Thames water.' The brute has some taste, then, I thought. 'A fire, dear boy, a *fire* was set in the parklands. A whole fair *tree* burnt. His Grace had three men despatched to York for wagging their tongues that some dark devilry was at work.' I said nothing. Doubtless, there would be some prophecies about burning trees and destructive Thames water. Still, the prophecies were coming true, in their fashion. Still, this creature was making them come true.

But why, when hardly anyone would understand their meanings?

'It is bad,' said Lutini. 'Most bad. My men, they not wish to work. Not with these other untameable creatures threatening violence. Every man say, why is this not brought before the king?' He cast a look at the apprentices and servants attached to Gosson and Cornish.

'Hmph,' shrugged Gosson. 'It is me and my men must make good.' He turned from us, frowning at the painting. 'It is my work now wounded. Such expense wasted.'

I focused on Lutini, as Cornish began whimpering some nonsense about dark forces at work. 'No one saw anything?' I asked.

'*Non*. Nothing.'

'Some creature. Comes in the night,' said Gosson, returning his attention to me. A mute agreement seemed to have passed between us to ignore the Revels Master. The painter's eyes narrowed.

'Ay,' I said, meeting his suspicion evenly. 'And in London too.'

'He kills the scholar. He kills Monsieur Visser. Who he come for next, huh?' Lutini looked at Gosson. 'You?' And then me. 'You, huh?'

He already has.

'He means to ruin your masque,' I said, trying to look at three faces at once. 'He means to stop it, maybe. To silence talk of the king's descent from King Arthur.'

'Huh?' asked Lutini.

I suspected that, as one, the trio had considered this before and were now putting up their guards. No one wished to speak of politics. Still less, I thought, working my tongue in my cheek as I stared at the Frenchman, a man whose king would have the motive to send an agent, and who had once been a servant of a Scotch king who was as good – or bad – as the French.

'We shall not stop,' said Gosson, breaking the awkward silence. 'We go on. I have no fear of ghosts. Bad spirits.' He put out his fleshy lower lip. Cornish crossed himself. 'We will have more canvas. Better. You, boy. You will tell His Grace he must open the purse. Wider.'

I gave a little shrug.

'Here is the lady, huh?' said Lutini. He was looking over my shoulder. I turned, as had every head in the room.

Sir Thomas Boleyn strode towards us, neither smiling nor frowning at anyone, ignoring the prentices and musicians who put their backs to the walls and their chins to their chests. The master craftsmen and I did likewise, only looking up as he drew near enough for us to smell his perfumed musk.

In his wake, I saw, was a girl of about my own age, with a sallow, slender neck held high. She wasn't beautiful. Her eyes were too large for her long, narrow face; but they were tilted, dark eyes, almost black, and looked up from under thick lashes. Her gown was black too, expensively so, and dark, almost black hair peeked up in a coiling braid from beneath the veil of her French hood.

'*La belle*,' said Lutini, loud enough to be heard. Boleyn silenced him with a slight widening of his eyes.

'My daughter, Mistress Anne,' he said. No 'Nan' here, I noticed – not outside of his private chamber. I supposed the other Boleyn girl must have been dropped – for whatever misdemeanour Wolsey had hinted at which might embarrass the emperor or the queen. I could imagine what it must have been, given he hadn't mentioned the king. 'I have told her that she need not attend on you. None of the other ladies or gentlemen to take part in the masque are attending, save the Moor.' He didn't look at me as he said this. 'But the Mistress Anne would have her way.'

The girl raised her chin higher. She stood, one hand down about her narrow waist, and the other on her hip. She gave only a brief look at her father before speaking. 'I would read the fair copy, if I may.'

Cornish dropped to one knee before her and reached out for her hand. She didn't give him it. 'Alas,' he said, before clucking his tongue, 'my fair copy is lost, mistress. Stolen away by some wicked fellow. And so we must rely on dance.' Realising she wasn't going to respond, he rose heavily. I could see his back stiffen. 'But of course – *you*, my dearest lady, are to be paired for dancing with the Moor. And a handsome pair you shall make, with your *night*-dark charm.' His flapping hand waved behind him.

I saw Anne's sharp eyebrows, like slashes of ink, lift. Her big eyes seemed to grow larger as the darkness pooled. And then they narrowed, her chin tilting downwards. 'A trumpet?' she asked, without expression. And then, with it, 'A trumpet?'

I saw something like smugness pass her father's face. 'As you wished, daughter, to make your presence known at this . . . this . . .' His fingers danced around the room. 'Then I shall leave you. As you have brewed, so shall you drink.' He gave her a bow and then began striding back down the room, again ignoring the sudden show of obeisance from dozens of inferior heads.

I realised two things. The coming of the girl, Anne, meant that I wouldn't be able to question Lutini about his Scotch connections, even if I could find a way of doing it subtly. And it meant that whatever conference there had been involving Wolsey and the great men must be over, for Boleyn was free of it. The cardinal would, I reasoned, thus be working on in his own chambers, reading whatever had been recorded or dictating to be written up what hadn't. I might approach him now.

Yet something kept me there, even as the craftsmen began awkwardly explaining to Anne Boleyn what was to happen, how the masque was to be staged, and what her part in it was to be. She seemed to take all of their talk of the painting, the music, and the dancing very seriously. With her little sharp baby teeth digging at her lower lip, she gave careful nods, and asked sensible questions about entrances and exits. The girl, I thought, was no fool. And she wanted, it soon became clear, a greater part than an anonymous lady trapped in and then freed from a tower to dance with a trumpet.

'I will have the foul copy, if it please you,' she said, addressing Cornish with a guileless smile.

'I'm sure,' he said, 'that we might find my lady a pretty book of poesy whilst we gentlemen attend to the work. Do you like to read, mistress?'

'People, sir, or books?' she asked. 'I perceive that you are better with one than the other.' Before he could work out her meaning, she added, 'I will read any foul copy of this masque that you have. Now, if you please. And I wish to see the guising weeds. The gowns and suchlike. I wish to see what you would have me wear. Now, if you please. It might be well that it is written to better mirror the words of *Le Morte D'Arthur.*' This she pronounced in exquisite French. 'And I will take my gown and have it amended to my father's wishes. Now, if you please.'

'Yes, mistress,' said Cornish. He wasn't smiling.

As she set the Revels Master off to his clerks with a request for a foul copy, and as Lutini and Gosson bent their heads and immediately began criticising him – accurately, I thought – I caught Anne watching his departing back.

'Night-dark looks,' she breathed. I thought, at first, that she was talking to herself; but then I realised that she was aware of me, standing close. 'I will do that fellow a mischief if it is ever in my power. I swear I will.' She half-turned, offering me one dark, glittering eye. Her nose was long, but thin and neat. 'Failing that, I should bite him.'

I smiled, careful not to let my lips spread and widen. 'I'll join you,' I said.

Her trace of a smile faded. 'Your sleeve,' she said. A little hint of disapproval coloured her words. 'It trails.'

'I . . .' My cheeks began to burn, my neck. 'I . . . my hand . . . it was damaged lately. It will heal. But until then . . .'

'Oh,' she said. 'And so you cover it.' I didn't answer her. 'Wise. Well, it seems you and I are to dance before the king. Have you danced before the king before, trumpet?'

'Before the French king,' I said, my chest rising despite the itch that would follow.

'The French king,' she echoed. 'King Francis.' A graceful hand, with incredibly long fingers, rose. She hooked one and held it before her face, just for a moment. It fell, just as that slight smile tugged again at her lips and one black eye gave a spider-lashed wink. Laughter bubbled within me. The girl had spirit, I thought, wit. And she would doubtless grow into her unusual looks in time. 'I have danced before the court before,' she said. 'And I would do so again. And I would know the steps and the measures better than any other. This is why I have come.' She sighed, looking around the room. 'A mistake.'

I could imagine her demanding to be brought to the chamber where the masquers were still preparing, assuring her father that she knew best, doubling and redoubling her efforts when he returned from the conference, ignoring his protests that no other ladies would deign to learn anything until the night itself.

'Alas,' she said, 'I am yet only young and simple.'

I said nothing. But I had the clear impression that little Mistress Anne Boleyn had been neither young nor simple since she'd been at her nurse's breast.

And I rather liked her for that.

I bowed my head. I could almost hear what Mark would say if I told him about the girl: that, again, I was tilting my cap at an unreachable maiden. 'Christ, man – first a nun and now some rich lady of the court?! You belong in the Bedlam.' I shut down the thought, even the taste of it, and looked away from Mistress Anne, right down the hall.

'I have to go,' I said. 'Cardinal's business.'

She turned on me. 'Go? Go?' Her sudden explosion brought the attention of Gosson and Lutini. 'I must know my steps, what I am to do. You cannot go.'

Swallowing, I said, 'I'm not worthy to dance with you, my lady. Yet . . . before the masque, before Winchester . . . I hope to be. Now . . . I must find the library of this great house.' I bowed. When I looked up, her irritation hadn't softened, but something else had crossed her face. Something, I thought, like a grudging approval, either of my standing up to her or my flattery. She said no more; she turned her back on me in a whirl of black velvet.

I walked away, backwards, my eyes still on her slim form, until I was near the door of the hall. I didn't hear Cornish's barked entreaties as he stood, waving pages in the air with ink-stained fingers. And then I fled, trying to push the girl out of my mind, trying to think instead of Wolsey.

And of murder.

17

Wolsey was closeted in his privy chamber with Audley. Papers were everywhere. The cardinal seemed weighted down with them. He was sitting, with documents piled on his lap, others on the settle beside him, and more scattered at his feet.

It was late in the afternoon. After leaving the masquers and the charming Boleyn girl, I'd gone immediately to the cardinal, only to find his presence chamber in the guest block packed with chaplains and secular servants. All were toasting, French fashion, the new marriage treaty that Wolsey had apparently managed to induce the two sovereigns to sign. The little Princess Mary of England was, it seemed, to marry her cousin, the emperor himself. Wolsey himself sailed in to cheers, holding his hands up like a victor at the joust, and on into his privy chamber, but the way was barred to me by his chamberlain as dozens of greater men passed in and out. Gradually, the afternoon sunlight falling in through the windows faded, turning heavy and pearly. The gilded edgings of cabinets and sideboards turned dull, the plate displayed within losing its sheen. Only then was I beckoned in.

'Anthony,' said Wolsey. He rose, the papers on his lap sliding to the carpet. Audley scurried to retrieve them without a word. 'Mm? Oh. Yes. Good man, Mr Audley.

Anthony,' he said again, raising his palms to me. 'We were most sorry to hear of your accident.' His eyes lingered for a beat on my right hand, then travelled up to my collar. The lazy one twitched under its heavy lid. The cardinal was bathed in red, his robes only loosened a little at the neck, where his white shirt collar ruffled out and thick grey hair showed. His biretta lay forgotten on the settle, half covered by paper. I had the impression that he had been drinking – heavily, even for whatever feasting might have followed the great conference. A wine bloom had spread over his cheeks. 'Have a drink, friend, to celebrate.' He nodded at Audley, who went to the sideboard and poured a trickle of wine into a silver cup. He passed it to me, but I didn't drink.

'What news out of London?' asked Wolsey. He began walking, kicking papers out of the way as he went. 'You have heard our news, I trust. England's news.'

'Yes, Your Grace.' I had the wit to incline my head, in mute thanks at his accomplishing his treaty. It was, I suddenly realised, Wolsey's day. I was a dark cloud of unpleasantness come to spoil it. 'Has . . . has Mr Audley told you of the book? The book I have to find?'

'Book?' His confusion lasted only a second. And then his whole mind seemed to clear. The boisterous, slightly drunken cheerfulness dissipated. Wolsey became his old self again. Even his eyes, which looked like they planned on matching his robes, appeared to focus. 'Yes. Yes. Quite. Hm.' His fingers danced, both hands held out before him, as though he was tickling something invisible. 'Our naughty creature. You know, I trust, that this monster has returned to court? Since his . . . assault . . . upon your person?'

'Yes, Your Grace. But now – now I know what he's doing.'

'Speak, Anthony,' said Wolsey.

I took a deep breath. I told him all that I'd discovered of the murderer's attempts to bring the prophecies of Merlin to life, and of how the book containing them might yield more. It might even, I suggested, indicate the man's next moves – how he might strike, where. 'Even the dragon – the painting – that he tore. I think – I know, Your Grace, that something like that – a torn dragon – I think it'll be in that book. He has it. Or knowledge of it. He's using it.'

Wolsey hadn't interrupted me. He moved to the fireplace and stared into the flames, agitating the sides of his robes. And then he turned. 'Why?'

'Your Grace?' I asked.

'Why? To what purpose?'

I began babbling, about the French and the Scotch, and about his desire to stop the masque from taking place. At the word 'masque', he held up a hand. Rings, three of them, glinted on his fingers.

'The masque,' he said. 'It is now more important than ever. It depicts King Arthur and his nephew. Both valiant. A loving family. And now, from today, England and Spain, king and emperor, uncle and nephew, are knit in loving amity. Both valiant. And so, in our masque, we make the tale true.'

Make the tale true.

'But . . .' I began, 'but that's what he's doing. This murderer. Making prophecies from the history of King Arthur true.'

'Hm,' said Wolsey. 'Yes.'

I was lost. I looked down at the carpet. The man was trying to stop the masque by . . . doing what the masque was doing. He was trying to silence talk of King Henry's descent from Arthur by . . . breathing new life into the old tales, the prophecies that had been forgotten by everyone save a doubting old historian in London.

And the dead man. Gonzaga.

'I don't understand,' I said. 'If he seeks to stop us, why . . . why is he bringing the prophecies to life?' A thought occurred to me. 'Is it . . . could it be . . . he stole Gonzaga's book – this book I learned about – G. Cass. Cassiodorus and the Gothi. He killed Gonzaga, stole it, and now he's . . . making people think of the old histories. Or trying to – if anyone had bothered to read that old stuff, or care about it. So that he can present his proof when it pleases him. He didn't kill, and steal it, to hide it, bury it – but to use it himself . . .' I hesitated, unwilling to say, on or behalf of some enemy of yours'.

Wolsey seemed to think of it, though, at the same time. 'By God,' he said. 'Someone seeking to do as our masque would do, and with stolen proofs discovered by our man. To outwit us. To steal our glory and triumph. An enemy. Then we are glad the king has not been troubled by these bloody displays. They might . . .' He seemed unable or unwilling to finish the thought.

I swallowed. 'An enemy within, Your Grace.'

'What?' Wolsey fixed me with a look and began to move towards me, through the lake of papers and letters.

I leaned back on my new shoes. 'Someone who can move with ease. Between your house, the court, London. Maybe . . . maybe more than one man. Visser must have seen them talking, the person behind this and . . . whoever his . . . his . . .'

'His minion,' said Wolsey, stopping, turning to Audley, who was still picking up papers. 'His familiar.' He turned to me again. 'By God's touch, young Anthony – I think you may have it. You may have it, by God. Yes. Some wicked enemy seeks to unman us. To rob us, to kill our people, and to present our own proofs of King Henry's descent. And an enterprise begun in blood will only grow bloodier.'

I only wished that I shared Wolsey's enthusiasm for my sudden suspicion.

'So,' I said, not sure what would come out, 'not the French, then, nor the Scots?' Even though I'd suggested the new theory, I was loath to give up the old one, even if didn't fit what had been happening, not fully.

'Hm? What? Oh. Yes. You say that that foul old goat Vergil said there was no proof contained in this – what was it? – this book of the Gothi?'

I lifted my chin. 'He said there wasn't any anywhere. He said . . .' I hesitated, unsure what made a treason. 'He said there never was a King Arthur so no book could prove it. But he'd never read it. He just said there was no King Arthur and that was that.'

Wolsey strung his mouth into a neat little bow. 'Goat. Old goat. Well, I'll confess that I cannot imagine what some dusty book of ancient barbarians – pagans – can tell us about the true history of King Arthur. Unless some clever monk had written in it, some fellow wise in the art of genealogy. But I shall tell you something, Anthony Blanke, of scholars. When they say that something does not exist, or has not occurred, they mean that they have not found it. And their too-little brains are no bigger than their eyes. Oh, I know Signor Vergil well enough. A man full of fine ideas who cannot conceive that he is wrong on any matter. Given denizenship in this our realm and he proceeds to make light of our history. To deny it. I call that discourtesy. Poor breeding, ay.' He had grown colourful again, as though the wine had only released the reins for a spell, not given them up.

'What shall I do?' I asked.

'Hm? Oh. Yes. Go to the library, if you will. Find this other book, this *Historia*. If Vergil is right about that, the king shall have a copy. It might tell you something, as you say. And with haste, my boy. This night. We leave,' he said, his red chest puffing, 'for Winchester on the morrow. King Arthur's ancient capital. And you and the others – craftsmen, those in service – you must ride with the foremost to ensure all is ready for Their Majesties, when the masque is performed, and the Round Table is shown on Monday . . .'

I cleared my throat. It was Thursday already. 'I thought,' I said, 'there might be something in it. Something we can use to . . . to set a snare, perhaps. Draw him out.'

'A snare?' Wolsey began drumming on his chest. A big, foolish smile, such as I'd never seen before, split his face. 'You have a cunning mind, of a sudden. I said you were no such fool as you like to be thought. It pleases a man to see he has the right of it. Yes.' The smile faded and sobriety gained a toehold. Audley, who had moved to stand by a desk covered in damask, gave a cough, his fist bunched before his face. Wolsey's eyes slid to him and he gave him a brief nod, before looking again at me. 'Yet you are no scholar, young Anthony. No. No man to read ancient prophecies and divine their meaning, their mysteries.'

'His Grace would,' said Audley, 'choose a gentleman. To aid you, at the least, in your . . . studies . . . tonight. A man built for scholarship. A learned man. I have just such a man.' He smiled.

I felt my heart sink.

18

I hadn't spent any extended time alone with Harry Gainsford since our time together in France. From my brief talks with him at Hampton Court in the last weeks, I'd found him to be polite, cold, and, in some ways, a model of his new master, the smooth Mr Audley. It had ever been Harry's way, to emulate his masters, whether father or governors. He had once had a sweetness, a gentleness about him, a mildness. Now, if that was still there, it was buried under the hard exterior of good service.

We began our walk down from the gatehouse which led to the Upper Ward. Harry had been waiting for me there; he'd merely nodded his acknowledgement and said, 'Mr Audley has told me what is afoot, Anthony. I will aid you.'

I'd known, from the moment the secretary had said he had someone in mind to help me, that it would be Harry. And I'd dreaded it. The huge, ancient round keep was a fat candle no longer but an odd, dusky giant's tomb. As we slid down the Middle Ward's cobblestones, he said, over his shoulder, 'The chaplain who keeps the king's books at Windsor is a Father Bernardo. An Italian gentleman.'

I quickened my pace.

'An Italian,' I said. My voice sounded small in the cooling summer night. 'It's getting like it's not even an English court any more.'

Harry stopped dead. Turning, he said, 'The king and His Grace, my lord cardinal, are proud to have so many fine men from the continent in their service. Men of great learning and subtle craft from the finest schools and seats of education in this realm or any.'

Jesus, Harry.

He had always had a child's sense of humour – innocent – but it had, at least, existed. 'I didn't mean to offend,' I said, sounding even smaller.

He looked at me for a moment more, his face pale and blank, and said, 'Come. The tower is this way.'

He led me on, both of us deep in the shadow of the curtain wall, and said nothing more until we reached a plain oak door cut deep into a projecting, circular tower. 'Here,' he said.

'Thank you, Harry.' His name felt odd in my mouth, like a dish I hadn't tasted in years, though I'd spoken with other Harrys here and there. He inclined his head and then tugged at the polished brass ring, beating it against the door.

It took a while, and we stood in silence, hearing ourselves breathe, until the door was pulled open. There, his hard face lit in the bloom of a candle's light, stood a small man in black. 'Good evening,' he said. The Italian lilt was heavier than old Vergil's had been.

Harry made his polite explanations for our visit: we were seeking some books urgently, for Cardinal Wolsey. Father Bernardo nodded, his candleflame guttering a little. As we went in, I asked, probably bullishly, 'Do you know, Father, if there's a book called . . . I don't know the name – a book about Gothi. The Goths. By Cassiodorus.'

He didn't break his stride; his flame kept bobbing as he led us through the round antechamber and over to a door on the right, which seemed to lead into rooms within the wall itself. He passed a squashed little featherbed without looking down. A book lay next to it, its cover closed. Evidently, we'd roused the poor fellow from his own reading. 'I do not know this name,' he said. 'We have a very small, very little, library here. Books of poesy and fancy, mostly. And religion. For the king's pleasure. The king's Master of Books, Signor Duwes, keeps the great library at Richmond.' That rang a bell. I'd heard of the library at Richmond much these past weeks. My hopes hadn't been high anyway. Vergil had said he'd no notion of the book even still existing, and he was a royal scholar, or had been. He hadn't known Southwark had had a copy. And besides, every book in the world of any age was unique – even copies. As Wolsey had said, whatever was in the one Gonzaga had taken, it might have been the labour of some monk in the last hundred, the last two hundred, the last thousand years.

It only really struck me then.

The book had not been stolen to be destroyed, according to my new pet theory. The murderer had taken it. If he was a puppet, working on orders or with another man at least, one of the two would have it still – they'd have taken it from Gonzaga, killed him, and now have it hidden somewhere for their own use.

Someone had it.

And if it was only hidden, then it might be found.

Beyond the door, the library was a long, rectangular chamber, with books stacked, as I'd seen them everywhere, on their sides, their page-edges facing outward, some painted gold. They sat in cabinets and even on wooden shelves placed against the walls. 'We come,' said Harry, as Father Bernardo began applying his flame to braziers, set well away from the books, 'for a volume of – of – what was it, Anthony, the book?'

I swallowed. I had said the name a thousand times in my head. I pronounced it slowly. *'Historia. Regum. Britanniae.* By . . .'

Goddamit!

'Geoffrey of Monmouth,' finished Harry. 'Yes, I have heard of it. You have it, Father?'

'The old history, yes,' he said. 'The elder copies – originals, I think – are at Richmond. But copies, yes.'

'With the prophecies of Merlin?' I asked. I couldn't recall the name in Latin.

'Yes, I believe so,' said the chaplain. He set down his candle in its dish and shuffled off, humming quietly.

'Have you read it?' I asked Harry.

'No. I have read *Le Morte D'Arthur.'* I nodded; I had too. Wolsey owned several copies of the old romance of King Arthur, translated into modern English from French or the old language or whatever it had been: there were printed copies at Hampton Court and York Place, retitled *The Hoole Book of Kyng Arthur and of His Noble Knyghtes of The Rounde Table*, too. One of the great injunctions of his – not followed by everyone in service – was that his men should read, and these were preferable to devotional texts. That was where I'd gained what knowledge I retained of King Arthur, Guinevere, Camelot, and the whole saga. 'That is all anyone reads of the old history, unless they are making some special study of it.'

Making some special study of it . . .

'Here,' said the priest, shaking me out of my thoughts. He was padding back towards us with a large book in his hands.

It was about the length of a forearm, but not very thick. Nevertheless, Harry immediately leapt over the scrubbed tile floor to help him with it.

'*Grazie*,' he grunted. 'You said the prophecies of Merlin?'

'Yes,' I said, 'yes!'

'This contains them. This is the seventh book of the *Historia*. The one few men read. The other books, we have those too. We have all twelve, as at Richmond. Do you wish them?'

'No,' I said.

'Perhaps later,' said Harry.

He and I took the thing over to a lectern set between two shelves, and then pulled a brazier closer. Its light danced on the plain green leather cover of the book. There was no title marked on it; the leather itself was old, pressed and discoloured. The stuffed lizard which hung in the apothecary's shop in Aldgate swung into my mind and as quickly retreated.

Harry opened it – it moved stiffly – to the first page. Here, on the yellowed paper, was the title: *Libellus Merlini*. It was written in ancient script, the sweeping letters edged in faded gold leaf. Underneath it was an unpainted illustration of a crowned and robed man with a beard, beckoning to the reader.

'The book of Merlin,' said Harry.

As he began turning pages, my excitement faded. The writing was, I realised, in an old form of English I couldn't understand. Harry, however, began sounding it out, reading it, until the sounds made sense, took shape, became words and carried meaning.

Within fifteen minutes, we had begun a means of

working, with the help of papers, inkpot and quill from the obliging Father Bernardo. Pulling another lectern over, I set up the writing equipment. As Harry read from the book, I began to write my understanding of it in English. The idea was that I shouldn't write every word, every prophecy or line, but only those which either explained what I had seen or seemed potentially of use in what our murderer might do.

Excitement rose as he read beyond the introductory verses.

' . . . two dragons, one of which was white, the other red, came forth—'

'Dragons!' I called, making Harry jump. I leant to the side of my lectern, over to his, and, sure enough, there was a coloured drawing of a red dragon, locked in battle with a white one. The ruined painting rose in my mind.

'Yes,' said Harry, nonplussed. 'The red dragon is well known as a great symbol of heraldry. It was used by the king's father, the late king, and—'

'I know about that,' I said, regretting my tone. More softly, I said, 'Sorry. Read on.'

Harry cleared his throat, a little primly, I thought, and continued. ' . . . approaching one another, began a terrible fight, and cast forth fire with their breath . . .'

My pen darted from inkpot to page, hurriedly copying out, 'the redde and whyte drakons came foorth . . .'

The going was slow. The writing was tedious. Soon my wrist began to ache. I could only write with my right hand and I had no choice but to fold back the cuff, blessing the weak light. Maybe, I thought, it wasn't as bad as I'd thought after all. I stared awhile, trying to judge, before forcing my attention back to the page. After I'd managed a page of script,

I called Harry to a halt and reread it. 'This is wearying,' I said. 'I can see why no one reads this any more.'

'If what you say is true,' said Harry, 'someone has.'

Chastised, I began writing as he resumed his reading. But I would put down only what was of value.

The long evening ground onwards, with Father Bernardo refreshing the lights. There were moments of heart-tickling victory and my pages began to fill with them:

From Conan shal procede a warlike boar that shal exercise the sharpneff of hys tusks withyn the Gallic woods for he shal cut downe all the larger oaks and shalbe a defence to the smaller. The Arabians and Africannes shal dred hym.

Well done, Signor Vergil, I thought. Thus was explained my attacker. The bastard.

It shal gyve sustenaunce to byrds of foreyn nacions

The unfortunate Signor Gonzaga, I thought, ended by doing just that.

I was still looking down at my writing, careless of my hand, when I noticed that Harry had stopped reading.

'Go on,' I said. 'We'll find the rest. This is what he's done. There'll be more. Vergil said the book mentions the sulphurous steps and – I'll wager there's something about torn dragons and whatever else this bastard's been doing.'

'I'm sorry about your hand,' he said.

My mouth dried. 'It's nothing. It'll heal.'

'Yes,' he said. 'I am certain of it.'

He took a gulp of air. Silence reigned between us. I shuffled my thoughts, trying to find the right words, looking at him from the corner of my eyes.

'I'm sorry—'

'I am sorr—'

We had both said it, the same words, at the same time.

'Ha! You first,' I said quickly.

Harry stood back from his lectern. One hand rested on the edge. He wasn't looking at me any more but off into the shadow. 'I am sorry, Anthony, that we have not spoken in this long time. I could not . . . I did not . . .'

'I might've written too,' I said. 'I thought you must be busy.' That was a lie and I felt sorry for that as well.

He turned his head to me. 'I was. After you left His Grace's service, I sought to fashion myself a better servant. A good man. A trusted man.'

This was easy enough to imagine. It was all Harry ever seemed to wish for – to be a good, trusted servant. I wished I might put out my hand to him. But I didn't. Instead, I said, 'You are. A good man. Trusted man, I mean.' I swallowed. 'I'm sorry about your father.' There. His father had died years before, and I'd never said nor written a word to him about it.

His face blanched. He stared off. I shivered a little as I saw hardness and sadness wrestle for control of his soft features. Eventually, he looked back to me. He returned my smile, without much humour or warmth. 'I thank you.' The hardness fled his voice. 'I was sorry that you left. That you went off to make your way.'

I bit at my lip. 'Well, I didn't make much of a . . . I mean, I'm back now. Like it was before – me, and you, and Mark. All friends in service. Making our way together.'

'Yes,' he said. He recovered. The little display of warmth was suddenly guarded again, the walls rising. It was tiring, being with a courtly gentleman. 'Quite. And this is not the time to discuss the past, times past. We are set to work on His Grace's business. Shall I read again?'

I nodded, flexing my hand, ignoring the sting and ache as I reached for the quill.

He turned a page, his face set, and his eyes began moving before his lips. 'Sweet Jesus. Anthony!'

I turned to him, blinking. Harry Gainsford didn't swear, didn't curse. He was, as I'd known and loved him, the wettest creature on the earth. 'What? It doesn't say that, does it?'

He licked his lips. 'Listen. Oh, my blessed soul, Anthony – listen!' He took another breath and began reading, his voice suddenly animated. 'Three springs shall break forth in the city of Winchester.'

Winchester!

'Winchester!'

'Listen!' he hissed. I did, dropping my quill, letting ink spoil what I'd already written. 'Three springs shall break forth in the city of Winchester, whose rivulets shall divide the island into three parts. Whoever shall drink of the first shall enjoy long life and shall never be afflicted with sickness. He that shall drink of the second shall die of hunger and paleness and horror shall sit in his countenance. He that shall drink of the third shall be surprised with sudden death. Neither shall his body be capable of burial.'

My veins chilled with the words. Harry stepped back from the book, as though it had turned toxic. 'Winchester,' I said. 'We go there on the morrow.' It hit me suddenly. 'Christ, Harry.'

'Language.'

I gave a hard headshake. 'No – it's . . . the king, Winchester. These prophecies that have been coming true. They're not for me. Not for us. Never were. How should I know the prophecies of bloody Merlin. These murders – they've been meant for the king. Meant to reach his ears. He'd know, as soon as he heard – as soon as he heard about Gonzaga . . . or stolen books and sulphur . . . or me, if I'd been killed in London . . .' I closed my eyes. If one of Wolsey's servants had been burned to death in a room with prophetical words marked on the wall, no one could have prevented King Henry hearing. So strange a crime would have been sung so loudly in the streets it couldn't not have been heard in Windsor. 'The king's ear's sought. The king's eye.'

Harry digested this; I could almost see his mind working. 'Yet . . . His Grace has kept matters close.' He looked away from me. 'Mr Audley has been getting reports from His Majesty's household. Men employed there . . . to silence any bruits. To stop rumours reaching the king.'

His Majesty shall not be troubled. If he is, I shall know the source.

I nearly laughed. There was I, caught between a murderer seeking the king's attention and the cardinal dancing his hands before Henry's eyes. Fighting hysteria, I said, 'My God. God. This murderer – he's been hoping the king would hear of these murders and think of the prophecies coming true. And all along His Grace has been stopping him – without even knowing he was thwarting him.' All traces of wild humour sank. 'But he won't be stopped. Not at Winchester. Not with the king riding in himself.'

Harry swallowed. 'Some spectacle at the town. We must

take this book. We must show Mr Audley and the cardinal. If this creature has made the other things come true . . . If this is the plat from which he constructs his . . . his outrages . . .' He didn't need to finish.

'Let's go,' I said.

Father Bernardo made no objection to our taking the book – so long, he said, as he might mark our names, the cardinal, and the title of the book in his ledger. We left him doing just that and fled into the night, the book of prophecies tucked under Harry's arm. I had left my pages. They were, I decided, useless. They proved only what I knew; that the murderer was bringing to life the words in the book. It was those he hadn't yet conjured into the world that were important now.

Out and along the curtain wall we went, uphill towards the Upper Ward. We didn't go towards the royal lodgings, and the guards, their halberds resting against the walls of the gate, ignored us. Instead, we darted across the cobbled courtyard – a place of industry in the day, but eerie silence by night. Light shone down from the moon. Still more danced wildly from the windows of the pale royal apartments behind and above us and the block ahead, where Wolsey was sleeping – or working, as was his custom. Carts stood everywhere, their humped backs laced up with ropes. Much of the court would be ready for the ride to Winchester; the first carts and barrows would doubtless be set on the road before dawn, as the cardinal always was.

Please be up. You're always up; you don't sleep!

There were lights spilling from the windows above, too, the southern range being as packed with Englishmen, Spaniards, and everyone else as the main building. As we made to enter the gateway, a lone royal guard stood forward.

He had been there when we'd left, but still he seemed suspicious, drawn by the fact that we carried something.

'What's this, lads, wenching?' he asked, his eyes on the book. 'What's that?'

'A book for the cardinal,' Harry said. 'His Grace would have it forthwith.' He held it flat before him.

The guard, suddenly, became disinterested. 'Book. Hmph. Book of homilies, I 'ope. Not no naughty stuff.'

Harry drew up. 'How dare you, sirrah. His Grace is a man of God. I will not—'

Not now!

I was still thinking that when I realised that Harry had stopped speaking. The guard wasn't saying anything either. 'What is—' My own voice died in my throat.

A spot of something had dropped onto the cover of the book. Another joined it. They pooled, spread, and joined, a stray – *rivulet* – escaping and making for the edge. Some light from inside the gateway bloomed – a door opening or closing – and the wetness shone red.

I was still looking, still trying to make sense of it – *rain?* – when a torrent fell, drenching me in redness, in horror, in blood.

19

The three of us stood dumbly, blinking. Blood dripped from the rim of my cap. It had squashed the small white feather in Harry's hat and splashed upwards, spattering our hose. Even the guardsman had not escaped; his jaw was hanging slackly, and the front of his white-and-green livery had fingers of darkness streaking up it.

And then, as one, we looked up.

A window above us stood open. There was no one looking down.

Whoever it was had evidently waited for our return and then poured the blood over our heads.

From what?

From whom?

Time seemed to grow sluggish. The guardsman began swearing, cursing, saying something about foul pranks and wicked knaves. But he made no effort to move. He was shaking his head, still swearing, when I said, 'Up there. Now.'

Harry was rooted to the cobbles. His white face was streaked with blood and his eyes were huge in it. 'What . . . what . . .' The book was clutched in his hand. I tugged at it, trying to rouse him, and he pulled back. And then he began wiping the cover with a sleeve. 'Paint,' he said. 'Someone has spilled paint.'

'This isn't paint,' I hissed. 'He's upstairs!'

'Paint,' said Harry, petulantly. And then he seemed to see me. 'Upstairs.'

'Come on!'

I grabbed his wet sleeve and pulled, and together we pushed past the guard. He made no effort to stop us. From the broad antechamber, we darted through a series of plain rooms with wooden screens – servants' rooms. Here and there men were lying on pallets, their doublets folded as pillows. I had no clear idea of where I was going. The southern block was where Wolsey kept his rooms; it was where the masquers had been at work; I'd heard Spanish voices coming from men in foreign liveries as I'd moved about the place. What else it housed, especially at night, I had no idea.

On the first floor, we left the staircase and passed into a narrow hallway. The square, leaded windows revealed the courtyard. The open window had only been one floor up; it was here, I thought – there!

Partway down the hall, the window gaped.

He was here! Moments ago – here!

I realised I was still holding on to Harry. Nor did I release him. He followed me, mumbling to himself, heedless of my fingers tight around the stained sleeve of his shirt.

Is he still here?

As we neared the window, something took shape on the polished floorboards. A little mound, I thought, dark; the hallway was unlighted. In the low shafts of weak light which knifed their way in from the courtyard, it began to look round.

I stopped before it and nudged it with the slipper of my now-filthy leather shoe.

It was, I saw, a bucket. It rolled in a semi-circle, coming to rest against the wall, right beneath the window, with a soft tap. For the first time, I noticed the smell. It was foul and coppery. My stomach rebelled, sending vomit up my gullet. I swallowed it down and forced myself to bend. Picking up the bucket, I looked inside. The smell was deeper, stronger, and I dropped it, turning my head to the open window and sucking at the night air. Then I looked down. We were directly above the gateway indeed, and there was the round, silvery helmet of the guard. It was replaced suddenly by his face as he looked up. 'You find 'im? Damned naughty pup,' he called up, one hand cupped around his mouth. And then, more quietly, 'This is blood what 'e's thrown!'

I ignored him, pulling the window in but not quite closing it. I needed the cool air about me.

Harry was quivering, holding the book to his doublet. I ignored him, looking up and down the hall. Opposite the window, a series of doors were set. I'd no idea what they led to, whether storerooms or lodgings. But Wolsey's room and the large room in which I'd met Mistress Boleyn were above us. I looked down again at the bucket. Where the blood had come from, I couldn't say; but at least there was no corpse here, no bleeding body.

'We should see the cardinal,' I said. My voice, though low, carried in the long hallway.

'The cardinal,' said Harry. 'Yes.'

He followed me as I returned to the narrow staircase and passed it, going to the set of stairs next to it – the ones which led up. The air around us became noisier as we drew closer to Wolsey's rooms.

The presence chamber was quieter than when we'd left it, though a few men still lingered by the huge fireplace, looking devilish in its dancing flames. Household officers, they were: the chamberlain, ushers, and even a couple of chaplains. All seemed a little drunk, laughing and passing around wineskins. They ignored us, but I tried to keep my back to them as I passed through the large room, which was thankfully lit only by the fire.

At the door to the privy chamber, Harry finally seemed to come around a little. 'We cannot,' he said. 'We cannot.' I reached to tug at his elbow again and he pulled away. 'We are begrimed.'

I opened my mouth to argue and then shut it, turning to the door. I rapped softly.

When it was opened, I saw the black outline of Audley. He was in a nightshirt, with a sable mantle over his shoulders. If the state of undress robbed him of his superiority, the mantle and his frown restored it. The room beyond him was well lit with candles and braziers. I could see that he had tidied it; the mess of documents had been ordered. I couldn't see Wolsey, who must, indeed, have retired to his bedchamber beyond. There was no hope of reaching him there: it was a space fit only for himself and his body attendants.

'What is this?' hissed Audley. And then, as though realising, he asked, 'By God. Are you hurt? Were you attacked?' He was looking at Harry, not me.

'The murderer,' I said. 'He . . . he dropped blood down on us. From a window. A bucket of blood.'

'Sweet Jesus,' said the secretary. He raised his hand, rubbing his chin between thumb and forefinger. 'Did you see him?'

'He was gone,' I said, 'by the time we got up. Gone. Again. But he's in this place somewhere. He's here.'

Audley appeared to consider this. 'As you said. An enemy within.'

'Might we speak to His Grace?' I asked.

Audley drew up. 'Certainly not. His Grace is abed. And you are begrimed.'

Harry's back snapped up. He nodded, military-style. 'Yes, Mr Audley. You are quite right.'

'But—' I began.

'Wash yourselves well and sleep. The great train leaves at dawn,' said Audley. 'This blood, you say, from a bucket?' I nodded, too eagerly. 'Then we must pray that he drew it from no man. Go, now, to the great hall with His Grace's other people. Wash and sleep. I will inform His Grace of this accident in the morning. Who else saw this outrage?'

'Only the guardsman, sir,' said Harry.

Audley stared, unblinking, for a moment. 'Good. I shall instruct the palace guard that if word reaches the king, he shall be the sorrier. Or you shall be, of course.'

Before I could say anything, Harry said, 'Yes, sir. Goodnight to you.'

The door closed on us.

Already, Harry was marching away behind me. Still, I stood looking at the door, cursing Audley, cursing Wolsey, cursing the creature who had been waiting on us.

Who had known, I realised, who we were and where we had been.

Turning my back on Wolsey's privy chamber, I hurried after Harry. He said nothing as we descended down the two flights of stairs and ignored the guardsman as we left the southern range and moved across the courtyard, between the humped carts and wagons. The royal guards, recognising our liveries, did not comment on the reeking stains. They were drying now, anyway. I wondered if they had seen the attack, seen the window opening across the way and the man leaning out. But I supposed not. The distance was too great, and the yard was heaving, crowded with goods.

When we reached the great hall, tiredness descended. As it had been before, the place was packed with sleeping servants: gentlemen, pages, chamberers, belonging to just about everyone with the power to command. Harry said, 'The ewer will be foul. With so many people.'

'Can't make us any fouler than what we are,' I said. A ghost of a smile passed his lips, and he reached up to clap my arm. Even his hand, I could see in the low light, was coated in the ugly stains that blood leaves, flaking and patchy. He left me, taking the book with him, and stepped between bundles and sleeping people as he made his way to the gentlemen's area at the top of the hall.

I, for my part, huddled around the middle ewer, and scrubbed at myself, my back to the sleepers. Pain danced across me, through me, but I was heedless of it. The smell of blood weakened, becoming watery. The water in the ewer darkened as I dipped my hands in; the dried blood regained its potency in it, spreading outwards.

When I was clean enough – my doublet had protected the front of my shirt, at least – I found an empty spot on the floor and bedded down.

I tried to think, as I lay amongst the rushes, of where a bucket of blood might be found. Where a bucket might be found. The smell invading the great hall from beyond, of smoke and baking bread and roasting meats, dulled my wits. Surely I had seen buckets in use? Yes. At some point. Somewhere. I nearly had it . . .

Sleep claimed me before I could grasp it.

★ ★ ★

I woke without realising I'd even slept. My sleep, if such it was, was somewhere between a doze and a blink. And I would be allowed no more. Something was jabbing, carefully, at my left side.

'Up, you!'

'Harry?' I asked. My mouth was sticky. I'd drooled on my hand. Rushes were stuck to my back, broken now and scentless.

'Do I sound like the gentle Mr Harry Gainsford?'

I opened my eyes properly. 'Mark.' I blinked crusted sleep from my eyes. He was there, towering over me. The sight of him got me moving; I hated being caught unawares, caught cringing about on the floor when others were up around me.

And the great hall, I saw, was rising – although the windows were admitting only a greyish light. The smell, which had been brewing when I'd first lain down, was stronger.

I got to my knees, taking Mark's hand as he held it out and dragged me up.

'Here, you stink.'

'Good morrow to you too,' I said. He was right, though. 'Can you find me something clean? Hose, doublet, shirt – clean?'

He shrugged, nodded, and disappeared into the thicket of men dressing, men laughing, men washing, and men arguing. When he returned, he wasn't alone. Harry was striding before him.

'Anthony,' he said. His shock had worn off. Worry lines were etched on his straight brow. 'You must hear this.'

I looked over his shoulder at Mark. Harry seemed to notice him too. 'It's only Mark,' I said. 'He knows everything.'

Harry accepted this with a nod. Mark stepped around him, handing me the fresh clothing. I made no effort to put it on; I wouldn't change in front of them. 'Go on,' I said to Harry.

'I could not sleep,' he said, 'when I lay down to rest. After . . . after our attack.'

'Attack?' asked Mark. 'Pardon me, sir,' he said, touching his cap. 'But . . . attack?'

I quickly told him what had happened. 'For Christ's sake,' was his answer to it.

'But listen,' said Harry. 'Mark me.' He seemed to realise his unintentional wit. 'Mark me – Mark – mark.' Neither of us smiled and a blush blossomed over his cheeks. 'Hear me,' he said. 'It shall rain a shower of blood, and a raging famine shall afflict mankind.'

Mark whistled. 'And that's from this book you both found?'

'Yes,' Harry said. 'Right there in the prophecies.'

I said nothing. I wasn't surprised.

'Shouldn't be messing with no prophecies,' said Mark. 'A bad business, that. He'll get no good of it.'

'You're right,' I said. 'He won't.'

'I must go,' said Harry. 'Mr Audley will be expecting me. I

must report all that has passed properly. Before we begin the great journey.'

I nodded. The great journey to Winchester, I thought. Where a prophecy foretold death. As though reading my thoughts, Harry added, 'I shall show Mr Audley the writings against Winchester. He will know what to do. He will inform His Grace.' He nodded the truth of his words – or the sincerity of his belief in them, at least. And then he gave us a slight bow. Mark doffed his cap to him, and I made a vague gesture towards my bare head.

When he'd disappeared into the crowd, Mark said, 'He's an odd one, him.' I didn't answer this. 'Anyway, you get yourself washed and ready. I'll have to stay back. Cardinal's going with the rear. With the king and all them lot. Everyone else to go ahead, make sure everything's clean and sweet for when they arrive.' A thought struck him. 'Ay, and that masque you're in – the parts all to be, uh, assembled, in the castle there. For Monday, ain't it?'

I adjusted the bundle in my arms. 'Mark, do you know who stays over in the lodgings across the way? Overnight, I mean. Who sleeps there?'

Mark flipped his cap off and scratched behind his pink-tipped ear. 'Over there. Lot of Spaniards, Flemings, Frenchies. All the foreigners. And the cardinal. His officers, secretaries, craftsmen, their prentices. It's just us lot in here. English, I mean. Gentlemen and lowers. Those what don't get their own space. You just know the foreigners'd start fights if we had to lie abed with them. Animals. Here, I heard some lads was going to give them a bit of sport, like they did at Hampton.'

'What?'

'Ah, that's right. You hadn't come back yet.' Mark rubbed at his chin. 'Them foreign lot. Some of our boys had a bit of fun with 'em. One gobbed his spit in their beer. Oh, ay – and one lad – dunno how he did it, mind – he got all their pallets stuffed with dried turds. Scooped right out the middens. Showing them Frenchies and Dutch or whatever they is whose house it is.'

'Jesus, Mark,' I said. I felt my colour rise, felt my cheeks darken. I could imagine, to be sure: foreigners – or people who looked foreign, or sounded foreign, or acted foreign – had to endure much. Even in great houses – especially in great houses – the native folks liked to let them know how hated they were. I'd been the butt of other people's jokes in the past, never meant kindly – if pranks *could* ever be meant kindly.

'I didn't do nuffink,' said Mark, shifting his gaze to the floor.

'Right,' I said. I forced my mind away from the thought of foreigners, from the arrows they faced. 'Damn it. I should have lifted that bucket. Kept it.' It was evidence of something. Probably, by now, it would have been carried away either by the murderer or by some unwitting domestic.

'Here,' said Mark. He snapped his fingers in my face when I didn't answer. 'Anthony!'

'What?' I asked. I'd been staring at nothing.

'Tried the kitchen?'

My stomach rumbled. 'Kitchen,' I said. 'I could eat. Should.'

'I'm not thinking of your belly, you ass,' he said. I frowned at him. 'A bucket of blood?'

'What about it?'

Mark sighed, rolling his eyes to the medallions on the ceiling. 'Jesus save me from asses. If there ain't no dead man you've found, the blood had to come from somewhere.' I shrugged, still not smiling, not understanding. 'The kitchens. They slaughter all kinds.'

'I . . . and they keep the blood?'

He shrugged. 'I had an uncle once, when I was a little lad.' He mimed swinging an axe. 'Butcher. I remember buckets of blood. Maybe made puddings or something with it. I don't know.'

My mouth fell open. 'Mark – that's it. You've a genius spirit to you today.'

'Every day,' he said, having another scratch. 'Born with it.'

'Come on!' I began pushing my way towards the ewer. 'He's not so clever as we are. We'll have him yet.'

* * *

The great kitchens at Windsor lay across a spacious courtyard – the unimaginatively titled Kitchen Court – from the great hall. The yard itself was cobbled, and channels were dug into it, criss-crossing everywhere, to carry away the vast amounts of waste the kitchens must produce. They ran now with a watery mix of vegetable peelings, bones, and the scum skimmed from the top of pottages. Thankfully, their smell was masked by the good, hearty smell of roasting flesh and stewing fruits, seasoned with the yeasty undertone of baking bread and brewing ale. Hopping over the channels was a small army of boys, some of them stripped down to their breeches, carrying dishes and trays, some empty and some laden. Women were huddled around a well, drawing up water and singing as they worked. Crates stood here and there, some of them already packed with bottles, others holding only grey packing paper and cloths. The ubiquitous ushers and pages darted about too, some barking orders at the boys, others standing their ground against stout cooks in white aprons who refused to budge from doorways.

Across the yard, several of those doorways opened into the kitchens themselves. Mark and I – I had cleaned myself up properly – stepped past one pair who ignored us, intent on their sparring.

'. . . will spoil on the road!'

'I've never yet let anything from this place that'd spoil in the span of a day or two!'

'You are wrong, sir! The king will not have his Imperial Majesty insulted with spoiled fruits!'

Beyond them, the kitchen spread – a cavernous, vault-like space. The ceiling rose and fell in a series of whitewashed arches. The heat, from the huge ovens and the hectic movement of people, was unbearable, like stepping into a desert. Everywhere there was shouting: over the wide, scarred wooden tables; from beside boiling pots set over hearths; from each of the pairs of naked boys who were turning spits upon which were skewered dripping sides of pork and beef. I tried to say something to Mark but gave up. Voices were everywhere, crying over us.

'Is it stewed?!'

'For the queen!'

'Where's that fucking fruit-man?'

'Argh!'

This last came from one of the spit boys as a spurt of sizzling fat lanced across his chest, leaving a scald.

Mark leaned close to my ear. 'Fancy turning to life as a cook?'

'No,' I mouthed back.

He set out ahead of me, making for a tall man in a white apron who was scolding the burnt boy. ''Scuse me, sir,' he said.

The cook turned blazing eyes on him. 'Get out of my kitchen!' he cried. His accent was unmistakeably French. 'Sortez! Sortez!' He clapped his hands for effect.

Mark held up placatory palms. 'We seek blood,' he said.

This had an effect. Confusion wiped away the cook's imperiousness. 'Eh?'

I stepped forward. 'Buckets of blood,' I said. 'Do you keep them?'

'What is this?' the man asked. 'What nonsense?'

'His Grace requires a bucket of blood,' I said. And then, because I could think of no better reason, 'For a masque. For a feigned killing in a masque.'

The cook closed his eyes, mumbling and swearing in French. 'I don't know nothing about any such madness. Go and find the scullery. We cook here, monsieur. We do no killing.' He proceeded, at Mark's request, to direct us to the slaughterhouse, listing a whole host of other chambers: the pastry yard, the bakehouse, the dry fish house, the wet and dry larders, the great buttery. Beyond them all, like a guilty secret, we should find the scullery where the slaughtering was done.

We thanked him. He ignored us, immediately shouting at another boy to baste, baste, baste.

Back out into the yard, we made our way through the network of kitchens and kitchen houses, getting farther away, it seemed, from the main one with each step. Eventually, we came to the wooden hut that housed the scullery.

There was no door – only a square opening. Inside, however, all was stone and metal: large grey basins and paved floors with guttering cut into them; metal hooks hanging down menacingly from wooden beams. Some of them were tenanted with sides of beef hung up to age. Others boasted whole pigs, fresh-killed.

With buckets set underneath to catch the blood.

I watched as one drip . . . drip . . . drip-dripped, silently, irregularly.

There was only one butcher present in the scullery, though two boys were on all fours scrubbing at the paving stones. The big man turned to us. His apron, of leather, was scarred and stained. He caught me staring at the dead beast. 'There's a creature put its meat into a good skin,' he said, without preamble.

'What?' My eyes flew down to my cuff.

'Yonder animal,' he said, with a tilt of his head. 'A fine fattening brute.'

Out of the side of his mouth, Mark said, 'It's just a saying. Country folk.' The butcher gave us both a sour look.

I didn't bother with politeness either. 'Have you had any buckets of blood stolen?' I asked.

'Stolen? Blood?' The man's confusion matched that of the French cook, though he had no Gallic fury to spice it.

'Just so,' I said.

Mark added, 'Someone threw blood about the Upper Ward. A prank.' I nodded.

The butcher dug into his beard, as though an answer

might be there. 'Don't know nothing about that,' he said. I cursed inwardly. 'We leave the blood out,' he said. 'For the cooks, if they need it. Or the builders.'

'Builders?' I asked.

'Ay.' He made a curious little motion with his hand, as though wiping an invisible wall. 'For whitewash.'

Something chimed in my mind. But it was distant, dulled.

'Touch of sow's blood,' the butcher went on, 'for the Suffolk pink. Rich folks' houses.'

'I see,' I said. And I thought I was beginning to.

'So none was stolen?' asked Mark.

'Wouldn't know. Blood's blood. It's what it comes out of is my business, lad.' He tugged at his beard and looked into the sunny doorway behind us. 'No buckets taken, far as I've heard. That all?'

'That's all,' I said, before Mark could say anything else. 'Thank you.'

I turned and stepped out of the scullery. It was, surprisingly, not so foul-smelling a place as I'd imagined, but still I needed a breath of sweeter air. I silenced Mark's questions with a shake of my head and was spared any more by the eruption of noise as we wound our way back through the kitchen complex. My thoughts were running wild, like a team of frightened horses turned loose, each one threatening to trample the next.

When we finally reached the great hall again, he said, 'Bloody hell. It's getting late.' It was still early morning, but already the hall was thrumming with activity. The floor had had been cleared, as the gentlemen and lowers had packed up their meagre belongings ahead of the journey to the southwest. 'A waste of time,' said Mark. 'Nothing taken, far as he knows. Must have got that blood somewhere else. Killed a hare, maybe.'

'Yes,' I said.

No buckets taken.

But what about the blood within them? I wondered. It would be an easy thing to pour the blood left outside into the bucket I'd seen.

So where did that come from?

'Well,' he clapped my arm, 'I'd better get the old trumpet. It was worth a try, though, wasn't it? Better get over to the cardinal. Riding,' he added, lifting his nose in the air, 'with His Grace. To let every place we pass know who's coming.' He turned his back on me but, over his shoulder, repeated, 'Worth a try, though. Sneaking, creeping bastard. You'll get him.'

I watched him go.

Yes, I thought. I would.

20

There were cheers, and blank looks from children dragged out to the front of houses by their parents, as we passed through the scattered jumble of buildings that made up the tiny hamlet of Littleton, just outside Winchester.

It was Sunday.

Having left on Friday morning, I'd spent the two nights since sleeping in open fields thick with midges and smelling of fresh-cut hay and mown grass. I rode alone, on my old friend Abraham, at the rear of the body of servants sent ahead. We were an assorted lot: the master craftsmen and their prentices; grooms; heralds; purveyors; cellarers; the whole body of domestic and kitchen staff. Our passage had made dusty roads dustier. Whenever the highway dipped or sloped ahead, I could see endless bouncing heads, men's and horses. If I looked back, a similar, endless body of people snaked backwards, growing more colourful as it turned from servitors to gentry in travelling-vizards and from gentry to nobility of church and state – all the way, I supposed, to the royals and the cardinal, and those servants deemed needful during the nights of travel.

Snake, I thought, King Henry's face in my mind, was the right word.

We, the whole court, funnelled onto the road, had become a great devouring snake. We stopped only when a juicy mouse took our fancy: a fair inn, or a local palace or good countryside lodging. And there we fed, the royals claiming beds for the night, the nobility retiring to tents hastily erected in the fields, and the rest of us relying on the stars for a canopy and good country air for blankets. And then, at first light on Saturday and now Sunday morning, we had slithered on. Banners were raised above and behind, from mounted men and those on foot. They displayed the Tudor Rose and the double-headed eagle of the Emperor Charles. Occasionally, a post-horse and rider would whip through fields, overtaking our lumbering progress or darting towards the great ones at the rear with some message or other.

As Littleton and its bemused country folk fell behind us, the city walls of Winchester began to take shape, grey, ancient, and windowless. An opening yawned. Like London, the town had its own gates. Unlike London, it had not overspilled them. Those ahead of me disappeared through the gates, spreading out into the town's streets. The lesser men at the very front would be clearing out citizen's houses for their masters, ensuring that inns were free, turning residents out with protestations that it was the king's will that the town and its houses – private or public – be turned over for the use of the court and its servants.

We're infecting the place, I thought, strangely. Odder still, the image of blood spreading in every direction through cobblestones formed in my mind, just as the glazier Visser's blood had run everywhere, unconfined by his broken body.

The gate led onto a wide street, which appeared to continue onwards, running straight through the town to its eastern side. Ahead, spires – at least a dozen – jabbed heavenward. Winchester, I knew, was a cathedral town, and the great hulking building rose above the lesser thatched and slated rooftops, ahead and to the right. Canopied wooden stands had been erected on either side of the street – which was broader than any London thoroughfare – much like those which stood beside tiltyards. They were still empty, but I supposed they would be for the use of the civic authorities – magistrates, aldermen, clerics, and perhaps a mayor if they had one – when they came out to welcome the king. There was no need for them to bid welcome to the blind head of this snake; it was the tail which glittered.

The only people, indeed, who were already out were several companies of raggedy beggars, their bowls already in their hands, being shepherded by friars. I ignored them, looking over my shoulder as Abraham clattered forward. People were still streaming through the gate behind me. It would a good while before the great men and women even saw the town walls.

I relaxed.

The castle clung, I'd been told, to the southwest portion of the city wall, like a growth. The bulk of us were already turning off down streets to the right, beyond the welcoming stands. I followed the crowd, ignoring the occasional head popping out from a window hanging over the streets, until I passed through another archway in another wall, and found myself in a large, roughly rectangular courtyard, enclosed on all sides by turreted walls.

It was, after the neatness and King's gold-painted splendour of Windsor, a little disappointing. Everything was neat and tidy, the gravel only beginning to show signs of our disturbance – but it was all so painfully grey. Only the royal lodgings ahead and the cathedral-like great hall suggested splendour.

Why Winchester?

I wondered. But I knew. It wasn't just the masque that was to be put on – such a thing could be performed anywhere. When I'd first been recalled to Hampton Court, Wolsey had said that Gosson had refashioned the Round Table which had once belonged to the ancient king. Everything on the emperor's visit, every demonstration to him of English glory, was to involve King Arthur. Even the choice of Winchester conjured memories of a vanished world – of the ancient king's capital.

I dismounted, finding a groom, and leaving Abraham to be led into the familiar world of clanking steel and flying sparks. Then – with much elbowing, stopping, starting, and darting through the mass of people still pouring into the yard – I crossed to a deep-set oak door on the southern side of the great hall and stepped inside.

My breath stopped in my chest.

The great hall seemed far larger on the inside, somehow. My neck instinctively craned upwards as I stepped from stone onto purple carpet. The soaring roof was crossed with overhanging eaves. From each of them hung banners with, again, Tudor Roses and Charles's eagles. Light caught the gold thread in them, falling in through great dormer windows. Stout stone columns, painted to resemble marble, met in a series of archways the full length of the long chamber, and between each, against the inner walls of the hall, were hung tapestries showing individual Knights of the Round Table, staring directly into the room's huge, open centre.

It was old, I thought – very definitely in an ancient style.

But it was impressive in its heavy, foreboding oldness.

Ahead, crates were being unloaded. Gosson, Cornish, and Lutini were all at work already, commanding their prentices, clerks, and musicians to begin putting together the setting for the masque. It was to take place the next day; there was little time. I ducked behind a column as I heard Cornish's voice rise above the others and echo around the room.

'It must be *done*, gentlemen, by this *evening*. I wish to see a *tower* in this room, ay, and with windows which do *open*. All must be in readiness for tomorrow.'

Peeking around, I saw Gosson break free of the activity. He walked quickly down to the head of the hall, where the royal dais was raised. Two servants were polishing the carved and gilded thrones – three of them – which sat there. Turning to slide between them, the Master Painter went to the wall behind. I moved around to see what he was doing.

Again, I drew my breath.

Gosson licked his finger and wiped at the bottom, outer edge of an enormous, perfectly circular tabletop. The thing was real, it was there, hanging up: the Round Table, King Arthur's Round Table. In the slanting shafts of light, its colours changed in vibrance from top to bottom. It was exactly as it had been in the painted cloth plat which Wolsey had had spread before him at Hampton Court. A Tudor Rose was painted at its centre. Around it, narrow writing – I couldn't see what it said – scrolled in a tight circle. Beyond that, alternating sections of identical size were painted in green and white. Rising from the top of the rose, covering one section which fanned upwards, was the throned King Arthur, swathed in red and blue, a closed crown on his head and Excalibur rising from his hand to his right shoulder.

Around the outer rim of the table, more writing scrolled. Squinting, I could make out 'GALAHAD'. Each section, I realised, green or white, must represent one of the knights.

As I watched, transfixed, the Master Painter removed his hat, freeing his cropped blonde head and pink scalp, and used it to wipe again at the table.

It was perfect, I thought.

When the court assembled to watch the masque and saw King Henry, on a throne set before such an antique thing, there would be no doubt in anyone's head that he was descended from the ancient king.

Judging from this room, one day his new Camelot might just be built, with himself at the centre.

Cornish's voice interrupted my thoughts. I saw Gosson's back stiffen too. 'And *how* might we construct a staircase within the tower in mere *hours*? To be fully dressed and fit to be used by a dowager *queen* on the *morrow*? I would have the ladies peer through *windows*, do you hear me? *Windows*? That odd little Bullen chit can be the lowermost. Have you the Moorish creature's *mask*? I wouldn't have him *frighten* any country ladies.'

To hell with you. I hope the 'Bullen chit' does bite you.

I crept out of the great hall, even as more crates were being brought in on rollers. 'Oi, have a care,' breathed one of the grunting servants pushing it. 'Mind yourself.' I bit my tongue and looked down in apology. 'We need to be fast. Royals is coming.'

My heart skipped.

I couldn't say why. I had no great desire to see the entry into the town, but I had a vague idea that if something was going to happen – *three springs shall break forth in the city of*

Winchester – then it would happen at some great moment. A prophecy hadn't come true unless people saw it come true.

I made my way out of the courtyard, which was hastily being cleared. Grooms with rakes were furiously plying them, trying to tame the gravel we'd so recently riled up. From there I walked out into the streets. Everywhere, people were pressed against plaster walls, clear of the horses which would soon come, clear of the filth the beasts would kick up. Some of them, I supposed, were our people – of the court, I mean – but others were Winchester folk. Already, children were up on the broad shoulders of fathers and women were chattering together, their rags in their hands ready to wave as they begged a blessing from the queen.

I made it back to the main street running in from the West Gate. Here, the crowds were thicker. The stands were heaving with men in red robes, chains of office around their collars. All were standing. From the houses above, people hung from windows – our people, I guessed: the ones who had commandeered the houses and upper floors of citizens. Many were dangling streamers, ribbons, and pennants, waving them so that they didn't just hang down the plaster walls in the windless air. Just after the wooden stands ended, a banner was being tied from the shutter of one house to that of the building on the opposite side of the street. Its writing shone through in the early afternoon sunlight. From where I was standing, my feet sinking into trampled mud by a house on the corner of a street which led down to the castle, it read:

WELCOME, ILLUSTRAT EMPEROR,
AND OUR KYNGE!

A hush descended.

I stretched my neck to see what was happening. I heard it first. The city officials in the stand began shouting, in a gruff chorus, 'God save the king! God save His Majesty!' They repeated it, over and over, until the chant was taken up by the people. I joined in, just to be part of the crowd.

First, the courtiers came in a blaze of colour, the lords and ladies on fine horses with footmen marching at either side. They inclined their heads towards the Winchester authorities, who doffed their caps; but they ignored the rest of us, as we ignored them, riding on to the castle or, if they were not quite so favoured, wherever their servants or the surveyors – if they were grand enough – had found for them. I saw the king's great friend, the rosy-faced Charles Brandon, Duke of Suffolk, and his wife, the king's sister, Mary. She was beautiful, pale and frail. He wore a perpetual look of slightly confused, jocular buffoonery (a cover, as I've said the whispers went, for a cunning, spiteful mind).

After the parade of nobility came the officers of the king's household, carrying their white staves of office before them like swords in some kind of military inspection. And then came a palfrey-drawn litter, with a canopy of cloth of gold. Women on white horses surrounded it. Seated on cushions within was Queen Catherine. Even from a distance, as soon as the horses carrying the litter emerged through the gate, I knew it was her; a chorus of cheers louder than anything I'd yet heard rose from female throats. As the litter and its escort of white horses and glittering ladies reached underneath the overhanging welcome sign, it paused. Murmurs of confusion ran through the crowd.

Two groups approached the litter: a small number of

coiffed ladies bearing flowers, which were accepted by the queen's women, and, on the other side, their heads bowed and hatless, a group of beggars. The mounted women on that side scattered coins.

And then the queen's party rumbled on.

As it passed me, I tried to get a look – and there she was – dumpy, tiny, solemn little Queen Catherine. I owed it to my stepmother, I felt, to record Her Majesty's dress: an ermine over-gown over a sea of dark velvet. Colourful jewels sparkled on her headdress. In a wink, she was gone, a happy smile – a genuine smile, I thought – on her round, pleasant face.

The rest of the queen's household followed.

Before it had cleared completely, the blasting of trumpets split the air.

Mark!

There he was, on a fine horse, his trumpet jabbing upwards as he came. And then, also mounted, came Wolsey's household officers: his chamberlain, ushers, chaplains. I didn't see Audley, who had undoubtedly come in advance with the rest of us, to see that the cardinal's letters were all organised and awaiting him in the castle, but Harry rode with the liveried gentlemen of the household. He looked, I thought, suddenly very young, but trying to look very old. I smiled at the sight of him.

Wolsey came next, incongruously, on his mule. The men in the stands greeted him, I noticed. But no one cheered. He didn't bother smiling out at us either, but followed his household, looking over his shoulder every few seconds as though still trying to control what went on behind him, to ensure it all went on smoothly. He clattered past me without looking down, just as Mark and Harry had – and I had no wish to trouble any of them when they were, as it were, at work.

That expectant silence fell again.

And then the cheers, the frantic cries of 'God save His Grace' torn from hundreds of throats.

Through the gateway came two huge horses: one black and one white. On the right was King Henry, in cloth of gold. He was grinning, one beringed hand on his bridle and the other in the air. The men in the stands began stamping their feet, waving their hats in the air. Next to the king rode Emperor Charles on his sleek black mount.

An odd-looking man, the emperor. In addition to his jutting chin, he seemed somewhat shrunken. His suit was dark blue and his jewels fewer and selected with what looked like a private man's preference rather than a public sovereign's. He was, I noticed, looking at his uncle, King Henry. But there was no love on his face. Nor was there respect, or affection. He did not look impressed.

He looked, I thought, amused.

Worse, there was a hint of contempt. I thought of Polydore Vergil – of how the old man had worn contempt in the curve of his lips and the sparkle in his eye. I saw that again on the face of the Emperor Charles. Whilst King Henry waved, grinned his wolfish grin, and seemed to bask in the cringing subservience of his people, the much younger emperor – he couldn't have been much older than me – seemed almost to be laughing at the older man behind his sleeve. And the worst of it was that our king seemed utterly oblivious to it.

Despite being a bigger man, a handsomer man, a far more impressive sovereign in his gold and his jewels, the ruddy-faced Henry seemed diminished, shrunken. If he could be looked at with smiling contempt by such a stunted little foreigner – a relative too, who owned half the world – then I was embarrassed for him.

Cheap, I thought.

King Henry, the most extravagant king in Christendom, as far as I knew, was made cheap and laughable by the twinkling eyes and nasty smile of his nephew.

I wished they would ride on, would go away, both of them. My father had once warned me against kings. There was something wrong with them, all of them. But King Henry was enjoying himself. He took hold of his nephew's hand and held it up, to more of those hollow cheers and cries. Still, they had not got beyond the stands.

And then, farther down the street, the quality of the cheering changed. It became wilder, shriller. I turned, looking on into the town. Around me, others had begun to notice it. I gave up on the king and the emperor, leaving them to their dull words of welcome from the city fathers.

Others close to my part of the street, beyond the high banner, joined me. We were all intent, now, not on the royal entry, but on whatever it was that was causing a commotion in the town.

Someone beside me – a woman it was – saw it before I did. Her scream, inches from my ear, rose higher than the cheers for the king and emperor that were still going on behind us.

From the open shutter of a tall house midway down the main street was hanging no banner, no streamer or pennant, but a wasted, scrawny body.

21

I pushed away from the screaming woman just as her friend, an older one in laundresses' grey, clapped her hard on the back of the head, silencing her. And then I strode, my gaze fixed up on the dangling body, across the turning which led down to the castle. The thing – the hanging body – was already being drawn back up into the window in a series of convulsive jerks. Whoever was pulling it managed to get the fellow up high enough to grip him under the armpits.

A crowd had gathered outside the house and was looking up. Men in royal white-and-green liveries were trying to restore calm, to quiet the anguished moaning, to direct attention away from the gruesome spectacle above and turn it, instead, down the street, to where the king and emperor would soon pass. They were having little success.

I found myself repulsed, pushed back by the people being pushed back in front of me, as the legs dangling from the open shutters above slithered inside. The shutters closed.

Desperately, I looked around the crowd, straining to see someone – anyone – who might be standing back, as the creature had stood back to watch for whoever might arrive at the Crutched Friars in his wake. But it was no use. There were too many people of every stripe, from citizens to servants to monks, beggars, wives, children, and guardsmen. With the body gone, they lost interest and turned, muttering, to add their voices to the general cheering going on farther up the street. I only gave a brief look over my shoulder, away from the now-shuttered house, as King Henry and the Emperor Charles rounded the corner behind me and set off for the castle. But it was enough.

King Henry, his eyes sunken pinpricks, was looking at the building too, as he reined his charger to my left.

And then they were gone, leaving only the remnants of the royal household to trail in their wake. With them went the sense of excitement. With them went the cheers. A frenzied, gossipy muttering took hold of the crowd outside the house, shaking it. Others, who had been closer to the West Gate, joined.

'What is it?'

'What news?'

'What happened?'

'It was up there.'

'Ay, I saw it. A man.'

'It's true!'

Fingers were pointed. A pair of men in their red civic robes, their chains not touched by a sun which struggled to reach down into the high-roofed street, marched towards us. A path was cleared for them as they made for the house. I remained there, watching, biting at my thumbnail, until they left. One of them was ashen. The other looked furious. The latter beckoned for a monk to step forward. After a brief conference, the holy man went inside whilst the two officials stormed off, their heads bent together.

I was still standing there, still debating what to do, when, from the direction of the castle, Richard Audley emerged, his black robes tight against his body. The crowd parted again, as though the man gave off an unpleasant smell. He didn't, of course; it was his stony face, his air of importance and ability, which drove them from him. If he saw me – I stepped forward so that he should – he gave no indication. Instead, he continued on, crossing the street and entering the house.

After a useless look around – no one seemed to know what was happening – I followed, not bothering to knock.

Inside was a plain counter. The place might have been a shop, with living quarters behind and above. It had been cleared now; presumably the stock had been dumped in the back rooms. I ignored the counter and the open archway beyond, making instead for a wooden staircase which led up into shadows to the right of the open space. My riding boots – another boon of service – made hollow, tumbling thuds.

The staircase was narrow. It stopped at a landing and then curved round, going up to the third storey. Voices droned from up there. After a brief look at the second floor – shadowed, quiet, empty – I climbed up.

Upstairs was one large room which stretched from the front to the back of the house. The floorboards were dusty, and the only furniture was a pair of straw beds, without frames, lying against the back wall, where the shutters were still open. In the centre of the room, the monk and Audley were speaking. Audley's arms were folded over his black chest. The monk's hands were clasped in supplication and his head was bent.

Between them, on the floor, lay the stretched body.

Audley, if he was surprised to see me, or even angry or alarmed, gave no sign. He didn't even break off his flow of words as I approached, my left hand raised in a grim salute.

'. . . how many have seen. And how you, Brother, did not see him leave your company.'

The monk bowed his head lower. 'A most sorrowful thing.'

'Indeed.' Finally, Audley spared me a look. He remained expressionless, but his nostrils widened a little and the darkness of his eyes flared. 'You may go,' he said, speaking to the monk but still looking at me. 'Arrange burial for the creature.'

'But,' said the monk, crossing himself, 'if it was a . . . by his own hand, as it appears—'

'It was an accident!' snapped Audley, turning to him. 'A tragic accident. This poor creature had hoped to see His Majesty – Their Majesties – from above. To drop some small show of welcome. And therein he did become entangled and fell. Entangled about the neck. You will make this clear. I will inform the king's own coroner of the same.'

The monk, refusing to meet Audley's eye, bowed deeply and fled, not looking at me. When he had gone, I opened my mouth to speak. Audley held up a finger, cocking his head until the echoing footsteps faded on their way downstairs.

'An accident,' I said. My tone betrayed me, as I meant it to.

'Look,' said Audley. 'Go on. Look.'

I did.

The body on the floor was male, clad in beggars' weeds: patched dun and brown. He looked identical to the companies of beggars I'd seen outside, waiting for the royal party and approaching Queen Catherine's ladies. He was old – I might have put him as high as seventy – but it was difficult to tell; he was painfully, awfully thin. His cheekbones seemed to be holding up a face that was sinking inwards. The nose was beaky, all gristle. And his staring eyes were sunken deep under the bony brows.

He that shall drink of the second shall die of hunger and paleness and horror shall sit in his countenance. He that shall drink of the third shall be surprised with sudden death. Neither shall his body be capable of burial.

'Suicide,' I said. It was a word I couldn't remember ever having said before: a word of horror, to be avoided. I wished I might have a drink to wash it away. 'But not. Did Ha— did Mr Gainsford tell you of the prophecy?'

'Yes,' was all Audley gave me.

'He – the man who did this – he's attempted all three, there. Hunger. Sudden death. Look of . . . it by his own hand.'

'Yes.'

I couldn't stand the secretary's gaze any longer. I bent down. The dead beggar's neck was encircled with a red welt. There was some bruising on his veiny, claw-like hands. A bruise, too, had risen purplish on his cheek. Sadness blanketed me. I could see the old man, promised food or wine or alms, lured up here. And then, at some point, he must have realised he'd been cozened. Perhaps he'd thought it some game, some cruel mockery. Yet, at some point, the horror had struck him. He'd fought back. Useless of course; he was old, weak, spent. Easy prey. But I was glad he'd fought back. Something my father had once said came back to me.

Sometimes da dying is fouler than death.

I looked down at my dangling cuff, feeling foolish.

Thank God that there is a rest of your life.

'He was forced,' I said. 'He was brought in here – up here – and forced.' I sought the right word. 'Constrained to it.'

Audley's light steps drew my head up. He had passed to the window. From a brass ring which hung from the shutter was a short length of rope. 'Yes,' he said. 'Hanged. Like a criminal. Beaten. Forced. Hanged. His Grace has heard of it. Doubtless the king will have seen something. I will make a report. As I've said. An accident. The fellow accidentally hanged himself in his attempts to make a welcome.'

'Where did he go?' I asked.

'What?'

'The man who did this. The murderer. The more you act to stop the king hearing of all this . . .' My words tumbled. 'The king would see the prophecies as soon as he heard – he's a . . . a true believer. He knows the prophecies of Merlin – the cardinal said he'd read every word about Arthur. You'll just push this creature into doing something more. Don't you see? He started with murder – he silenced the scholar. And it didn't reach the king. His other outrages haven't reached him either. And see how he grows bloodier? What next, Mr Audley? Something bigger, something that can't be kept from the king's ears. Where did he *go*?' Before Audley could answer, I stepped away from the body and across the room. Sunlight, warm and incongruous now, bathed me as I reached the open shutters near the beds. I pulled my cap down against it and leant out. One of the shutters, hanging open over a small, unkept kitchen-yard, had another length of rope attached. It dangled, like a dead serpent, downwards. Easy enough to get hold of rope if he was part of the great train. It was used on every cart, to secure every box and bundle.

Young, I thought. He was, as those who'd seen his face

had said, a young man, to be able to escape from a house by rope.

'Outwards,' said Audley. I jumped. He'd approached me silently. 'Clever. Into the yard. The back. When all eyes were to the front.' I said nothing. The yard spread backwards, meeting the adjoining garden of a house on another street. Similar yards and houses stretched on to the right, and a few lay to the left. It was possible, I thought, that someone might have been looking out, might have seen him. But all they would have seen was a distant figure.

And then, I realised, that didn't matter.

Turning to Audley, I said, 'Do you know whose house this is, sir?'

'Yes.' He lifted his chin. 'A seller of woollen cloths. Holbrook is the name.'

'Where is he? Do you know?'

'I have only just got here,' he said, a little peevishly. And then something like respect came into his eyes. 'Ay. Discover him. Find out if he let his house to . . . find to whom he let it.' I nodded. It was, as Mark might have said, worth a try. 'I will report this affair to His Grace. And the king's coroner.'

'An accident,' I said.

Something like a smile twitched at the corner of Audley's lips. 'An accident. Most tragic.' His usual not-quite-a-frown returned. 'If you discover anything, come to me at the court.'

I gave him a little bow, replaced the cap I'd taken off when I came up the stairs, and left the room and the house.

★ ★ ★

The Oak, the town's largest tavern, stood in a back lane, parallel to the high street but on the opposite side from the cathedral. Several men had their arms braced against its low, whitewashed walls as they painted them in thin streams of yellow. An old sign hung listless under the eaves of an overhanging gallery.

When I'd emerged from the house, I'd found that the crowd had largely dispersed. Evidently, people had decided that, on balance, an accident – however oddly timed and placed – was of lesser interest than the invasion of their town. I'd had to ask a fellow as he spat into the gutter whether he knew where I might find Holbrook the wool-seller. 'Down the old Oak. Old sot,' was his answer. Several other enquiries had led me chasing through the warren of streets which threaded, vein-like, from the artery of the High Street – and so on to the tavern itself.

I ignored the pissers and stepped inside. It was a low room, with a bar across the far wall and benches around the rest. There were no tables or chairs. The floor, though paved, was criss-crossed with muddy footprints. No music-men greeted me, begging a penny a ballad. The thrum of conversation dimmed as men, some sitting on benches and others standing by them, turned to look at me. Hostile looks, I thought. They were all of them run-down fellows, grizzled and heavy-bearded.

I stepped across to the bar, keeping my head down and my cap low. After rapping a few beats on it with my fingers, the tapster sidled out from the rooms beyond. His eyes raked me. I realised – I could see – that he, like the drinkers, held me in suspicion. I was a coloured bird of paradise in my good livery. I was an exotic, court-coloured bauble.

'We ain't got no beer left nor no wine,' announced the tapster, before I could speak. 'You lads've had it all. We're dry.'

I held up my left palm. 'I seek no drink.'

It was the wrong thing to say. I could see that in the narrowing of his eyes. 'We not good enough for you, then, is it? Good honest English beer not enough for a lad from . . . where is it, Italy? The Africs?' He began warming to his theme; some laughter and grumbling agreement behind me told him he had an audience. 'The New World?'

'London,' I said. Anger was bubbling – I could feel it. I swallowed it back down. 'I'm looking for a man named Holbrook. Is he here?' This time, before he could speak, I said, 'The Lord Chancellor of England, my master, seeks him. Now.'

The tapster made a noise somewhere up his nose. 'Which Holbrook?'

'A man. The wool-seller. Is he here?' I turned my own nose to the room. 'Is one of you Holbrook the wool-seller?' They began laughing at me, and then turned their faces into their tankards, as though wishing the whole court and its creatures drowned at the bottom.

'He's gone,' said the tapster.

Shit.

'Where?'

'Off to his brother's. One old drunk gone to one mad lout. Says as how your lot kicked him out of his house and so he'd to go off to that giant of a brother.'

I said a silent prayer before speaking. 'This brother. Is . . . is he in town?'

'Maybe,' said the tapster. And then, shrugging, 'Ay.' He

gave me the address: a tenement of almshouses hard by the eastern wall of the town, fourth hovel on the left. 'Don't reckon any other town would take a mad great brute like young Holbrook.'

I didn't care – it made no difference to me what this brother was like. If that was where Holbrook had gone, then that's where I would go. The fellow had seen the old man's killer – must have been coerced into giving his house over.

And, I thought, if I had to, I'd drag him to the castle and have him look at every face, from low to high, until he pointed out the man.

I gave grudging thanks to the Oak's master, ignored the laughter of his patrons as I left, and set off. Closer, I thought – I was getting closer.

And yet I was getting farther away.

After regaining the broad High Street, I hurried deeper towards the far end of Winchester. The long, tall walls of the cathedral passed in a blur of grey stone and sun-dappled glass. Houses, I noticed, grew a little shabbier. Thatch replaced slate. Whitewash became less fresh. The spires of friary chapels poked upwards, seemingly every few steps. I ignored the groups of grumbling people – Winchester people, all. And, finally, I reached the city wall and turned right, into another narrow lane. Shabbiness turned its back on poverty. Somewhere, over the sagging roofs and chimney tops, the turrets of an ancient castle poked.

I had no need, however, to go that far. The tenement of old almshouses hung next to the wall on my left. The street became a flat, muddy path, untroubled by cartwheels or horse's hooves. I counted each thin wooden door as I passed.

One.

A little herb garden, barren, stood before it.

Two.

The wooden shutters were cracked.

Three.

The path took a dip, and stones were scattered across it. A low stone wall began, shielding the next run of gardens a little from the street, with breaks leading to the doors of the houses.

And then I drew up short.

There was a something in the road ahead.

I couldn't see it all; the wall screened most of it.

No!

The door to the fourth almshouse opened suddenly. I looked over, looked up, away from the thing in the road.

'Roger? Rog?' An enormous, bearded man bent under the low lintel and stepped into the garden. He drew up to his prodigious height. 'Roger?' he bellowed. He didn't see me; he wasn't looking. I hopped the last few steps, to the break in the stone wall. As I rounded it, the thing sticking out onto the road took shape.

It was a pair of feet and calves.

They were, of course, attached to a man, who lay face down on the little path leading up to his brother's house.

22

'Roger! Rog!' It didn't take me long to realise that the younger Holbrook, the giant, was not quite as other men.

One mad lout.

He saw me. His face reddened. 'What've you done to my Roger?' he asked.

I held up my hand, speaking softly. 'Peace. I'm . . . I'm with the king,' I said, bending the truth. I thrust my chest forward. His eyes danced over it.

'The king,' he said. His expression changed. He wasn't, I realised, an idiot or a fool. He understood well enough that I must be a man of authority. 'My brother. Look. He ain't well. Get the monks. Monks'll help him.' He nodded the truth of this. I cast a look farther down the street, across the other gardens, and back the way I'd come.

Where are you, you bastard?

And then I bent down to the body of Roger Holbrook. Two in one day, I thought. I could see already what the cause had been. His coat – his back – was perforated with bloody, ragged wounds. They were scattered randomly. His blood had turned the mud of the little path a darker brown as it soaked in. I touched his hand. It lay, palm facing downwards, stretched out beside him. The other was tucked beneath his body. His left hand it was, and it was hairy, pink, and still warm. I knew enough to know this meant that he'd been freshly killed. Death hadn't yet chilled him.

I swallowed, straightening and removing my cap. 'Your brother, uh . . . Goodman Holb—'

'I'm Thomas.'

Wolsey's name, I thought irrelevantly and irreverently. 'I'm sorry, Thomas. Your brother is dead. I'm very sorry.'

'I didn't do it!'

His reply surprised me and I stepped back. I had half-expected him to accuse me. 'I . . .'

'I didn't do it. No, sir. Not this time.'

This time?

I swallowed again. Fear trembled in my voice. 'No,' I said. This time my surprise was at just how level I sounded.

'I didn't do nothing. Not this time. Not like that last time when I broke that bastard's head. No, sir.'

'No.' I looked down at my livery, hoping it would bring reason back to me. 'I'll . . . I'm sorry. About your brother. I'll alert the . . .' I had no idea. Undoubtedly, I thought, this was no prophecy. Roger Holbrook had been hastily stabbed in the back because he knew too much – because he had let out his house to the murderer. He was, I suspected, a victim of necessity rather than design, probably as Visser had been. He had had to be silenced because of what he might say.

And, I realised, because I was trying to speak with him. It was as though the demon – again, I thought he must really be one – knew exactly what I hoped to do. And poor Holbrook had paid the price.

'Who done this to Roger?' asked Thomas, looking at me with brown, cow-like eyes. 'Who killed him?'

'I don't know,' I said. How to explain to a Winchester

loose-wit that his brother had been murdered by a man – men, I insisted to myself – who had stolen and were concealing proof of the king's descent from King Arthur?

There's a question for the ages.

'I'll find out,' I said. 'He'll hang.'

'No. You bring him. You give me him. I'll break his head.'

I bit my lip, looking down at the body. Signora Gonzaga's face hissed its way into my mind, swearing justice, swearing vengeance. When I found the man who had done all this, he wouldn't want for spectators spitting at his gallows.

When I found him.

'Perhaps we should put him inside, Thomas. In your house. Would you help me? I'll – I'll send someone. But we shouldn't leave him here. Like this.' I spoke slowly, as if to a child, and he sensed it.

'I know that. I know that. You young brat. I'm not a dumb, stupid fool. I'm not a lack-wit. I know that.' He spat on the sparse grass at his side. And then, as though his brother were a doll, he lifted the corpse up on one mighty shoulder, heedless of the blood. I looked away. The sight was unpleasant, almost comic.

As Thomas Holbrook turned, swinging his dead brother around, an idea struck me. 'When you've put the corp— When you've put Roger inside, will you come with me?'

'Yes, sir,' he said.

I smiled. I hadn't even needed to say why or where.

It didn't take him long and, uncomfortably, he spoke to the body as if it were alive, mumbling, 'Easy, there. You rest easy, now. Soon inside, heh?' as he carried his brother in. I looked up and down the street again. Opposite the almshouses were only the butt-ends of some old timber buildings. Was he watching me? I wondered. He had tried to get me before.

A thought began to form, just as Thomas re-emerged from the almshouse. He was spattered with blood and began wiping at his frieze coat, disturbing the weave, rubbing it in. 'Sir?'

'Come with me, please.'

Perhaps to my discredit, I had no plans to do anything official involving Thomas Holbrook. Rather, I'd wished for an escort: a big, hulking brute of an escort who could, apparently, break heads. Thus, I had the poor fellow walk me all the way through Winchester, right to the walls of the castle. People, I noticed, made way for him, trying not to look. A few boys laughed and I shouted at them to hold their tongues or the king would have their ears nailed.

I debated, as we reached the gatehouse, whether to send him home. He was looking at me with eyes which had, I noticed with horror, begun to glisten with tears. 'You going to send the hangman for the man who killed Roger?' he asked.

After a breath, I said, 'Not right now. We have to find him first. I have to find him.' I exhaled again. 'Come with me, Thomas.'

'In there?' he looked up, a little hesitantly, at the walls which dwarfed even him. We stood aside as a pair of cattle were herded into the yard ahead of us. Bound for the scullery, I thought. Their blood might be collected, but it wouldn't do for Suffolk pink. That was sow's blood.

'Yes,' I said. I felt I owed him. I did owe him. He might

come with me and say his piece, at the very least, to Mr Audley.

* * *

For once, the secretary looked ruffled. It was the sight of Thomas Holbrook, all six feet of him and more, that did it. His pale face whitened until it was almost blue.

If the circumstances had been different, I might have laughed in it.

Cardinal Wolsey was, apparently, enjoying a small, private banquet with the sovereigns. Audley therefore had the run of His Grace's privy chamber. In its appointments and furnishing – already unpacked and laid out – it resembled the one in Windsor. It was, however, smaller, cramped, its walls made of painted stone with only the tapestries to warm them. The carved sideboards and velvet-lined desks therefore looked as out of place as Thomas. They were just too much for such a little space.

I told Audley about the body of Holbrook being found outside his brother's house. Thomas stood, his eyes continually rolling about the room, his mouth agape, occasionally saying, 'Ay, ay,' when I prompted him.

'And this man saw nothing of . . . any other? Any who might have left these bleeding wounds?' Audley asked. Although he kept darting glances at Thomas, I noticed that he seemed unable or unwilling to address him.

'No,' I said.

Audley moved, like a drifting shadow, over to a horn window and opened it. He took a deep breath of the Winchester air. The lowing of the cattle below boomed up. He turned. 'Well.' A dart of his dark eyes to Thomas. 'It seems, then, that no man was there. This was an accident. A bull, a loose bull, might have gored the poor fellow. His Grace shall inform the king. Put His Majesty's mind to rest.'

Jesus Christ, I thought. Right in front of the man's brother!

'A bull! I'm surprised, Mr Audley, that you don't just say that being dead was an existing condition he suffered from before we all even came to town. I'm sure you might find neighbours willing to testify that he'd been awfully bloody quiet this last week.'

Audley's cheeks drew taut over his high cheekbones. 'You forget yourself, Anthony.' He said my name with emphasis, reminding me what I was and what I wasn't: low, and a gentleman. 'You have grown naughty-mouthed and overbold since your accident. You must calm yourself.'

The air stilled between us. I wouldn't apologise.

'What's this . . . a bull? Dead before? Are you two lads simple?' asked Thomas. 'It warn't no bull. It was a man did it. This day.'

'Anthony, would you show . . . Goodman Holbrook . . . from my lord cardinal's privy chamber? It is, I think, no place for him. And he should be happier somewhere downstairs. Tell him he might be given some pottage. Some bread. A cup of ale, perhaps. Downstairs.'

'Why don't you tell him? You're standing right there.'

I'd gone too far, and I cursed myself, for now the unwilling apology should have to come. 'I'm sorry,' I said, through gritted teeth. I ignored his thin-lipped smile as I sent Thomas out of the room. I'd had no business bringing him in at all, and I'd known it. An urge had simply come upon me to disturb and discomfit Audley. And it had worked.

'Well, sir,' I said, when Thomas had gone, 'it was no tragic accident. I brought the big man to . . . to watch over me. In case he lingered. The murderer, I mean.'

'Hm.' Audley moved to a desk and began stacking papers with neat, deft movements. He started tapping them so that the edges all met. They whispered softly. As he did so, he said, 'And so he kills a witness and escapes. To kill again, perchance. You were too late.' He set the papers down but didn't turn back to me. 'It was not your fault. You must have been close. Very close.'

'Yes,' I said.

'Let us pray he attempts nothing on the morrow,' said Audley. Monday: the day of the masque, I thought. 'His Grace shall have some of his friends – his especial friends, you understand – abroad about the town tonight. To listen for scurrilous talk, yes, but to watch for any . . . strangeness.'

'The town,' I said. 'It's not the town. It's here.' Audley turned and gave one hard, downward nod. 'I'd like to be about the town myself. Tomorrow. About the castle, too. I wonder . . . if you might do me a favour,' I asked. One of his eyebrows rose. 'Might you get me a weapon?'

An idea, which had occurred to me just after I'd asked Thomas Holbrook to escort me to town but before he'd come back out of his house, had taken shape.

* * *

We couldn't bed down in the great hall of Winchester Castle that night; the master craftsmen, though they had their own lodgings, had set their men to hammer and bang the night away. Canvas panels of false stone, I supposed, would be nailed together or locked with wooden pegs. A scaffold-like stage would be constructed. Velvet and tissue would be unrolled. Guising gowns and masks would be unpacked in a makeshift tiring room, probably hidden behind one of the massive stone arches. Trestle tables would be set up around the whole length of the great chamber, one on the dais before the three thrones.

Thus, our beds for the night were rushes on the ground floor of the royal lodgings, hard by the kitchens. But I managed little sleep. Instead, I told Mark and Harry of my plans, and set them to work.

By the time I said my silent prayers and closed my eyes, the whole of the court knew that Anthony Blanke the musician would be searching the town on the morrow, because he had discovered something about the unfortunate accidents that had plagued the emperor's visit. The court – any great concourse of people – made it easy, the easiest thing in the world, to ensure that word spread. The trick was controlling what that word was.

If I was right, the news would soon reach the mysterious, demonic murderer's ears.

23

I had almost no experience with a sword. I had played as a child with wooden ones, but my father – and how I had hated him for it – always insisted that it was a useless exercise. Swords were for gentlemen. I'd be better, he said, playing with a wooden club that might at least teach me how to beat away thieves and cutpurses.

And he was right.

But it wasn't using the thing that was important. It was being seen with it. If I was right, the whole court would know that I planned to be out with the guard. Probably they thought it madness. Or, I thought ruefully, they might think it some wildness in my blood coming out to play: the mad Moor, they'd call me, practising to play the Black Knight in the evening. I had to admit that Audley had been as good as his word. He'd found me a well-maintained cutting sword that had apparently seen use in France. Its scabbard was rusty but the sword was good, and the feel of it striking at my leg reminded me of my trumpet, which was gathering dust in London.

When I was dressed and armed, I crossed the yard from the little guardhouse and went into the great hall.

The room had, as I'd imagined, been transformed, though still the trestle tables were being dressed, with domestic servants holding damask tablecloths at each end, dropping them and caressing away the lumps.

The stage had been set up in the upper third of the room, so that the royals could have a good view and those nobles of high favour would be closest. On it, at one side, stood an amazingly real-looking false tower, its turreted top touching the rafters. Its painted stones were grey; a small, working door had been set into it; and, similarly, opening glass windows, stained white and green, had been set from its bottom to its top. On the other side of the stage stood a canvas painted with rolling green hills and, of course, a red dragon, near identical to the one I'd seen but untorn. The boards of the stage had been covered with green cloth, some of which stood over small boxes to make mound-like platforms.

It was impressive, I thought. Combined with the real backdrop – the Round Table on the wall behind the thrones – it was magical.

The air was filled, however, with anguished moaning.

I rolled my eyes. 'All is lost! *Lost!*' groaned Cornish the Revels Master. Lutini was speaking to a group of musicians, and occasionally pointing up and over to a small, railed, wooden minstrels' gallery which had been set up at the foot of the room. Gosson was standing apart with his painters, making L shapes with his fingers and occasionally clapping one of the men on the shoulder. Cornish, thus, had for an audience only his fool, his tumblers, and his clerks. He was, as usual, waving pages in the air. The fool, Patch, seemed to have inherited his master's distress and was wailing in harmony, whilst the others tried to comfort him. He looked up and pointed at me. Cornish, his sobs suddenly ceasing, turned.

'You!' he cried.

'Me,' I said.

Cornish rose from where he had been sitting on the open floor before the stage, and said, 'You must be *dressed* for your part. Only that *Bullen* creature has bothered to learn when the ladies are to leave the tower. What are the steps of the dance? *You* will partner her and stand thither.' He pointed at one of the covered green platforms. 'You *see*? Yet we are *lost*. Poor Patch . . . he cannot learn the *words* of the masque. No matter how often I sing them to him, they will not *take*. It was to be such a great *toy* to have a fool speak the words whilst the noble lords and ladies – and you and the Bullen girl – stood by. And *danced*.'

Lutini left his musicians. 'The music. My music. It – it shall do this talking. We need no words.'

'Ha! Music is wasteful air,' said Cornish.

I watched as Gosson, his back ramrod straight, moved down from his painters who were grouped before the dais. 'They come to look,' he said. 'Not listen. Look. And from this . . . many more commissions, I think.' He put his hands on his hips. 'Many more.'

'I have no *greed* for more commissions,' said Cornish. 'Do you think of nothing but *filthy* and *sordid* coin? My heart is *here*. On *this* day. On *this* night. And in the beauty of *my* words, spoken fairly to tender hearts.' I turned to go. 'And where are you going *now*? You *forget* yourself, young sirrah. You are *our* creature.'

I lifted my left hand, waggling my fingers. 'I'm going to capture the man who's killed two of you. He's made an error. Goodbye.'

Job done, I thought.

As I stepped back into the yard, into the glare of the sun and the sight of countless windows, I felt sweat begin to creep up, sparking the itching on my chest, my arm, everywhere.

* * *

I walked the streets of Winchester alone. Yet everywhere I could see evidence of Wolsey's 'friends', as Audley had called them. These were his spies – faces I recognised – out to sniff out scandalous talk and report back. As far as I knew, there was never any real punishment for those caught. Rather, they might find their tithes increased, their rents due early, their parish priests replaced with harder men. Wolsey was a man of subtle means. His motto might well have been 'loose tongues make empty purses'.

His spies would have their work cut out, I thought, amongst the working men and women of Winchester.

Up and down the High Street I went, matching my gait to the plodding style of country folk rather than the busy stride of the city men. Occasionally, I gave a small, suspicious nod to a courtly face I recognised. Towards the eastern end of the street – it was here, I hoped, that he might make his move – I saw a more pleasing face.

'Mistress Anne,' I said. I raised my hand and removed my cap, bowing as I crossed the street. She was coming out of a shop, with two maidservants carrying wrapped packages in their arms.

She didn't answer me at first; I think I took her by surprise. When I looked up, I noticed her unusual dress. She was wearing a fine, plum-coloured gown over an olive kirtle and square-cut bodice which buried her small breasts. It was the attached sleeves, though, which had caught my eye. Rather than showing the usual ruffle of white silk at the wrists, they were long and heavy, dangling down to points. She caught me looking and her face broke into a mischievous grin. She looked, I thought, very young.

'The trumpet,' she said. The grin faded but amusement lingered on her sallow face. Her lips were dark too – dark and full. She inclined her head downwards. 'Oh. I see you are become a gentleman.' I turned a little to hide the hanging sword, stiff against my hose. She was so direct in her looks. It was discomfiting. It was exciting. 'I have decided that such long sleeves and cuffs are pretty. They make a mystery of a lady's hands. And I have fine enough hands. I have had the tailor here alter my guising weeds to be likewise. You see.' The maids behind her held up their tied bundles. Anne held up her arms and shook back the heavy material, revealing those shapely hands. Fine enough indeed, I thought.

'It will become a fashion,' I said, a little shyly.

She reached out to my right hand with long, sharp-nailed fingers. Instinctively, I pulled it away. 'Indeed. I will wear my sleeves so. And that means that you, my friend the trumpet, cannot any more.'

I frowned up at her. Still, she wore amusement lightly, like gossamer. She was, I realised, trying to be friendly. Trying, in her odd way, perhaps, to be kindly. 'I . . .'

'No one is looking at your hands. You have no need to make a draggle-tail of yourself. You will not wish people to say you ape a lady's fashion, I think.' I must have looked unhappy because she sighed and lowered her lashes. 'Well, well . . . for the masque, perhaps, you might follow me in hiding your hands.'

Follow you?

'Uh,' I said, looking to the ground myself. 'The masque. I . . . it might not be me who partners with you, mistress. As I said, I'm not worthy. And being . . . wounded . . .' The word 'crippled' came into my mind and I banished it. Never, never that. 'It would not look well.'

'What?' All good humour fled her face. 'What?'

If my plan worked as I intended, I would not be taking part in the masque. Someone else would. But I dared not insult her by telling her who. 'A better man. A lustier man.'

'But you are the Moor. To play the Black Knight. Else what is the point?'

'I was to be masked, mistress. For . . . for not being . . . Moorish . . . enough.' I hated the words, hated even thinking them. Quickly, I added, 'This other fellow shall wear my mask. All will be well.'

'You, trumpet,' she said, her head tilting back on her long neck and her French hood sparkling, 'are a deceiver. A wicked deceiver. Good morrow to you.' Without another word, she turned away from me and began gliding up the street, her cringing maidservants scurrying behind her. People, I noticed, made way, bowing. The men looked up afterwards, sharing dirty looks with each other. I had lost a friend there, I thought. I had upset her plans, and Mistress Anne seemed a young lady who liked things to go as she anticipated.

Still, at least she hadn't bitten me.

When I was alone again, I gave myself a little shake. I had let my guard down in being drawn into conversation with the girl. The afternoon was wearing on and still the demon-creature had yet to strike. He must have heard that I had some means of catching him. I would have to go deeper into the town, to somewhere he might try and come at me without being seen by others. I had stuffed old rags down the back of my doublet, over the shirt, all held up by my tied points. Just in case, I thought.

Something moved behind me.

Turning, I saw only a random scattering of women carrying pails, nearer to the eastern wall than to me. I tried to look between the shabby houses fronting the street, but I could see only their blank walls. Perhaps the hanging sign of the tailor's shop had caught in the wind, or a shutter had been opened or closed.

Perhaps.

I began moving back down the High Street. The cathedral loomed ahead, on my left now. Several side streets snaked away. As I approached the mouth of one, a figure stepped out, into my path. I had briefly time to think of Ironmonger's Lane, of a man who could be behind but get in front, to fumble at my sword hilt, when I realised who it was.

'Harry!' I shouted, hoarsely.

He stood there, his own hand on his sword, his head high. 'How fare you?' he asked. His chin rose higher.

'What are you doing here?' Harry was no part of my plan. His only job had been to help spread the word that I'd be abroad in the streets, alone and unguarded.

'I followed you,' he said. 'Did you not mark me?'

'Follow . . . no.'

'Then it is clear you have need of me. Young Mark guessed that you were not truly going out to find this brute but to lure him. He wished to come himself, but His Grace must needs be played in and out of the king's presence. And so, I begged leave of Mr Audley to be amongst the company keeping order in the town. It is a poor and dishonourable knave who lets his friend risk danger and destruction without aid or succour.' All of this he delivered in the high tones of a chivalric master. Dropping it, he added, 'I wished to help you.'

Irritation fought with love in my charred breast. 'Oh, Harry.' His blonde hair, curling under his hat, glinted. I reached out and patted his hand – with my right one. 'I've missed you,' I said. 'I really have. But I have a plan here. A design. This creature – he must think he's hunting me. But this hare will bite back.'

'But a friend in danger must be honor—'

I looked at him, appeal stretching my lips.

'Very well,' he said. He gave me a stiff little bow. 'I will go. Have a care.' He backed away from me. I slid off my cap and gave it a little wave. When his back was turned, I decided to make again for the eastern reaches of the town.

I didn't get far.

When I reached the lane down to the almshouses, I felt, again, that twitching sense of movement behind me. Turning, of course, I saw nothing. The lane, stretching ahead, was empty.

He's here. Somewhere.

I set off down it, as though returning to Thomas Holbrook's house. This, too, was part of my plan.

Deliberately, I slowed my pace. I stopped, even, to rest against one of the walls of the buildings opposite the almshouses. If I'd had the sense to bring a wineskin, I'd have drunk from it.

Give him time.

I knew the creature's tricks. He wouldn't fool me again.

After my rest, I again began my walk down the lane. My heart rose up into my mouth as I passed an alleyway on the right. I forced myself to keep my eyes ahead. And then it was behind me. I had passed the Holbrook place. I didn't want to go too far from it.

The light behind me changed in quality, dimmed, shadowed.

I wheeled, my hand already pulling my sword free. It was heavy, as well I knew, unwieldy.

No Harry stood before me, nor even Mistress Anne Boleyn.

Instead, there stood a young-looking man in an apron, with cropped hair, the lower half of his face hidden by a vizard. He stepped towards me with the same careful, deliberate steps I had seen in his relentless pursuit through London.

I didn't run.

I hopped to the right, leaping over the low stone wall which led into the scraggly almshouse gardens. This seemed to confuse him. He knew me to be a coward, a frightened hare. But he turned with me. A dagger seemed to grow from his fist, just as before. I wondered, wildly, if he meant to make a display of me or if, this time, like Visser and Holbrook – I just had to be silenced.

I didn't engage him with my sword. Instead, I began running up the gardens, crushing weeds, in the direction of Thomas Holbrook's house. Over my shoulder, I saw him quicken his pace.

Yes! Just seeks to silence you!

My plan, now that it was happening, seemed incredibly stupid. And my record of planning was piss-poor. I'd have to adapt it, change, shift. I should've knocked on the door earlier, not wandered the town; told him to be in; he wouldn't be in – I'd really have to fight.

Too late now!

Reaching the door, I kicked at it.

And then I turned.

He'd gained the Holbrook yard – he was only a few feet away.

I lifted my sword and swiped diagonally through the air. He hopped back. I chanced another kick at the door.

Answer, you great ox!

'I know who you are,' I shouted. He didn't answer, but he did pause. I waved the sword again. 'I know what you have. About Arthur. The king. I know who you are. You're finished!' His eyes, tilting over the vizard, narrowed. And then he slid to the ground, as through falling backwards, his boots kicking out, kicking at me.

And I was falling. He had caught me in the shins, knocking my feet from under me. The sword, useless with no weight behind it, cut a loose, powerless arc through the air.

Shouldn't have let him get close.

'Thomas!' I screamed.

But it wasn't Thomas Holbrook rearing over me. It was the masked murderer – the creature who had killed four men. His heel caught my hand, pressing into the grass, shredding the tender new flesh. His dagger rose, shimmering in the air. I closed my eyes; I couldn't see, couldn't imagine, the sharp edge slicing into me.

'Ahhhh!'

It took a moment for me to realise that the sound wasn't coming from me.

Thomas?

But no giant had bathed me in shadow.

'Have at you, knave!'

Harry!

The pressure on my wrist intensified in a furious burst of pain, and then it disappeared. Opening my eyes, I saw that the masked man had turned. This time it was his blade waving uselessly. He had time to hold it up, to hold up his whole arm over his face, as Harry's darted forward.

And then, suddenly, the whole weight of him came down on me, crushing my belly, my breast. I gasped. The wind was knocked out of me, stopping me from giving voice to the thousands of points of pain. My neck strained backwards and my cap flew off, as my head sank into the grass.

The weight stiffened.

It disappeared.

He had rolled off, or fallen aside. Only then did I feel the wetness soaking into my chest, my arms.

Harry stood over me, his sword dripping, his face rigid with determination. 'Are you hurt? Anthony, are you—'

Finally, the door to Thomas Holbrook's house opened. I could see him, upside down, like an enormous carved statue. He rubbed sleep from his eyes. You, I thought – I was supposed to deliver him to you to break his head open.

His head.

Him.

The pain seemed to wash away, replaced with fear, with excitement. I rolled myself over, my sword forgotten on the grass. Thomas's and Mark's voices became a distant hum. I was numb to them. The blood, rushing through my ears, drowned them out. Instead, my attention focused on the dark shape lying beside me, staring up at the sky. His eyes had softened. They looked frightened.

Who are you, you bastard? Who are you, who did this to me?

Gaining my knees, I reached out and tore away his mask.

24

There was no great moment of recognition. I hadn't expected one. I had suspected – I had known – for some time now that the masked creature was but the real murderer's weapon. Someone else had wielded it.

And I thought I knew who.

I looked down at him, at the man who had ruined my skin for life, who had murdered Gonzaga, Visser, the beggar, and Roger Holbrook; who had burnt and stolen books; who had caused mischief in the preparations for the cardinal's masque. He was young, about eighteen, with cropped hair. Beardless. His hands were, as I'd been told, stained, though the fingers were long and fine. His apron was spattered.

He was dying.

Harry had cut deeply into his side, as he'd turned in surprise, and must have twisted the blade as he withdrew. The grass was already slick. Blood bubbled up from between his lips, popping at the air as the sun touched it. Still, Thomas and Harry were shouting. Still, I ignored them. 'Who sent you?' I asked him. 'Who do you work for?'

He said something. More blood bubbles burst.

I looked for his dagger. It lay a few inches from his hand. I flicked it farther, before leaning down to his red-rimmed lips. 'My . . . mast . . .'

'Your master,' I whispered. 'Tell me his name.'

'He'll . . . avenge . . . kill you. Moor . . . scum.' His words were hard and clipped but shorn of any accent; he didn't give me enough to detect anything, not even London.

Fury overtook me. I reached down and began shaking him, kneeing him in his ragged, bloody side, hastening his death.

Suddenly I was jerked away. Harry had caught me under the armpits. I thrashed out at him too. His words, shouted in my ear, began to sink in. 'The brute is dead. And may God have mercy on his wretched and black-spotted soul.'

Dead.

'Goddammit!' I barked. I was still thrashing in Harry's grip. The aftermath of excitement and fear had set me wild, set me to a terrific trembling. 'Dead! Dead! He has to tell me! To tell me his name!' Sudden pain flared across the side of my head, knocking me sideways. My eyes widened. Harry had struck me.

'Calm yourself,' he said. 'The brute is dead.' I looked down and saw that he was right. Goddammit, I thought again. 'Do you recognise him?' He'd let me go now, and I sat cross-legged on the blood-soaked grass.

'Do you know him?' Harry asked again.

I looked again at the pale, white features.

I didn't, not exactly. Or if I did, he had made no impression. But that didn't matter.

I remembered, on that first day that I'd returned to Hampton Court and met Audley, Lutini, Gosson, Cornish, and Visser. Their servants had all been finishing off cakes and wine in the New Court. Harry had hurried me past them.

And when Gonzaga had been found, the birds had been lured by crumbled cake. My fingers, when I'd tasted them after picking up the breadcrumbs, had been sweet. Before I'd got there, perhaps a good while before, this creature had been in that yard. He'd stolen off with a pocket full of cake, much as I'd done often enough, to await the historian.

He was a servant, certainly, of one of those men.

Other things began to slot neatly into place.

I didn't need him to tell me. I knew who he worked for. I had suspected since the torrent of blood, since the discovery of what it meant. All I lacked was proof. Proof, I thought, and a clear and certain reasoning behind the creature's actions. The second would follow the first. Once I had some proof against him – ideally, the stolen book, if it still existed – then he might be forced to explain all he'd done.

'I didn't do it,' said Thomas Holbrook, intruding on my wandering, feverish thoughts.

I turned and looked up at him. He repeated himself. The poor fool. I had been planning on using him, shamefully, to beat and capture the beast once I'd lured him down to the almshouses. That part of my plan had not come off. Thankfully, as it turned out, Harry was unable to let his ideas of honour and chivalry die.

'No, Thomas,' I said. 'Perhaps we should get him inside. Until some men from the town can take him away.'

As though it were an everyday occurrence – and it apparently was, now – Thomas pushed me and Harry aside and lifted the dead, bloody creature up, disappearing with him into the house. 'We will return soon,' I said. A closing door was the answer.

'Was that the creature you brought to Mr Audley yesterday?' asked Harry. He was wiping his sword on the grass.

Audley.

Ignoring his question, I fumbled about on the ground until I found the vizard I'd torn from the dead murderer. 'I need to see him,' I said. 'But . . . Harry, I have to be dead.'

'What?'

Fixing the vizard over my own face, I explained the rest of my plan. It didn't impress him. 'Stupid,' he said. 'Foolish, Anthony. It's foolish.'

'He has to think me dead, the man behind this – and his own creature alive. He has to. You have to disguise me. I don't want any word of me returning to the castle. Alive or . . .'

'What?' asked Harry, a little doubtfully.

'Forget it. Forget that. Doesn't matter. This is a clever man. He'll be watching to see if I come back or not. He'll see through a disguise, a mask. Better I do come back. Brought back by my friend. Slain.' He began muttering, questioning, as I looked down to ensure I was well stained in the dead man's gore.

* * *

So it was that I was carried through the streets of Winchester with a bloody cloth draped over me, lying on a door borne by Harry and one of Wolsey's spies, who knew nothing of the deception. It had not, I thought – as I tried not to breathe too deeply; tried not to roll over or fall off the door; and tried to ignore the halting, jerking movements – been my plan. Originally, I would have had Thomas kill or wound the murderer and then crept back into the castle in disguise.

This late addition, this embroidery, was better.

But it was hellishly uncomfortable.

All sense of place and time fled as I lay there, in the dimness of my makeshift shroud, on an old almshouse door. I was bumped and jogged, but I remained as still as I could. Harry, at the forefront, at least tried to make the journey a comfortable one. He had procured the door and the cloth and had likewise sent word up to the castle that Anthony the trumpet had been slain.

I hoped that he would also get word to Mark that it was all a feint.

The quality of sound reaching through my cloth changed. The town's hubbub, which rose and fell in excited chatter and respectful silence as we passed, we left behind us. In the courtyard, the echoing sound of cattle and distant pipe music came to me.

He would be out there, I thought.

He would be out there, watching, ensuring that I was dead – that his weapon had accomplished this time what he'd failed to last time. An urge to throw back the cloth and terrify him came upon me. I resisted it.

I was being borne to the chapel. The board shifted. Was turned. Was turned again. Was lifted higher. I thought I heard Harry's voice. I thought I heard Mark's, louder and more insistent. If I did, it turned angry and then stilled.

More jouncing. More voices.

And then the door was set down. I didn't move. Somewhere, the banging of doors.

I remained still, unwilling to breathe. The cloth was thick and heavy, but a rising and falling bump might be noticed. Still, I had no clear sense of time. But the sound of music was louder now, though it came from far away, through stone and glass and wood.

And then light poured over me.

Someone had snatched away the cloth.

I sat up, stiffly, one hand tightening on the crumpled vizard and the other around the hilt of my sword. Just in case.

Audley!

'Thank God,' I said. I'd never expected to be pleased to see the dour secretary. Yet I'd needed a man of authority, and there was little time. I'd asked Harry to tell him everything and send him to me, ensuring he was not seen or followed.

'I am pleased,' he said, 'that you are not dead.'

I ignored this. 'Were you seen?'

'No.' He looked annoyed at even being asked. 'The masque's fore-banquet is beginning. Already the tumblers are at their labour. The better sort are entering the great hall. Now.'

'The craftsmen – Wols— His Grace's craftsmen – are they inside?'

'They are.'

I sat up, letting my legs dangle over the edge of the table my door had been set on. We were in a little chamber with a low, wooden ceiling: the kind of room which clings to a chapel. On shelves were assorted golden chalices. Some gilt rosary beads dangled over the edge. And, thankfully, there were writing things: inkpots, a silver jar of quills. 'Is there paper?' I asked.

'What?'

I repeated myself. He didn't ask again but bent to a large coffer in the corner. He drew out an armful of cassocks and dropped them to one side, before reaching in again and retrieving paper. I slid to the floor and brought down the ink and a good quill. As I took the paper, Audley's interest overcame him. 'What fresh foolery is this?'

'The murderer – Harry told you he's dead?' I asked. He nodded. 'He works for someone. And I know who. Please, sir – just give me a moment.'

Before I wrote anything, I screwed my eyes shut. In my mind, I tried to recall the handwriting I'd memorised on the ride from Hampton Court to London – the writing on the false note penned by the murderer but signed 'Mark'. I could see it – more or less – and I set about copying it. I wrote:

The Moor ys ded. I haue slayne hym in secrecy, but one other knows of ye book, he did say. Come at masque tyme to the chappel.

I didn't bother to sand the paper; I fanned the air gently above it with my hand. It was hardly a perfect imitation, but I hoped it would be enough. I passed it to Audley. 'Can you give this to a chamberer, sir?'

'To give to whom?' he asked.

I told him.

Audley's eyes widened. 'You are sure of this?'

I swallowed. 'I . . . yes. But I know how to be more sure. Do you know where the craftsmen lodge at night?'

He nodded. 'Yes. They have their own chamber here. In the royal lodgings yonder.'

'Could you – whilst the masque is on, the court busy – could you search his things? Everywhere – look hard.'

'I am aware,' he said, coolly, 'of how things might be concealed.'

I said, 'Sorry, Mr Audley.' A book, I reasoned, must be too big to carry on his person. He would have hidden it. 'If you find it, bring it here.'

He said nothing but, taking the paper, made to leave. He paused at the small door and looked over his shoulder. 'Are you going to wait for him?'

'No,' I said. Already I was fixing the vizard over my face. 'I'm going to watch him observe the masque and receive the note.'

25

Dressed in a priest's cassock, with another wrapped about my head so that only my vizarded face peeked out, I emerged into the evening. Braziers had been set up all around the courtyard, giving it a festive air. The windows of the great hall were blaring and flaring with music and light. I had no need to worry about being spotted – even spotted as an odd, lumbering monstrosity – because everyone was either going into or hanging onto the outside windows of the hall. A carpet had been set up, leading from the royal lodgings to the eastern door of the large building. Servants were scuttling, beetle-like, about the cobbles, bent under the hard shells of their silver-domed dishes.

It was the poorer entrance on the southern side, of course, to which I made my way. I stepped inside without comment, stooping a little. I might have been an elderly chaplain – the type of wizened old creature who wraps up against the cold even on warm nights.

Inside, the hall glittered and winked and echoed with genteel chatter. Hundreds of candlesticks shone brightly on the long tables that formed an enormous, stretched horseshoe, the base of which stood farthest from the dais. The private table there, before the thrones, was piled with dishes and glasses. Queen Catherine was nearly lost in her seat, despite it being the smallest. Next to her sat the Emperor Charles, looking out on the hall, whilst his aunt continually leant over and spoke up to his ear. He didn't bother bending to aid her.

The king hadn't yet arrived. The third throne stood empty, its carved, pointed top and velvet back-cushion looking bereft without the padded bulk of the sovereign. Next to the empty throne sat Wolsey, as low on his stool as Queen Catherine on her throne. The look on his face was pure, shining pride. His hands were clasped over his red-clad chest.

And he had reason for it, that overweening pride. A rainbow of courtiers descended along the long trestles leading down either side of the room, turning duller as it reached the bottom table. The stage set for the masque, with its tall false tower, false meadow, and painted dragon, was still empty. Before it, however, in the open space between stage and bottom table, jugglers and tumblers were careening and capering for the guests, trailing pink, blue, red, and green streamers as they leapt and twirled. The cardinal's fool, Patch, darted amidst them, taking comfits from the tables and scampering off.

The bottom table.

There sat the three surviving men whom Wolsey had commissioned to devise the masque: the blonde, gruff Gosson, the elegant Lutini, and the dramatic Cornish.

One of them a serpent.

Trumpets flared.

Every head looked towards the minstrels' gallery, above the lower end of the room. The entertainers ceased their dancing, turned to the dais and bowed, as though the stage wasn't in the way. They filed through a gap in the trestles and left, amidst scattered applause and calls of, 'Well played! Well played!'

And then, through the same gap, came Sir Thomas Boleyn. The trumpets issued another blast. He had no notes, no sheets, but he took up a position before the stage and began to speak. I recognised the words. He was not working from the mangled text which the Revels Master had written and claimed lost, but from a variation of the original prose – a book I had read: *Le Morte D'Arthur.*

'So came a damsel into the hall,
'And saluted the king most highly
'A favour, sought she, and an end to her woes,
'So from Arthur she sought right succour.'

He spoke well, nearly singing the words in a rich, high voice. Nor did he neglect to move, lithely, like a dancer. In his reading, Sir Thomas Boleyn ceased to be a cold, dry man, of pure black bile, and became a fellow I could see winning friends as an ambassador.

Not that anyone was looking at him.

As his words soared upwards, a lady I didn't recognise came through the gap. A painted mask, of painted dried paper, shone with gold leaf, as did her dress. She took her place on the stage, facing the dais rather than the longer length of the hall.

But still King Henry hadn't arrived.

Perhaps it was the Emperor Charles who was to be the off-stage King Arthur; it was he the gold-clad lady faced. I frowned under my vizard, confused. If the thing was to imply that King Henry was Arthur and the hero of the piece, his nephew, Gareth, was Charles, then it wasn't working.

Unless . . .

Oh, God.

'For whom? said the king, what adventure?'

As Boleyn read this, the pointy-chinned emperor gave a vague lift of his hand. His expression, however, was one of barely suppressed contempt, as though the whole thing was fiddle-faddle, pure mummery.

Isn't it?

I was glad suddenly of the emperor's languid disinterest. I couldn't afford to watch the masque unroll across its little stage. Boleyn continued speaking: of the golden lady's sister besieged in a tower (here the top window of the tower opened and the dowager, the king's sister Mary Tudor, Duchess of Suffolk, popped out her masked face); of the Red Lands, whereupon a masked man in red took the stage, and stepped onto a platform; of the king recommending her to take Beaumains from the kitchen to rescue her sister.

Whilst the stage began to fill, I kept my gaze fixed on the bottom table. The three master craftsmen remained seated. Evidently, Audley hadn't trusted me, or he wouldn't send my note until he'd performed his search.

Or I was wrong.

I shrugged away that possibility.

I wasn't.

A hush suddenly descended over the hall. Glasses and dishes stopped clinking. The scurrying servants froze.

Beaumains.

Of course.

Onto the stage had come the hero of the piece, 'Beaumains', who in the tale was really King Arthur's nephew in disguise.

I'd been told, by Cornish, that he was to be played by the Duke of Suffolk, opposite his wife. And Wolsey, of course, had said that the part was designed to flatter the emperor, Henry's nephew.

I ought to have known better.

King Henry hadn't arrived to watch the masque because there he was, on the stage, tall and broad and unmistakable. He wore the costume of a kitchen slave, draped over a spotless Holland shirt, and his face was covered by a mask (this one in pink, depicting a smiling, dimple-chinned face), but it was clearly our king. No one spoke or cheered, no one cried, 'God save the king.' We were, all of us, supposed to play along with his deception. Doubtless he had arranged, all along, to take on his brother-in-law's role, telling no one but Suffolk. The part of the noble hero was one I couldn't imagine the king allowing anyone else to enjoy.

Oh God, poor Mark.

'And they came to a black land,
'Where grew a black hawthorn
'From which hung black banner and shield.
'And riding beside it,
'His black spear most fearsome,
'There came a black knight in black harness.'

In through the gap and onto the stage walked Mark, stiffly, all in black. His mask was grotesque: a painted thing (black, naturally) with eye holes. The mouth was a pair of oversized red lips with white teeth grinning between them. I had told him, in the morning, when I'd asked him to take my place, roughly what to expect.

'I could . . . you know . . .' he'd said, gesturing to his face, 'with the soot.'

'No,' I'd said. 'You couldn't.'

Yet I'd no notion of any other surprise changes of players; and I didn't envy him the shock of finding himself before the king.

Hopefully, I thought, he would know when to fall down dead – Boleyn's words would tell him – and when to rise to dance – when the heroic Beaumains freed the ladies from the tower and led them all in their pairs.

I gave another narrow-eyed look at Mark and his ugly mask – this they would have had me in, to show the world how fearsome and hideous I was – and then turned to the bottom table.

There was the gap.

I froze.

The note must have come.

One of the three craftsmen had indeed left, going, so he thought, to meet with his young hunting dog in the chapel.

26

The figure, lit in an ethereal glow from the braziers and the dancing light which cast the dregs of its cheer out from the great hall's windows, hurried across the courtyard, making, as expected, for the chapel. He was some distance ahead of me, but I didn't hurry. Instead, as I walked, I began to shed my disguise. There were few people about – the very old, mostly, who had no interest in what was going on in the great hall. Everyone else was pressed against the glass windows. I remained outside for some time, listening to the excited chatter and cheering from the servants, and to the music drifting from where the masque was taking place. Let him sweat, I thought. Let him think his creature is coming. The longer I could delay, the longer I'd give Audley to perform his search.

He had closed the chapel's slab of a door behind him by the time I crossed to it.

My sword was fastened tight against my filthy, bloodstained hose and doublet. This man wasn't a killer, as far as I knew; he was simply the mind, the engine, behind all the unspeakable acts. But he might well be skilled, and so I gripped at the hilt. Just in case.

Pushing the door open, I stepped into the soft light of the candles I'd left burning about the porch. He wasn't there.

He had gone straight in, probably looking to see where his minion was.

Through the narthex I went, and on into the nave.

He was there, standing halfway down the aisle, and he spun, his hands on his hips.

'Good evening, Herr Gosson,' I said.

Yes! I've got you!

Piece by piece, I'd constructed his guilt. The blood might have been stolen from the scullery at Windsor, but the bucket itself had been one of those I'd seen him and his men mixing their paints in when they were making the false walls. And that paint, too – being ground and mixed with water in the buckets – though it had been grey, had struck a chord. The dragon's fiery breath and its yellow eyes had been the same yellow as the false sulphur at the Crutched Friars. What I had taken to be yellow dirt or dust had been whatever stuff painters ground down in the making of their colours. When Harry had killed the minion, his apron had been spattered not with blood or dirt, but with paint; and those dirty hands which were noticed by all had their explanation in the fellow's job of work. And Mark – poor Mark – had had his face blackened by the painters, advertising my plan, giving Gosson time to send his creature ahead and trap me. Even the drawings he'd left on the wall of the Boar's Head – as well as the painted mask – had been useful.

A boar. Tusks, you know. Quite well done.

What I didn't yet have was firm proof, though I understood the motive well enough. From the beginning, Gonzaga had had to die – he knew too much. The manner of it – that had been devised as a gruesome masque in itself. The silencing of the poor man had worked; the advertising of the spectacle around it for the king hadn't. Thereafter, I supposed, the following outrages were simple enough to devise. Murder must get easier after the first. Wolsey's words came back to me.

An enterprise begun in blood will only grow bloodier.

The apprentice, of course, was nothing. I knew well enough such creatures were bloody brutes, rogues and rascals. And, when I thought of what Mark had told me about our Englishmen stuffing their beds with dried turds and spitting in their beer . . . I might have jumped at the chance to turn my club or blade to staining English soil myself if I'd ever been stupid enough to become a prentice lad.

'You!' he growled. His eyes darted over my shoulders.

Should have brought someone.

'Alive, Herr Gosson,' I said. 'Though your young dagger isn't. I killed him.' I wished the lie were true.

Fury crossed his hard features. He removed the hat from his cropped blonde head and, when he replaced it, studied blankness had forced away the anger. 'I do not know what you speak of,' he said.

'I think you do,' I said. 'It was you. You've been behind all of this. Worried, perhaps, that when work on Hampton Court was finished you'd be despatched back home? Hoping to inspire someone to launch a greater project to keep you in riches forevermore?' Another thought occurred to me, though I hadn't really appreciated it before. The tiresome Cornish had said something about sending out for supplies to London. Doubtless Gosson's pet killer had been as free to ride in and out of the court as I was. 'Setting your creature out to do murder. Sending him into London to kill me. To steal and destroy.'

'I am glad you are unharmed,' he said tightly. 'But I think your wits are loosed.' He tapped the side of his head.

'We'll see,' I said. I had to keep him talking. He was too clever, I thought, to incriminate himself – he had shown that by his devious actions. Like the rest of the craftsmen, he was not a fool.

Men of great learning and subtle craft from the finest schools and seats of education in this realm or any.

'Gonzaga was your friend,' I said. I'd become aware, suddenly, of the dozens of eyes glaring at us from the frescoes on the walls. Saints and sinners both were watching to see how this might play out. 'When I first came to Hampton Court . . . when his body was found . . . Monsieur Lutini said that you were his friend. It was you who told me where he lived.'

Gosson crossed himself. 'I mourn the loss of so high a friend. Now I must return. I hope you are soon restored.'

He began to move towards me and I put my hand more firmly on my sword. Pausing, he swept me with his cold, angry gaze. In the low light, I thought I saw his hand twitch and wondered if he carried a weapon. I thought not – not if he'd been in the king's presence.

Didn't stop you.

I swallowed. 'You read the book. Merlin's prophecies. The cardinal said right at the start of all this madness that he'd set you men to study. You did. And you knew that Gonzaga had found proof of King Arthur. Of King Henry's true descent from him. And you had your creature kill him and steal it for you. And to kill two birds by making the scene a . . . a spectacle. Why?'

For the first time since his initial anger, his own mask broke. His head cocked to one side. 'Proof? You idiot. You stupid fool. You know nothing. About anything. Get out of my way.' This time he made to push past me, and I stepped back.

'Halt,' announced a sharp voice. 'And make way for His Grace.' Audley strode into the chapel, something clutched across his chest, with Wolsey at his back. I saw Gosson's hand clasp around his throat before he hastily swept off his hat and bowed.

'We might spare you only a moment,' growled the cardinal, 'whilst the king is re-dressed. Your masque, Herr Gosson, was a success.'

The painter looked up, his face now blank, with just a few webs of confusion on his brow. 'I thank Your Grace.'

'Hm. Yes. Now, Herr Gosson, perhaps you can tell me why this,' he gestured to the book Audley was clutching, 'was found in a leathern pouch in the false bottom of one of your coffers of paint powders.'

'I . . . I cannot say, Your Grace. Some mischief. Put there. By someone. I know nothing.'

'Hm. And we hear, also, that a young prentice of yours lies dead in the town. That he has, in fact, been a most wicked fellow. That he has murdered two of our most special servants. Attacked another and damaged him foully. And killed and attacked and made mischief in divers ways. How came this, Herr Gosson?'

The painter licked his lips. 'I . . . I cannot say.' He eyed the book. 'I have never seen this. This prentice you speak of. He has stolen it. Hidden it. He . . . these . . . prentices. You know. They like to make great ruffles. In the state.'

'Yet you know it was stolen?' said Audley.

Gosson's gaze flicked to him, his mouth clamping.

'Peace,' said Wolsey. 'It is late. And this is a most troublesome matter. Do you know, Herr Gosson, what this book is?'

'No,' he said.

'It is a history of the Gothi. By one Cassiodorus. It bears in its margins notes by our special servant and your friend, the late Signor Gonzaga. Notes touching the once-sovereign lord of these isles, King Arthur, of great fame and memory.'

No one spoke. I chewed on my bottom lip. Wolsey had his proof – this book, taken from a dead man, had been found in the painter's possession. Hidden, no less. And yet he did not seem angry. In fact, he seemed a little annoyed, as though he were truly wearied and troubled by having been dragged from the great hall. He shook out his silk handkerchief and wiped his brow. It seemed the game had begun to pall. 'There are men outside,' he said. 'Trusted men and armed. They will take you to the house of the late Mr Holbrook. You will be warded there this night. Until we have better intelligence of this matter.'

Gosson straightened. He worked his mouth dumbly, as though measuring what he might safely say. 'Am I to be judged on the deeds and delations of one servant? The word of a mere trumpet?'

'What?' barked Wolsey. And then, more gently, 'I am the Lord Chancellor of England. I would hardly put the law out of office by avowing you guilty. I shall have no wild instigating and inspiriting of rude justice. And you are a master craftsmen of considerable skill.' He drew a breath. 'We would not lose your talents lightly, sir, when you have done us such fine service. It might be that Hampton Court is not the last of our great works and we should indeed have need of you again. No; we would not lose you. You will be lodged, for your comfort and safety, in that house. We would speak with you further on the subject. Tomorrow, perhaps. Yes. Tomorrow. Go now.'

As Gosson, with a trace of a smile, walked down the aisle and disappeared, I began shaking my head. 'He's guilty, Your Grace. That dead man was the blade, but he was the head. From the start. All he's done. You must discover why.'

'Shut your mouth,' said Wolsey. He mopped his brow again and then turned to me, blinking slowly. 'I am sorry, young Anthony. Truly. This book . . . this night . . . it has wearied us.' Audley held the thing away from himself. 'We shall have no need to speak further with that creature. No, not tomorrow nor any other night. We know what he did. And why.' He took a deep breath. 'Mr Audley has read the late Signor Gonzaga's writings. He made notes in his own hand in the margins of this cursed book.'

'But I . . .' I crossed my hands over my chest. The book was thick, tall and heavy-looking. 'It's the king's descent. The truth about King Arthur. Gosson wanted it for himself.'

Wolsey clucked his tongue. 'Alas, my dear boy, we were wrong. All of us. Wrong about what Gonzaga was up to.' He spat the name of his pet scholar. 'He has indicated names in that book. What is the name?' He shot a look at Audley.

'Riothamus, Your Grace.'

'Yes. Pagan name.' He shook his head and fetched another weary sigh. 'Signor Gonzaga found no descent of our king from Arthur. Not in this book or any other. No. The opposite, I fear. He was bent on doing as that old goat Vergil has long meant to do.' The hawk-like face of the old Italian, with its mop of grey hair, smiled smugly in my mind. 'Signor Gonzaga was set to . . . argue . . . that there was never any King Arthur as appears in the old tales. That . . . he calls them "false legends" in his writings . . . that they were spun out of pagan warriors such as this Riothamus. And others. He named others, which he found in other books. Each abominable ancient text led him on and on to the next, and finally to this thing. He would have sought to prove, on the eve of this masque, that the old chroniclers were as women at their embroidery, making a whole false picture out of divers threads. Read it, Mr Audley. What does it say?'

Audley stepped towards a pew, spreading the book open. 'The late Signor Gonzaga writes,' he said, before clearing his throat, '". . . simple legend . . . arising from the false and fabricated constructions put upon this . . . and other ancient Romans and the like barbarous men of war . . . in antiquity . . . mine own late master and the only begetter and setter forth of my zeal in learning, Signor V, speaks truly when he disdains the English love of Arthur. The said Arthur is a fond fantasy drawn from this Riothamus and the said other barbarous pagans of ancient history."'

'Disdains,' said Wolsey, with plenty of it in his voice, 'the English love of Arthur. A dangerous man, was my poor late scholar.'

I barely followed.

All I heard was, '. . . there was never any King Arthur . . .'

And my mind rebelled. Wolsey might as well have told me that Gonzaga had proven there was no Henry V or Robin Hood or Julius Caesar. I shook my head. 'Are . . . do you mean that . . . Gosson . . . he was saving the masque?'

Of course, I thought. The staging of the murders – those that weren't sudden attacks of necessity – was to bring the prophecies, the tales, Merlin and Arthur and Camelot, to life. Gosson was keeping King Arthur alive – or returning him and his court to life by enacting the old prophecies. And the audience he'd wanted – and which Wolsey had blocked from seeing it all – was King Henry.

'In his manner, possibly,' said Wolsey. 'Yes. Perhaps he thought so. He has, at any rate, saved His Majesty embarrassment by preventing Gonzaga from spreading his vile studies and constructions, his desire to make trash of King Henry's . . . His Majesty's lineage.'

Saved His Majesty embarrassment.

Such evil, I thought, done in the name of this king.

'Yet he retained the book,' added Wolsey. 'He did not destroy it.'

'Why?' I asked, looking at the thing.

'I suspect,' said Audley, 'that this book will be worth a great deal. More, if it becomes known what it might suggest. Herr Gosson is a man driven only by money. If the tales of Arthur were proven false, the masque would have been quickly cancelled. No more commissions of its like. It is a fine business for a painter, the tales – the history – of Arthur. And by those foul murders alone . . . had His Majesty's belief – his belief in his descent been given encouraging signs . . . I daresay our painter might have found himself at work on a new Camelot.'

'Eighty pounds!' Wolsey croaked, his face reddening. 'For the repainting of yonder table alone! Eighty pounds he had of our purse, just for that. And more on masks. On false walls and much else. Ay, Mr Audley. Money. I doubt he could have brought himself to destroy a book that might one day be sold. Even if we succeeded in keeping these false prophecies from the king . . . well, His Majesty would have paid handsomely to have in his possession a book which disturbed his beliefs and threatened his policy.' He repeated the last word, almost spitting it. 'New Camelot. The glory of his age. All torn down and mocked. Ay, His Majesty would have paid anything to prevent such a shameful thing being sold elsewhere.'

Either way, Gosson would have profited.

I closed my eyes. All those men dead just to keep a legend alive. To ensure a rich painter might continue to grow richer. 'He's a murderer,' I said. 'Whether he struck anyone with his own hand or not. A murderer.'

Wolsey tilted his head back and breathed in. It was cool in the chapel. It smelled of stale water and polished stone. He rolled his tongue in his cheek. 'The dead wool-seller – this Holbrook. He has family?'

'A brother,' I said. 'Thomas.'

Wolsey clucked his tongue softly. 'Ah yes. Mr Audley spoke of the poor creature.' He turned to his secretary.

'One Thomas Holbrook,' said Audley. 'The other body lies in his house, I believe.'

'We must write him our blessings. Tonight. Have someone send him a kindly note to take when they retrieve the body of the corrupted young prentice.'

'Yes, Your Grace,' said Audley. 'I've informed the coroner to expect the corpse of a young painter of your household. Who has been gored by a bull.'

Drawing from that well again, I thought.

'Mm. Yes,' said Wolsey. 'Most tragic. Write this note to Thomas Holbrook forthwith and have the messenger read it to him. Telling him how sorry we are for his loss, and that the Church is sorry also to hear that the very doer of the wicked deed is even now in his murdered brother's house. Alone and unguarded.' He gave another little cluck. 'So sad. Yes.'

I stood, open-mouthed, as Wolsey turned and his broad, red back began to descend down the aisle. He turned only once. 'Get you a night's rest, young Anthony, and prepare a tale by which to explain how you are turned Lazarus.

'And . . . Mr Audley?'

'Yes, Your Grace?' answered the secretary, stepping carefully after him.

'Burn that book.'

27

News of my remarkable resurrection was swiftly buried. I wasn't that important. Instead, in every man's mouth was the woeful news that good Herr Gosson, who had done all that lovely work in the great hall, which had so pleased the king, had been found dead. The superstitious said that he had been attacked in the house where he was lodging by a giant, or by the ghost of its former owner, or the man who had been hanged from its window, and he had tried to escape. He had been found in the little garden at the back, having attempted to climb out of an upper window and fallen. His head was quite broken.

'Reckon he was pushed, or jumped?' asked Mark. We were standing in the courtyard, eating hunks of manchet bread. He had already told me how the king had looked right at him – cold eyes, he'd said – and how the young Mistress Anne had gone from being furious at being paired with a nobody to smiling upon him. He was, like me, quite taken with Mistress Anne, so that I found that it had been me teasing him rather than the other way around. But, of course, the conversation had turned, as it had turned everywhere in the yard, to the mysterious death of Herr Gosson.

'Who cares?' I said. I meant it. I would have liked for Thomas Holbrook to have dashed his brains out and thrown him from a window, as long as the Church assured him his soul wouldn't be tainted; but I suspected that a cowardly creature like Gosson would have tried to climb out the window and fallen. I didn't judge the cardinal for what he had done.

Instigating and inspiriting!

Wolsey could, I knew, make people disappear. I don't mean anything so grubby as murder; no, His Grace's doings as Lord Chancellor simply involved erasing the wicked by subtle means. If evil men looked set to darken the pages of history, Cardinal Wolsey wrinkled his nose and inked them out, so that they never were. Even, I knew, to their own families. Gosson would be forgotten. Gone.

Dead was dead.

'Well, it's a dark business, all of it. The cardinal's Revels Master is leaving His Grace's service, I heard. Says that some wicked plot's aimed at him and he's the target for . . .' His brow wrinkled, '"cruellest practices of murder", apparently. Old Lutini's dancing as well as playing to see him go. But people's saying the house in town's cursed. From all them deaths. They're wanting it torn down, I heard.'

'Pfft,' I said. 'Men make things happen. Men make curses.'

He looked set to argue when another voice interrupted us.

'Good morrow . . .' Harry joined us, looking scholarly today in his black robes, so redolent of his master's. 'I trust you heard the news of the accident?'

'*Accident,*' Mark sneered. And then he remembered who Harry was, and so did I, and we took off our caps.

'An accident it was,' said Harry. 'But . . . but I trust one desired and compassed by God. Mr Audley told me of the evil that the Master Painter did.'

I shrugged, as an old woman chased a flock of wandering chickens across the yard. Their wings rose and fell flightlessly. 'Mark,' I said, 'enjoyed playing in the masque.'

'Yes,' said Harry. 'I was there. You did well.'

'I was going to . . . with the soot. He said no.'

'You're goddamned right I did,' I said.

We stood a while, content in each other's company: an unlikely trio, I thought – a bookish gentleman with a dark history and a pair of trumpets, one who belonged and one who didn't. I might be small-friended, I thought, but they were good friends. 'Well,' said Mark, 'I'd better go. Cardinal will be out of mass soon.'

'And I,' said Harry. 'Mr Audley will have letters to be sent out.'

It was only me, I realised, who had no more business at court or in Wolsey's service. The revels were ended, the masque done, and the murderer and his agent unmasked. As they walked away, I swallowed down the last of my bread.

'I say,' said Harry, turning. 'It has been good to see you again. To work with you. And I should think your . . . your hand will heal soon enough. Why not come back into His Grace's service?'

'As what?' I asked. 'Cardinal Wolsey's murder-hound?' I regretted the question, but the delicate Harry didn't pale.

'He's right, though,' said Mark. 'What else you got to do? Hide in your house, getting drunk on all that woe-is-me you'll have to enjoy? Remember what I said. You love you a bit of misery. Well, don't. Come back into service and earn an honest crust like the rest of us.' He winked. 'And we can take turns lingering outside old Sir Thomas Boleyn's rooms and asking if the lady would like a lesson.'

I laughed as they went away, Harry castigating Mark for his intemperate speech about a knight's daughter.

I watched them go and then looked around the courtyard, at the teeming life: animal and man and woman and glass and song and gilding. And I considered the reverse of it: intrigue and scheming and murder and suspicion and death. At Wolsey's court I could be someone, however little, however gawped at.

You should be proud of having such a father, coming from strange lands with a headful of strange knowledge.

On the heels of the thought came images of Aldgate and London, of my father's house and my stepmother, and the Minories and its thinning, sparkling infirmaress. And I considered the reverse of it: obscurity, the perverse joy of being forgotten and unseen, longing for something that would never be, revelling not in hopes but in self-inflicted miseries which tasted good and sour, like ale.

Smiling now only to myself, I made my decision.

Although Anthony Blanke and his book are fictional, John Blanke was very much a real person. Little concrete is known about his life, which has allowed me to create a first wife and a son for him.

It is supposed (but not known for certain) that the real John came to England in Catherine of Aragon's train, when she arrived from Spain in 1501. Some documented facts thereafter are available. Treasury payments were made under Henry VII to 'John Blanke, the blacke trumpeter'; he received 8d a day, as he would continue to do under Henry VIII. John is very likely the black man shown twice, in different coloured turbans, in the Westminster Tournament Roll, indicating that he played at court to celebrate the birth of a prince in 1511. He successfully petitioned Henry VIII for a pay rise, though the date of his petition is unclear. He was also provided with a wedding gift in January 1512, supplied by Henry's 'great wardrobe' (though we know nothing about his wife). That is all that is known of him. After this, the records fall silent. In the novel, John has died by the early 1520s, but I've allowed that he had hitherto inserted his fictional son into Wolsey's service.

Charles V, nephew of Catherine of Aragon and thus of Henry VIII, landed in England on the 25th of May 1522 and remained for six weeks, departing on the 16th of July. At the time, the two sovereigns were engaged in planning, with Cardinal Wolsey's eager assistance, a marriage treaty between Charles and the Princess Mary (his first cousin) and a joint invasion of France. It would be Wolsey who secured the Treaty of Windsor 1522 (ostensibly guaranteeing these things) and Henry who unilaterally declared himself governor of France. Like most of Henry VIII's celebrated meetings with foreign potentates, the ostensible goals were never ultimately met (the invasion of France fizzled out, and Mary did not marry Charles, though she did, decades later, marry his son, Philip) but the revelry and spectacle were considerable. Henry's Thameside palace of Bridewell was connected via a specially built wooden gallery with the emperor's lodgings at Blackfriars, and a triumphal entry with pageants featuring Samson and Hercules – representing the kings – was staged along the traditional route through the city. As depicted, the pair dined with the Duke of Suffolk in Southwark on the 9th of June before moving on to Hampton Court for two days, Windsor until the 20th, and then on to Winchester.

At Winchester, Henry and Wolsey had had repainted the Round Table, which according to contemporary belief was the true table used by King Arthur at Camelot. The masque which I've had Wolsey arrange is entirely fictional, but the emphasis on Arthuriana during the visit is based on that recommissioning of the table. In order to understand the early Tudors' fixation with King Arthur (and their own supposed descent through Cadwaladr) it is necessary to recognise that Henry VII's and Henry VIII's grasp on the throne was rather shaky. Descending as they did through the female line, there were better candidates (at least until Henry VIII's virtual massacre of them) for the throne. Thus, from the beginning of the Tudor dynasty, Henry VII sought to emphasise his supposed descent from Arthur. The lyrics mentioned in the novel as being used during Henry VII's accession really were. I would recommend, as an introduction to this interesting topic, Sydney Anglo's 'The British History in Early Tudor Propaganda' (1961: *Bulletin of the John Rylands Library* 44 [1]: 17-48. Both King Henries were, however, up against the development of history as a discipline. Henry VII commissioned Polydore Vergil to write a history of England. His *Anglica Historia*, though, was to consistently demonstrate his anti-Arthurian position, as Vergil placed himself in the vanguard of those who rejected the mythical and legendary origins of nations, which had hitherto been popular (he also criticised the mythical origins of Scotland via the Egyptian Princess Scota, for example). An interesting man, Vergil found himself in the Tower of London for slandering Wolsey in 1515, but he was released and thereafter continued to write until his death, living largely in England (where he was granted papers of denizenship in 1510) until his retirement back to Italy in 1553 and death in 1555. Despite his life in England, he was never a slavish pawn willing to peddle propaganda about the Tudors' origins. The full – true – Tudor story can be found in Leanda de Lisle's wonderful *Tudor: The Family Story* (2013: Chatto & Windus).

Yet the myth of Arthur and the quest to find out if he, or someone similar, ever lived has remained a popular topic (one can find documentaries still being made on the subject). All of the books mentioned in the text are real and have at one time or another been cited as the inspiration for what would become King Arthur. The *Getica* (*The Origin and Deeds of the Getae*) professes to be a summary of a lost account of the Goths by Cassiodorus featuring a Romano-British general,

Riothamus, who battled the Goths in the fifth century. As a 'king of the Britons' last noted to have been in Avallon in Burgundy, he is considered a viable inspirational figure for the mythical king. The historian Geoffrey Ashe was the first to propose Riothamus as one of the prototypes of the composite Arthur (with others claiming that Riothamus and another apparent prototype, Ambrosius Aurelianus, were one and the same – the latter also mooted as a potential Merlin template). Other texts, such as the *Historia Brittonum*, supposedly by Nennius, present Arthur as a historical figure. The *Annales Cambriae* also presents an Arthur, although he might be a later addition. At any rate, even modern views differ on who, if any single person, inspired King Arthur. The legends, however, took on their most identifiable forms in Geoffrey of Monmouth's *Historia Regum Britanniae*, which includes as its seventh book the *Prophetiae Merlini* (or prophecies of Merlin). The prophecies used in the novel are all from the *Historia*, and I'm indebted to Aaron Thompson's 1718 translation, which has been recently published with revisions by J. A. Giles (1999: In Parentheses Publications). Those interested in all things Arthur will enjoy Tony Sullivan's *King Arthur: Man or Myth* (2020: Pen & Sword).

Undoubtedly, the reason for showing off Winchester and the Round Table to Charles V was Henry VIII's way of demonstrating the strength and supposed antiquity of his dynasty ahead of the mooted marriage alliance. It obviously didn't work. The curious relationship between the cynical, deformed Charles V and his dangerous uncle is well covered in Lacey Baldwin Smith's *Henry VIII: The Mask of Royalty* (1971: Chicago Review Press). Though the masque in the novel is, as noted, a fiction, 'sumptuous masques' were indeed put on at various times during the royal visit. These included a play in which a wild horse (representing Francis I) was tamed by the gentle persuasions of his Spanish and English superiors. Entertainments at early modern courts were seldom staged for their own sake; masques, plays, and 'interludes' were forces of political discourse throughout Renaissance Europe. My concession here to a later period is including readings (in the novel delivered by Sir Thomas Boleyn). Masques with scripts – at least by professional playwrights, such as Ben Jonson – came later. It is unclear exactly how early Henrician masques were planned and conducted, but I suspect there must have been more than just dancing, even if written material has not survived. Thus, I think having the masque-makers loosely adapt other written sources (rather than writing hugely elaborate poems, as Jonson would later do) seems a reasonable halfway house as to how these things might have been performed. Neither masques nor Arthuriana, it should be noted, were frivolous or whimsical. In addition to bolstering the Tudors, the pressing of Arthurian descent supported King Henry's periodical claims to suzerainty over the whole of the British Isles; Henry VIII's own singer and playwright, John Heywood (not to be confused with the later playwright), did indeed write a now-lost *Masque of King Arthur's Knights*. Henry was, throughout his reign, engaged in trying to establish England as a fully hereditary monarchy by stressing dynasty; before, the country had not seen many sons inherit directly from their fathers.

On the subject of Thomas Boleyn, it is interesting to note that, throughout the first decade (and more) of Henry VIII's reign, it was he who was the star of the family. A champion jouster and a skilled diplomat and ambassador, Boleyn was a workhorse with a mean streak (in financial terms) who was very much one of those who rose to prominence through skill under the early Tudors. Few could have predicted, in 1522, that this distinguished and talented fellow would rise far higher through his charming daughter. Nor could anyone have predicted how far both would fall.

Anne Boleyn is one of the most fascinating women in English – perhaps in world – history. However, one of the many remarkable things about her is how little is known of her life prior to her explosion onto the political scene in the mid-1520s. Indeed, we cannot even be sure when she was born, with dates ranging from 1501 (the most likely) to 1507. It is, however, known that she was sent by her father – who likely recognised her intelligence and linguistic skills – to the court of Margaret of Austria in the Netherlands, where she was educated, and on into the French court (hence why Genevieve Bujold gave such a wonderfully authentic performance in Hal Wallis's *Anne of the Thousand Days* in 1969).

What is so beguiling about her history, though, is that she returned to England in 1521 as part of a marriage project her father approved that would see her marry an Irish cousin, James Butler, and thereby settle a family dispute over the earldom of Ormonde. This allowed her to take part in a masque at the English court (alongside her future sister-in-law, Jane Parker; her sister, Mary Boleyn; Mary Tudor, Duchess of Suffolk; and Catherine of York) in March 1522, just months prior to the historical events in the novel. Anne became betrothed – perhaps – to Henry Percy, heir to the earldom of Northumberland, in the spring of 1523. What is fascinating here, however, is this rather long period between

1521 and 1525-6 during which the Frenchified and dazzling young Anne introduced continental fashions to the English court and became, in modern parlance, an 'influencer'. Throughout, Henry VIII was fully aware of her – indeed, at some point (the dates cannot be known) he carried on his infamous affair with her sister Mary. Yet the king paid, as far as we can tell, no attention to the woman he would later tear his kingdom, his people, and his long-suffering wife's heart apart for. Henry VIII did not fall in love with Anne in 1521 or, indeed, in 1525-6 (indeed – I'm unconvinced that he ever fell in love with anyone other than himself). However, monster of ego that he was, he became overwhelmed by a monomaniacal desire to own and possess her at the later date. Thus, this 'lost' period of Anne's life – the time between her return to England and her falling victim to Henry's frenzied courtship – is a wonderfully interesting one.

What was Anne like?

This is a question that continues to divide opinion, as it did in her day. A number of myths about her have gained traction and refuse to die. Perhaps most tiresome is the notion that she had six fingers on one hand, and that she popularised trailing sleeves to hide it. This extra digit was invented by the later Catholic propagandist Nicholas Sander, whose aim was to blacken her name (he was an inveterate enemy of her daughter, Queen Elizabeth). In addition to giving her a sixth finger, Sander's Anne was deformed by 'wens' and, bizarrely, she was Henry VIII's daughter as well as his lover. However, George Wyatt, grandson of Anne's admirer Sir Thomas Wyatt, inadvertently added fuel to a fire he was trying to extinguish by writing his own biography in c.1605. His Anne has 'upon the side of her nail, upon one of her fingers, some little show of a nail'. At first glance, this appears to corroborate the idea that there was something about Anne's hand.

Wyatt's claim – written long after Anne's death by a man born nearly twenty years after it – has indeed led some historians, such as Antonia Fraser, to conclude that Anne did indeed have some minor imperfection on one hand, which was exaggerated by Sander and corrected by Wyatt, who might have had some (unproven and unrecorded) insider knowledge gleaned from his family connections. However, it is, I think, far more likely that Wyatt invented the little double nail in direct response to Sander's original outright fabrication; his goal was thus to ameliorate an existing popular image rather than to provide a true picture of the unfortunate queen. In short, there is nothing – not a suggestion or whisper or fragment of a sentence – from Anne's lifetime which indicates that there was anything unusual about either of her hands. By all accounts, Anne was 'not the handsomest of women', being somewhat sallow rather than milky white, but had remarkable eyes which she knew how to use. She was inherently charming and graceful, witty, au fait with fashion, and possessed of dark – perhaps black – hair, dark – perhaps black – eyes, a long face, and a long neck. The definitive biography of Anne is Eric Ives' *The Life and Death of Anne Boleyn* (1986: Wiley). More recent books include Elizabeth Norton's *Anne Boleyn: Henry VIII's Obsession* (2008: Amberley) and Alison Weir's *The Lady in the Tower: The Fall of Anne Boleyn* (2009: Jonathan Cape).

In trying to reconstruct Cardinal Wolsey's 'shadow court' and the various palaces and castles, I relied on a number of books. Foremost was Simon Thurley's *Houses of Power: The*

Places that Shaped the Tudor World (2017: Penguin). Thurley's older *Henry VIII's Hampton Court* (1988: Architectural History Reprint) was also useful, as was June Osborne's gorgeously illustrated *Hampton Court Palace* (1984: Kaye & Ward). Much of the palace was altered by Henry VIII – the famous astronomical clock, for example, was his addition – but floorplans of Hampton Court as it looked in the late 1520s are available, construction under Wolsey having taken place in two waves, in the 1510s and mid-1520s. Patch, the fool who appears briefly in the novel, was a gift from Wolsey to Henry VIII, preceding the better-known Will Sommers. Unlike Sommers, Patch (his real name was Sexton) appears to have lived with some form of learning difficulty, which required him to have keepers. He did not dress as a fool – his head was not shaved, and he wore no particoloured coat and silly hat – but as a favoured retainer. Wholly fictional are the master craftsmen and Richard Audley. However, I had some leeway with Audley in that Wolsey's most famous principal secretary, Richard Pace, had gone into royal service by this time. Pace did continue to work secretly for Wolsey; nevertheless, he was on a diplomatic mission to Venice during the period covered in the novel. Ultimately, part of Wolsey's downfall was that he lived and ruled as a prince, not a cardinal. Those interested in the less opulent surroundings described will very likely enjoy Stephen Porter's fascinating *Everyday Life in Tudor London* (2016: Amberley). Liza Picard's *Elizabeth's London: Everyday Life in Elizabethan London* (2005: St Martin's Griffin) and Ian Mortimer's wonderful *The Time Traveller's Guide to Elizabethan England* (2012: Penguin), though focusing on the later Tudor period, both look back to the ways in which things had changed since Henry VII's (and

Henry VIII's) time. The monasteries and convent depicted are real, the Abbey of the Minoresses of St Clare Without Aldgate being run by one Abbess Alice Fitzlewes until 1524. All would be dissolved by Henry VIII in the 1530s, with the Crutched Friars being noted by Cromwell as particularly licentious and badly run.

What is next for Anthony Blanke? His decision on whether to go back into Wolsey's increasingly dangerous service has been made. When I know what it is, so will you.